BY DEGREES

Books by Elle Casey

CONTEMPORARY URBAN FANTASY

War of the Fae (10-book series)
Ten Things You Should Know About Dragons
(short story, The Dragon Chronicles)
My Vampire Summer
Aces High

DYSTOPIAN

Apocalypsis (4-book series)

SCIENCE FICTION

Drifters' Alliance (ongoing series)
Winner Takes All (short story prequel to Drifters' Alliance,
Dark Beyond the Stars Anthology)
The Ivory Tower (short story standalone, Beyond the Stars: A
Planet Too Far Anthology)

ROMANCE

By Degrees
Rebel Wheels (3-book series)
Just One Night (romantic serial)
Just One Week
Love in New York (3-book series)
Shine Not Burn (2-book series)
Bourbon Street Boys (4-book series)
Desperate Measures
Mismatched

ROMANTIC SUSPENSE

*All the Glory: How Jason Bradley Went from
Hero to Zero in Ten Seconds Flat*
Don't Make Me Beautiful
Wrecked (2-book series)

PARANORMAL

Duality (2-book series)
Monkey Business (short story)
Dreampath (short story standalone, The
Telepath Chronicles)
Pocket Full of Sunshine (short story & screenplay)

BY DEGREES

ELLE CASEY

Elle Casey

PO Box 14367

N Palm Beach, FL 33408

Website: www.ElleCasey.com
Email: info@ellecasey.com

ISBN/EAN-13: 978-1-93945509-3

SECOND EDITION

DEDICATION

For my husband, my forever guy.

CHAPTER ONE

SPINNING PARTWAY AROUND ON MY back while still holding onto her ankle, I use my feet to defend myself. My ribs are aching too much to throw a punch, so I kick the ever-loving shit out of her thighs and crotch and don't stop, even when a voice finally comes over my cell phone.

"Nine-one-one ... what is your emergency?"

I don't know exactly where my phone is, but it's near my head somewhere, so I just start yelling.

"Intruder in the house! Tarin Kilgour's residence! The musician from the band *By Degrees*! Beverly Hills!" I can't for the life of me remember his address. I hope I've given her enough information to find me.

"I need your name and a description of the intruder, ma'am."

"Fuck you!" yells my attacker. "Give me that goddamn phone, dammit!" She struggles to sit up and reach for my cell, but I give her a running shoe to the face, making her fall back again.

I keep kicking, but her foot slips out of my sweaty grip. She's crawled out of my way, but I can tell by the way she's eyeing my pinwheeling legs, she doesn't want to eat any more of my sneakers than she already has. All those hours on the stationary bike are paying off.

I yell again, hoping the operator can hear me. "My name is Scarlett Barnes and I work with Tarin Kilgour! The intruder's name is …" I'm cut off by her struggle for my phone. When I kick her away, I continue. "She's an unwelcome fan of Tarin's! She broke into the house while he was out and she's in the process of taking some of his things!"

"I was not taking anything!" she screeches as she stands somewhat unsteadily on her feet. She sways there, out of her mind with anger. "And I'm not an intruder! Tarin loves me and I love him!"

"Get over it, freak!" I yell at her. I've officially lost my cool and I don't care about her delicate psyche anymore or the fact that all of this will be on the operator's recording. "You're just another bimbot deluded fan! He doesn't give a shit about you!"

She freezes in place, hunched over, her make-up starting to smear a little and her hair a crazy mess. Backing up, she points a shaking finger at me. "You don't know anything about Tarin and me." Her voice is quavering.

The operator speaks again and I can barely hear her. I look over and see my phone turned upside down, the speaker facing the carpet. I pick it up in time to hear her say, "We're sending someone to the house now. My advice is to not engage with this intruder and just leave the premises until she can be apprehended."

"Yeah, sounds like a good idea," I say, attempting to stand. My ribs are killing me, and as I get more upright, I shift to the side a little. A sharp, stabbing pain sears into my guts and makes my breath catch in my throat. "Fuck," I grunt out, bending towards the pain, trying to make it stop. "You fucking broke my ribs, you freak." I look up in time to see her nostrils flare.

"You broke your own ribs, coming after me like that."

"Coming after you? After *you*? Are you fucking kidding me? How deluded can a person possibly be?"

"Ms. Barnes, I suggest you leave the premises," says the voice over the phone.

"Yeah, well it's not that easy, actually."

"I'm not deluded," says the freak, lifting her chin, "I'm in love. Love can make you do crazy things, but that doesn't mean it's wrong."

"Yes, actually, it does. What you're doing is wrong. You need therapy and medication." I resort to begging. The pain is bad. I can't move enough to escape. "Please just get out of here."

She's crying now. "Tarin loves me."

I shake my head, backing up until I'm leaning against the wall. "No, he doesn't. He doesn't love anyone but himself."

"No!"

I nod. "Yes."

She moves around the side of his bed, never taking her eyes off me. "You don't know anything about love. You're empty inside. I can see it."

"Wrong." I slide down the wall a little, my legs apparently deciding that injured ribs are too heavy.

She stops when she's in front of Tarin's nightstand. "You want Tarin for yourself, don't you?"

I shake my head. "God, somebody shoot me." Her words combined with the pain make me nauseated. I'm afraid I'm going to barf right here on Tarin's silk carpeting. With my luck I'll probably fall in it too, making the thought of it doubly awful.

Her eyes flash anger, and her color goes up again. "Oh my god! That's it! You want Tarin for yourself. That's what this is all about! This isn't about him not loving me or me having problems … this is about you and your sick little infatuation with Tarin!"

My butt hits the ground, and I drop my face into my hand, using my other to prop myself up. I half whisper, half moan, "Jesus Christ save me from delusional nutbags." I swallow over and over to keep my stomach contents where they belong.

I hear a drawer open and lift my eyes in time to see her pulling a handgun from the nightstand.

My heart stops beating for what seems like forever. My salivary glands go into overdrive. The vomiting is near.

The gun comes up and she stares at it, almost mystified. And then a big grin comes over her face as she looks at me. "Tarin keeps a gun in our bedroom to protect us from people like you."

"Jesus, Mary, and Jerome." I lift the phone to my ear with monumental effort. It jitters against my head, I'm shaking so bad. My heart starts beating again, only now it's going a mile a minute. "She's got a gun," I say to the operator. My voice is all over the place. "I'm pretty sure she's going to shoot me."

CHAPTER TWO

TWO WEEKS EARLIER...

I'M SITTING in the office reception area of Hollywood super-agent, Mel Warner, waiting for him to finish a meeting with one of his clients. The secretary pays me no mind, busy clicking away on her computer.

I take the time before our appointment to look around the office. Lots of framed awards and pictures of Mel with three generations of famous people adorn the walls. Healthy plants and colorful orchids make the place seem less sterile. The furniture isn't too modern, which is a nice change from what I'm used to seeing in places like this.

When Mel's previous appointment comes out of his inner sanctum, I recognize her as an actress who has starred in at least six feature films. She commands a high salary with generous terms, but she's not why I'm here. I'm here for a superstar who needs my particular brand of help, and this actress is too on-track with her career to worry about that kind of business.

I wait for them to exchange air kisses and promises to see each other again before I stand.

"Scarlett Barnes, I presume," Mel says once she's gone, looking me up and down as I walk over to him.

I hold out my hand. "In the flesh."

He's short and round with a really daring comb-over, but he has a firm grip. He holds on longer than necessary, but I don't fret over it because I know he's not coming-on to me; he's taking my measure, wondering if I can do what they say I can ... if I can pull off a miracle in a month or less.

I'm taller than he is, but only because he's barely above five feet himself. I have dark gray eyes and blonde hair that's lighter with help from my hairstylist. Looking older than my twenty-five years is a definite asset in my little niche of the entertainment business. I dress professionally until I'm actually knee-deep in the work; then I dress as casually as possible, so I can be ready for anything. Today I'm in my favorite gray pantsuit. It's cut in a casual business style that strikes the perfect balance between professional and trendy, its light fabric perfect for this scorchingly hot Los Angeles day.

I'm fairly certain I know what's going on in Mel's head as he looks me up and down because I've dealt with people like him before, several times now over the past couples years. He wants to know who the hell I really am and what exactly it is that I can do for him. My job in the next half hour or less will be to convince him that I can do what I promise and that I'm worth the money.

"Come on in to my office. Nanette, get Scarlett some coffee."

I look at the receptionist who's taking his terse command in stride and hold up my hand to keep her from going too far in her mission. "I'm not a coffee drinker, but thanks anyway."

"Tea or water, maybe?" she asks, frozen partway out of her chair.

"Nothing, thank you."

Nanette goes back to her work, and I follow Mel into his office, taking the chair across from him. I gaze around the room, casually taking in the details. It's a big place, but then again, they all are. Hollywood money demands that agents' offices be something to brag about. The view behind Mel's chair of the Los Angeles skyline is amazing, even though the brownish smog is easier to see from this high up. The chair I'm sitting in is smooth leather and slippery. I'm glad I chose to wear pants instead of a skirt today. I hate when my bare legs leave sweat marks behind.

His desk is big enough to have sex on, and I wonder if he's ever indulged. Rumor has it that he's been happily married to the same woman for over forty years, but you never can tell in this industry. He could be boinking the girl who fetches the coffee every morning before nine a.m. for all I know.

"So," he says, folding his hands and resting them casually under his belly as he leans back. "I hear they call you The Normalizer."

I nod once. "Some do." It's not a name I use for myself, but it does describe pretty accurately what I do for a living.

"Do you know why I called you here?"

"I suspect it's because you have a problem client who needs some redirection ... recalibration."

He smiles, but there's no warmth or happiness to it. "Recalibration. That's an interesting way to put it. As if he were a machine."

"In some ways, he is. He's human of course, but he's also a money making machine, right?" I find there's no need to beat around the bush or pretend why I'm here with these people. Agents, managers, and producers don't hire me because they miss their old friends. They need their income sources back online and functioning at optimum levels.

He frowns. "While it may be true that they're like machines to some degree, I'm not sure I'm comfortable with the coldness of it."

I smile tolerantly. "You've worked your entire life in Hollywood. Surely you jest."

He shrugs, moving his hands to the arms of his chair. "I may be old guard, but that doesn't mean I have a heart of stone. My clients are important to me as people, too."

"Good to know. It helps if the client actually *likes* his agent." What he's saying confirms what I've heard from others. Mel Warner does care about his clients and their welfare, at least more than the average Hollywood agent does. But I'm no fool. It doesn't mean he isn't all about the bottom line when everything's said and done.

"That's not always the case. That stars don't like their agents." He says it like a statement, but I know he's curious for details. It's the nature of the beast, to want to know more than what is polite to know. And guys like him don't get to the top of the food chain without wooing away a few clients here and there. But I don't give out details like names and dates. Confidentiality and privacy are key in my business.

"No, it's not always the case. Sometimes I'm fighting the agent at the same time I'm helping him. I prefer not to do that."

"Is the fee cheaper if we play nice?" He's smiling genuinely now. I don't smile back. "No. I never discount my fees."

He sits quietly for a little while and then sighs long and loud, staring at me the entire time. I wait for him to speak, which he eventually will. No one can ever just let me walk away with this much left unsaid.

His thumbs rub the edges of the arms of his chair rhythmically as his measured words break the silence. "You're pricey. My question is, are you worth it?"

Here's where the rubber meets the road for the agents. For my clients, the celebrities who've gone off the range, it's a different place in the process where they finally have that come-to-Jesus moment. But for the agents, managers, or producers who hire me, here's where I sprinkle my magic dust over the one who hires me. It's a special medicine I like to call 'reality'.

"You tell *me* if I'm worth it. I assume with your agency contract you're pulling in at least a couple mil a year with him, right? And with your declining roster of clients, this relationship becomes more valuable and important every year, especially with your retirement looming. You've put a lot of eggs in this basket. That's dangerous."

"How do you know about that? That information is confidential." He doesn't seem angry or surprised, and there's no reason he should. He knows as well as I do that secrets don't stay secret for long in our world. The key is to keep them secret long enough that their eventual revelation doesn't matter. We all have secrets. Even I have skeletons that I keep under lock and key.

"I have contacts in the industry who keep me informed. Right now, for example, I know you and your client have commitments for a full, twelve-stop European tour and two movies. Without even considering all the promotional work and endorsement deals, we're talking a considerable sum for your agency. My fee is just a fraction of that."

"But if you fail, I lose it all and then some."

"I don't fail. Ever. And if I do, you don't pay. That's how it works. It's a no-risk proposition for you." I finish silently with, *You'd be stupid to say no.* I don't have to say it out loud, though. That would be overkill, and I never do overkill. I hit strong and I hit quick, but then I pull away and let things settle out. Eventually, he'll figure it out for himself. Hopefully, he'll do it before his client ends up dead. I ignore the slight twinge in my chest as I think those words to myself. *Dead. No, I can't let that happen.*

He rocks back in his seat, now in pensive mode. His chair squeaks as it goes back and forth, back and forth, back and forth. I can practically see the figures swimming around in his head, right next to the visions of his retirement trip to Fiji and the around-the-world cruise his wife already booked for two years from now.

"But if you fail, even if I don't pay, I lose."

I stand in front of my chair, preparing to leave. I've accomplished almost all I came to do. Now for the *coup de grâce.* "Like I said, I don't fail. And without me, you're going to lose it all anyway. He's on a downward spiral straight into hell, and if you don't do something to stop it, he'll be gone or at least out of commission within sixty days, unable to do anything but *cost* you money. That's my prediction."

He stopped rocking, coming to sudden halt. "How accurate are your predictions?"

I stare him down because this is important. I feel very strongly about my work, and not because I like the money. The money is just something that allows me to do other things I'm passionate about. "I'm never wrong about downward spirals." My expression softens. "But you don't need me to tell you what's going to happen, do you? He's clearly off the rails. He's been arrested five times in the last two months, he's doing massive amounts of drugs including H possibly, and he's out every night of the week wrecking cars, hotel rooms, and cameras. He has six civil suits pending against him, five of which will stick, half of his road crew has bailed, and you're about to lose his drummer, who, incidentally was in the hospital for a heroin overdose just last week. Who do you think was shooting up with him?"

"How could you possibly know that?" he asks, sitting up straighter and staring at me with a mixture of fear and respect.

"I have eyes and ears everywhere. It's my business to know these things. Besides, I've had my eye on your man for months. He needs me. You both do."

"Why didn't you contact me and offer me your services?" He's a little offended now. Hearing the truth so unvarnished tends to have that effect, but it's one I intended.

"That's not how I work. I don't solicit. People come to me."

"What…? Is that some kind of ego thing?" He's angry. Frustrated. But not at me. I know this, so it doesn't bother me.

"No. It's about privacy. It's about ethics. I only come to those who need me and who know they need me…those who are willing to let me into their private worlds and relinquish control to me. In my experience, until people recognize they need help, they won't be in a position to accept it and do what needs to be done. I don't like wasting my time or making empty promises. There are other people out there who need me."

"But it's not the agents who need your help … it's our clients."

I shake my head, letting my disappointment show through. He needs to see it … to *feel* it. "No. It's *both* of you. And your client's friends, family, and crew. Everyone is involved. You're all enablers. Everyone will be involved if you hire me."

He waves his hand in a downward motion at me. "Please sit. I didn't mean to upset you. I'd like to talk some more about this."

"You didn't upset me." I shrug casually. "I get this all the time. It's a natural reaction. But I have another appointment, so I have to get going." I sidestep away from between the chair and desk to begin my walk to the door backwards.

He frowns and stands. "But what if I want to hire you?"

"Sign the contract my assistant emailed to Nanette and send it back along with a receipt for the funds in trust."

"Funds in trust?"

"You put my fee into a trust account with your attorney, and he or she pays me when the job is done. All the terms are in the contract."

He nods. "Smart."

I turn to go, not reacting to his approval of my financial and legal acumen. Power shifts are very important in my world, and I never let it shift out of my hands when dealing with anyone in this business. I wouldn't last an hour if I did. Mel can never think for a single second that he's in any position to control me or issue demands. It makes my job ten times harder and my motto is always to work smarter, not harder.

He comes out from behind his desk. "Wait one more second … I just have a couple more questions."

I turn back and raise an eyebrow, waiting for it. I know what's coming next.

"Are you a psychiatrist? I mean, what are your qualifications? And how do you do this… thing you do? Because he has a lot of commitments, and we really can't afford for him to disappear for a month. That's why he refuses to go into rehab. He says he doesn't have time."

"My qualifications are that I do this and do it well. You can talk to my references. I'm sure you know most of my former clients at least casually. And *how* I do it is my business. I'm not big on sharing. But I'll tell you this … I get complete control. Every aspect of his life, I will control it. I have ultimate authority. Anyone who crosses me or pisses me off, gets fired. And by fired, I mean permanently gone. You agree in our contract not to re-hire anyone I let go during the process. It's non-negotiable."

"Whoa, that's pretty harsh, don't you think? I don't know if we can do that." He's looking at me like I'm a little crazy. And maybe I am, but crazy is the only thing that works in these situations.

"Then I'm sorry I've wasted your time." I finish my walk to the door, hesitating before I'm completely through to say one more thing. "Just keep in mind that I work on a first-come, first-served basis and I only work with one client at a time."

"I'm going to think about it!" he says to my back, as I step out into the hallway leading to the exit.

I say nothing in response. It's better that I let him have the last word. Sometimes meetings with me can take the wind out of very big sails, and I don't need bruised egos standing at my back when I'm trying to work.

Walking past the reception desk, I nod at the woman still clicking on her keys. "Have a nice day, Nanette."

She looks up, her surprised expression telling me she wasn't expecting the courtesy. "Thanks. Uh, you too."

I'm on my phone before I'm out of the building. My assistant answers in two rings.

"Scarlett Barnes and Associates. Did you bring that mother to his knees?"

I smile. "We'll see. Book me a table at Scoto's just in case."

"Consider it done. Eight o'clock?"

"Perfect. See you in an hour." I hang up the phone and walk out the glass front doors of the building. If Mel doesn't come through for me, I can always bring my assistant Scott out to dinner. He's never offended over being my back-up plan, and he's always more fun to have around than clients, so it works for both of us.

A Lincoln Town Car with black tinted windows pulls up to the curb as I'm stepping out into the sun. The large, black chauffeur gets out and jogs around to attend to the passenger door. He's younger and bigger than most of the chauffeurs I've seen around town, making me think he doubles as a body guard.

As soon as the car door is open, a person falls out of the backseat and onto the sidewalk, his sunglasses flying off his head and skittering across the concrete towards me.

As I bend to retrieve them, another person comes out of the car, laughing in a raw, high-pitched cackle as she slides out and lands on top of the man on the sidewalk. Her skirt rides up around her waist to reveal a black thong. Both of them are either drunk or high, laughing, snorting, and flailing around limply.

I shake my head sadly, waiting for the chauffeur to pick up the girl and set her on her feet before walking over calmly with the glasses in hand.

"Thank you, ma'am," says the chauffeur, taking them from me with a humiliated expression.

Hmmm. Curious. He seems to care about his passenger. I look down at the man still on the ground. He's staring up at me from the sidewalk, squinting his eyes to see around the sun.

"Who're you?" he asks.

I can smell the stale booze and cigarette smoke coming off him from three feet away, and I work very hard not to let it upset me. *What a waste.* My heartstrings twang with distant but still shockingly painful memories. *So much youth, so much talent ... gone in the blink of an eye.*

I hitch my bag up higher on my shoulder and give him a tight smile, letting my past slip away into the darkest parts of my mind. "I'm the person watching you make a complete ass of yourself in broad daylight."

I walk away, a bitter smile forming as I realize how likely it is now that I'll be getting a call from Mel Warner. Scott will be bummed to miss out on his favorite restaurant, but a girl's gotta do what a girl's gotta do. I predict that my date tonight will have a righteous comb-over and a pinky ring.

"Do you know who I am?!" The man on the ground yells out after me, his words slurred and rough like he's been smoking and drinking for twenty-four hours straight.

I say nothing. I just keep walking.

"I'm Tarin Kilgour! You hear me?! I'm Tarin Fucking Kilgour!"

"Yes," I say softly to myself, pressing the unlock button on my keychain, "I know who you are."

CHAPTER THREE

THE SIGNED CONTRACT ARRIVES IN my office three hours later, along with a letter from Mel Warner's attorney advising me that funds have been placed in his trust account for my fee. I walk through the door with my hand held up. Scott is waiting there to give me the high five he always throws up when we close a deal.

"He's on for eight o'clock," Scott says, frowning. "That rotten bastard. I was so ready to inhale that filet mignon with the béarnaise sauce."

"Have you noticed your taste has gone from Mad Dog 20-20 to Champagne in less than six months?" I drop my purse down on the small table near the entrance. The place is homey - nothing like the swanky offices I visit to see prospective clients - but we like it that way. None of my business contacts ever come here, so there's no one to impress but us working stiffs.

Scott is my only employee. He's pretty much responsible for making sure my entire life is organized. He's the little brother of the man who stole my heart, and now, after ten years of being up my butt every day, he's finally found his place in my life: Right hand man. Neither of us could be happier with the arrangement. It's a little weird because I used to babysit him when we were younger, but it works. No one would guess that he's only eighteen.

"I don't know about the Mad Dog, but I *do* notice that my paychecks have gone up and I enjoy spending them." He examines his fingernails critically. "Do you think I should get a manicure? I hear straight guys do that out here."

"If you get a manicure, I'm calling your father and telling on you."

He scowls at me and drops down into a chair with rollers on the legs, slouching until he hangs over one of the arms. He ticks off one finger at a time. "Mean. Ugly. Uncalled for..."

I laugh. "I'm kidding. I kid, I kid. But seriously. Don't go all metro sexual on me or I'll have to fire you. I hate that shit. Gay is okay. Faux gay is not."

He sits back up and gasps like a woman, fluttering his hand to his chest and affecting a strong southern accent. I think he's trying to channel a woman from *Gone With the Wind*. "How dare you threaten me with job loss! Who do you think you are? My master? I'm not your slave, you know. I'm a *free* man. *Free!* Do you hear me?" His voice goes back to normal. "Fire me? As if. You wouldn't know how to wipe your own ass without me around."

"Thanks for the visual." I grab him by the hand and pull him and his chair around to my side of the desk before sitting down. "Who I think I am is your worst nightmare if you piss me off. Take a look at this." I quickly type out a search on Google and come up with a set of images.

He leans over and stares at the gallery for a few seconds. "Whooaaa. Ho, ho, ho, Santa's slutty mistress has come to town. Hello, plastic hooters and bee stung lips." He wiggles his eyebrows. "Me likes."

"Yes, I'm sure you do. Put your hormones away, though, before I'm forced to b-slap you." I enlarge the picture a little, trying to see if she looks sober. "Scott, meet Jelly Summers, Tarin's latest party girl. God, is that even a real name?" I shudder at the girl's stupidity. "Does she stay or go?"

He puts his finger to his lips in concentration. "Hmmm. Scroll down. Let's see how *much* she likes to party. Maybe she's his soulmate-of-the-month. If she is, we're better off keeping her."

There isn't a whole lot to look at, most of the pictures showing her carefully posed in front of cameras that are catching her looking her best. But near the end of the collection of images is a mug shot.

"Badda bing, badda violà," I say softly as I click on it. Scott and I read the article silently and learn that this delightful young lady was arrested a few months ago for driving under the influence and possession of cocaine. Judging by the shape she was in today, I guess she hasn't done much to straighten her life out.

"She's out," I say, clicking off the search. "Do you have that list I sent you?"

"Do you even need to ask?" he quips, handing me a stack of paper about a half-inch high. "Profiles on all of them, including police records."

"Anyone clean?" I flick through the head-shots of the known friends and hangers-on who spend a lot of time with the lead singer of the band *By Degrees*: Tarin Kilgour - the man I need to bring down to Earth so he can get on with his life as a living person and not end it prematurely as a drugged-out corpse.

His bandmates, managers, and crew people are on top of the pile. Occasional girlfriends, ex lovers, and leeches come last. I need to find a core group of people I can count on to get Tarin's ass in gear. Thirty days is not a lot of time to wrestle a tornado to the ground.

"The driver, Ricky Williams, looks good. Two of the bodyguards who've been with him the longest do too, Leonard Skites and Zach Boston. The manager's been with them from the start, so I have to believe he's good. I didn't find anything saying otherwise. Bassist, rhythm guitarist, and drummer are probably fine, and there's not much we can do about them if they're not." Scott yanks those pages out and puts them on my computer keyboard. "Most of the road crew that's left is okay. I don't think they spend a lot of time with him outside of setting up and breaking down the equipment." Scott pulls a few sheets from the back. "These are the real problem children. I'd dump these suckers in a hot second if I were you."

I look carefully at the profiles Scott has pulled together on these unlucky souls. "Who's this?" I ask, holding up a sheet that has a picture of a good-looking guy with wavy brown hair and dark circles under his eyes.

"New best friend. Brett Campbell A total scab. I think he's the drug connection."

"Okay. What about this one?" I ask, pointing to a guy with a buzz cut and a tight t-shirt. He looks fit. *Wowza.*

"Another user. I'm not sure what his gig is. His name is Clay Matthews. I think he started out as a back-up dancer for someone and then just became a part of the scene. I think some chick gave him a truck for his birthday last year. Remember her? Country singer? Blond hair? I can't remember her name. Tanya? Tabitha? Twinga? Twila? Tabouleh?"

Without taking my eyes off the paper, I brush my hand down his face to make him stop. "Shut up, your voice is hurting my brain."

"So *she* gave him the truck and *he* gave her a case of crabs."

I look at him, trying to figure out if he's serious.

"Jay kay. But that would make an awesome country song, right?"

"Jay kay?"

"Jay kay … Just kidding. Come on, don't make me grow up too fast. This job will be totally lame if I have to act all businessy all the time."

I snort once before going back to the profiles. "That'll be the day."

Scott stands up and starts playing air guitar, singing with serious country passion. "I bought my man a car … he gave my heart a scar … we did it in the cab … and now I got the crabs … oh, loooove, you done me wroooong! Oh, loooooove … you done me wrong, and noooow there's no more schloooong…"

"You had me right up until schlong," I say as he rips out another few invisible silent chords with a pinwheeling arm. Except for the ridiculous lyrics, he actually did come up with a catchy tune. He's got serious talent. He knows it and I know it, but we also both know that he'll never do anything with it. His brother made sure of that.

He drops his air guitar and sits back down. "Yeah, well, I was hurtin' for a rhyme. Sometimes as an artist you just have to go where your heart takes ya. Screw common sense."

I push his chair away to make it roll across the floor so I can go back to my papers. He scoots two inches at a time over to his desk, using his swaying, jerking body to ambulate the chair. I shake my head at his goofiness. He's good at keeping life real, and that's what we're in the business of doing so I don't complain. When things get out of hand, we're there to get it real again. We've both lived through enough misery in our own lives to know that being able to laugh at ourselves is the best way to stay sane. Being too 'businessy', as Scott calls it, usually forces a disconnect with our clients, so we keep it cool, fresh, and current when we're in the trenches. Otherwise, we're just our goofy selves. The only time I really step into my serious shoes is when I'm getting new clients or meeting with lawyers. Most of the lawyers I've known have zero sense of humor - at least the brand of humor that Scott and I enjoy.

I collect the papers neatly together and slide them into the briefcase that will go with me to the restaurant tonight. I'll withhold judgment on this batch of people until I talk to Mel and meet them in person. I need a chance to observe them in their regular habitats, but the ones Scott has identified as those who have to hit the road are on my high-alert radar. Something about having lived through a nightmare and making it out the other side gives a person a special sense about those things. He's almost never wrong.

CHAPTER FOUR

WHEN I ARRIVE AT THE restaurant, Mel is already there and sitting at the table Scott reserved. As I walk up, he's saying goodbye to someone who stopped by to chat. I don't recognize this stranger, so I pay him no mind.

Mel gets up and comes around to pull my chair out for me and then sits down after pushing my seat in. I'm charmed by his manners. I don't see that a lot out here in L.A.

"Thank you."

"My pleasure," he says. "I'm glad we could meet on such short notice."

"I often book a table here. It's not a problem."

"You don't cook?" he asks, putting his napkin in his lap.

"No time for it." After putting my own napkin in my lap, I lean down to open up my briefcase. He doesn't need to know my main home-cooked meal is macaroni and cheese or re-heated Chinese take-out.

"Aren't we going to have dinner first?" he asks as I pull out my sheaf of papers.

"I'd prefer to get this part out of the way if you don't mind. Then we can relax and enjoy the food."

He shrugs as the waiter walks up. "Whatever you say. It's fine with me."

I order us a bottle of wine. The waiter knows me so it's easily done with minimal fuss. Once he's gone, I begin the process of narrowing my focus. I review the papers in my hands.

"I have profiles on all the people who I believe spend a significant amount of time with Tarin. You can let me know if I've missed anyone." I name all the people Scott researched, briefly showing Mel their pictures.

"That Jelly person isn't someone to be concerned with," says Mel, when I get to the leeches. "She's just passing through. Ship in the night kind of thing."

"I agree in theory, but she was with him as recently as yesterday, so for now, I have to assume she's part of the group I'll be dealing with."

"He goes through women like underwear," said Mel. "If you spend a lot of time on them, believe me, you won't have time for anything else."

"I understand. Thank you." I have a man-whore on my hands. Nothing new there. Girlfriends who aren't special were easy to deal with. It's the Sid and Nancy types that are a nightmare.

"What about these two?" I ask, holding up the guys Scott identified as possible drug connections.

"I don't know 'em. I've seen them, but who they are? … It's a mystery to me. Tarin hasn't been very forthcoming lately." Mel takes a sip of his water. He looks distracted.

The waiter comes and delivers our wine, allowing me to taste it first, giving Mel time to collect himself.

I put my fingers on the base of my wine glass, moving it in circles on the white tablecloth to circulate air over the deep ruby-red liquid inside. "Tell me about Tarin. I mean, before he was having problems."

Mel smiles, a little sadly. "He's a good person, underneath the brash exterior. A little bold, a little over the top, yes. But good. I met him when he was just seventeen, playing a few small clubs with his buddies. It was just a fluke that I caught his act. I was there with a younger agent showing him the ropes, and we'd come for another group that ended up having to go on late because something happened to their equipment. I can't recall what it was at the time, but anyway, that's neither here nor there ... I saw him, I heard him, and I knew he was going places." He smiled. "I walked right up to him and gave him my card, something I hadn't done in years and never again since. The agent I was with thought I was nuts. He said Tarin was too raw, too uncivilized for the market. But he was wrong. I knew it then, and I've been proven right a thousand times over. Kids like it raw. He's rock and roll at its very essence."

"No one can argue his success or your vision for him."

"No, they can't." Mel leans forward, now speaking passionately about his protégé. "And what so many people don't fully appreciate yet is that he's *versatile*. He's not just a one-trick pony." Mel pokes his index finger into the table several times, in staccato rhythm. "He's going to take those movie roles and he's going to blow people's minds."

"That's you're prediction?" I give him my ironic smile, the one that says it's his turn to impress me, like I did with him in his office earlier today.

"Yes, that's my prediction." He leans back in his chair, back to being his calm self once again. "And my predictions about superstars are never wrong. Tarin is a superstar."

I hold up my glass of wine and smile. "Here's to your prediction being right, then."

"I'll drink to that," he says, touching his glass to mine before taking a sip. He frowns and looks closer at the wine, using the candlelight to illuminate the shades of burgundy swirling around. "This is good. What is this?"

"Something sent over by a friend. The restaurant keeps it here for me and special clients." *Thank you, Jack.*

"You have nice friends," he says, obviously curious but perhaps too polite to press me for details. It's a refreshing change from the nosey people I usually deal with.

"Yes, I do have nice friends." I put my glass down. "So, back to business. Here's how this will play out: Tomorrow I need to meet with Tarin's bandmates and his homeboys, the ones who've been around since the start. They need to be on my side in this before he knows what's going on. After that, maybe later in the day or the next, I'll need to meet with just him, you, and me. I suggest a place he can't run away from."

"That'll be tough. What do you suggest?"

"Do you know anyone with a boat?"

He smiles. "I have a few friends with boats."

"Great. Find one with a couple bedrooms that have locks on the doors - the kind that will lock from the outside."

"Sounds ... serious." He laughs like he's not sure if I'm joking. "Are you planning on taking him prisoner?"

"No, not at all. The locks are to keep him *out* of the bedrooms, not in. In my experience, celebrities who hear things they don't want to hear like to run. If we're on a boat, he can't go far, but if he locks himself into one of the rooms, it just takes me longer. I don't have time to play. And I don't do well on small boats, so that's not an option."

Mel nods. "I think I can figure something out. You haven't given me a lot of time, though."

"Do your best. After I meet with Tarin and explain how everything will work, I'll meet with him and his people all together - an intervention of sorts to kind of solidify what we've gotten him to agree to in theory. After that we'll deal with the crew, and then the others. Tarin won't be there for those meetings. I don't want him giving them any impression that they'll be protected by him."

"Aren't you worried that Tarin will tell everyone to blow you off?"

"Tarin can try, but I can be pretty convincing when necessary. And I have you and his friends to back me up."

"But there's nothing tying Tarin to anyone. He can fire his manager, me ... anyone ... whenever he wants. If we all tell him the same thing, and he doesn't like it, he can get rid of all of us and start over new."

"He won't do it. First of all, all of his most trusted friends will be right there standing with me. And the way he's behaving now? That's a cry for help. He wants someone like me to come in and take over. He's under too much pressure. He has no boundaries. I'm the walls that are going up around him. Once he feels secure again, we'll take them down. I'll teach him to put his own boundaries in place."

Mel shakes his head. "Well, more power to you, is all I can say." He takes a healthy chug of wine. "But I hope you realize that they don't call him Tear-It-Up Kilgour because it looks cute on t-shirts."

I smile. "I'm aware. When I'm done, he'll be just regular old Tarin. And if he's not, you don't pay."

Mel stares at me for several seconds before he responds. "I *want* to pay you because I want you to succeed. I've talked to your references. They say you're some kind of miracle worker."

I shrug, a little embarrassed about the moniker. "I don't know about *that*. But I get results." I take another sip of wine. For some weird reason I'm perfectly comfortable talking about my own success, but when someone else does, it makes me feel weird. I prefer admiration to be more understated when it's directed at me, I guess.

"You get results that save lives and careers. Tarin needs you. If he can't see that, I don't know what'll happen to him." Mel shakes his head and lowers his eyes to the table, suddenly lost in thought.

I reach over and put my hand over his, patting it gently. "You don't need to worry about that. I promise. I'll get him under control and back on track."

A rough voice comes to us from over my shoulder, startling me and giving Mel a near-heart attack when he looks up. "You'll get *who* under control?" the man asks.

I turn around in my seat and find Tarin Kilgour standing behind me.

CHAPTER FIVE

MEL STANDS, CLEARLY FLUSTERED. "TARIN, my boy. What are you doing here?"

Tarin grabs a chair from a nearby table and swings it around with one hand, straddling the seat and wrapping his arms around the back of it. He's oblivious to the several sets of eyes staring at him, many of them obviously recognizing who he is.

"Looks like I'm late to the party." He holds out a hand in my direction, leaning the chair over onto two legs so he can reach me. "I don't believe we've met." His expression has a smile, but he doesn't fool me for a second. Talk about intense. I feel like a piece of chocolate in the sun.

I take his hand for a brief moment and give him a tight smile as we shake. "Not officially, no." I pull my hand back, even though he's holding on tight enough to keep it longer. I'm not comfortable with the sparks that are flying between us. This has never happened before with anyone I've ever worked with. My palm is already sweaty.

He tilts his head, frowning at me in concentration. "We sleep together before?"

I shake my head, not smiling or blushing like he expects me to, even though I'm having a minor heart attack. "Never ever." My damn brain is actually visualizing him shirtless right now. There are tattoos involved.

A cocky grin slides out and some of his intensity falls off, giving way to an easier mood. "Wow, that sounds definite." His eyes actually twinkle at me. I'm torn between blushing and slapping his face, but I play it super cool.

"Trust me, it is definite." I turn my attention to Mel. "We can finish this another time if you want."

Mel's at a loss, looking from Tarin to me.

Tarin waves in Mel's direction to keep him from answering, all of his attention focused on me. "Where do I know you from?" He rests his chin on the back of the chair, looking much younger than his twenty-three years. He reminds me of someone I used to know and it makes a pain of regret and sorrow shoot through my chest. I so don't need those reminders right now, especially when Tarin is my next fixer upper.

I sigh. He's not going to let the subject of how he knows me drop until I tell him. "I saw you today outside of Mel's office."

His face brightens and he points in my face. "That was you! Ha!" He drops his hand to the table. "You look different upside down."

I have nothing to say to that so I just stare at him. I'm all business. I will not fall for his playboy act.

He looks over at Mel. "She was in your office, wasn't she?"

Mel nods. "Yes, she was. And we were talking about you."

Tarin grabs the sides of the chair and leans back, yanking on it a few times before leaning forward again and resting his chin on the top of the chair back. He's oblivious to the fifty pairs of eyes watching everything he does and the whispers of recognition coming from the other diners.

"I'll bet you had a really interesting conversation." He raises his eyebrows up and down and smiles. He's completely full of himself. I don't find it attractive at all, but my guess is he thinks I do. I sense he's giving a performance, and I understand now why

Mel says he'll be great as an actor. I agree wholeheartedly, even with only this small sample. The women and girls will love him.

"We did have an interesting conversation actually," said Mel, pulling his napkin from his lap and putting it next to his plate. "But this isn't the time or the place to discuss it."

Tarin flops his arms down on the table in front of his chair. "Why not? You got a hot date somewhere you need to get to?" He starts drumming out a beat on the table with the sides of his thumbs.

"No. Suzanne is waiting for me at home."

Tarin winks at me while he responds to Mel. "I'm glad I didn't catch you cheating on her over here. I'd have to tattle or blackmail you or something."

Neither Mel nor I jump to the bait Tarin is dangling. He's acting like he's in a jovial mood, but there's anger or frustration there, simmering just below the surface. It will only take one small thing to set him off, and he's daring us to find his trigger and pull it.

"I need to get going," says Mel, standing. He's smart. He obviously knows his client well and realizes he's better off disappearing than staying to watch a spectacle.

I raise an eyebrow at him, letting him know I'm not crazy about being left to tame this tiger alone. He ignores me.

"See you tomorrow or Friday? On the boat?" I ask.

"Yep. I'll send you the details by email."

"Boat? What boat?" asks Tarin, looking from Mel to me and back again. "What's up, Mel? You going on that cruise already?"

"Hardly." He pats Tarin on the shoulder. "Stay. Have dinner. You look like you haven't had a decent meal in a while."

Tarin scowls, shrugging Mel's touch off. "I'm too busy to eat." Then he stands suddenly, grabbing Mel by the arm. "Wait! Stay. We can chat like we used to. Talk about my future and all our big plans." His word drip with angry sarcasm.

Mel looks at him sadly. "Please don't do that, Tarin." He reminds me of a disappointed grandfather and my heart hurts for Tarin. I pray he's not too far gone to feel the pain too.

Tarin drops his arm and looks like he's about to spit. He's angry. "Whatever. I'll see you around."

"Yes, you will."

Tarin watches him leave and then he looks at me. "What's the deal with you two? Why are you here with old man Warner in this sexy place if it's not a date?"

I gesture to the chair across the table from me, ignoring his insult to his agent and me. "Have a seat and I'll discuss it with you."

He takes a few exaggeratedly casual steps over to the chair, eyeing me suspiciously. "You a shrink?"

I shake my head silently.

"Good. Because I don't need a shrink."

No, you need a set of parents who will whoop your butt. "I agree."

He gives me a brief smile. "Great minds think alike."

"I wouldn't get ahead of myself," I say, giving him the challenge he's looking for.

He drops into the seat, sliding and slouching down until his legs bang into mine. He leaves them there, daring me with his eyes to move away.

I don't move an inch. I stay there and let the heat coming through his jeans seep through the thin material of my pants. I refuse to allow it to distract me. I will not let it do that.

"So, what's on the men-yooo," he says, giving me what I think is his best sexy look. If I weren't so disappointed in him as a person, I'd probably fall for it, or consider falling for it, anyway. Right now, it's just irritating.

"Food. Not me."

He laughs softly. "Touché. You're good. So seriously … who are you and why are you eating dinner with my agent and having meetings with him in his office?" Some of his asshole façade is slipping away and I feel like I'm catching a glimpse of the real Tarin behind the mask. It gives me hope.

"We'll discuss it Friday. On the boat."

"I'm not going on a boat."

"Yes you are." I take a sip of my wine.

He backs his head up, like he can't believe I just said that. "Says who?"

"Says your agent, the person you're contractually obligated to give your best efforts to."

He snorts. "Bullshit."

I shrug. "The rest of the band will be there. It'd be shame to have a business meeting without you there, but if you force us to, we will."

"Who the hell are you to talk to me this way?" His façade is firmly back in place, and he's spoiling for a fight. I'm not going to give him one, however. Not here. Not now. But later? Oh yeah. Most definitely.

"I'm a friend."

He stands suddenly, grabbing the edge of the table. I snatch up my glass just in time as he lifts the table up, like he's going to dump the entire thing over onto me. But then he just bangs it down. "Fuck that!" he growls. Other diners are looking at us with worried expressions. Two men sitting nearby stand and assume defensive postures. It's possible they've heard about Tear-It-Up Kilgour and how he's famous for destroying rooms and furniture.

I sit dispassionately watching his tantrum, slowly lowering my glass to the tabletop. I will not react like he wants me to.

"Mel doesn't pick my friends for me. I pick my own friends." He sounds like a small child. It's sad, not scary like he intends it.

"And you do such a good job of it," I say, deliberately egging him on. It will help my case to have something to talk about with him later … when I'm convincing him he needs me.

He walks around the table and bends over, his face only inches from mine. I can smell old booze on his breath and the stink of cigarettes. I remind myself to bring an extra toothbrush on the boat.

"Listen, girl … I don't know who you are or where the hell you came from, but you stay the fuck away from me and my friends, you hear me? Stay away."

I blink once and give him a bland smile. "Have a good night, Tarin. Try and stay out of trouble." I say this knowing it will make him crazy. Maybe it isn't the best approach, but something about him is making me act a little reckless. More reckless than I probably should be.

"Fuck that," he says. He stares at me hard for several seconds, either waiting for me to respond or just trying to wrap his head around who I might be. Either way, he gives up when I say nothing and storms off.

The waiter comes over and looks at me nervously. "Are you all right, Miss Barnes?"

I nod. "I'm fine. All in a day's work, right?"

"If you say so." He picks up the tipped over glass on Mel's side of the table and puts a fresh napkin down over the small amount of wine that stained the linen. "Will you be staying for dinner?"

"Yes. I'm just going to find myself another date. Bring me a shrimp cocktail while I wait, would you please?"

"Of course." He walks away and leaves me to make a phone call.

"What's up?" comes the voice on the other end of the line.

"Feel like eating filet mignon with bearnaise sauce?"

"Does the Pope eat pizza?"

I laugh. "I don't know. Does he?"

"Fuck yeah, he does. The guy lives in Italy. I'll be right over. Fifteen minutes max. Order for me."

"You got it. See you." I hang up and pour myself another glass of wine and smile to myself. Everything is going according to plan. Now all I have to do is convince a bunch of rock and roll stars and their best friends that Tarin Kilgour needs to be reined in and managed before disaster strikes. *Piece of cake.*

CHAPTER SIX

I WAIT UNTIL THE LAST person has arrived before I signal Mel to start the show. We're gathered at his private residence, a place most of these people have never seen. They know this is a big deal, all of them talking softly among themselves, probably speculating about why they're here. Some are seated and some are standing, all together in the huge living room Mel uses to entertain. It's much too big for a childless couple to use on a regular basis.

"Is this going to take long? Because we have a session in a couple hours." I look for the source of the voice and recognize the rhythm guitarist standing off to the side, looking annoyed.

Mel is in front of the crowd, holding out his hands for silence. "It shouldn't take more than thirty minutes unless you want it to take longer." Mel lets his not-so-subtle hint sink in before continuing. "I've asked you here for Tarin. It's that simple. The people in this room are his closest friends. We're starting with you and then we'll move on to the crew and the others."

"Starting what?" asks the guitarist.

"The intervention. Of sorts."

The guitarist shakes his head. "No way, man. Don't even bother."

A few of the other people look over at him. I see they're neutral on the subject for now, but they could go either way, deciding it's not worth the effort or that it's definitely worth trying. It will depend on who does the better job of convincing them. Now I know who I'm up against. I narrow my focus on the guitarist, reading his body language and facial expressions, trying to gauge the best plan of attack.

I stand and walk over to be with Mel.

"This is Scarlett. Maybe some of you know her. They call her The Normalizer."

Eyebrows go up around the room, but no one gives any indication that they've heard of me. They're probably wondering what the hell he's talking about.

"I'm going to let her talk to you now, but understand that she has the label's support and mine. She has complete authority over Tarin's business. Let there be no mistake about that."

The whispering starts again, and several people don't look happy.

"Hello, everyone." I stand straight with my shoulders back, being sure to make eye contact with several people as I scan the room. "My name is Scarlett Barnes. I've been hired to get Tarin back under control, back on track, and back to doing what he does best: making music. Lately, as I'm sure you've noticed, making music has kind of taken a back seat to partying, drug use, womanizing, and general hell raising." Several smiles bloom. "Not that there's anything wrong with those things in moderation, but at this point, Tarin has long passed doing any one of those things in moderation. If he keeps going at this rate, he'll be dead within the year."

I've shocked several people, but there are a handful who don't look as if they disagree. I count the bassist, the chauffeur, and the two bodyguards in that group. *Good. Four down, three to go: Drummer, guitarist, manager.*

"Wow, man, harsh," says the drummer. His stringy hair and stained t-shirt makes him look almost homeless.

"You're fresh out of the hospital for a heroin overdose, right?" I ask him.

The guy's jaw drops but he doesn't say anything. Several people snicker, but stop when he shoots them the evil eye.

"Who was with you when you were shooting up?"

He sets his jaw mutinously, but still doesn't respond.

"Yeah, that's what I thought. I know Tarin's your friend. I know you don't mean to cause him any harm. But right now, he's on a one-way path to self-destruction. It's not just having fun for him. He's lost control. He's off the rails. I need your help getting him back on."

"Yeah, but who are you?" asks the bassist. He's smiling, obviously not as bitter as the drummer. "Not to be rude or anything, but…" He shrugs.

The guitarist gives me a mean smirk as he's nodding in agreement.

"Thanks for asking, Randy. Actually, I'm a consultant. I have thirty days to get his ass in gear. It's not a lot of time so I need your help."

"You a doctor or something?" Randy asks.

"No. But I do this for a living, and I'm good at what I do."

"We just have to take your word for it?" says Stick, the rhythm guitarist. He's obviously not as convinced. "Sorry, but we're not that naive. People come after us for our money all the time."

"I've vetted her credentials, and they're impeccable," said Mel, sounding offended. "And in case I wasn't clear enough before, let me be more clear now … she has the label's and my full support. Period. This is a done deal."

I hold my hand out to calm him and the others down. "I'm not here to make anyone upset. I'm here to ask for your help. I assume you want Tarin healthy and happy …" I look around for confirmation, knowing full-well that anyone who disagrees with me right now is going to look like a complete ass. All the heads in the room either nod or just remain still.

"Good. That's what I want. It's what Mel wants, it's what you want, it's what your label wants … and believe me … it's what Tarin wants."

"I wouldn't be too sure about that," mumbles the drummer.

"Oh, I'm sure. And anyone who stands in the way of Tarin getting healthy and productive is gone." I wait a few seconds for that to sink in.

"Come again?" says Stick, on the verge of losing his temper. The anger simmers beneath the surface of his cool exterior.

I repeat in a calm voice. "Anyone who interferes in this program to get Tarin back on track is gone. Crew, bodyguards, drivers, friends …" I look directly at him and finish, "…and even bandmates if necessary."

The guitarist and drummer look at each other and then bust out laughing. They get themselves hysterical over it, so I wait for them to finish. I get the sense that the last bit of their mirth is forced, but that's okay. If they don't learn now, they'll learn soon enough.

I smile indulgently as they look at me, now obviously feeling very full of themselves. Once I'm sure I have their attention, I continue. "I recommend that you check the terms of your contract with the label. Have your attorneys verify too, if you want. Specifically take a look at paragraphs forty-three subsection 2a and forty-four in its entirety."

The smiles disappear from their faces and they exchange a worried look.

I gaze over the group, forcing my grin to stay away. This would be the wrong time to gloat. "The good news is that anyone on board with helping Tarin get his life back has nothing to fear from me. My only goal is to get rid of his problems and bring him back to his creative, happy place. I need your commitment today that you're with me in this. Thirty days or less of absolute dedication to helping Tarin."

"What are we going to have to do?" asks one of the bodyguards.

"We'll have a strategy meeting where I'll ask for your input. Then we'll start right away. We'll get rid of all the bad influences in his life, the drugs, the booze, the pills, the cigarettes. All of it. We'll get him exercising, writing, singing … doing the things that will get him whole again. We'll talk to him, remind him what he means to us, help him remember what's important in life."

"Isn't that what rehab's for?" asks the chauffeur.

"Rehab is for addicts. My information is that Tarin is not an addict." I look pointedly at the drummer. He drops his gaze.

"He has no particular drug of choice, he takes whatever's around. And he doesn't do drugs all the time, just when he's around certain people." I don't bother pointing anyone out. Everyone already knows who the culprit is in this room.

"Why don't you do a package deal?" says the bassist, looking at his bandmate. "You can get two of them sober instead of just one."

The guitarist holds the drummer back from punching the bassist in the face. I watched them work it out, waiting to speak until they're done.

I would never say this to them, and it's not that I'm a cold person, but I don't do this work for drummers unless they're the Phil Collins type. If the drummer for *By Degrees* suddenly becomes unavailable for whatever reason, they'll find a replacement in less than a day. If Tarin disappears, *By Degrees* is over. Finished. No longer able to make music that changes people's lives, lifts them up when they're down, and allows them to connect in ways that they can't without the songs. He's the singer, songwriter, and face of the music. I don't value one life over another or one career over another, but I can't save everyone. I save the ones I do because of the one I didn't.

"What's good for Tarin will be good for everyone here," I say, being as politically correct as I can.

The time has come for passionate advocacy, for me to show them exactly how and why we are going to do this. I take a deep breath and settle myself as much as possible, preparing my mind and my heart for what I'm about to say, preparing my soul for the ghosts I'm going to temporarily resurrect. I give these strangers everything I have, reaching down into the darkness and pulling out the piece of me that only sees the light of day once in the presence of strangers I will be working with: when I need them to know why I'm so dedicated to this task and how far I'll go to succeed at it.

"Many years ago, I was in love with a musician. Maybe some of you knew him. His name was Austin Betzer." I pause and see the shock on their faces as I continue. "We grew up together. We were in love for a long time, since we were in junior high, thirteen years old. I was with him when he picked up his first guitar at fourteen. I went to every show he played, from the garage parties to the arenas. I stood by his side for everything, from his rocket ship ride to superstardom to his descent into madness. I watched him slowly lose track of who he was, where he came from, and what he was all about." Everyone in the room remains silent, many of them obviously shocked.

"First his relationships suffered. Then the music did, too. And then there was nothing left for him. He couldn't stop the downward spiral and I didn't step in and do it for him. No one did. I let him go, and in doing so, I had a hand in his death. I'll never ever forgive myself for that. But what I *can* try to do is make sure it doesn't happen to another great musician like him ever again."

I look around at their expressions, seeing tears from several. I take a deep breath and give it my last bit of emotional strength. "I will fight for Tarin with everything I have, and I will personally kick the ever-loving shit out of anyone who gets in my way. But I can't do this huge thing myself. I need your help. Tarin needs your help. Please tell me now if you're in or if you're out."

The room is dead silent for about five seconds. And then the bassist speaks up. "I am so fucking in right now, you have no idea. Austin was my idol, man. I fucking died a little that night with him, you know?" He wiped a tear out of his eye. "Fuck, that was awful watching him go. We lost a fucking rock icon that night."

I nod, not trusting myself to speak. He's absolutely right, but what he doesn't know is that the world lost a gentle, loving soul that night too. There will only ever be one Austin Betzer.

"I'm in too," says the driver, his voice rough with emotion. "All the way. You just tell me what you want me to do. I didn't know Austin, but Tarin is my friend. One of my best friends. I'd do anything to help him find his way back."

"Us too," says one of the bodyguards, pointing to his colleague. "You won't have to kick anyone's ass. We'll do it for you."

My hearts soars with hope, but I just nod without smiling.

"Damn, Austin Betzer? You're his girl? I heard about you but never saw a picture." The band's manager walks up and holds his hand out. "Whatever you need, I'm in."

I shake it firmly, looking around at the rest of them.

The drummer takes a huge breath and lets it all out at once. Then he looks up. "I guess this is where I say, 'My name's Dave and I'm a drug addict,' or whatever."

I smile. "No need. Just tell me you're in and I'll see what I can do to get you whatever help you want."

He nods. "Fine. I'm in. I don't know about committing to anything else, but I can commit to Tarin. He's my best friend."

Stick is the last man standing. He's conflicted, that's clear. I can almost see the battle going on in his head. Everyone in the room is uncomfortable except me. I wait for his answer.

"Come on, man ... you remember Austin," says the bassist. "He was totally there for us. He got us that show where we met Mel."

"Yeah, remember that?" says Dave, laughing while he travels down memory lane. "He snuck around and fucked up that band's amps so they couldn't go on. We got their slot and then *bam*. Mel saw us and that was the start of it all. Where would we be without Austin? Probably still in my parents' garage."

I try not to let my shock show on my face. It feels like someone just walked over my grave. I imagine Austin's ghost whispering in my ear, telling me he was the one who set me on the path into Tarin's life all those years ago. *It's a small world, babe. There are hidden connections everywhere.*

I shake my head to get the specter out. There's no such thing as destiny. Only memories, regrets, and the desire to do better next time. I will do better this time. I *will* save Tarin's life.

"Fine." The guitarist looks at me with a guarded expression. I know I haven't won the entire war with him ... just this one battle. "I'm in until I see shit going wrong. Then I'll be out, and I won't be going anywhere." He glares at Mel. "No one can force me out of the band I helped put together."

Mel raises an eyebrow but wisely says nothing. I do the same.

Once I see all the expressions relaxing around the room, I smile. "Excellent. Thank you for coming. Please put your contact information on that sheet over there. Be sure to fill in all the boxes. My assistant Scott will be in touch for our next meeting. He's Austin's little brother, so please be gentle and forgive him if he drops a load of f-bombs on you." I pause to wait for the laughter to stop. "Please consider yourselves on-call for the next thirty days. If I call, I'll expect you to answer and respond ASAP. Last, but not least, please do not say anything to Tarin or the crew or any of the other people who hang around. I'll be discussing this situation with Tarin personally tomorrow and then all the rest of them after." I pause to scan their faces. "Are we good?"

I get affirmative nods from everyone. Some of them are reluctant, but I'm okay with that. Acceptance will come slower for some, but I *will* get it. Failure is not an option.

"I'm meeting with the crew and other people who spend time with Tarin tomorrow. I'll be getting rid of the ones who I deem to be counterproductive to our task. Just to be clear, anyone I dismiss is permanently gone, so if you have friends who are not here right now, who you know I'll speak with, please wait until after I've talked to them to discuss it with them. I don't mind if you try to get them on board, because we need all the help we can get, but just know that I don't give second chances. Once they're gone, they're gone. Even after I've left. But I don't want any of them speaking to Tarin until I do, so mum's the word." I put my finger to my lips for effect.

Eyebrows go up, but no one argues. I let out a long breath in relief as Mel walks up to me and the crowd filters over to the door where my contact sheet is waiting for their information.

"That went better than I expected," he says quietly, standing very close so no one will hear as they leave.

"I was happy with it. I know you wanted to discuss our plan for tomorrow, but would you mind if I call into my office first?"

"Not a problem."

"Do you have a quiet spot where I can do that?"

He walks me to his private office and waits until I'm seated to leave me alone. At the door he turns and faces me. "Thank you, Scarlett. And for what it's worth, I'm sorry for your loss. Austin was very special. Now I understand why you do what you do, and I respect it very much."

I nod, unable to answer.

He seems to understand, leaving me to my thoughts.

As soon as he shuts the door, I drop my face into my hands and cry, unable to keep the memories at bay any longer.

CHAPTER SEVEN

TARIN COMES SAUNTERING DOWN THE dock wearing board shorts, boat shoes, a white surfer t-shirt, aviator sunglasses, and a blond on each arm. One of them is the ding-a-ling I saw outside Mel's office falling out of Tarin's car. Jelly is her name if memory serves. That kind of name is hard to forget.

She looks much better today than she did in her mug shot. It's amazing what makeup and a hairbrush can do for a girl. I try not to dislike her on sight. It's not her fault she's a groupie. Like so many other girls before her, she's caught up in the image and the music. I'm willing to bet she really has no idea what it's like to live with and love an artist. She's living in a fantasy world right now, and I can hardly blame her for holding on with both hands.

Tarin's swagger is perfect, no drunken swaying or stumbling to mar the effect. He walks like he has a golden prick between his legs and he wants all the women of the world to know it. I force myself to think of other things as the giggles from the girls carry over to us on the ocean breeze. Memories of him in the restaurant with his cocky casualness overlaying a crazy intensity make me go uncomfortably warm.

"We're not letting those women on, are we?" Mel asks quietly as we watch them approach. He shifts from one foot to the next, nervous about our plan for Tarin. It's strange to see such a powerful man so worried about a simple thing like taking on a rock star. It makes me just a little nervous too, which pisses me off. I cannot afford to be nervous right now. I conjure up an image of Austin, wasted on the couch, to solidify my resolve. I have lots of those memories to prop me up when necessary.

"No, they are definitely not coming," I say. "You take Tarin into the salon and I'll escort them off the boat. He'll never know they're not with us until we're gone. Make sure you put some music on kind of loud in case they yell."

"He's going to be angry."

"Good."

My goal is not to avoid emotional outbursts, believe it or not. Tarin has a lot of things going on that are torturing him; the sooner I can get him to exorcise those ghosts, the better off we'll all be. Guys like him do it though music and sometimes yelling if the mood is right. If he yells at me and Mel today, I'll consider that a win.

"Well, well…if it isn't little miss uptight," says Tarin, sneering at me as he lifts his glasses and leaves them on the top of his head. They settle into the messy, spiked hair. He looks like a cover model advertising cologne for bad boys, his arm tattoos and dark beard stubble standing out in stark contrast to his white shirt and pale skin. He's thin … too thin, and it makes his shorts slip down too far. Without the shirt on, I'm sure I'd be seeing way too much. I'm glad for the shirt. I don't need any more distractions than he already offers.

"Tarin … manners," chides Mel.

"Yeah, whatever." He turns to the girl on his left, the one from the car. "Why don't you go find the bedroom, love."

"What about me?" asks the one on the right, pouting.

"You find the bar and mix me a drink. Then come join us." He smacks her on the butt and she practically coos.

Working really hard not to smack her myself for being so stupid, I put on my cruise director smile. "Actually, if you two could just come up to the front of the boat for a couple minutes, the captain wants to be sure you know where the lifejackets and things are."

"What's that all about?" Tarin is suspicious.

I shrug. "It's not my boat. I don't make the rules, the captain does." I turn around and wave at the man in uniform who's standing up in the glassed-off command center, and he waves back. Then he points to bow of the yacht, just like we planned. He's good at looking stern.

"Fine," says Tarin, his mood only slightly deflated. "Go do your little life jacket thing and then get to the fun stuff. Drinks and bedroom." He looks at Mel. "Lead the way, Mel. You have ten minutes before I get my drink on."

Tarin takes a big step from the dock to the boat, and I make sure to get far enough back so he can go by me without stomping on my toes. He gets close enough to brush up against me anyway, and I can smell his scent as he goes by. It stirs my blood enough to throw me off a little. He chuckles, and I know that he's done it on purpose. He's trying to intimidate me with his male-ness, but I won't fall for it. I never do. Guys like him bag girls just because they can, not because they care. I won't ever be one of those girls.

The men leave me standing with the girls who are still on the dock, and I breathe a sigh of relief. *Little things first. These chicks, I can handle.* Tarin's two bodyguards come out of the door behind me and stand there. I can't see them but I can sense their hulking forms.

"Change of plans, girls," I say, once I'm sure Mel has Tarin inside. "You won't be going on the cruise today."

The girl assigned to get the drinks looks confused. The one assigned to be head prostitute narrows her eyes at me. "Says who?"

"Says me."

"Who are you, his wife?" She's pissed.

The other girl snorts, but then stops abruptly at a glare from me.

I turn my attention back to my interrogator. "No, Jelly, I'm not his wife. I'm worse than a wife. But don't worry ... he'll be back in a few hours. You'll be able to hook up with him then. Feel free to wait right here on the dock if you want."

"Bullshit. I'm coming on board." Jelly takes a step forward and the other girl looks ready to follow her.

"Don't even think about it, Jelly," says Zach, the bodyguard on my left.

"Shut up, whoever you are. You don't tell me *or* Tarin who goes on a boat with him." She's not just pissed, she's furious. Her nostrils are flaring and her hands are in fists. Her fake boobs are bouncing around as she flexes her chest muscles.

I look up at Zach and am impressed with his complete lack of expression. He's a total badass, immune to her anger and her plastic beauty.

Jelly hesitates just a moment before moving forward again.

I step out of the way so Zach can get by. He blocks her entry by standing in the way.

"Move!" she says loudly, leaning over from the dock and pushing on him. It's about as effective as trying to move a brick wall.

I turn around and signal again to the captain. He puts his hand on his cap and jerks it down at me once, signaling he understands. Then the horn sounds loudly and the engines rev, churning up the water behind the fifty-foot yacht.

A small, skinny guy dressed all in white walks quickly to the front of the boat and unties a rope from the dock, making quick work of coiling it and stowing it in a cabinet. He moves down the side of the boat and passes behind me to do the same with a rope at the back of the boat. He whistles loudly when it's done, and the boat begins to drift away from the dock under the power of the engines and the slight current in the marina.

"Hey! You can't leave without me!" shouts Jelly.

Zach is standing just at the edge of the boat, keeping her from jumping on. She tries to sidestep around his barrier, her obvious plan to leap to the space next to him, but he easily moves over to block her once more.

"Move, you big ogre!"

"Just go give it a rest, Jelly," he says. "You can catch Tarin later."

"I don't *want* to catch him later! I want to catch him *now!* You have no right to keep us apart!" She turns her attention to the back of the boat, the last place she saw Tarin before he disappeared. "Tarin!! Tarin, they're not letting us on!"

The other girl joins in and they're both screaming by the time the boat is ten feet from the dock. There's no more danger of them jumping on board, so Zach backs up to stand with his partner behind me.

"Taaaarinnnnn!!" They're both beet-red in the face with their screaming, and they look ready to tear someone's hair out. I'm glad I'm too far for them to reach, because the murderous expressions they're sending my way are making it clear it's my hair that would be their target.

"You are going to be so sorry!" Jelly yells at me. "Don't think for one second you're going to steal him away from me!"

"I'm not interested in your man, Jelly, don't worry. We'll deliver him back to you in one piece by the end of the day. Why don't you go get a manicure or something?"

"Why don't *you* go get a manicure you plain-as-shit bitch!" she screeches, stomping her foot with her fists at her sides.

I smile and turn my plain-as-shit self around, leaving the vultures on the docks. The last thing I hear are threats to call the police for the kidnapping of boyfriends. I'm not worried, because we'll be in international waters in about fifteen minutes and that's when the fun will begin.

Now that everything is well underway here, I have to call Scott and let him know to set up the meeting with the crew and others for later. While I'm on the phone, I remind him to add Jelly and her friend to the list of attendees and tell him he can call the dockmaster right now so he can speak with Jelly directly before she gives up and leaves. I wait until we're far from shore before going to join Mel and Tarin in the salon.

CHAPTER EIGHT

I WALK INTO THE SALON and find Mel and Tarin alone. Zach and Leonard, the bodyguards, are out of sight, but I know they're somewhere close. They promised to be there in case things get out of hand, and I trust that they'll follow through.

"Hello," I say, shutting the sliding glass door behind me. "How's it going in here?" I ask. I walk over and put a glass of orange juice down in front of Tarin before taking a seat across from him. Mel and I are in single armchairs on the opposite side of a low coffee table from Tarin who's sprawled out on a couch, one of his legs dangling off and the other propped up at the end.

"What's that? A screwdriver?" he asks, looking at the drink while reaching for it.

"Yep. Virgin screwdriver."

He snorts, and pulls his hand away. "Bring me a couple shots of vodka."

"No." I stare at him mildly, not trying to get him worked up, but letting him know I'm not his servant. "We have a meeting to take care of before you start having anything to drink or smoke."

He gives me a lazy smile and then sighs happily as he turns his head to look at the ceiling. "Wake me up when you're done with your meeting. I need to go get laid." His smile remains as he begins to fake-sleep.

Mel glances at me, but I shake my head briefly, telling him to let me handle it. He gets up and stands behind his chair, watching me nervously.

"Tarin, this meeting is between you and me, so I'd appreciate it if you could give me your attention."

"I didn't call any meeting." His eyes are still closed.

"I did."

"And that might matter if I even knew who you are, which I don't. You aren't my agent, you aren't in the band, and you aren't from the label, so unless you're here to put out, I've got nothing to say to you."

Since he's determined to be crude, I decide to skip the niceties and just go for the throat. I have to snag his attention before he actually falls asleep. "I work for the label and your agent, so I called this meeting, and I expect you to pay attention. As of today, your life is going to change. The game is over. No more bullshit. It's done."

He lounges there silently, not saying anything. But his smile has slipped a little, so I know he's hearing me.

"The drugs are gone. The booze is gone. Cigarettes are gone. You're on a new exercise regimen that starts this afternoon. Consider yourself in active outpatient rehab."

He opens his eyes and looks at Mel, scowling. "Who is this crazy bitch and why'd you let her on your boat? Is this some kind of joke?"

Mel shakes his head sadly. "This is no joke, Tarin. This is the rest of your life. I suggest you sit up and start acting like the man you really are and stop making this so difficult on yourself and everyone else."

Tarin sits up quickly, his anger clear in his tone. "Fuck that, Mel! What the hell? What'd I do to you anyway, other than make you a shit ton of money, huh?"

"It's not about the money, Tarin. It's about you, as a person. I'm worried about you."

Tarin stands, the muscles in his chest pulsing through his t-shirt. "Bullshit! All any of you care about is the money. Are you worried I won't show up for the tour? Is that it? I told you I'd go, all right?! I told you I just needed to let off a little steam first. Jesus, why is everyone always up my fucking ass?" He runs his fingers through his hair, knocking his sunglasses off. They bounce off the couch and land on the floor.

Mel looks at me, disappointment shining out from sad eyes. "I need to let you do this without me. I'm liable to ruin everything with what I want to say right now."

I shake my head, hardening myself to his distress. "No. Tell him what you're thinking. He needs to hear it."

"Oh, what … you're going to blame me for some bullshit right now, is that it? Well, *fuck you*, Mel, okay? Fuck you." Tarin moves around the coffee table towards the door leading out to the back deck of the boat.

Zach appears in the entrance and shakes his head no. Crossing his arms, he makes it clear he's not going anywhere. Tarin will have to pass through that mountain to get to his destination.

Tarin throws the sliding glass door open. "Get the hell out of my way, Z."

"Sorry, man. Can't do it. Just give the girl a chance to talk to you."

Tarin shoves him with both hands in the chest, but Zach barely moves.

"Get the fuck outta my way!" Tarin yells in his face, his entire body tense.

"Don't touch me like that, man," says Zach. He sounds sad.

Tarin growls and turns around, rage in his eyes. "Mel! Tell that bitch to get off your boat or I'm outta here!"

Mel gestures out the windows to the deep blue ocean that surrounds us. "Where are you going to go, Tarin? We're at sea." He pauses for the reality to sink in before continuing. "Why don't you just sit down here and listen to what she has to say? You need to hear it, and when it's over, it's over. Like a bandaid. Rip it off. Get it over with."

Mel walks closer to Tarin, holding out a hand in my direction. "Go sit. Relax. I'll be back in a little while."

Tarin shifts to the side and watches Zach let Mel by. As the door slides shut he turns his ire on me.

"I don't know who the fuck you are, but you're going down for this." He pulls out his cell phone and presses some buttons. "I'm calling my attorney. He'll file the lawsuit before we even get back. Kidnapping and … fuck. Other shit. I don't know what but it's gonna put your sorry ass in jail."

He puts the phone to his ear and then frowns. Pulling the phone away, he stares at the screen. "Fuck. No signal." He points the phone at me. "I'm calling when I get back. You're fucking going down."

I walk back to my chair and sit. "Come talk to me. We'll discuss the upcoming lawsuit later."

He turns his back to me and stares out at the water. "Tell them to let Jelly in and I'll talk."

"Jelly's not here."

"Yeah, I know. She's in the bedroom waiting for me. Bring her here and I'll talk."

"No, I mean she's not on the boat. She's still on the dock."

He spins around and looks at me like I'm crazy. "What?"

"She wasn't invited. She'll be waiting for you when you get back."

He slowly shakes his head at me, biting his lower lip as he walks over. It's impressive how he goes from flaming pissed to deviously angry. "You are something else, you know that?" He walks around my chair until he's in front of the couch. Dropping down to sit on the edge of the cushions, he points a finger at me. "I don't know how you managed to brainwash Mel and Zach, but you're not going to get away with that shit. There's laws against taking people against their will."

I nod. "Hopefully once you hear me out, you'll decide not to sue."

He leans back, lacing his hands behind his head and letting his legs drop to the sides. I have a straight-on view of his crotch, and I'm glad his board shorts are so long that they cover up things that would normally be revealed in this kind of pose. He pulses his pelvis up once, either to get comfortable or to make me ner-vous. I suspect the latter when I see him give me a lascivious smirk right after.

I yank my attention back to why I'm here, hoping he doesn't notice my ears going red. "Thank you, Tarin. Really, I appreciate you giving me a chance to explain."

He says nothing. He just stares me down, trying to intimidate me or too busy keeping a rein on his anger to respond, it's hard to tell which.

"I've been hired by Mel and your label to help you get your life back under control."

His nostrils flare but that's the only sign I have that he's heard me. It's like he's attempting to stare holes into my face the way his gaze never falters and his expression stays so serious. I wonder when I'm almost under his thrall like this why no one calls him Terror instead of Tear-it-up. It seems a more appropriate nick-name. I'm not afraid of him; I'm more afraid of what he could make me do than anything. I have a feeling he can be very con-vincing when he wants to be. It's probably what's gotten him in all this trouble in the first place. I can picture him being hard to say no to.

"I've worked with several other artists in the same situation you're in right now. Whether you realize it or not, you've lost your way. I've talked to Ricky and Zach and Leonard along with your bandmates, and they all tell me the same things."

Tarin shifts in his seat, but otherwise gives me no indication of what he's thinking.

"You're incredibly talented and a nice person. You like to play practical jokes, you'll give a friend the shirt off your back, you loan money you never expect to get back. You're generous and fun loving and you used to be happy-go-lucky."

As I shift gears, I can see it's having an effect on him. He drops his arms to his sides, still staring at me. I continue. "But now you're angry a lot. You're taking drugs that you know ar-en't good for you or your music. You're hanging out with users, people who don't care about you. You're not healthy. You blew off your grandfather's birthday last month, and you didn't even visit Dave in the hospital after he overdosed. And you were there when it happened. You didn't stop him when you could have."

Tarin's uncomfortable now, breaking his gaze away to look at the walls and floor. His legs twitch, his knees going towards each other and apart, over and over.

"You're using women who don't know any better than to throw themselves at you, you're treating the people who helped get you to where you are rudely and accusing them of using you … all of these things are symptoms of a bigger problem."

"Oh, yeah?" he says, his voice not as loud now but just as emotional. "What's that, Miss Know-It-All?"

I shrug to ease the sting. "Lost. You're lost. You're wandering around in a scary place and you don't know how to find your way back. That's why I'm here. Let me be your guide."

He jerks his eyes back to me glares. "Fuck you. I'm happy."

"Be honest. You're not happy. You're miserable."

He frowns at me, frustrated. "Who the hell are you to tell me I'm not happy, huh? You don't know me. You don't know me at all."

"I knew a man like you. Once."

"What'd he do, dump you?" He laughs at his own cruel joke.

I look down in my lap, gripping my hands tightly together in the hope it will keep me together too. "No, he didn't dump me," I say softly. My strength has abandoned me temporarily. I lift my head, tears making my eyes bright. I will them not to fall.

Tarin loses his smile. "What happened?" His voice is softer this time. I catch a glimpse of the humanity inside him, the man his friends tell me he is when he's not high and drowning in darkness.

"He was a brilliant musician. The love of my life, actually. But he got caught up in the fame-and-fortune part of the life and got lost. I never got him back." *And I never brought him back, either.*

"What do you mean, you never got him back?" He's scoffing at my pain, trying to remain cruel and unconcerned, but I recognize it as a protective measure so I didn't take offense. I try not to let it hurt too much.

"Or maybe I don't want to know," he finishes.

"His name was Austin Betzer." I pause, waiting for the words to sink in. "You tell *me* what happened." I want to hear him say it out loud. He won't listen to me, but maybe there's a chance he'll at least listen to himself.

Tarin looks like he's seen a ghost. He whispers, "Fuck me," as his entire body goes slack, the aggression draining out of him in an instant.

His reaction is stronger than I'd expected, but I don't let that stop me. "So now you know. Now you know why I'm here. You and I are going to work together and get your shit fixed, so you don't end up in a body bag like my boyfriend did. It's time to pay the piper for all the mistakes you've made. Time to man-up and turn your life around."

Tarin leans over and grabs the orange juice, gulping it down. His gaze never leaves my face. When he finishes, he leans back, using the back of his hand to wipe the orange juice mustache off his upper lip. "So what's that mean, exactly? Like what is it you want to do? Are you the fucking ghost of Christmas past or something? Are we getting lawyers involved?"

His abrupt change of attitude makes this situation completely different than the ones I experienced with my other clients. I hadn't expected it to go this smoothly, so I'm temporarily at a loss for words. My silence seems to make him nervous, so I throw something out there until I can collect my thoughts. "Lawyers?" is all I can manage.

He gets a burst of energy and starts gesturing with his free hand while he talks. "You know, shit happens with people, right? I mean, you go out and you party it up ... and shit happens. You have no idea when you're about to go too far. You do one more hit or drink one more shot. No one ever knows when it's too much until it's too late, right?"

He leans forward suddenly and puts the empty glass on the table before dropping his head into his hands. He runs his fingers through the hair above his ears, like he's massaging the sides of his head because he's stressed out. "Fuck! ... Fuck!"

I begin to wonder if he's high. I hadn't detected that he was under the influence when he arrived, but it's the only explanation that makes sense. I hope I've been speaking with a semi-straight person this whole time, otherwise I'm going to have to do it all over again once he's clean.

"Are you okay?" I ask.

He laughs bitterly and then sits up, staring at me intensely. "Okay? No. I'm far from okay, as you've so clearly pointed out."

I stand, feeling like having a friend around right now is a good idea for him. "Mind if I invite Zach and Leonard in?"

He shakes his head, back to staring at the ground. "Do whatever you want. I don't care."

I signal the bodyguard to come in. When he opens the door, I say, "Would you get Leonard and join us in here?"

He nods and disappears around the corner.

I sit back down and wait for Tarin to say something. I don't want to stop his flow of thoughts with my own spoken ones.

"I can't fucking believe it," he says. Then he throws himself back into the cushions, staring at the ceiling. "After all this fucking time...Austin."

"Austin's been gone for two years. It's not that long."

He angles his eyes down to look at me. "Feels like forever. I've been looking over my shoulder for fucking *ever*."

It seems like a strange way to describe the situation, but he's the poet-musician, not me. "I know what you mean." I lie when I say that, because to me it feels like it was just last week that I was staring into Austin's bloodshot eyes for the last time.

"So when do we start this deal?" he asks as the door slides open to admit Zach and Leonard. He acknowledges them with barely a glance, before looking back at me.

"We have a deal, then?" I ask. "You agree to my terms?"

"Yeah, fine." He tips his head back into the cushions and looks at the ceiling "We have a fucking deal."

"Good. To answer your question, it starts today. You're going to make an announcement to all your people and your team that I'm in charge and that they follow my direction. Tomorrow morning starts your healthy living campaign. You will get you up at six for your first workout. We'll discuss the rest of the plan while you're running on the treadmill after."

Zach and Leonard take seats next to me and Tarin. "Don't look so freaked out," says Zach, nudging him in the leg. "We'll do it with you."

Tarin says nothing, he just lifts his head and stares at his friends with his mouth partway open, his jaw off kilter.

I continue, not wanting to break my rhythm. "I'm going to be firing some people. Whoever I let go, you need to support me on it." Tarin presses his lips into a thin line but still says nothing, so I keep going. "Who's supplying you with drugs? Is it Brett Campbell?"

Tarin sighs loudly before nodding and answering. "Yeah."

"Okay, he's gone. Zach and Len, I need you to make sure he stays away."

"Consider it done," promises Zach. Leonard nods his head in agreement. They both look happy about the prospect.

"What about Clay?" I ask. "Is he bringing drugs in too?"

Tarin folds his arms. "No."

"What's his function in your life? Because I know he's not a friend."

"He's a friend." Tarin acts offended but it's too much. He's defensive.

"Truth, Tarin. No more messing around."

He rolls his eyes. "Fine. He brings the party guests."

"He means the hoes," says Zach, smiling mischievously.

Tarin scowls at him, but doesn't deny it.

"Nice. So he's the pimp." I look at the bodyguards. "He's out too." They nod.

I address Tarin, putting the full weight of my determination in my gaze. "You'll call them when we get back to the dock and tell them yourself that they're out. If they have any stuff at any of your properties, they have until the end of the day to get it." I shift my attention to Zach. "Make sure they have escorts so they don't steal anything."

He nods at me and then at Leonard. They exchange a look and some sort of silent agreement.

"Oh, man, no," says Tarin, sounding desperate, "don't make me do that. Please don't make me call them and tell them to fuck off." He's begging and both Zach and Leonard look shocked at his tone. I can't help but be surprised too. He's always struck me as tougher than that. Maybe he's not as heartless as he seems. Or maybe he's just worried about missing out on the parties and the chicks.

"Sorry, but it'll be easier on them in the long run if they hear it from the horse's mouth. If they hear it from me they're going to get their asses beat by these guys when they try to force themselves back in."

Tarin bows his head and rests his face in his open palm. His voice comes out muffled. "Fine. Anything else?"

"How close are you to Jelly?"

He lifts his head suddenly. "What the *fuck?* I have to give up sex too?!"

Zach snorts. Leonard looks away to hide his face.

I smile, noting that he considers her for sex before companionship. I have a feeling she won't be around for long if that's the case. I don't know why that makes me happy, but I shove the feelings away. "No, you don't have to give up sex. But you have to give up all bad influences."

Tarin looks at Zach. "Do you think she's a bad influence?"

"Don't ask me, man. I'm just the enforcer."

He punches him sloppily in the arm. "Don't be a fucking pussy, just tell me."

Leonard joins the conversation. "She did get busted for DUI and possession. She's got shit in her purse every time she comes to see you. She likes to get high."

"So I'll tell her to clean her shit up. She can stay clean with me."

I shrug. "I'm willing to give her a chance. If she can do it, she can stay."

"Fine. She stays then." Tarin looks like he's won something, and I'm happy to see it. I don't want him going into this all beat down. He'll do better if he has a hand in his recovery. Plus, his relationship to Jelly is nothing to me. Nothing at all.

"Anyone else on the chopping block?" he asks, some of his spark back.

"Maybe your drummer. We'll see."

He laughs, but more with shock than anything else. "What…? *Dave?*" He looks at Zach. "She's kidding, right?"

Zach shakes his head silently.

"Fuuuuck me. That's just fucking *crazy* talk right there." He stares at me, half challenging me and half fearful of me. "You can't kick people out of the band. That's going too far."

I narrow my eyes. "I can do whatever I want. We have a deal."

He swallows with effort and then throws up his hands. His voice comes out an octave higher than normal. "Fine. Fucking kick Dave out, see if I care. Fucker's an H fiend anyway." He looks away, but not before I see his eyes going shiny.

"Don't worry about Dave," I say, hoping to calm him down. Tears aren't a good thing right now. He'll feel too vulnerable and I need him strong. "We're going to try and help him too. I don't want to do anything with the band. You guys are great. You just need to get your shit together again, that's all. Dave sounds like he wants to help, so if he accepts it, he stays, not a problem."

"I don't even know if we have shit to get together at this point," Tarin says, staring out the window at the ocean.

I stand, preparing to leave him alone so I can use the ship's phone to call Scott. "Sure you do. The garbage you've been filling your life with has blocked some of your creativity, but we'll get it back. Don't worry."

"You're going to do all that … get our lives back and clean our shit up … in how long? A year?"

"Thirty days."

"Thirty days," he deadpans, looking at me like I'm nuts.

"That's the deal."

"Good luck with that," he says, dropping his head back on the cushions and closing his eyes.

I leave the salon, sliding the door closed behind me.

CHAPTER NINE

SCOTT IS MORE NERVOUS THAN I am. I slap him gently on the arm. "Would you please chill? You're going to freak us both out if you keep doing that."

He's bouncing up and down and flicking his hands around. I don't tell him, but whenever he does that it reminds me of his brother. Austin used to do it before a show; he said it limbered him up and got the blood flowing. I should have known Austin was in trouble when he stopped doing it and just sauntered out onto the stage without caring. There were so many signs I ignored. Or maybe I felt powerless to control them. Either way, it was no secret Austin was in trouble and I didn't do anything to stop the train wreck from happening. I was too weak and afraid. But not anymore. Now I'm in complete control. I will not let Tarin down.

Scott's bending his head left, right, front, and back, like he's exercising his neck. "I can't chill out. What if he flips? It could get seriously ugly. You know I hate scenes."

"We've been through this several times with other people and it always worked out. Why are you so jittery this time? You've never done this before." He looks lost, so I grab his hand and yank it once before letting it go, trying to pull him back into our reality.

"This one is different." He looks at me, real fear in his eyes as he grabs my arm with two hands. "Can't you feel it? Tell me I'm not crazy and that you feel it too. It's like … a tingle in my butt cheeks or something."

"Ew. Bad visual. And for the record, you *are* crazy, but I know what you mean. He reminds me … of … stuff." I shake Scott off as I look away, hoping to see people walking through the door; but it remains closed.

Scott isn't done pestering me. "It's Austin, right? I know he reminds you of Austin. He reminds *me* of Austin and I haven't even *met* him yet." Scott's bouncing again. "This is fucking nuts, man. Nuts with a capital T for testicle."

"He has the same intensity as Austin, but other than that, there's no similarity." I'm not sure I'm being exactly honest about that, because I sense the possibility of a lot of other similarities, but I don't want Scott fixating on that stuff. He needs to keep his head in the game just like I do, and he's even more sensitive about Austin's death than I am. Austin was his hero and his only sibling. Aside from his dad, I'm his only family now.

The door opens and people begin to filter in to Mel's living room. The relief that washes over me is calming, and it gets me back to the place where I need to be mentally. We're here for the big meeting followed by a buffet dinner in the garden after. This is where the last group of people will be let in on our plans, surrounded by all the others who've already been notified. Tarin has promised to come and to be on time. Ricky assured me he'd get him here. I look at my watch. He has fifteen minutes left.

"You don't really believe that, do you?" Scott stops bouncing as he stares at me. "Don't play hardass with me. I know you see it too. It's more than just their intensity that's the same."

I sigh. "Maybe they have the same intensity and their music style is similar, but that's it."

Scott snorts. "And they're the same size, same color hair, and same attitude."

I shrug. "Maybe."

He crosses his arms over his chest. "I'm calling you out. Truth."

I press my lips together and scowl at him. We have an agreement, so I cannot deny him what he demands. "Fine. I see it, I feel it, and to be honest, I fucking hate it. I've been trying to pretend it's not there since the minute we started following his story. But it's awful, Scott, okay? It's really, really awful to feel Austin so close again, so I don't want to talk about it anymore."

He nods, his good humor gone. "Yeah, I get it. I do." He throws an arm across my shoulders. "I'm sorry I pushed you, sis."

A lump develops in my throat over that name. *Sis.* We both thought I was going to be his sister one day, but that never happened. Austin was gone too soon for us to make our family connections official.

I punch him in the ribs, making his arm drop. "Don't worry about it, bro. We're all good." I never let Scott see how hurt I still am over what happened to Austin. I need to be strong for my almost-little-brother.

After he recovers from my abuse with some exaggerated deep breaths, Scott swings his arm up again to rest on my shoulders. "So … who's ass shall we kick first?"

"I'm giving everyone a free pass today, unless they do something stupid in the meeting. We'll see what shakes out after. And, Scott … I have something special I need you to do."

"Yeah, you name it. I'll all over it. Your wish is my command."

"We're moving in to Tarin's place for at least the first week. I need you to stick to him like glue."

His arm drops away. "Uhhhh … no."

I smile, not even looking at him. "Uhhhh … yes."

"Bitch be smokin'."

"No, bitch be serious."

He shifts to whining to try and convince me. "But I've got really important shit to do! I can't be running around playing babysitter all day. This isn't in my job description."

I put my hands on my hips and face him. "Oh yeah? What important things?" He thinks he has me fooled.

"*Very* important things. Really, very, super important *things*."

"Video games are not really, very, super important things, Scott. Try again."

"Maybe not to you!" His face gets pink with indignation. He's sensitive about his gaming. I think he spends so much time doing it just to avoid contact with other humans, and it makes me hate the games like they're bad people. He thinks he's developing hand-eye coordination which will somehow be critical to future plans he hasn't even made yet.

"If it makes you feel better, you can bring your stupid games to his place if he doesn't already have what you need."

His arguments go silent. Then he sighs. "For how long, did you say?"

"A week or until we're sure he's playing fair and doing what he says he's doing."

Scott shifts from his whining voice to his negotiating one. "I'll need a raise. And money for expenses, too."

"I figured."

"And lots of mint chocolate chip ice cream."

"Done."

"That was too easy. Fuck. I should have asked for a car or something."

"I already bought you a car on our last job, remember?"

"Okay, a Vespa, then. I should have asked for a Vespa."

I smile. "Play your cards right and maybe it'll happen."

He grabs my arm. "Are you serious? Because don't play with me like that if you aren't. You know how much I want a Vespa. I'm Vespa Desperate. It's a medical syndrome, you know. I see Vespas and I want to chase them down the street like a rabid terrier."

I smile and say nothing more. It's going to be fun torturing him with his scooter obsession. For some reason he denies himself the things he wants most, even though he makes enough money at this job to buy pretty much whatever he wants. The only nice things he has are gifts from me and the video games his brother gave him before he died.

"I need a red one. Or blue. But *not* pink. Don't you dare make me ride a pink one. Because it's a Vespa, so I'll have to ride it anyway, but everyone will think I'm gay, which I'm not. Not that there's anything wrong with being gay. Unless people think you are when you're not. That would suck major donkey balls. Not that I'd know anything about sucking balls, but I assume it would be really unpleasant..."

"Could you shut up now?"

"Yeah. Right now, I can. I'm shutting up. Right this second. I'm not going to say a single other solitary word to you. Not one. Not even one. Just don't forget about the Vespa and it not being pink."

I step close enough to elbow him sharply in the ribs before moving off to join Mel at his side.

"Ready for the big reveal?" I ask.

"I think so." He glances at me. "Call me hopeful at this point, but I thought the meeting this afternoon went really well."

"Yes. Better than I expected, actually."

"That isn't how it usually goes?"

"Not necessarily." I don't give him details about how Tarin flipped a switch in the middle of our negotiation and suddenly became perfectly amenable to changing his whole life. Mel's already stressed enough as it is; I don't need him trying to figure out the mystery that is Tarin when he has so many other things to manage.

We both turn our attention to the group that's gathering. It's a motley crew with everything from straight-laced preps to drugged-out losers. None of them is Tarin. The last person in the door is Zach. He walks over to us, his expression dark.

"What's wrong?" asks Mel before Zach is even close.

"Can't find Tarin."

My heart sinks. "Did you call Ricky?" I ask.

"Yeah. Tarin ditched him earlier today and left him driving around town looking for him."

"Who's responsible for this? … Because I know it's not Ricky," I'm pissed, ready to kick ass and take names. No way am I going to let Tarin get dragged down any farther. I had him for a moment today, totally connecting on an eye-to-eye level, and it was enough to tell me this can work. The conversation I just had with Scott about Tarin being so much like Austin only makes the whole thing feel more urgent.

Zach responds. "My guess who's responsible? Jelly. She was with him at the time. He got a phone call, told Ricky to wait for him outside a restaurant, and when he wasn't out an hour later, Ricky went in looking for him."

"Where was he?" Mel asks.

Zach shrugs. "He wasn't anywhere. He hadn't even stayed to eat. Must have gone right back out the front door when Ricky wasn't looking." Zach's shoulders sag. "I should have been with him. I should have known he was being too easy about the whole thing. Tarin never does anything the easy way."

I push away the anxiety that wants to take over. "Don't worry about it, Zach. Now we know he's going to fight us a little. We'll do better next time." I'm pulling out my phone to start making calls to people who might be able to locate him when the door opens and three laughing, snorting people come stumbling into the room.

Tarin. My heart skips a beat at how messed up and handsome he is. I have to work really hard to not shoot daggers at the idiots with him. Tarin, Jelly the dingbat, and Brett the druggie are all standing together, laughing at some private joke. The three stooges. Maybe it's just paranoia, but I suspect their mirth has something to do with me, since they keep looking at me and giggling rudely all over again.

Zach looks like a bird with ruffled feathers, so I put my hand on his arm. "Just leave them to me."

He stares down at me for a few seconds and then nods. "Probably better that you do it. I'm about ready to crack a couple skulls right now."

"I know the feeling," I say, earning a smile from him. I turn my attention to Mel. "You can stay or go, your choice."

"I'll stay. No need for you to have to do this on your own. I hate to admit it, but I feel somewhat responsible for this whole mess." His face sags and he looks every bit his age for a change.

It's sad to see him resembling an empty balloon. An empty balloon with a comb-over is about as pitiful as it gets.

I pat his arm. "You're not to blame for his bad choices. And if you hadn't called, things would be worse. Let's just get tonight over with and tomorrow morning we'll start getting him back."

Mel nods. "Good. I leave him and the rest of us in your hands, then. I'll be over in the corner with a triple scotch if you need me." We share a wry grin before I move to confront Tarin and his buddies.

Tarin's head comes up from Jelly's neck as I approach. Zach is behind me and Scott is behind him. Everyone else is watching intently and the room goes quiet. Dave and Stick take a few steps and get behind their bandmate. At first I worry that it's going to be a showdown between all of them and me, but then I see the shame in their eyes. They're pissed at their friend, and it fills me with a new strength of purpose. I have their support and it's going to make a world of difference.

"You're late," I say.

Jelly, Brett, and Tarin all giggle, Jelly more than the other two. She's clearly wasted, barely able to stand without Tarin's help.

"Not much," Tarin says. "We're here now. Go ahead and do your worst."

I give him a tight smile. "Fine." I turn to Zach, happy to see that Leonard has also arrived with Ricky right behind him. "Zach, would you do me a favor and escort Jelly and Brett off the property? I need you to take them back to Tarin's place, clean out their stuff, and deliver them to their own houses."

Zach nods once and steps up to my side, waiting for me to finish.

I look at Jelly who has finally stopped laughing. She's staring daggers at me. "Jelly, I'm sorry this didn't work out between you and Tarin, but you have to go. Consider your relationship over."

Her jaw drops. She gives a half-hearted laugh but then stops suddenly. "Go to hell," she spits out. "You don't decide where I go." She looks to Tarin and whines, "Tell her, babe. Tell her to go fuck herself." She tries to put her hand on his chest, but she hits his chin instead.

Tarin instantly gets angry, pushing her hand away, causing her to stumble back against Brett. He catches her, his expression leaving no doubt as to how he feels about me.

"Just go for tonight, Jells. I'll come get you tomorrow. I just have to do this meeting shit." Tarin's words are slightly slurred and his lids are heavy.

I shake my head. "Sorry, Tarin, but that's not gonna happen. I told you, I don't give second chances. I also told you no more booze or drugs." I look at her, my expression showing all of them what I think of her messed-up ass. "She's a bad influence, so she goes." I look at Brett. "Him too."

Brett looks at Tarin, incredulous. "You're gonna take that shit from her? I thought you said she was just a consultant."

Tarin's chin comes out. "She is just a consultant."

"What the hell then, man? You gonna let her talk to your friends like that?"

"You ain't no friend, man," says Dave.

Brett whips around to confront the drummer. "Fuck you, dude. You're one to talk."

Dave holds up his hands in a gesture of surrender. "Yo, don't get worked up about it. I'm just sayin' … friends don't let friends … whatever it is you just did together before you showed up here." Dave looks at Tarin, regret in his eyes. "I was a shitty friend too, Tare, but I'm gonna fix that for you, man. For us. For the band."

As inelegant as the delivery was, I give him points for having his heart in the right place. And he's right about one thing for sure: Friends don't let friends piss me off.

"Listen, Brett. I'm sorry to have to be the bearer of bad news, but Tarin's about to make some big changes in his life, and one of them is cutting the dead wood. That means people like you." I look at the other people gathered, the ones who haven't yet officially met me. They share the same expression: confusion. I can practically see the WTF word bubble over their heads.

"Heads up to everyone in the room … I have a contract that says I can fire and get rid of anyone who I deem in my sole discretion to be counterproductive to getting Tarin on the right track.

No second chances, no appealing to Tarin, Mel, the label, or anyone else. You either get on board with helping Tarin *my way* or you're out. End of story." I pause for a moment to let that sink in. "Anyone who has a problem with that can save us all a lot of trouble by walking out now."

No one moves a muscle at first. Then heads turn to look at Stick. Clearly they consider the guitarist to be the one making decisions for them.

I have to give him credit. As against the idea of me as I know him still to be, he still does the best thing I could have hoped for. He turns his head slightly to show them the side of his face. "What she said." Then he looks back at me, giving me his full attention. His snub of Jelly and Brett is bold and sharp. Everyone is on pins and needles now, waiting for their response.

"Tarin, man, you gotta do something about this," says Brett, laughing uncomfortably under his breath. "We go way back, man."

"Tarinnn," whines Jelly, wiping her hands all over his upper arms and chest, "come on, let's just go…" She tries to push him towards the door, but he digs his heels in, shoving her hands away again. He's upset, but he can't seem to bring himself to either argue against me or make Jelly and Brett feel better.

"Go," I say to Zach, softly so only he hears it. There's no need to rub salt in any wounds, and I don't need anyone giving Zach a hard time for following my bold orders.

Zach and Leonard move forward, Zach gesturing toward the door. "After you, Brett. Jelly, come on. Don't make a scene."

Brett points at me, his face screwed up in anger. "Fuck you, bitch. *Fuck you!* You're nothing, you hear me! Nothing! I'll be back tomorrow and you'll be fucking *gone!*" He looks at Tarin. "I'll call you, man. We'll talk."

I stare Brett down, saying not a single word.

Jelly's crying, her fat tears causing her mascara to run down her face in bluish-black smears. She looks a lot like she did in her mug shot, the only difference being that her hair is brushed this time. I have a feeling it won't stay that way for long the way she's flopping all over the place as she tries to hold on to a struggling Tarin.

"Get off!" he says, turning his attention from her to Zach. "Get her off me, would ya?" He's annoyed. I take that as a good sign.

"But Tarin, I *love* you!" she screeches as Zach pulls her away. She tries to hit him, but it's like a piece of paper battling a hurricane gale. She's halfway to the door before she can get her next sentence out. "But I'm pregnant! You can't make me leave, I'm pregnant! With Tarin's baby!"

I'm instantly sick to my stomach. I don't know why, but I see my life flash before my eyes. Why Tarin's future as a father has any connection to *my* life, I have no idea; but this definitely adds a new wrinkle to the plan. A big fucking hell of a horrible awful wrinkle.

The room goes mostly silent, the only sounds left to be heard being Jelly's cries and struggles to get free.

Tarin's face has gone white. At the same exact time, both Scott and Tarin say precisely the same thing.

"No. Fucking. Way."

Scott looks at me, his eyebrows practically up in his hairline. "I totally called it. I told you this shit was going to be bad."

CHAPTER
TEN

LEONARD ESCORTS BRETT OUT THE door and promises to watch over him as he removes his belongings from Tarin's house. It takes me a good half hour to calm Jelly down and get her to believe me when I say that I'll let Tarin talk to her.

I've given up on cutting her out of the equation entirely, but for sure she can't be here right now during this meeting, because otherwise I'll get nothing accomplished. She's too big a distraction, although now in a much more complicated and heinously awful way.

Ugh. I can hardly stand the idea of her and Tarin making a baby together, especially with her being such a drugged-out mess. All I can picture is a baby in a stroller wearing a bustier and high heels while her mother blows cigarette smoke in her face. Jelly does not strike me as the good mother type, and I should know; I was raised by a wingnut myself. It's partly what drove me into Austin's arms in the first place. He was my shelter from the storm that was my life.

Jelly finally agrees to let Ricky drive her home, and even though Tarin looks like he's still in shock, I start the meeting up again.

"Okay, well … that was … unexpected." I wait for the nervous twitters to go away. "So, as I was saying, we have a project ahead of us. Getting Tarin back." I look over at him and he's just staring out into space. I don't know if it's the mood-altering drugs he's taken or the life-altering confession of a girl named Jelly, but either way, he's lost right now, lost more than usual. I continue to address the group. "Anyone here feel like they can't support the cause?"

No one responds. I look at each and every face in turn, trying to figure out if anyone's playing games. I see nothing but unasked questions and confusion. The only one with a hint of attitude is Stick, but I know for now at least that I have him on my side.

"Good. Tarin starts a new program tomorrow at six a.m. It continues for at least thirty days. No drugs of any kind unless they're prescribed by a doctor I've approved in advance, no alcohol, and no cigarettes. Anyone who supplies him with any of the above is out, no questions asked, no second chances."

"No cigs? Man … harsh." Dave is shaking his head.

"Rots your lungs," says Tarin in a distracted voice. Everyone looks at him. He's staring at the floor, like he's in a trance. "I saw a lung once. In biology class. Remember that, Stick? Black as shit."

He's traveling down memory lane, stoned. I can only imagine the horrible images his warped brain is conjuring for him right now.

Stick smiles vaguely. "Yeah, I remember. Why do you think I don't smoke? That shit was nasty."

"You think my lungs look like that?" Tarin asks him, finally looking up.

Stick looks sad. "Nah, man. Your lungs are fine."

Tarin looks at me next, his eyes not exactly focused. "You think my lungs are black, don't you?"

I shake my head silently. He looks positively tortured.

He's almost in a trance as he speaks. "Black lungs. Black soul. You think I have a black soul, don't you?"

I stare at him, wondering what kind of mood-messing-up drugs he's been taking. He looks like he's ready to jump off a cliff. Moving forward, I take his hand. It's cold and clammy. "I don't think that about you, Tarin. If I did, I wouldn't be here. We just need to get you on the right track. You don't have any black lungs or soul or anything ridiculous like that. Trust me."

"Trust you."

"Yes. I never lie."

He smiles a little. "What are you doing in L.A.?"

I smile back. "I'm taking care of Austin's legacy."

His smile disappears in a flash, leaving a pale, fearful expression behind. "Yeah. How could I forget?" He pulls his hand away and sighs heavily before facing his group of friends and co-workers. "Yeah, so," he says, stopping to clear his throat of its rust, "what she said … I, uh… I support it or whatever." He flops his hand in the air in my direction. "Just do what she says and we'll get through this shit, okay?"

Everyone nods. A few people give him their verbal agreement.

"Happy?" he asks, looking at me. I could swear he's about to cry.

"Yes. I'm happy." I look out at the group. "Let's eat! Dinner's in the garden. Please no smoking around Tarin. If you want to smoke, go around to the front of the house."

I hold out my hand to Tarin, palm up.

"You want to hold hands now?" he asks, his expression tortured.

"No." I give him my thousand-watt smile. "I want your cigarettes and the pipe you have in your pocket."

He slowly reaches into his front pockets and pulls out the items I could see outlined there. "It's not a crack pipe, you know. I don't do crack," he says.

"Crack is whack," I say, trying to lighten the mood.

"I just smoke a little dope every once in a while to relax."

"Not anymore," I say, motioning for him to give me more.

"What?" he asks.

"Don't act like you're not holding," I say.

He stares at me intently. "Who's your informer?"

"I don't need an informer. I can see the bulge in your pants."

A slow, sensual smile slips across his mouth. "How do you know it's not just my dick?"

I laugh in spite of myself. "Oh, you mean … is that a bag of pot in your pants or are you just glad to see me?"

His sexy look turns into a straight-up grin. "Something like that."

"Sorry. I don't mean to damage your man-ego, but I've been around the block a few times. I know the difference between a bag of weed and a cock." The c-word flies out of my mouth before I can reel it back in.

He nods, the sneaky smile back. "Cock, huh? Dirty girl. Dirty, dirty girl." He reaches slowly into his pocket and I hold my breath, almost thinking for a second he's going to show me it isn't weed in his pants. But then some plastic comes out and the brownish green stuff inside it becomes visible, and I let my breath go.

"What? You thought I was going to show you the money?" he asks, chuckling at his own joke.

"Yeah, right." I play it off, grabbing the bag from his hand. "Go eat, would ya? You're too skinny."

He runs his hands from his chest down to his abs, watching them go down. He looks over at me when he's got his hands on his pelvis. "What? You don't go for the emaciated rocker look?"

I shake my head. "No. I go for the healthy artist look, personally. But I guess since you got Jelly knocked up, it doesn't matter what I like, right?"

I want to slap my own face for saying it. I don't know what possessed me to take the fun we were having and throw it into the shredder like that. Maybe he was getting too close, or maybe I was getting too close to him. Either way, I did it and I don't want to take it back. I cannot afford to let anything happen between us, and neither can he, whether he knows it or not.

His face drops. As he walks away, his head hanging low, I hear his mumbled reaction. "Fuck you."

Hearing it brings the sensation of being stabbed in the heart with a very sharp and painful weapon.

CHAPTER
ELEVEN

DURING DINNER I GATHER TARIN'S inner circle around me, now focused on talking strategy. Scott's at my right taking notes. There are nine friends at the table with Scott and I making eleven. Jelly's in the house being tended to by a house-keeper of sorts.

"Thanks for agreeing to meet with us to discuss our plans for the next thirty days." Almost everyone nods, but not Tarin. He's looking a little too shell-shocked to be able to contribute much. I don't mind; it's the people who care about him who will be the most help to us right now.

"First of all, I just want to give you a quick overview of what we're doing. Number one is healthy living. Tarin's going to be on a strict diet and exercise program. Any of you are welcome to join us, and some of you I will expect to be there." I look at the bodyguards. "Zach and Leonard, you two need to be involved since some of this stuff will be happening in public and Tarin will need security."

"Count us in," says Zach. "We exercise everyday anyway."

I nod, silently thanking them for their enthusiasm.

"Count me in too," says Ricky. "I need to get in shape." He looks down at the giant piece of cake in front of him and puts a big bite onto a fork. "Might as well enjoy it while I can." Winking as he puts it into his mouth, he gets the table laughing at his good-natured joking. I'm happy for the levity.

"Good. Anyone else?"

The band manager gives me an uncomfortable look. "Actually, not that I want to bail on this whole deal, but I had a big vacation planned starting next week. And I was going to work in some meetings while I'm out of town, too, so I wasn't planning to be back for almost three weeks."

Stick nods. "Yeah, with the tour coming up, we were all going to take off." He looks over at Dave and Randy, and all three of them are nodding like bobble head dolls.

Scott and I exchange a look before I turn my attention back to the table. "It's no big deal, actually. As long as I have security and a driver, we can take care of the rest."

"We're all in, so it's good, right?" asks Ricky. He's still enjoying his cake, but it's almost all gone. He looks at Zach and Leonard. "Security and a driver." He nods at me.

"Yep, we're good. The rest of you enjoy your time off and when you come back, Tarin will be almost where he needs to be."

"Chicken shits," Tarin says in a low tone.

Everyone ignores him, but I can tell from their expressions he's made them uncomfortable.

"Now's your chance to give me some insight into Tarin's life. Into his psyche. We'll use the information to help put together a gameplan."

Tarin glares at everyone, and I laugh.

"Don't let him intimidate you. He'll eventually realize you're doing it to help him, not hurt him."

"Well, maybe you can have him leave the table, then, because I don't particularly want to get punched in the face," says Dave.

Randy nods silently.

"No, I think it's better that he hear it coming from the people he cares about."

"Fuck that," says Tarin, trying to stand.

I grab his arm and squeeze it. "Stay. I want you to hear this."

He looks down at me, glaring at me. I refuse to be intimidated by it. "I insist. Take a seat."

Letting out an annoyed sigh, he flops back down into his chair, slumping back and lowering himself down. "Fine. Hit me with your best shot." He looks out over the back lawn like he could care less about what's about to be said.

"Who will go first? Give me some insight into Tarin as a person." I scan the faces at the table, waiting expectantly.

No one says anything. This is normal. It doesn't dissuade me in the least.

"Okay, I'll start," I say. "I've noticed that Tarin has a great sense of humor. He likes to tease." I smile at his friends. "How's that? Did I get him right?"

Everyone nods, a few of them smiling. "Yeah, that's about right," says Randy. "He likes to play practical jokes on people, especially the crew." He pauses, some of his smile slipping. "Some of them quit over it, actually."

"So what you're saying is that sometimes his jokes have sharp edges to them, is that it?"

Randy doesn't want to respond, but eventually his head wins out over his heart. "Yeah. Sometimes."

A long hiss comes from Tarin, but he's still staring out into the distance.

"He doesn't realize it, though," says Randy, trying to do damage control. "He just gets wound up and gets carried away sometimes."

I look at Stick. "What do you think? Do you find Tarin getting too wound up sometimes?"

He sticks his lips out like he's thinking or doubtful. Then he shrugs. "Maybe. I mean, he's an intense guy. I guess … I get the impression he's a little tortured, you know? Like the jokes are a form of self-therapy."

Tarin whips his head around and glares at Stick. "What the fuck, man?"

Stick is angry now too. "What? Are you saying it ain't true? Because you're a fucking liar if you do. Come on, asshole, don't make this harder than it has to be on everyone else. We didn't do anything wrong."

I shake my head. "You let it get this far, though, didn't you?"

Stick stands up. "Listen, whatever your name is ... sorry, I already forgot it ... I get what you're trying to do here, but I'm not going to sit here and take the blame for Tarin's shit, okay? The guy's a fuck-up. He doesn't show up for practice, he's forgetting lyrics at shows now, and he's got terrible taste in women. None of that is on me. None of it." He throws his napkin down on his plate. "I have a plane to catch in the morning, so I'm outta here. Good luck with everything. I'll see you in a few weeks." He leaves the table after bumping fists with Randy and Dave. No one else even gets a second look, not even Tarin.

I chance a look at my client and he's just sitting in his chair stunned. Now's my chance.

"Okay, that was some good stuff. Honesty. That's what Tarin needs right now. Who's next?"

"He doesn't write anymore," says Randy. "All the new stuff we're getting is coming from Stick." He lowers he voice and his head to finish. "And no offense to Stick, but it's not half as good as Tarin's stuff was."

"I wrote something two weeks ago, what the fuck are you talking about?" Tarin's trying to defend himself, but it loses some of its force with his weak delivery.

"First of all that was like two months ago, not weeks ... and to be honest, it sucked balls. We're not including it in the next album."

"Fuck you, we're not."

"No, dude, we're not. Seriously. We took a vote, but you weren't there of course, so that's why you don't know about it."

"Yeah. He doesn't come to our sessions anymore," says Dave, sounding sad. "He's too busy partying."

Tarin grips the arms of his chair and leans over, practically spitting in his friend's face when he responds. "You're one to talk about partying, you fucking H fiend. You're the one I've been partying with! How can you stand there and tell me I'm too busy partying? Fucking hypocrite."

Dave stands up, looking both frustrated and guilty as hell. "Whatever, man. I'm just doing what she asked." He gestures at me with his fork before dropping it on his plate. "I've got my issues, yeah. Okay, I admit that. I'm going to deal with that too. But this was about you, and you might not want to hear it, but I love you, man. You're like a brother to me, and watching you throw your whole life away is killing me. It's half the reason I try to escape all the time."

"Oh, that's rich," says Tarin, his voice going snotty. "Now I'm to blame for you being a fucking user. Nice."

Dave looks at me. "I think I'm going to schedule a stay at a clinic. I appreciate what you're doing here, but I don't think I can stick around and try to participate on the side. Sorry." He turns to leave.

"Good luck, Dave," I say, sincerely hoping by clinic he means a rehab place.

"You love me but you're fucking running away!" yells Tarin at his back. "Nice! With family like that, who needs enemies!"

Dave flinches but he doesn't respond or turn around. He disappears into the house through the terrace doors.

"That's not nice, Tarin," says Mel. "You really need to think about what you're saying before you let it out. Some things you can't take back."

"There's only one thing I've ever said or done that I wish I could take back, Mel, and that ain't it." Tarin gets unsteadily to his feet. "I'm going to bed. Ricky, take me home."

Ricky looks to me for my input.

"Don't look at her! Look at me! I pay your paycheck." Tarin shoves his chair back so hard it flips over backwards and lands against a fountain behind him.

"Not right now, you don't," I say. "Right now, I run the payroll. But I'm fine with him taking you home to sleep off whatever it is you took." I stand too and look at Tarin's bodyguards. "Will you please go and make sure he doesn't take anything else? Tomorrow's going to be enough of a shock as it is."

"Don't talk about me like I'm not standing right here next to you," says Tarin. He's breathing like a bull, huffing and puffing with his anger.

I face him, taking in his rage and hurt expression. "Okay, fine. Tarin, you need to go home and sleep off your high. Zach and Leonard will go with you and watch over you to make sure you don't get into any more trouble until tomorrow when I move in. Ricky will drive you home and nowhere else. Jelly will not be going with you. Tonight, you sleep alone and without the aid of medication."

"Move in?"

I smile. Of all the things I've said, that's the one he's clued in on. He looks afraid. "Yes. Scott and I will be moving in to your house. We'll be with you twenty-four/seven with around-the-clock supervision."

"Sounds like prison."

"It won't be. I promise. Just consider us like boundaries."

"Boundaries. What the fuck." Tarin turns around. Halfway to the door, he turns back. "Well come on, fuckers! If you're gonna babysit my ass, might as well get moving away from the goddamn cake."

Chairs scrape back and everyone's standing. "Good luck, everyone," I say. "See you tomorrow morning early."

"Later!" Ricky jogs away from the table, trying to outrun Tarin to the car. Zach and Leonard are even faster, reaching Tarin before he gets to the back door.

I'm left with Mel, Scott, and the band manager.

"Well," says Mel, breathing out long and slow, "I guess that went okay. At least he didn't throw anything at anyone."

"He wanted to," says the manager, holding out his hand. "Best of luck to you, Ms. Barnes. Call me if you need me. I don't know how much of a signal I'll have, but I'll try to check voicemails from the hotel."

I shake his hand. "Thanks. Don't worry about us. Tarin's going to be fine." I truly believe this, which is why my smile is so confident and strong. I feel high on life right now. Tarin not flipping the table and throwing dishes is indeed a step in the right direction.

Mel moves off to join his wife and some of the crew members by a chocolate fountain, leaving Scott and me alone at the big empty table.

"Get some good notes?" I ask, leaning over to look at Scott's pad.

"Yep. I have a great profile all built up." He looks down at his chicken scratches. "Rude, angry, hurt, undependable, short-tempered, and a man-whore drug user." Scott looks up and grins at me. "The only thing he hasn't done that I can tell is kill someone."

I grin back. "Then we're all good, aren't we?"

He puts his arm over my shoulder. "Austin would be proud of us, I think."

I'm choked up, but I answer anyway, my voice a little raspy. "I know he would be. Come on. Let's go get some cake."

"Awwww, yeah buddy," says Scott, dropping his pad in his chair and abandoning me for the dessert table.

I follow behind him, my heart beating slow and sure. I feel like Austin's spirit is guiding me every step of the way and it makes me strong.

Slow and steady wins the race babe. You got this.

CHAPTER TWELVE

SCOTT AND I SHOW UP at Tarin's front door at five the next morning. Ricky lets us in, dressed for our morning's activities in navy blue basketball shorts, a white t-shirt and glowing green running shoes. He and Scott look like they're on the same sports team, their clothes are so similar in style and color. Scott's shoes aren't nearly as flamboyant, and I catch him staring at Ricky's with envy. Normally I can count on Scott to keep the footwear interesting, but Ricky wins today in that department. I make a mental note to add bright green shoes to Scott's Christmas list.

"Looking good," says Scott, holding out his hand to Ricky.

"Thanks, man. You ready to hit the pavement?" They exchange hand slaps and knuckle bumps. Scott has tried several times to teach me that intricate set of maneuvers that they all seem to know how to do instinctually. He's given up on me ever learning, but I haven't. I study their movements and try to memorize them for my next attempt.

"As ready as I'll never ever be," says Scott, dropping his duffle bag on the floor in the front entrance and looking around at the opulent foyer. He's not a huge fan of exercise. Like me, he does it as part of the job, but he's one of those guys who doesn't have to do anything to look lean and fit.

"Can I get that for you?" Ricky asks me, gesturing to my bag.

"Sure. There's another in the trunk, but you can leave it there. Is Tarin up?" I eye the stairs leading to where I assume his bedroom is.

He smiles. "Yeah, but it ain't pretty. He's in the kitchen having some coffee."

I smile back a little evilly, a piece of me happy we're making him work for this. *Stupid jerk, getting that ding dong pregnant. Maybe. We'll find out soon enough if she's really pregnant, if I have anything to say about it.* "How'd last night go?" I ask Ricky as he takes my bag from me.

"Good, I guess. Jelly had a fit and Tarin kicked her out after listening to her for a hour. Nobody gave him any trouble after that. He went to bed early. Early for him, anyway." Ricky puts my bag on the bottom stair and then goes to the front door.

"What time did he go upstairs?" I ask.

"Two in the morning."

I roll my eyes. "Great. He's going to work out on three hours of sleep and a hangover."

Ricky talks louder to be heard from out in the front valet area. He's disregarded my offer to leave the other bag in the car, pulling it out of the trunk. "The caffeine will get him to lunchtime. Maybe he can take a nap or something before we do anything later."

I don't commit to anything. I'm going to play these first few days by ear. I pray to any god listening that Tarin's drug use hasn't messed him up too bad. I'm still fairly confident he's not a drug addict, even if he is addicted to bad behavior and destructive users.

One thing at a time - first the physical health, then the mental health. Rome wasn't built in a day. It wasn't built in thirty days either, but I've been called a miracle worker before for good reason. This is what I was meant to do. *Rescue party, reporting for duty.*

Scott is in another room, but his exclamation of happiness makes him easy to find. I walk into a big family room to find him glowing with joy, staring at a huge television screen and a boat-load of stereo and video equipment.

"Did you see this?" he asks, his voice an octave too high and cracking like it used to when he was fourteen. "Every single awe-some video game known to man ... it's like a frigging video store in here!" He's staring into a cabinet that goes from floor to very high ceiling. "I'm pretty sure I've just died and gone to heaven."

"Oh yay," I say with zero enthusiasm. "Now you can kill off a few million more brain cells."

"Hush your mouth, woman. Can't you see I'm in church right now?"

"You let him talk to you like that?" asks Ricky, standing be-hind me, obviously amused by what he's seeing and hearing.

I walk out of the room and gesture for him to go in front of me. "Once a week he gets a pass to be a complete fool. He just used it all up in there. Could you show me to the kitchen? It's time to get this party started."

"I'll be with you in a minute!" says Scott at our backs.

"Yeah, come on," Ricky says, his long strides carrying him swiftly down the hall.

I follow Tarin's driver and sometime babysitter through the large house, taking in the details as we make our way to the kitch-en. An interior decorator was hired to do the designing, that much is clear. It has a cold, beige, perfectly-put-together look about it. I can't picture Tarin being happy here or being involved in the buying of any of these items other than to sign a check. The place could go up for sale tomorrow and be purchased by a wealthy couple not at all involved in the entertainment industry, that's how *not* Tarin it is.

It makes me sad knowing that maybe this is the whole point for him; he doesn't want to connect here and needs to be ready to fly the coop at a moment's notice without any attachments hold-ing him back. Maybe this should bother me on Jelly's behalf, but it doesn't. I don't want him to be with her, and the idea of them being a couple out of a sense of duty over a child makes me want to rage at the world. It's because I care about him as a musician and a person, nothing more. I hate to see a wasted life. It has nothing to do with the fact that I find him attractive and annoying and maddeningly similar to someone I once loved with all my heart. Tarin deserves that kind of love and dedication. Not from me of course, but someone. Someone who wants to be with him for who he is, not because of his money or status. *Grrrrr … Jelly.* I smile bitterly, thinking how it's those two things that make him the completely wrong person for me. He has too much of both the money and the status. Never *ever* will I get involved with someone in this world again.

"Hello? Anybody in there?" Ricky is stopped in the middle of the hallway and I do the same behind him without even consciously doing it. He's caught me staring off into space.

"Oh, ha, yeah…" I giggle, trying to play off my space cadet act, cringing when my goofy laugh makes it worse, "…just lost in thought for a second there."

"Looked serious." He's probing.

"What's behind that door?" I ask, letting him know without exactly saying so that I'm not the sharing type.

"That's the music studio. No one's allowed in unless invited."

"Do you get invited?" I ask, staring at the door handle, wondering if it's locked. My curiosity is instantly off the charts. This would be the room where Tarin can be himself. I really want to see that, and then again, I really, really don't. I have a feeling it would do something irreparable to me, and I've already had those kind of things done to me before. I'm not fond of being broken like that.

"I've been in there once or twice maybe. But I don't stay."

I look up at him. "Why?"

He shrugs, looking sad. "I don't know why. I guess … I don't like to see him doing something he should love and looking unhappy about it."

A lump develops in my throat as a picture of Tarin's tortured expression comes to mind. I nod, taking a moment to collect myself before responding. "Yeah. I know what you mean." It's exactly how Austin was near the end. I'm so glad I'm here to help Tarin.

Everything I learn about him makes me feel stronger about my goals for him. This is *so* going to happen. We're going to get Tarin back on his feet and performing healthy again if it's the last thing I do.

I'm jerked out of my inner pep-talk by Tarin's voice coming from the kitchen. It's loud, and he's clearly angry.

"That's not going to happen! I'm telling you right now, it's just *not!*"

"Uh-oh," says Ricky, loping down the hallway and turning a corner ahead.

I follow behind, stopping at the entrance to the kitchen.

Tarin's on the phone. He looks at me as he listens to the person on the other end of the line and throws his hand up while rolling his eyes. Apparently, I'm the icing on his poo-cake.

"No … *no.* Fuck that. No." He pauses before launching into another tirade. "You tell them they can kiss my fucking ass and suck my dick twice while they're at it. I'm not paying them shit."

I walk over and stand in front of him. "Lawyers?" I ask softly.

He nods.

I hold out my hand.

His eyebrows go up, but he shrugs and hands the phone to me, placing it in my palm. "You want to deal with 'em, go for it. I'm over that shit." He leans back against the counter and snatches a plastic bottle filled with orange stuff, preparing to take a swig.

I take the container from his hand and sniff it before putting the phone to my ear. "Hello?" I take a quick sip of the drink to make sure it's alcohol-free. When I'm sure it's just orange juice, I hand it back to him. Tarin's mouth is hanging open at my nerve, but I ignore his reaction and concentrate on the phone call.

"Who's this?" asks a frustrated male voice.

"This is Scarlett Barnes."

"Oh … Hi, Scarlett." His tone goes from angry to conciliatory in the blink of an eye. "This is Nick Galanos. I was told you'd be getting involved over there."

"Hi, Nick. Nice to meet you. So what's going on?"

Tarin takes another swig of his juice and I watch his Adam's apple bounce up and down in his throat. When his head tips down again, he stares at me, licking a couple droplets of juice off his lips. It sends a tingle through my body that I work desperately to ignore. *Such a bad idea, Scarlett. Stop looking at him.* I cast my eyes to the floor.

"We have a possible civil suit I need input on. A settlement offer's been made. Two people from the press are claiming Tarin hurt them when he grabbed their cameras and trashed them a few weeks ago. They've made a demand and they're threatening to sue for damages."

"I know you're busy, but is there any chance I could come in to see you soon to discuss all his outstanding legal issues?"

"Sure. How's tomorrow look for you?"

"One o'clock works."

"I'll make a space for you. See you then. In the meantime..."

"In the meantime, just put anyone off who calls about Tarin. He's unreachable for the immediate future. We'll come up with a plan when I see you."

"Great. I've heard good things about you, Ms. Barnes. Glad to have you on board."

"Call me Scarlett," I say, finally warming to him. He doesn't sound like the man-eater I know some of his kind to be.

"Good. And you can call me Nick. Gotta go, see you soon. Bye."

"Bye." I give the phone back to Tarin after shutting it off. "We'll go see him tomorrow together."

Tarin's brought his anger down a notch or two, but it's not gone entirely. He wipes his upper lip off with the back of his hand. "I'm not paying them jack shit. They came after me and hit me in the face with a camera. I was just defending myself."

I put my hand on his shoulder but quickly pull it away when the heat coming through his shirt surprises me. I can smell him too, so I take a step back to clear my head. Talking while under the influence of Tarin would be a bad idea. "Don't worry about it now. I'm not into rewarding the bad behavior of paparazzi. It just encourages their bullshit."

Tarin smiles for the first time since he flirted with me about the drugs in his pants. It's a slow movement across his face, transforming the dark clouds that had gathered there into rays of sunshine. He truly is a beautiful specimen of a man … if you like that type, which I don't really. Not anymore.

"I like you," he says, before taking a careless swig of his juice.

His words make my heart do a flip. The look on his face probably means nothing to him, but it makes my ears burn anyway. I feel like I'm developing some kind of schoolgirl crush on him and that just won't do. Not at *all*.

I press my lips together. "You shouldn't. I'm about to bring you pain in the worst kind of way. Liking me will only confuse you. Better just stick to the hate for a little while longer."

He's still smiling when the juice bottle moves away from his lips. It distracts me temporarily from what we were talking about. I like how his eye-teeth look sharp and one of them kind of overlaps the tooth next to it. His face is unique, handsome in a dangerous kind of way. He's careless and it shows everywhere, even with the way he wears his hair and how he looks around at the people nearby. He's got the world at his feet and he knows it.

This is the closest I've been to him, and I can see his imperfections. I list them mentally so I can tally up all the reasons why he's really not all that good-looking and definitely not someone I should be paying any of *that* kind attention to.

His nose has been broken before and not perfectly set. His lips are full but his mouth too easily twists into a smirk. He hasn't shaved in a few days, and the almost-black beard growing in is sparse and patchy. Both of his ears are pierced with a couple holes each, but there are no earrings there. His eyes are a dark green, so dark they've always seemed brown to me until now. He's about two months overdue for a haircut, but the unkempt look goes alarmingly well with the rest of his careless attitude. *Ugh.* I hate him for being attractive even while being ugly.

"Sounds like a challenge," he says, pushing himself off the counter to stand more squarely in front of me.

"Nope. More like a warning."

"I don't scare easy. I thought you knew about my reputation."

My heart is hammering behind my ribs, making it very likely he can see it moving my shirt ever so slightly. I step to the side, brushing off the silly flirting he's trying to play at, acting like it's all just a big joke to me, like I do this kind of thing all the time.

"Oh, I heard all right." I grab his orange juice and hold it up as I move towards Ricky and Scott at the entrance to the kitchen, walking backwards. "If you have any more of these, might want to grab a couple." I spin around and leave them all standing there, taking off at a fast clip down the hallway.

Yes, I'm running away like a total chicken-shit, but it's better than getting caught up in a game that I cannot win. Tarin has me at a distinct disadvantage. He's full of himself and has nothing to lose in his mind, so it makes him bold, fearless. I, on the other hand, doubt myself almost every second of the day where men are concerned, and for the last two years, I've had no heart left to break. *I'm* the one with nothing left to lose, and I'm full of fear that I'll never have anything worthwhile in my life ever again.

CHAPTER THIRTEEN

I GREET THE OWNER OF Charlie's Gym warmly. He and I go way back. I practically grew up in this neighborhood, and Charlie and my dad were friends for years before my father passed away.

"Sweet Mary, look at you," he says, giving me a hug and then holding me out so he can see me better. "All grown up. Where does the time go?"

I chuck him in the shoulder, unable to hide my smile. "You say that every time you see me, Charlie."

"I only have memories of you as a little girl, that's why. Short term memory's shot all to hell." He shifts his gaze over to the others. "Who've you got with you this time?"

I follow his gaze. Ricky looks only a little uncomfortable with the fact that we're in a boxing gym that saw its best days about thirty years ago. Tarin's nodding his head in appreciation, most of his attention fixed on the ring near the center of the big space. It warms me to think he likes Charlie's place despite its shabby parts. Hopefully, the rough-edged clientele who'll be showing up later won't scare him off.

I put my hand on Charlie's shoulder and hold out my other towards my crew. "You know Scott, of course." I remind him because it's not a joke that his short term memory is gone. He never remembers Scott. Too many punches to the head as a youth has taken its toll on his brain matter.

"Nice to meet you, young man."

Scott shakes his hand, scowling. "Come on, Charlie, you know you remember me. I've been here hundreds of times now."

"Nope," Charlie says matter-of-factly, "never seen you in my life." He turns his gaze to Ricky. "Who's this big guy? My next project?"

"No. He's just here for the fun. Your project is Tarin." I nod my head in his direction.

Charlie shakes Ricky's hand first and then eyes Tarin up and down. "He's pretty skinny."

"Yes." I try to hide my smile at the frown on Tarin's face. He's finally paying attention to what we're talking about.

"He looks soft," Charlie continues.

"He most definitely does," I say, having a very difficult time not laughing my butt off.

"Hey, now!" Tarin puts his right arm up and flexes his muscle. It's lean but small, and when he looks at it, he frowns again. "Oh, shit. What happened to all my muscles?"

"They went up in smoke," says Ricky. He looks instantly chagrined when Tarin cuts him with a sharp look.

Charlie ignores their banter. "If we're gonna do this, you gotta get him to eat. I mean *eat*. None-a that La Jolla froo froo garbage. Real food. Meat and potatoes with two desserts minimum. Six meals a day."

"Trust me, I plan on it," I say. "So you think you can do it?"

Charlie chews on something, maybe his cud or his tongue, I don't know. I don't *want* to know. Charlie doesn't invest much of his income in dental care.

I know the expression on Charlie's face well; he's considering Tarin, his physique, his structure, his overall look. He's taking his measure. Charlie's trained more middle weight champions than anyone else in the state. If he can't get Tarin in fighting shape, no one can.

Tarin stands up straighter, his shoulders going back. I'm not even sure he's aware of the fact that he's trying to give Charlie his best, but he is, and that makes me very happy. Charlie's routines are not like going to the local workout gym and pushing a few plates up and down on a machine. Tarin's going to need a lot of motivation for this to work. I find that bringing men to a badass place like this is almost good enough to spark that flame. The rest has to come from hope, lying somewhere inside the man. I pray he hasn't lost all of his.

"Where you from?" Charlie asks Tarin, as if that matters in his calculations.

"Chicago."

"You do drugs?"

"Sometimes."

"Gotta stop that. No drugs, no alcohol, no smokes."

"I heard."

"Hearing and doing are two different things. Don't waste my time. You willing to quit, cold turkey?"

Tarin shrugs. "Sure. I'm no addict."

"Good." Charlie looks at me. "I'll give him a shot. Just one. He messes up, I'm done. I'm too old to play games. I got people banging on my door all day to train them, but I say no to everyone. Everyone but you." He sighs as he puts his rough hand on my cheek. "I never could say no to you."

I hug him to me. "You're not old. And I'm glad you can't say no to me. Never say no to me, Charlie." When my dad passed on, Charlie took up the space that was suddenly there. I think I did the same for him when he lost his best friend.

He pats me on the back, his voice going soft. "Easy now, chickie. I have a gym to run here. No tears allowed."

I back up and smile. "Tears? Who's got time for tears?"

He grins back. "That's my girl. You ready to throw a few?"

I nod and then look at Tarin. "Oh, yeah. I'm ready." A thrill goes up my spine when I see the look on Tarin's face. First he's confused, then intrigued. His expression reveals the exact moment he fully realizes what's about to happen. *Challenge accepted. Yeah, baby.*

Charlie helps Tarin and I get into our gear, all the while giving a safety and rules briefing. I've heard it a thousand times if I've heard it once.

"…And remember … when I call the match over, it's over. You throw one more punch after I ring-a-ding and you're banned for a week, you hear me? This isn't one-a them MMA cage matches." He's grumbling again, never having gotten over the idea that boxing could turn into something so brutal. He's an interesting man, born and raised to fight but believing in a very strict and finite set of rules of engagement. He doesn't like change much. I'm convinced his memory loss is a self-induced refusal to acknowledge that the world has changed into something he's not comfortable with.

Tarin's holding up his gloves and looking at them through his face pads. "These things are pretty big." He looks at me with concern. "I'm afraid I'm going to hurt you. I'll just give you like half-punches or something."

Charlie snickers. "I don't recommend it."

"But she's a chick," Tarin explains, as if Charlie doesn't understand. "I was raised not to hit chicks."

"Fine. Don't hit her," says Charlie. The glee in his voice is impossible to miss. I know he's hoping Tarin won't, just so he can enjoy the show.

"You worry me, old man," says Tarin.

"It's not me you should be worried about," Charlie says, patting my wrist now that he's finished closing up my glove. "Go get 'im, girly."

I climb into the ring, coming easily to my feet. I do some light bouncing to get the blood flowing, reminding myself of Scott. I nod at him and he smiles at me, giving me a thumbs up.

He and Ricky are standing ringside, both of them with arms folded across their chests now. Ricky seems nervous, but Scott has seen me at the gym before. This is almost as much fun for him as video games. I think the only thing that would make it better for him would be to have me hooked to a game controller he was holding.

Tarin rolls under the ropes awkwardly and gets on his feet. He walks around the ring, like he's getting the lay of the land or something. I can see him warming to the idea of doing this, but not necessarily against me. Every time he looks in my direction, he acts guilty, his shoulders hunching and his eyes darting away.

"Gloves up!" orders Charlie.

Mine go up automatically. They feel natural there, like I should always be walking around protecting myself this way. Tarin's come up slower; he's watching me and mirroring my actions. He's wary, and I admire him for having such good instincts.

"Engage!" is Charlie's next order. He bangs the bell once with a tiny hammer that rests near it.

I wait for Tarin to follow Charlie's call.

He walks around the ring in a circle, like he's taking a stroll. I side step, keeping my gloves between us. I'm on my toes at all times, just like I've been taught.

Tarin's nervous, full of anxiety. I'm sure it's all about the idea of hitting a girl. It's good to know he doesn't relish the idea, but he needs to get busy. I have other things to do today besides dance in circles. I close the distance between us and throw out one easy punch, catching him in the shoulder.

"Hey! Watch it, now. I don't want to have to hurt you." He moves out of the way, watching me over his shoulder as he retreats.

Charlie's frustrated. "Get back over there, boy! What's wrong with you? She's throwing down the gauntlet and you're walking away! What are you, a pussy?"

Tarin stops in his tracks. "Say what, man? Did you just call me a pussy because I don't want to hit a girl?"

He's so busy bitching at Charlie, he doesn't realize I'm there until it's too late. I land a solid punch to his shoulder, knocking him sideways a few steps. I dance out of the way.

"What the …?" He turns around and stares at me. "Did you just hit me?"

"Of course she hit you! That's what you do in the boxing ring for crying out loud! Whaddya think this is, a beauty parlor? Now get over there and give her a tap!"

Tarin snorts a laugh and then takes a tentative step in my direction. "Give her a tap," he mumbles under his breath, "I'll give her a tap…"

I wave him towards me. "Come on then, Tear-It-Up Kilgour. Let's see what you got." I'm grinning like a fool, the adrenaline coursing through my veins. I'm probably enjoying this too much, but I don't care. I haven't punched anyone in the head in way too many weeks.

"Oh, you wanna see what I got, huh?" He raises his gloves up and takes a few more steps in my direction. "You sure about that?"

I rush him and give him three quick jabs in his chest, easily knocking away his gloves. I dance away and laugh. "Yeah, I'm sure."

"Hey! Cut that out!" He's moving more assuredly now, walking sideways, reminding me of a caged tiger the way he's watching me. "No sneak attacks allowed."

I let out a whoop because I have too much energy built up inside me. I punch my gloves together to aggravate him. "Come on, sissy boy … bring it."

"That's not a sneak attack, that's boxing!" yells Charlie. "Now get in there and throw some punches before I get so old waiting for it I fall over dead." Charlie uses a towel to snap Tarin in the ankle when he gets close. "Go! Fight!"

Tarin jumps. "Shit! What the hell!" He turns around to scowl at Charlie, and I take the opening he provides.

I jump in and pummel him. Chest, shoulders, abs, and then when he turns around, his jaw. He flies back into the ropes and I dance away again.

As he bounces down the ropes to land on his ass, Ricky and Scott are laughing loudly.

"Damn, girl," says Ricky, his joy echoing around the gym, "you ain't gotta kill the poor boy his first day."

Tarin shakes his head a few times and then scrambles to his feet, his face beet red under his pads. "You are so going down right now," he growls.

"You wish," I say before I can stop myself.

"*You* wish," he says, advancing on me.

He takes a swing at me, but it's sloppy and obvious. I lean back just the slightest bit to let it breeze by and then cut in with a quick jab to his ribs. When he leans over his injured parts, I give him a left hook to his other side and then move away again, avoiding getting too near the corner of the ring.

Ricky's laughing like a lunatic now and Scott's right there with him, adding some hoots and hollers for good measure. It's having the desired effect on Tarin, making him angry and frustrated. I smile, knowing he's about to live up to his nickname. I'm totally ready for him.

Tarin lets out a roar and comes for me like a bull, head down, planning to tackle me.

I wait until he's almost on me before jumping to the side and slamming his upper back first with the back side of my left fist and then a roundhouse from my right. He falls to his face on the mat with a loud boom.

I expect him to stay there and catch his breath, so it takes me by complete surprise when his hand shoots out and grabs my ankle. One quick yank and I'm on my back on the mat next to him. He reaches for me, his gloved hand landing on my thigh and squeezing.

I panic. His hand is way too close to places it shouldn't be, and his face isn't too far behind. This isn't boxing, it's wrestling, and we're sweating and breathing heavily. I can't be here like this. *Too close! Too close!*

I sit up in an instant and bash him in the arm several times before hitting him in the head. When his hand finally falls away, I scramble back and jump to my feet.

Shaking my arms and head, I dance to the opposite side of the ring. I'm totally amped up now, a little afraid of what I'll do to him if he gets up and comes after me. The fight or flight instinct is raging inside me right now, and the ropes are keeping me trapped in here with him. He's got me backed into a corner, and it goes against everything I know to leave the ring and not keep fighting. The smart thing would be to slide under the ropes and end the match. I am not always smart.

Tarin gets up, his heavy breathing sounding like a freight train. He stumbles towards me, his body language telegraphing his plans. He's against hitting girls, but apparently has no problem with wrestling them to the ground.

As soon as he's close enough, I hit him with a volley of quick jabs to the chest and face. He holds up his gloves, avoiding the worst of it, but I still get a couple taps in. At first he responds with some weak moves, but with egging-on from the guys, they become stronger, more assured.

"Come on, come on, show us what you got!" yells Charlie. "I've seen ten-year-old girls fight better than that!"

Tarin finally gives me something decent to look at, but I block it easily. Swatting his attempts away like flies, I land another couple solid punches to his abs. This is how I motivate men to do crunches. Now he knows I go for the soft parts.

"Short, sharp, quick! Jab! Gloves up! Jab!"

Tarin quickly gets into the rhythm Charlie's calling out for him. I'm impressed with how easily it's coming for him now. He's got a certain grace to his moves, reminding me of a professional boxer. Raw, yes, but with a certain natural talent. He'd be a hell of a street fighter if he had any finesse.

"Left, left, right! Go! Sharper! Harder! Right, right, left!"

Tarin will never beat me with this kind of workout, since Charlie's giving me the entire playbook through the natural megaphone that is his mouth, but it doesn't matter. The goal is to get Tarin interested, and I can tell we've won. He's on his toes, he's moving, he's swinging with abandon but listening. I let him get a few punches in so he doesn't lose hope entirely.

Tarin backs away when Charlie takes a break from yelling. He grins at me. "You had enough yet?" He asks me. He can barely get the words out he's breathing so hard.

I smile evilly. "The question is, have you had enough yet?"

He shakes his head and dances closer. "Enough? Please. I haven't even gotten a taste yet." And then he launches some of his own moves on me.

I block all but one, taking a hit to the chin. I bend over and turn partially away, pretending to be hurt. Waiting… waiting…

He stops immediately and comes to my side. "Oh, shit. Did that hurt? I'm sorry, I didn't mean to.."

I wait until he places a hand on my back before turning around and punching him right in the gut. As he bends over I meet him with a solid uppercut and then a combination, left-right-left. He's on his back staring up at the ceiling about three seconds later.

Applause erupts around the gym. Several of the regulars have come in and are giving me thumbs up. I wave to my fans before sticking my right glove in my left armpit to yank it off. I walk over to Tarin and hold my bare hand out. "Need some help?"

He reaches up, his gloved hand limp. His head lolls to the side a little. "Yeah. Help … me." He's exhausted.

I smile, triumph feeling especially good for some reason. As soon as his wrist clamps around mine, though, I know I've been foolish. *Oh, you silly, gullible girl…*

One second I'm standing on my feet, and the next, I'm on my back with his heavy, sweaty, smelly body on top of mine. I struggle to get away, but he's got more energy and strength left than I would have thought possible.

"Say uncle," he demands, his sweet breath blowing into my face. It doesn't smell like cigarettes for a change. I can feel his heartbeat pounding into my breasts.

"Screw you," I grunt, trying to wiggle out from under him.

The people in the gym are hooting like teenagers.

I punch him in the back of the head with my gloved fist as best I can, but he traps my arm with a strong grip, pressing his chest harder into mine. His face is even closer. I can feel a hard-on starting for him, as his crotch settles in on top of my leg. "I wrestled in high school," he says, his hot breath washing over me and giving me shivers. "You're not getting away until you say uncle and admit I am the champion of all champions." The more I wiggle, the harder he presses into me.

Panic level nine. Get out! Get away! The feel of his body this close to mine is freaking me out. I don't know why, I just know it has to stop.

"I guess you had different rules in high school wrestling than I have," I say, sweating coming out of my every pore, my pulse going so hard I can feel it pounding in my neck. I'm giving him fair warning, but he doesn't get it.

"What's that supposed to mean?"

I bring my knee up into his crotch only half as hard as my fear wants me to, immediately immobilizing him. His expression goes from smug to surprise and then to pained in the space of a single second.

I easily push him off me and watch as he rolls into the fetal position around his nuts. The relief washes over me like a giant ocean wave. My pulse begins to return to normal immediately. The threat has been removed.

The hoots turn to laughs and then shouts. "Damn, girl! You ain't gotta do that!"

"Next time just kiss him and get it over with!" yells someone else.

Ricky and Scott walk up to greet me as I flip over the ropes and land on my feet next to the ring.

"That was coooold-blooded," says Ricky, holding up his hand for a high five. "Respect, girl. Respect."

I smack his palm with mine and smile. "I don't play for anything but keeps."

"Remind me not to mess with you *ever*," he says, cupping his jewels with one hand. "I plan to have lots of kids in the future."

I smile. "Just don't try to wrestle me to the ground, and we'll be just fine. I don't do wrestling."

Scott puts his hand on my shoulder. "Well, sis, you've done it again. Brought a man to his knees and made him see the error of his ways. What's next? Chest waxing?"

"Yeah," I say, knocking his arm off me. "And you're going first."

Scott rubs his chest nervously. "Do you mean it? I only have like five hairs there and I'm kind of attached to them."

I punch him lightly in the arm. "Shut up and get this stuff off me, would ya?" I hold out my still-gloved hand at him and wait for him to oblige me.

He smiles. "Do you have any idea how much I love the first day in the gym with these guys?"

I grin back. "About half as much as I do?"

He laughs. "Yeah, maybe."

Once I'm out of my fight gear and my hair is back in a somewhat decent ponytail, I turn to look at my latest victim. Tarin falls out of the ring and lands on the ground, letting Ricky get him to his feet. He walks with a limp over in my direction. I can't tell if he's angry by his expression. Even with his pads off now, he's wearing a mask.

Charlie joins us. "Well, that was educational." He slaps Tarin on the back so hard it makes him hunch over and cringe. "See you in a couple days?"

Tarin stands up and looks at me sharply, something akin to fear in his eyes.

I smile. "Absolutely." I give Tarin my best challenging look. "You in, Tarin?"

Tarin's eyes narrow and then he smiles too. "Oh, I am *so* in. You have no idea."

"That's my boy," says Charlie, smacking him one more time before ambling off to yell at someone not using the punching bag properly.

Tarin lifts his chin at me and then winks once before walking over to the water fountain. As I watch him walk away, the thrill that runs through me tells me that I really don't have any idea what's happening here, but I want to find out. My better judgment has definitely abandoned me.

CHAPTER FOURTEEN

I LEAVE TARIN TO SHOWER while I discuss the menu for the week with the cook I've hired to do all of Tarin's meals for the next month. I met Josh when he was working at one of my favorite restaurants. When he went into freelancing, I hired him immediately, and since then, we've done several gigs together. He's always a part of my contract because no one can cook a healthy, interesting meal like Josh can, and he does it over and over again. I don't think I've ever eaten the same thing twice with him in the kitchen. Good food tends to ease the pain of my workouts and demands, and I am not too proud to manipulate a man through his stomach.

He's wearing his cooking uniform: black and white checkered pants and a white t-shirt, the entire thing covered in a white jacket. He's always formal in the kitchen, even when he's just working for my clients in their homes.

"So nothing special, is that it then? Just the usual?" Josh asks.

"You can ask him if he has anything he prefers, but you know the routine. Heavy protein, high glycemic carbs, no refined sugars, light on the gluten."

"Yum-*eee*. Sounds like I'll be eating chicken and cardboard," says Tarin, walking into the kitchen. His hair is wet and hanging down around his face, his board shorts, t-shirt, and flip flops making him look like a surfer. The tattoos that run up both arms only heighten the effect. My heart flips when a vision of him in the shower jumps unbidden into my head.

I stand there with my eyes bugging out, trying to get myself together as Josh introduces himself.

"Love your stuff, man." Josh holds out his hand.

"Thanks." Tarin shakes Josh's hand and looks down at the two plates on the counter that contain our pre-lunch snack. He doesn't seem very excited. "What's that?"

I clear my throat, my voice finally ready to work again. "That's your snack before lunch."

"Good. Because if you said that was my lunch, I was going to have to call Charlie and tattle on you." One side of his mouth goes up in a smile. "Meat and potatoes. Charlie says."

I smirk, glad he feels that what Charlie wants, Charlie should get. Maybe next time we're in the ring together he'll throw a few real punches and give me a decent workout. "Come on. Let's go eat by the pool." Picking up the plates, I nod at Josh. "Thanks. We good for the rest of the week?"

"Yeah. Just try to give me some advance notice on numbers if you can."

"That's easy, I can do that now. We'll have seven for dinners, six for the rest of the meals."

"You want me to plate-up the rest of them now?"

I nod. "Yeah. Keep it with Tarin and me for the snacks, everyone together for the meals."

"Gotcha." Josh goes to the stack of dishes on the counter and pulls four of them out so he can put the food on them.

Tarin frowns but says nothing until we're outside sitting at a poolside table that has already been set for two with silverware, glasses, and an iced down pitcher of lemon-flavored water.

"Who are the seven coming for dinner?" Tarin asks as he takes his seat.

"You, me, Scott, Ricky, Zach, Leonard, and Jelly. She'll be here for dinner but that's it. The rest of us will eat together for main meals, and you and I will be alone together for snacks. It gives us time to talk about what's going on and the plans for the day or week." I don't tell him this, but it's also the time for him to talk about his emotional issues and other things getting in the way of his success. He's not ready for that yet. He needs to trust me first before I broach the subject of unloading his deepest regrets on me.

Tarin pulls his napkin out and drops it into his lap. "Jelly." He shakes his head.

I swallow the lump in my throat. I don't know why I have such a visceral reaction to her name, but it's there. I can't deny it. I just keep my mouth shut to make sure I don't say something I'll wish I hadn't later.

"What the hell was I thinking?" he asks.

"What do you mean?" I can come up with all kinds of things he could be referencing. Picking her up in the first place … dating her … sleeping with her … impregnating her. I don't know how deep his regret goes, I only know how deep my regret goes for him: profoundly so.

"I don't know," he says, running his hands through his wet hair, making it stick to the sides of his head. The top part flops over onto his forehead. No matter what his hair does, it never detracts from his amazing good looks.

He looks sexy. Lost. Tragic, but on the edge of greatness again. I want to take a picture of him just like this and save it in my head forever. An energy hums out from him that inspires me to do whatever I need to so he can be all he is again. I have to restrain myself from grabbing his hand and pledging my undying support. *Holy groupie alert.* I take a deep breath to calm myself. I've never felt this way around anyone in my life. Not even Austin.

"Never mind." He picks up his fork and pokes at the food on his plate. "What is this stuff, anyway?"

"Tuna." I clear my throat because my voice is coming out strange. "Lentils. Cucumber salad. Try it. I promise, you'll like it."

"I'm not a fan of any of the things you just said." Tarin pokes his food some more. "Fucking rabbit food."

I take a bite of the crunchy vegetables. "Rabbits don't eat tuna, dumbass. Come on, have I steered you wrong yet?"

He looks up at me, mild shock on his face. "Did you just call me a dumbass?" He laughs a little. "You're kidding right? Steer me wrong? Call me crazy, but even though I just met you, in the last few hours you've turned my entire life upside down, fired a bunch of my people, punched the shit out of me in a boxing ring, racked my balls, and turned my kitchen into a … what did Charlie call it … a La Jolla foo-foo restaurant."

"Froo-froo, not foo-foo. But *have I steered you wrong*, is the question." My eyes are sparkling with happiness. Everything he just said makes me so psyched about my progress. I really have accomplished a lot in just short time.

"To be honest, I'm not sure yet."

"Try the tuna. Decide after you eat."

Tarin slides the smallest morsel of food onto the fork that a human tongue is capable of tasting and puts it in his mouth. He hesitates a few seconds as the flavors register in his brain, and then the fork goes down to scoop up a healthier portion. He's nodding his head as he puts that one into his mouth too. There's nothing like fresh tuna the way Josh prepares it. I've never been able to go back to the canned stuff since.

"Not bad," he finally admits.

"Try the lentils."

He pokes his fork at the brownish green beads. "Those things?"

"Yeah." I eat a big bite of mine. Josh is a master at taking a thing I'd destroy in the kitchen and making it magical.

"Rabbit turds," he says quietly. But he bravely tries more of the food and soon enough is shoveling it in without stopping.

We eat in silence for a little while and I try not to stare at his arms as they move around, picking up utensils, taking his glass and moving it to his mouth, the way his throat moves as he swallows.

I jump slightly, startled when he suddenly turns to me and speaks. I'm afraid he's caught me checking him out.

"So, how do you know Charlie so well?" he asks between mouthfuls.

I'm relieved to know the question wasn't *'So how long have you been a stalker?'*

"He and my dad were good friends. Since they were kids." This is safer ground than where my mind was headed. It's not exactly my favorite topic of conversation, but it's definitely safer.

"You're from around there?"

I nod as I wipe my mouth with my napkin. "Yep. Born and raised."

"You're just Scarlett from the block." Tarin starts doing a riff on the Jennifer Lopez song *Jenny From the Block.* I can't help but smile at how he takes a song *so* not in his genre and turns it around into something that sounds like a cross between rap and rock. He puts my name in for Jenny. For a few lines it makes me smile, but then when he grabs a knife and uses it as his microphone, staring at me while he raps, it reminds me too much of Austin. The smile drops off my face as a cool breeze blows through my world and cuts off the joy.

Tarin's song ends prematurely and he puts the knife on the table. "That bad, huh?"

I shake my head, reaching out to touch him but then pulling back before I make contact with his skin. "No, it's not that. I like the song."

I put my napkin on the table and stand, the awkward moment too much for me to deal with. "Ready for your next workout?"

He takes me by the hand and pulls me a little, keeping me from leaving the table. Where his fingers are touching mine I feel a tingling. I almost can't breathe.

"Wait. Don't go," he says. "Sit. I just need to relax for a few more minutes. You kicked my ass in the ring." His fingers slide away and I'm suddenly without his touch. I miss it already.

I hesitate, hating myself for letting my out-of-control personal feelings interfere in my work. And I don't want to have this conversation, especially when I see so many unspoken questions behind his eyes. Maybe dangerous ones. This is not going as planned.

"Please?" he begs.

And just like that, I cave.

He looks so sincere and sweet for a change, finally not angry or depressed. I can't resist. Despite my misgivings about getting too close and letting him in, I take my seat again.

When I sit back down, he smiles. It's slight and it's only half there, but it's charming anyway. I can see why girls would totally fall for him, even if he wasn't a rock and roll star. Other girls, though. Not me. I don't fall for rock stars. The shell I've built around my heart can be bruised, but it cannot be broken.

"Fine. So, what's up with Jelly?" I ask. I need to be in control of the conversation to keep it from going places I can't manage; might as well get the conversation rolling on the worst, least sexy subject I can think of.

He leans back in his chair and closes his eyes, letting out a long sigh. "I don't know," he finally says. His head is resting on the back of the seat.

"Are you going to have her move in here with you?"

He tilts his head towards me and opens one eye. "Are you kidding? We'd kill each other in less than a week." He closes his eyes again and turns his head to face the sun.

I battle the smile to keep it hidden. I'm sickly gleeful about them not getting along which obviously means I'm a horrible person. "Why do you say that?" I ask, forcing my voice to remain even.

He shakes his head. "She's fun, don't get me wrong. But she's … high maintenance and she likes to party too much. I like to party too much. When we're together, we party *way* too much. It's stupid." He rubs his closed eyes with his fingers, digging in deep.

"And she's pregnant. With your child."

He sits up slowly as his fingers fall away and his now bloodshot eyes open. "Do you believe her? That she's pregnant, I mean."

"Do you?"

He looks down into his lap as he fiddles with his fingers. "No. I don't think I do. That makes me an asshole, right?"

"Not necessarily. Why don't you believe her?"

"Because ... would she keep partying if she knew she was pregnant? I mean, what kind of woman does that? Besides, my motto is no glove, no love. But maybe when I was really wasted ..." He looks at me, his expression telling me he's sick over it.

I say nothing. I sense he has his own answers to his question about Jelly, and I don't like mine. They're not nice at all, and I'm not necessarily a very good judge, especially since I can't stop staring that this man's face, arms, and hands. I refuse to let my gaze stray lower, even though it keeps trying to go there.

He gestures angrily. "She's either lying and partying, which makes her a fucking bag and a half for doing that to me, or she's telling the truth and filling my baby full of drugs and alcohol, which makes her a fucking two-bagger and not worthy of being a mother. I'm fucked no matter what."

It wouldn't be right for me to just agree with him. I feel uncomfortable, like a part of me is trying to get her out of the way for some reason and that it's more than just me looking out for his best interests. The little devil inside my head wants me to yell, *'Yes! She's a total ho-bag! Dump her ass!'*, but that's not why I'm here. I can't let my personal feelings get in the way of him living his life the way it was meant to be lived.

So I take the high road. I say the thing that the professional Scarlett Barnes would say. The Scarlett Barnes who feels a pull towards Tarin like she did towards another guy once, a long time ago, will now and forever remain totally silent. I will not let the weak Scarlett's voice be heard.

"Maybe Jelly just loves you so much, the idea of me telling her she had to go was too much to deal with. So maybe the lie was kind of justified in her mind."

He frowns at me and leans forward a little. "Are you serious?"

It's kind of freaky how intensely he's studying my face.

"Do you really mean that?" he presses.

I can't hold his gaze. I look down at my feet, pretending to care a lot about my shoelaces. "Yeah, sure, why wouldn't I?" My heart squeezes painfully in my chest. I never lie to clients like this, ever. I feel like a fraud and an asshole and a girl who shouldn't be here.

He says nothing. The silence goes on for so long I have to look up to see what's happening.

He's still staring at me. His green eyes are so bright, I'm struck by how they remind me of emeralds. Of Ireland. Of places where magic happens in worlds we can't see.

"Why are you staring at me like that?" I ask, my voice barely above a whisper.

He looks sad. "I don't know why. I guess I'm just waiting to hear your answer." He shrugs and there's a bitterness to his expression.

"I already answered you," I say, my heart feeling like it's going to explode with withheld emotion. What emotion that is, I can't say.

He taps my forearm with the side of his index finger a few times before letting it slide away. It leaves a trail of heat behind. "You're just blowing me off. I want your real answer."

I look away, the rose bushes off in the distance my only escape from his intense gaze. *Time to bail.* "I forgot the question. You ready to go yet?" I put my hands on the arms of the chair and use them to leverage myself up.

I grab my plate and glass and am partway across the lawn to the back door of the house when his next words hit me.

"Chicken shit."

Disappointment laces his tone. It's like an arrow piercing my heart. Real pain slices through me. I feel like I let him down, but I'm not even sure how.

I say nothing as I walk into the house. My face is burning and I want to run. *Chicken shit is right. What in the hell am I doing?*

CHAPTER
FIFTEEN

MY PHONE RINGS AS TARIN is walking into the kitchen. I press the green button to connect the call and turn my back to him, wandering into the hallway for some privacy.

"Scarlett Barnes," I say.

"Yo, Scar, what up? It's me, Jack."

"Jack who?" I smile, laughter bubbling up inside me. I keep it down though, at least for the few seconds it takes for my joke to play out.

"Are you shitting me, girl? Jack Sprat who ate no fat, that's who. Come on, don't fuck with me. I need you."

I sigh, the smile in my voice letting him know he's still one of my best friends. Now that we don't work together anymore, anyway. Before that, when we first started working together, we weren't friends. Not at all. Bitter enemies might be a better word for what we were when his label hired me to get his ass out of a very dark place.

"Fine. What's up? You need me to go shopping with you and help you pick out an outfit for the premier? Because I see you in baby blue. Call me nuts, but I think you could pull it off. Ruffles… Lots of ruffles around the cuffs and down the front. Think: old school prom tux."

"Seriously, Scar, you need to stick with what you know, and fashion is *not* what you know. The reason I'm calling is I got this gig tonight and I want you there. It's kind of a last minute thing, but it's big."

"No, I can't. I'm up to my ass in work right now."

"Ahhh," he says, his voice going softer, "another lost soul needs finding, is that it?"

"You could say that." I look over my shoulder. I don't see Tarin, but I sense he's near. There's no noise coming from the kitchen anymore.

"Bring him along."

"How do you know it's a him?"

"Because in all the time I've known you, you've never taken a chick for a client. Just the lost boys get your attention."

I smile sadly. "Yeah. The lost boys." I want to cry for some reason.

"Bring him."

"I can't. I really can't. I don't want him to see you." I can only imagine what that would do to Tarin at this point in his rescue. Jack can be overwhelming sometimes, and he's one of my biggest fans.

"You're thinking he's not ready, is that it?"

"Something like that, yeah."

"Listen … nobody's ever ready for you Scarlett, you know that. You make them ready. You drag them kickin' and screamin' and you make them ready. So bring him along. I promise to behave. Mostly."

I sigh. "Where and when? No promises, but maybe I can stop by. I've missed seeing you."

"Yeah, me too. Tonight, nine o'clock the show starts. I should be on around ten. I'll text you the address."

"That's late. You know I go to bed early on work nights."

"And I also know you break the rules for special occasions, if you recall."

I smile with the memory. "Yes. When it's really important, I will do that. But only on special occasions."

"Trust me. This is one of those. I hope I see you there. Two tickets will be at the door for you. I want you to come see me backstage."

"If I come, I'll stop by and say hello."

"Don't forget to bring your lost boy. I like Scott and all, but I'd like to meet this new man of yours."

His choice of words makes me go warm inside and then just as quickly freaks me out and causes me to get the cold sweats. "He's not my man."

"Okay, if you say so. It's all just words, though, you know? That's not what matters. It's the doing and the feeling that means something to people like us."

He hangs up before I can argue the point any further or ask him what in the hell he means by his mysterious comments. He has a way of throwing me off whenever we talk, often giving me the feeling he has so much more to say but doesn't. It's one of those issues we never fully worked out before my time with him was over and I moved on to my next lost boy.

"Who was that?" asks Tarin, coming out of the kitchen. I can't tell from his expression if he heard any of the conversation or not.

"Just a friend. Someone I used to work with."

"Someone like me?" he asks.

I answer honestly. "Yes and no. Do you want to spend some time in your studio before we leave?"

"Where are we going?"

"A couple places. First to a friend's and then a meeting with your attorneys."

His nostrils flare and a storm passes over his face. His mood changes abruptly, from day to night. "When do we leave?"

I look at my watch. "Half hour."

"I'll be in the studio. Knock loudly when you want me to come out."

I nod, following his progress down the hall. He's slouched over and tense. He bangs the door to the studio closed behind him.

I wait, and a few minutes later, the weak sounds of a guitar being played come out of the room and leak into the hallway. The chords are dark. Angry. Frustrated.

I leave before I can hear too much more. Our morning went well, but I know that there's so much work for me to do before I'll be able to sleep well at night again. The words of an old poem come to me as I take the stairs slowly to my temporary bedroom and office. I have promises to keep and miles to go before I sleep.

CHAPTER SIXTEEN

I TAP ON THE STUDIO door when it's time to go. Ricky's in the car waiting and Scott's goofing around with video games. He worked his butt off all morning organizing things for us, and I know he'll be up late tonight at Jack's show, so I don't give him any crap about it. He'll stop in time to finish his work; he always does.

I hear a crash on the other side of the door, coming from the studio. My blood goes cold and my blood pressure spikes up.

"Tarin?" I ask.

Another crash comes, followed in close succession by more banging and crashing.

I try the handle, but the door is locked. "Tarin!" I say louder, trying to be heard over the noises coming from inside.

Zach appears behind me. "Need help?"

I turn to him, my pulse hammering with nervousness. I hate this part of my job. "I think he's having a meltdown."

Zach nods. "Sounds like it. You want to ride it out or get in?"

"What do you suggest?"

"We usually just let him ride it out."

"Then let me in." Whatever indulgences they've given him before are what contributed to him being what he is now: a spoiled brat. Time to change the program.

Zach raises an eyebrow at me, but reaches up above the door and brings a key down. "Better step back and let me handle this part." He slides the key into the slot as I step to the side a little.

Banging on the door, he shouts, "Tarin, I'm coming in."

"Fuck you, Zach! Don't you dare touch that fucking door!" Something crashes into the door, making it shake in Zach's grip.

Zach looks at me. "You sure you want to do this?"

"Yes. But be careful, I don't want you to get hurt." I take a deep breath and hold it.

Zach pushes open the door and then shuts it really quick before going in. Something smashes into it and drops the floor. He opens it again without hesitation and rushes in, shoving whatever's in the way to the side.

I'm right behind him, so I get a great view of what happens next. Tarin has part of a drum set held high above his head, his face bright red and sweating. Before he can launch it across the room, Zach gets him in a full-body lockdown, wrapping his arms around Tarin's waist and squeezing hard. The drum part falls out of his hands, bonks Zach in the head and then rolls to the ground.

"Get the fuck off me!" Tarin's grunting, trying to get away.

"Calm down!" yells Zach, re-adjusting his hold to include Tarin's arms.

"Fuck you! *You* calm down!" Tarin struggles to get free, but Zach's arms are like a straightjacket. All the little brat can do is turn bright red with his efforts.

I walk into the room, stepping around the garbage that used to be musical instruments and sheet music. I don't know what the place looked like before, but it's a disaster now. I want to cry over the frustration I see reflected here. *So much lost.* I'm afraid I won't be able to get it back. When a musician spends this much time wrecking his most valued things and places, it's never a good sign.

"Get the hell out of here!" he screams at me, spittle flying from his lips. "This is my personal space! You're not welcome here!"

I don't know what comes over me in that instant. Maybe it's the fact that he's acting like a spoiled child or that he's talking to me so cruelly, but I lose my cool. I walk right up to him and slap him across the face.

Taking a step back, I stare at him, trying not to let my shock at my own behavior show in my expression.

He immediately shuts up and his body relaxes in Zach's hold.

Zach looks at the ceiling, battling the smile that is coming over his features.

"Did you just fucking slap me?" Tarin sounds like he doesn't believe it himself.

"Yes, apparently I just did." I look down at my hand, surprised at the tingling there. I guess I smacked him pretty hard.

He looks up at his bodyguard. "Let me go, Zach. Seriously. It's cool. I'm not really down with the man love like you are."

Zach ignores the veiled insult. "You're not going to smack her back are you?"

Tarin scowls. "Come on, man, you know me better than that."

Zach loosens his hold. "I'll be outside." He stops at the door. "You want me to send someone in here for this?" He gestures to the mess on the floor.

"No. Leave it." I'll be damned if I'm going to let anyone but Tarin clean up after this ridiculous tantrum.

Zach walks out the door and shuts it quietly behind him.

Tarin and I stare at each other. The red handprint on his face makes me ashamed of myself, but I try to focus on the bigger picture and not let it overwhelm everything I'm trying to do here.

"You hit me," he says.

"Yes, I did. And I'm sorry."

"Why'd you do it?"

His question confuses me. "Isn't it obvious?"

"Is it part of your little program? Do you do that all the time?"

"No. It's not a part of my program." I feel the heat rising in my neck.

"Why'd you do it then?"

I shrug. "What difference does it make?"

"Is it because I hurt your feelings or because I was having a fit?"

I bite my lip as I consider his words. He's watching me like a hawk, making me nervous. His gaze shifts from my eyes to my mouth and then to my chest. I know he can see my breaths coming too fast. I could blame my reaction on me freaking out over the destruction, but I have a feeling he'll know I'm not being entirely honest.

I try to blow him off. "Hurt my feelings? Please." I gesture to the room around us. "It takes a lot more than you not welcoming me into your garbage pit to hurt my feelings."

He takes a step closer, the trash on the floor making loud swishing sounds as his feet pushes it aside. "Oh, so you're such a hardass, no one can get through, is that it?"

Every part of me wants to run away from him. He's invading my personal space like a boyfriend, but I can't back away. This is a challenge I *will* win. "No, that's not it. I'm not immune to harsh words. I'm actually very easy to hurt if you want to know the truth." My chin comes up, even though I don't mean for it to.

"You slapped me because I was having a fit, then. Not because I hurt your feelings."

I blink a couple times slowly. "Yes. That's it. You were out of control. I just brought you back down to Earth."

He studies my face for a few seconds and then shakes his head. "Nope. That's not it. I hurt your feelings."

I press my lips together to keep them from trembling. The reaction I'm having and this conversation reminds me way too strongly of another situation and another boy who hurt me terribly. It's all too much, how Tarin and Austin are so alike in that way, with the power they have to affect me so easily. My chin quivers from the effects of trying to keep my emotions from showing.

Tarin reaches up slowly and touches my chin. "I'm sorry I hurt your feelings."

I turn my head so his finger will fall away. "I'll get over it." I look around the room. "You'll be cleaning this up when we get back today."

He laughs. "Like hell I will."

I turn my head back to stare at him. "As soon as I leave this room, I will instruct everyone in this house not to touch it. No one will cooperate with you until you cooperate with me. From now on, you clean up your own messes."

"What the fuck is that all about?" He's on the brink of another tantrum, so I go for the jugular.

"It's about respect for the people who work for you. Who the hell do you think you are, anyway? Is your mind so warped that you actually think it's okay to act like a four-year-old child, destroy thousands of dollars worth of equipment and the work of other people, and then call someone in to clean up after you? Like they don't have other more important things to do? What … you want to pay Marta to wipe your asshole for you too?"

"That's what I pay them for."

"No. It's not what you pay them for, you jerk. You pay them to cook, to clean up after normal usage, to drive you, and to protect you. That's it. No one is here to babysit you. And you definitely can't buy friends … not real ones. And you keep this shit up and you're going to lose the only ones you have left."

"Then what are you here for?"

I turn to walk away, but he grabs my sleeve. "Answer my question."

I look down at his hand that's twisted in my shirt. I speak softly, but there's no hiding from the threat that lies underneath. "Get your hands off me, Tarin. Right now."

He lets me go. "Tell me why you're here."

Looking at his face, I can tell the answer means something to him. And I can't lie. I have to tell him the truth. "I'm here to save you from yourself."

"What if I don't want saving?" he asks, unshed, angry, frustrated tears making his eyes bright.

"Then I'm either going to drag you kicking and screaming back to where you used to be or die trying."

"Why do you think where I used to be was so great? Maybe it was worse than where I am now."

I sense there's more to what he's saying than just the bare words, but I don't have the time or the inclination to delve right now. "I don't believe that."

He backs away, nearly tripping over the junk on the floor. "You don't know shit about me." He's angry again.

"I know what I need to know. You have five minutes to get your ass out to the front door."

"Fuck that. I'm not going anywhere."

I sigh, pausing at the entrance to the room. "You will either come willingly or you'll be dragged. And if you continue to put Zach and Leonard in a position to get hurt, I'm going to have to let them go and hire some other people who are more … tuned in to that kind of behavior."

"You can't fire Zach and Leonard! They've been with me from the start! They're my friends!"

"I can and I will. You decide if they stay by your behavior. If you give me trouble about going where I need you to go, I'll take that as your tacit agreement to having them fired."

He spits on the floor. "You're a hardcore bitch, you know that?"

I give him a smile that carries no humor, ignoring the pain that his words cause. "I've been called worse."

I close the door softly behind me. A few more crashes follow but then silence. I go out the front door and get into the car, confident that Tarin will be out within the timeframe given.

I can say a lot of things about him that aren't very nice, but I cannot say he doesn't try to be a good friend when he needs to be. Something tells me leveraging his loyalty to the people around him will be the key to winning him over, so that's exactly what I'm going to continue to do.

CHAPTER SEVENTEEN

RICKY PULLS THE SEDAN UP to the warehouse I've given him the address for. "Is this it?" he asks, looking at the bland exterior with suspicion.

"Yep." I open my door. "Come on, Tarin."

"You want me in there?" asks Scott.

"Sure. Ricky, do you mind waiting out here?" I ask, dipping my head down into the car window to look at him.

"Not at all." He pulls a Kindle out from under the front seat. "Got about a thousand books on here I've been meaning to read."

Tarin snorts from the backseat. "You don't read books, who are you trying to kid?"

Ricky looks at him in the rearview mirror, his voice stern. "Don't pretend you know me that well." He drops his gaze to his Kindle and turns it on, decidedly ignoring the shocked and hurt expression on Tarin's face.

Boom. Shot to the heart. Everyone's mad at Tarin for having that tantrum, and I feel like singing and dancing in the rain over it. There's nothing more powerful than peer pressure to get someone like Tarin back in line. He may be an independent, crazy, loud-mouth musician on the outside, but inside he's like everyone else; he needs connections, he needs to be respected, and he needs love. His friends have given this to him without question and without demanding anything in return before, but that's over now. Now, he's going to have to work for their love, just like everyone else. *Recalibration engaged.*

Tarin gets out of the car and stands next to me. He won't look at me, but that's okay. What I'm about to do doesn't require that he like me right now. Or ever.

"What's this place?" he asks.

"It's a friend's studio."

"I already trashed one studio today," he says, sounding just a little bit disappointed himself. My joy edges up another notch.

"It's not that kind of studio." I take a key out of my small purse and fit it into the lock. Before I can finish unlocking the door, it swings open, and a man with disheveled hair and paint splatters covering most of his body is standing there in the doorway.

"Scarlett!" he exclaims, holding out his arms.

"Greg." I move in for a quick hug, hoping this time the paint is dry.

"Oh shit," he says, backing away. He searches the front of my clothes. "Did I get ya?"

I look down. "Not this time."

"Awesome." He looks over my shoulder. "Bring a friend?"

"Yes." I step inside as he moves out of the way. "And Scott, of course."

"Yo, Scotty boy." Greg holds out his hand and they shake.

Tarin walks in last with his hands in his pockets. He nods a silent hello.

"I know this guy." Greg points at Tarin with a smile on his face. Then he breaks out in a raspy rendition of one of Tarin's older hits.

Tarin smiles, even though I can tell it pains him to do it. Greg's kind of hard to resist that way and his voice isn't bad.

"Man, that piece was awesome," says Greg. "That reminds me … I gotta show you something."

Greg walks over to stack of paintings and starts shoving them around, obviously looking for something he can't remember the location of.

Tarin's gaze roams the room while we wait for Greg to join us again. I wonder if what Tarin is seeing scares or intrigues him. I hope for the latter. This warehouse has been Greg's home away from home for years. It's covered in acrylic paint splatters from floors to walls and even some spots on the ceiling. Good thing he owns the place or I'm sure the landlord would have kicked him out a long time ago. Canvases lean against the walls, four, five, and six deep. They're stacked up on almost all of the surfaces, sometimes a few feet high. Bigger pieces that are in the process of being worked on are attached directly to the wall. There are cans and bottles and tubes scattered throughout. One corner of the room is dedicated to making canvases with rolls of the heavy material, a chop saw, small pieces of wood, and various staple guns, hammers, nails, and wire.

"Here it is," exclaims Greg, sliding a canvas out from a big pile. The remaining ones teeter, and Scott gets there just in time to save them from crashing to the floor. He works on straightening them out as Greg walks over to Tarin to show him his find.

"I did this after I listened to *Break Me* for the first time. I'll bet I heard that song a hundred times as I painted this. Probably more."

Tarin takes the painting from him and just stares at it. Greg prattles on and on about the inspiration he received from Tarin's music and lyrics, but I can see that Tarin is hearing none of it. He's lost in the colors and the movement of the paint across the fabric. Greg is a genius. His pieces have never failed to grab my lost boys and pull them in, and now I know that Tarin is no exception.

Tarin's voice is rough when he speaks. "What's it supposed to be?"

Greg's tone holds traces of humor. "I don't know, man. What do you see?"

Tarin tries to give him back the painting. "Nothing. Just some colors, that's it."

Greg pushes the painting back at him. "Nah, you keep it. It's a gift."

"I can't. I don't want it."

I cringe inwardly, knowing how sensitive Greg can be sometimes about his work.

Greg pushes his lips out and then shakes his head. Finally he says, "You got it bad, dude. Better suit up." He walks away and grabs an old coffee can, looking inside it as he goes. At the sink on the far side of the room he fills the can partway and locates a few brushes lying on the draining board, making sure they're clean before dumping them into the water. He disappears into a large storage closet where I can hear him moving things around.

Scott walks over to Tarin and takes the painting from him. "If you don't want to ruin your clothes, you'll want to get one of those suits on." He motions to the rack of car-mechanic jumpsuits hanging from hooks near the door. They're in several sizes and none of them are clean.

"What are you talking about? Is this guy gonna start flinging paint everywhere or what?"

"Not him. *You.*" Scott carries the painting over to the door. "I'm going to go wait in the car." He leaves before any of us have time to say goodbye.

"What's he talking about?" Tarin asks me. I can't tell if he's angry or just confused.

"Three days a week you'll paint. Get a suit on and get ready to have your first session."

Tarin frowns, his face going darker than it already was. "I don't want to paint."

"So what? Paint anyway." I move towards the door. There's a stool there that's safely out of Greg's paint-splashing zone, and it gives me a great view of the room. I climb up on it and rest my feet on the bottom rung.

He puts one hand on a hip and gestures angrily with the other. "So even though I don't want to paint, you're going to force me to do it anyway?"

"Yes." I shrug, offering no apology.

"And if I don't follow your orders?"

"I think you know what happens if you don't cooperate."

His nostrils flare as he drops his arms to his side. "This is bull-shit and you know it."

"No, it's not bullshit, Tarin. You're a creative person. If you can't create music right now, you'll create something else. Work out your emotions in a way that doesn't destroy your house or your friendships."

He shakes his head, thoroughly disgusted with me. "Un fuck-ing believable." But he shuffles over to the wall and yanks a suit off a hook.

Before I can look away, he pulls his shirt off over his head. Tattoos I've never seen before glare out at me. A particularly rough-looking one across his abdomen jumps out at me.

Guilty is what it says.

I wonder what he did that was so terrible it inspired him to brand himself with such negativity. It makes me sad to see it. I turn to the side when his hand goes to the first button of his pants.

"What's the matter? Worried about seeing me naked?" he asks, finishing with a bitter laugh. He's taunting me. He's not happy.

I turn back around, my face expressionless. "No. Not at all."

He drops his pants, and I try not to let my shock show. He's not wearing underwear and his entire body is right there on dis-play, not more than five feet away. His tan lines only emphasize what I'm seeing just below his waist. My heart flips over at the raw maleness of it. My eyes roam north in self-preservation.

His body is lean, the tattoos roaming over muscle bulges and smoother sections of skin, wrapping around arms and ribs and shoulders. Some are old and faded, others brightly colored.

Guilty.

That tattoo keeps drawing my eyes back down to his waist.

I catch him smirking at me as Greg reappears, coming out of the storage room just in time to save me from saying something really stupid and embarrassing myself. I turn to face him instead of a naked Tarin.

"Ho, yeah, okay … all right," says Greg, nodding and shrug-ging. "Painting in the buff. I can hang."

"Nah, I'm getting dressed," says Tarin.

When I hear the suit being zipped up, I look at Tarin again, trying with everything I have not to appear affected by having seen him in all his glory. And glorious his body is, too. I'm going to have to drink a lot of alcohol to scrub my brain clean of that image. *Guilty, guilty, guilty...* I resist the urge to actually wipe my eyes.

Seeing him clothed in the painting suit should have been helping to get me back to Earth, but it isn't. I can't get rid of the sensation I experienced seeing him standing there naked with a knowing smirk on his face. He's completely covered now, from neck to ankle, but my libido still knows that all it would take is one downward yank on that zipper and he'd once again be standing there with just tattoos for clothing. And then it would be all over for me.

At this point, now that I've seen pretty much all of him, I'm going to have a hell of a time keeping myself from staring at him while he works and not fantasizing about all kinds of dangerous things. It's been way too long since I've had sex. The way I'm reacting to his body, in the middle of an art studio no less, tells me that I'm on a hair-trigger. God forbid he realize that and use it to manipulate me.

No matter what, I cannot afford to let that happen to either one of us. No matter how much certain parts of me might want it, there will be no sex or even a hint of that between us. And under no circumstances can he find out that he makes me think about these things between us.

I move around on the stool uncomfortably, my nipples suddenly too sensitive and other parts of me just as aroused. I seriously need an ice cold shower *right now.*

Tarin avoids my eyes as he zips the suit up the rest of the way. *Thank the universe for small favors.* I fan myself, pretending it's the weak air conditioning in the room making me sweat.

"Okay, so you ever work with acrylics before?" Greg, who's totally oblivious to my sexual distress, is pulling out a blank canvas and setting it on an easel in the middle of the room.

"No. Nothing. I've never painted." The tone of his voice belies his interest. Now that we're past the butting of heads, his natural interest is taking over. I'm secretly thrilled but I make sure to keep that emotion from showing.

"Okay, well, first thing you need to know is it's water-based, so if you want to change colors, you just rinse your brush in the can. Here's a rag so you can dry it off." He hands Tarin an old rag as he approaches. "The paints dry a lot faster than oils, so you don't have as much time to make changes before things start to get tacky." Greg gestures to a flat board covered in a rainbow of colors. "There's a palette. You can squeeze out the colors you want around the edges and use the center to mix new ones. You remember probably from kindergarten ... the primary colors are yellow, blue, and red ... you can mix them into whatever you want or use these colors that are already mixed in the tubes or bottles. If you want something lighter, add white ... darker, add black. Don't be shy about loading up your brush with paint. You don't want the canvas showing through." He gestures to the can with the water in it. "I've got brushes there for ya, but if you prefer to use a palette knife, I have some of those too."

"I don't need any of that," says Tarin.

Greg looks at Tarin and then at me, shrugging. "Whatever you say, man." He turns his attention more fully to me as he walks over. "Listen, I have to take off for a while. You okay here?"

I nod. "We're fine. Want me to lock up after I go?"

"Yeah, that'd be great. See you in a couple days?" He leans in to kiss my cheek. All I can smell is paint, turpentine, and dust. This is Greg's normal cologne.

"Yeah, see in you in two days. I'll text you if anything changes."

"Stay golden," he quips as he shuts the door behind him.

The room goes almost completely silent. Tarin stares at the empty canvas. The sounds of a clock ticking get louder as the sense of awkwardness grows. I say nothing, determined to wait his stubborn ass out on this chair until it's time to go.

Tarin sighs and grabs a tube of black paint. His back is to me, but I can see that the palette remains untouched. Seconds later he's pushing his hand into the canvas, leaving a giant black streak behind.

I shake my head. *Finger-painting? We're doing finger-painting?* I can't help but smile. He can't see me at this angle, so it's safe to let my feelings show. He is such a total brat. I should probably be mad about this, but I have to admit, I admire his spirit. Austin would have done the same thing.

CHAPTER EIGHTEEN

"CAN YOU COME OVER HERE for me?" Tarin asks about ten minutes later. He moves to the side as he turns to look at me, and I can see he's got the entire canvas covered in blobs and streaks of dark colors in black, blue, and a red so deep it reminds me of blood.

I get off the stool and move forward, not getting close enough to be touched. I don't trust him not to mess up my clothes out of revenge. When I'm parallel to him, I stop.

"I need you to pose for me," he explains.

My right eyebrow goes up. "Excuse me?"

"I need a model and you're the only one around. Just go sit on that table over there, would you?" He motions to a table behind his easel that has paintings stacked on it.

I search his face for guile but see none there, so I walk over and move the paintings to the side so I can sit on the table. I dangle my legs over the edge, my jeans and sneakers in no danger of being ruined. Everything over here is long dry, and the dust doesn't bother me when I'm dressed this casually.

Tarin puts some paints on the palette finally and picks up a brush, wiping the water off on his rag.

"So, tell me about you," he says out of the blue as he dips his brush into some yellow paint.

I frown. His face is hidden behind the easel and canvas, so I can't see his expression. The tone of his voice makes me think he's not even really paying attention to my answer much. He's concentrating on what he's doing with his brush, his arm moving in small circles. I can't imagine what about me says he should be painting in bright yellow, since my shirt is white and my jeans dark blue, but I withhold my comments. At least he's doing something other than staring at a blank canvas.

"There's not much to tell." I'm looking down at my nails, trying to decide if I should put polish on them later. Going to Jack's show is occasion enough to put up with the hassle. I love when they're painted but hate when they chip just hours later, and I never was one for acrylics.

He leans out and looks at me. "Chin up," he orders, gesturing with his own chin.

I drop my fingers and do what he says. His face disappears back behind the painting but comes out now and again as he pauses in his brush strokes.

"How about a husband? Got one of those?"

"No."

"Boyfriend?"

I squirm a little, hoping we aren't going to get any deeper into my life than this. "No."

He leans out. "In the market for one, or do you play for the other team?"

I can't help but smile. "Isn't there a third option?"

He disappears again. "No, not really. Isn't everyone looking for love?" His arm swoops around. I think he's picked up blue on his brush now.

"No, not me. I'm straight, unattached, and happy to stay that way. I'm not looking for love." *I already had my chance and blew it.* I push aside the pain, knowing this isn't the place to wallow in it.

"Bullshit." The frame jiggles with his efforts. I can't tell if he's reacting to my answer or using an especially inspired painting technique.

"It's not bullshit, it's the truth. Not everyone has to be in a relationship to be happy."

"You do, though."

My mood is quickly slipping south. I don't like his completely assured tone. "You don't even know me, Tarin."

"I talked to Stick about you. He knew Austin pretty well. Better than me."

I don't like where this conversation is headed. "I don't like to talk about Austin."

"Why not?" Tarin picks that moment to stick his head out from behind the canvas, and he catches me scowling. "Miss him too much?"

"Yeah. I miss him too much. Talk about something else."

His head is hidden again when he says his next words.

"Or maybe you feel guilty about something. Maybe that's why you don't like to talk about him. Guilt will do that to a person, you know? Makes them avoid things. Hide from things."

My throat feels like it's closing up on me. My face goes red with heat and tears threaten. I jump off the table without thinking and stride to the door. All I can think is that I don't want him to see me like this. He can't know that his deliberate jab hit me right where it hurts.

"Where are you going? I wasn't done." He sounds a little too happy about my departure and my reaction. Now I know he did this on purpose. This is my punishment for making him paint. *Fucking bastard.*

"I'll be right back." I step outside and close the door behind me, gulping big breaths of air.

Scott sees me through the car window and gets out, jogging the few steps it takes to get to my side. He puts his hand on my shoulder and stares at me.

I can't meet his gaze. I look away, forcing the tears to re-absorb themselves and not fall. I don't trust myself to speak right away, so I remain silent.

"What's wrong?" When I don't answer, Scott sounds alarmed. "Seriously, Scarlett, what the hell happened?"

I shake my head. "Nothing. Really, it was nothing. He just … said some shit about Austin that got to me. I had to get out of there for little while."

"What a dick." Scott lets go of my shoulder and moves towards the door.

I grab him by the arm and yank him back. Scott's shoes slide in the small rocks sprinkled over the blacktop with the sudden loss of momentum.

"No!" I say too sharply. I calm myself before continuing. "Don't say a word. He can't know it affects me like this, all right? He'll just keep pressing my buttons over and over. I have to show him it doesn't matter, that it won't change things."

Scott pulls his arm out of my grip. "What you *should* be showing him is that real people don't fucking *do* shit like that." He kicks a stone. "Spoiled, arrogant, ass fuck, prima donna, butt munch."

I nod, smiling at his outrage. "I know. You're right. But let's give him some more time. I have a feeling part of the reason he's acting out so much is because he's got a block on his creativity right now."

Scott takes a deep breath. I know he remembers when it happened to Austin. It was devastating for everyone at the time, and we're still living with the fallout. "Tarin trashed his studio," he finally says.

"Yeah. And the garbage he was playing before he did that was bad."

"I heard it. What are we going to do?"

"What we always do. Get rid of the noise that's drowning out the voice of his muse. Get rid of the poison. Get back to basics."

"What if it doesn't work this time?" Scott's brows are drawn together, and I can't tell whether his concern is for Tarin or me. I step over hug him without thinking about it.

"We don't fail, remember?" I say over his shoulder, trying not to sound weak. "We don't fail."

Ricky's standing next to us. I didn't even hear him get out of the car and suddenly he's just there.

"What are you?" Scott says to Ricky, pulling out of my hug, "a fucking ninja?"

Ricky doesn't smile. "What's going on? Do you need me to go in there?"

I shake my head. "No. Just leave him alone for a little while."

"Guy's being a dick," says Scott, not as ready as I am to forgive and forget.

"What'd he do?" Ricky looks angry, but not at us.

"Scott just let it go," I warn, but there's no stopping Scott when he's offended for me.

"He's fucking with her head. Saying shit about Austin."

Ricky's nostrils flare as he presses his lips together. He shakes his head and looks at the ground, saying nothing.

"Let's just take a breather out here for a little while and then I'll go back in," I say, trying to diffuse the anger building up around me. No matter how in control I am, Scott always knows when I'm hurt and jumps to my defense. Apparently Ricky is joining the party.

"You're not going in there alone again," insists Scott. "I'll go with you. He wouldn't say that shit with someone else there to hear it."

"It wasn't that big a deal," I say. Tarin's words were so simple and basic. The fact that they caused me so much pain is my fault, not his.

"Bullshit. He knew exactly what he was doing … punk." Scott is furious. The more we talk about it, the angrier he gets. "None of our other clients went there. They knew better than to talk about Austin." His voice cracks when it gets to his brother's name. "It's just … not cool. Not cool at all." He runs his hand through his hair, making it stand on end.

I grip his shoulder and shake him a little, trying to pull him off this track he's on. I can't forget that Austin was his big brother. Scott is hurting for me over Tarin's careless words, but he's hurting for himself, too. Being around people like Tarin makes the pain of Austin's loss especially raw for us, even though he's been gone for two years now.

"I'm going in there," says Scott, making a move towards the door.

I grab his shirt and yank him back. "No! I'm serious. Stop, Scott. Don't undo what we've accomplished so far by losing your cool."

"What have we accomplished? The guy's a douche! He needs to know."

"He knows. Trust me, he knows. He's just acting out against his loss of control. You know this is normal."

"No, it's not. He's fighting dirty."

I shrug. "So we fight dirty too. Come on. We're in this to win it." I punch him lightly in the arm. "Don't make our job harder."

Scott huffs out a breath. He looks at the sky for a few seconds, collecting himself, before finally capitulating. "Fine." He checks his watch. "But we're out of time, so we need to go anyway."

"I'll go tell him," I say, heading to the door.

Scott's right on my heels and Ricky's behind him. "I'm coming," Scott says. "Don't try to stop me."

I smile. He can't see my reaction, but I'm sure he can hear the gratitude in my voice. "I won't."

I open the door and step inside, my eyes taking a moment to adjust to the dimmer interior.

"I'm almost done," says Tarin, all of his concentration on his work.

The three of us stand in the entrance, waiting for him silently.

He looks over a few seconds later and freezes. "What?"

"Time to go," says Scott. He's making no effort to disguise the fact that he's not happy.

"Check out my masterpiece." Tarin puts down his paintbrush and picks up the painting, carefully turning it around so we can all see it.

I stare at it for a while, trying to figure out what the hell I'm looking at.

"What is that …? Pac-Man?" Scott looks at Tarin and then me. "Is it Pac-Man?"

"Yeah. That's Pac-Man," says Ricky.

"*No*, it's not Pac-Man," responds Tarin, obviously annoyed.

The Pac-Man conclusion seems perfectly reasonable to me. There's a big yellow blob in the middle of the picture and a blue blob near it.

Scott points. "Yeah, that's one of the ghosts right there and Pac-Man's about to eat him. Wabba, wabba, wabba, wabba…"

My face is flaming red. I feel like a fool for having sat on that table as his model.

"That's not fucking Pac-Man, okay? And it's not a ghost. That's supposed to be her." He gestures at me with the painting.

Ricky snorts and then turns around quickly, hiding his face.

Scott goes from amused to angry in a nanosecond. "You know what, dude?" He's so pissed I'm surprised there isn't steam coming out of his ears. "That's fucked up. You've gone too far this time."

Tarin raises his voice. "Fuck you, man! I'm not a fucking painter, okay!" He throws the canvas onto the ground and stalks over in our direction. We part like the Red Sea and let him through. I turn away when the sharp buzz of a zipper going down reaches my ears, only catching a small glimpse of his tattooed back before I can see no more.

I walk over to the painting and pick it up gingerly from the floor, resting it in the easel. I use the rag to wipe the black and blue paint from my fingers and a little dust from some of the wet paint on one of the corners. My smile will not go away as I stare at the finger-painted mess. For someone *not* trying to paint a video game character, he sure did a pretty damn good job of it.

"I hear you laughing over there," Tarin says. He's pouting; it's in his voice. "Just throw it in the garbage."

I turn back, hoping he's dressed. My blood pressure stays level when I realize he is, even though a slight trill of disappointment buzzes through me. "I'm not going to throw it away. I want Greg to see it."

"Why? So he can laugh at me too?"

"No. So he can give you some pointers next time." I walk to the door where Ricky is standing and holding it open.

"There's not going to be any next time," says Tarin, staring me down.

I shake my head slightly at Scott, sensing he's about to unload his temper on Tarin. Scott turns on his heel and leaves the studio, not saying a word.

"What's his problem?" Tarin asks, watching him go.

I don't say anything, not trusting myself to make the right decision with my words. A piece of me thinks Tarin should hear the straight-up truth about how his words hurt people like Scott and me; but the other piece of me worries he's too far gone right now to care. Neither Scott nor I can put up with too much more abuse before something bad happens. I don't like the idea of putting that kind of ammunition in Tarin's hands. I can't trust him enough yet.

"He's just having a bad day. Come on," I say, gesturing towards the door, "we have an appointment with your lawyers."

"I'm hungry."

"We'll eat on the way. I brought food."

"Of course you did."

I pass Ricky as he begins talking. "Tarin…"

"What?"

Ricky says nothing. I can't see them anymore because I'm outside and they're still in the studio.

"What?!" asks Tarin, more insistently this time.

Ricky walks out without saying a word and gets into the car. He starts the engine and just stares out the window. Scott joins him in the front seat, also staring off into space.

Tarin walks out of the building and stands just at the entrance. "What the fuck is everyone's problem today?"

I stare at Tarin and wait for him to finally look at me. His angry green eyes make my heart hurt.

My voice is soft, but strong at the same time. "You can't keep pretending you don't know what you're doing to people."

His nostrils flaring are the only sign I have that he understands me. "What's that supposed to mean?" He clenches his jaw and the muscle in the side of his face twitches over and over. I want to say this visible sign of his anger makes him unattractive, but that would be a lie. The darkness that's hovering over him right now only draws me in tighter. I have to battle to breathe normally. Oh, how that darkness pulls at me, tempting me to dive headfirst into danger with this man. *God, I am the dumbest girl alive.*

I decide against having a head-to-head confrontation right now. It's not the right time or the right place. Those things will come later, though. It's inevitable that we will have it out, and it's going to happen soon. "Just think about it," I say. "If you still want to discuss it with me this evening, I'll be available."

"Never mind. I don't care." He walks over to the car and gets inside, shutting the door so hard it rocks the vehicle.

I don't believe he doesn't care, and it gives me hope to know he's as bothered by this whole scene as we are; maybe not for the same reasons, but it's a start at least.

I take a deep breath, lock the studio door, and walk around to the opposite side of the car, not looking forward to meeting lawyers with Tarin when he's in this kind of mood. I get in and speak only to Ricky. "Take us to the attorney's office, please."

"Yes, ma'am," he says, putting the car in reverse and then pointing us back out onto the main road.

CHAPTER NINETEEN

WE'RE ON OUR WAY TO the lawyer's office when I notice Ricky glancing in the rearview mirror over and over. He appears nervous about something. I look over my shoulder at a minivan that's behind us. Nothing about it looks wrong to me.

"What's up, Ricky?" I ask.

"We're being followed."

I twist around in my seat more fully and this time notice a Jeep with at least three girls in it weaving around the slower moving minivan. One person in the backseat and another in the front passenger seat are leaning out of their windows and waving at our car.

I sigh. *Great. Because things aren't shitty enough right now, let's add lunatic chicks to the mix.*

Their expressions are classic psycho-fan: mouths wide open in grins so big they make the girls appear unbalanced, eyes bugging out, arms flailing, hands fluttering, screaming … In any other situation, people doing these things would be locked away in a mental hospital. In this situation, we just smile and try to indulge them without giving them false hope. Such is the life of a celebrity.

The problem is, you never know which fan is just a person carried away by the fantasy and which is one who is truly unhinged. I assume because there are three of them together, we're looking at the less-threatening variety, but you never can tell, often until it's too late.

"Fans," I say simply, even though it's anything but a simple issue. Tarin would be nowhere without them, singing in the shower without an audience. But some fans take their admiration to a whole other level that oversteps the boundaries between admirer and artist. They go from sane to insane in the blink of an eye, and there's almost nothing you can do about it but avoid them. They take innocent gestures as signs of mutual attraction and devotion. It's sad and scary at the same time.

These chicks seemed like the *temporarily* insane type, the way they were endangering life and limb just to get close to Tarin. I watch their Jeep nearly go up on two wheels as they turn a corner too fast trying to keep up with us.

In their regular lives they're probably perfectly nice, reasonable girls, but seeing Tarin pulls a trigger that pushes them over the edge and makes them act like drunken clowns. And drunken clowns are *so* not attractive. I cringe at the fools they're making of themselves.

I really wish I knew how they found out we were in this car. I make a mental note to do some checking into possible info leaks among the crew when we get back to Tarin's place. I notice Scott tapping out either a note or an email on his phone, and I assume he's thinking the same thing. He's the best assistant on the entire planet that way.

"Yeah, right. Fans. Awesome," says Tarin. He doesn't sound very happy about the idea. Slouching down farther into the seat, he stares out the window where he won't see them and vice versa.

"Scott, would you take care of this, please?" I ask.

He's already on the phone, talking to the attorney's office staff, doing what he can to plan for an uninterrupted arrival. I've never been to this attorney's office before, so I don't know what kind of security is available, but I'm hoping for an underground parking garage that has a guard shack in front of it.

"Ricky? What are the chances we can get in and out without contact?"

"Very little. I've seen these girls before." Ricky glances over his shoulder at Tarin. "It's Posey and the Pussycats."

Tarin snorts with disgust. "Great. Just what I needed."

"Is that really what they call themselves?" asks Scott, hanging up his phone.

"It's what we call them. The girl driving is Posey. The rest of them … we just gave them the tag to have something to call them."

"Is she a stalker?" I ask.

"Not exactly. She's harmless, but annoying." Ricky's frowning, I can see his expression in the rearview mirror. He changes lanes at the last minute so he can take a left turn and try to lose them.

Looking out the back window, I see Posey cut off two other cars in her efforts to follow Tarin, causing one of them to squeal its brakes and the other driver to lay on his horn.

"We're almost there. What do you want me to do?" asks Ricky.

"Just get us there as quickly as you can and we'll make a run for it. Scott, can you and Ricky do interference for us?"

"No problem." Scott looks over his shoulder at his targets. He's no match for three rabid girl-fans, but he can at least slow them down. He's used to doing this; he's been practicing since he was about fourteen.

Ricky pulls up to the valet area of the building and throws the car into park. It lurches forward with the sudden lack of movement as Tarin throws open his door and jumps out. I'm in the process of sliding over to get out after him when he reaches in and grabs my hand, pulling me out with him. I'm not expecting the extra power for my exit, so I stumble a little as I get out, landing against him. I'm still trying to get my feet under me when the girls' Jeep pulls up and screeches to a halt behind us.

The doorman on duty comes outside the glass doors from inside the building, and Ricky runs around the front of the vehicle to join Scott on the sidewalk. The three of them form a barrier between us and the girls.

As I stand up straight, Tarin puts his arm around my waist and pulls me near to him. Our bodies are touching from thigh to shoulder, and my engine is instantly humming with sexual energy. Having him this close is throwing me for a complete loop. It should mean nothing, but it doesn't. It means everything, and I hate myself for being affected like this.

I know he's doing this for protection - either mine or his own - but that doesn't stop my pulse from going through the roof and my heart from slamming against my ribcage. I picture the tattooed arms I saw bare earlier wrapped around my body while I feel the heat from his body seeping into mine. My ears are burning with embarrassment over where my thoughts are going and with the arousal that suddenly hits me like a truck. *BAM. Sex.* It's almost all I can think about, wondering what he might be like in bed, picturing him naked again.

"Oh my god, TARIN!" screams the one out in front, effectively jerking my attention back to the more immediate problem. She's taller than I am, with curly blonde hair and bright blue eyes. She looks like a Barbie doll and is probably no more than seventeen years old.

"Posey," he says, nodding at her while guiding us towards the door of the building. He pulls me along with him, keeping my body clamped to his side.

"Ahhhhh!! He remembers your name!" squeals the redhead on her left as she grabs her friend's arm and shakes it sloppily.

Posey turns to her friend, her eyes blazing as she jerks her arm out of her grip. "Of course he does, *idiot.* He's my man. He knows I'm his biggest fan." She turns her fanatically obsessed eyes back to the object of her desire. It's then that she finally realizes he's not alone and focuses her attention on me. Glowing eyes become dark with instant hatred. "Oh God, Tarin, who is *that?*"

No one answers her. We're almost to the door.

The girl on her other side says, "That's probably his new girl-friend. What happened to Jelly, Tarin? What happened to Jelly? Are you broken up now?"

The blonde smacks her friend on the back hard. "Shut up, Lindsay! Jelly Dumbshit Summers is *not* his girlfriend and neither is this skank!"

"Watch who you're calling a skank," says Scott.

"Get out of my way, twig," she says to him, stepping forward to shove him away.

He stands his ground, moving sideways to block her attempts to get closer. He's rewarded with a slap to the side of his head as she keeps trying to move forward. "Back off, Posey or whatever your name is," he warns, trying to trap her hands and keep her from girl-slapping him anymore. "Tarin doesn't want you to come that close."

"Shut up!" she spits out at him, yanking her hands away from his grip. "You don't know what Tarin wants. I'm his biggest fan. Tell him, Tarin! Tell him! You want me here, right?"

I stare at Tarin, a warning in my eyes. He looks down at me and for a split-second, I can tell he's warring with himself. The angel and the demon on his shoulders are in a wrestling match.

But then the devil takes him and he opens his mouth. "Yeah, she's my biggest fan. Nice seeing you, Posey, but I don't have time to hang out. I have to go talk to some lawyers."

Posey nearly passes out with the attention. She faces her girlfriends, flicking her curls around her face. "Oh my god, see? *See?!* I told you he loves me." She goes back to idolizing Tarin. "Tarin! I can go with you in there if you want! I can go with you and sit with you or whatever! I'll do whatever you want!"

I have ceased to exist as anything but an obstacle to be smashed through for this nutty chick. Right now if Tarin were to tell her to scratch my eyeballs out, she'd do it without blinking. It's scary to see someone so caught up in the moment and this obsessed. Reality has completely disappeared for her, and Tarin is doing nothing but making it worse. The worst part is, he knows it. He's having fun making her do this to herself, and it makes me sick.

Elbowing him in the ribs, I force him to detach his arm from my waist.

"Ow, what'd you do that for?" he asks, slightly amused.

"Shut up and get in the building."

His good mood begins to fade. "I'll go. Just give me a minute."

The bastard is enjoying this whole thing, how poor Posey is losing her mind over him and how I'm standing here being annoyed at both of them. He's playing with us like we're pawns in a stupid chess game.

It's in this moment that I begin to really dislike Tarin as a person, and that's never happened before with any of my clients. As I look at his twisted smile, I start to wonder why I even agreed to take this job.

Maybe he sees the shift of my thoughts in my expression, but something causes him to lose that smile. "What?" he asks me, like he's completely innocent and clueless.

"Just get inside," I say, leaving him out there to deal with his mess. I feel a little guilty about abandoning Ricky and Scott there too, but I know if I stay, I'll say or do things that will end this job. And as much as I'm disgusted by Tarin right now, it doesn't mean he is no longer worth saving. He's just not going to be one of those clients I become friends with and stay in touch with, like Jack. *No, definitely not.* He'll be the first one of the six that I normalize and then leave behind. *Forever.* The fact that he might be beyond saving barely enters my mind, and as soon as it does, I throw the thought out like garbage. I will not accept defeat.

CHAPTER TWENTY

I TAKE THE ELEVATOR UP to an office on the twelfth floor. The view of downtown is spectacular, making me wonder what the rent is for a place like this. Probably more than I make in a month. Everything is ultra-modern, down to the hard black leather couch with chrome legs that sits in the corner of the reception area with two matching, equally uncomfortable-looking armchairs.

Mostly women are coming and going out of the reception area, and all of them are dressed in tight-fitting, tailored suits. I'm so glad I'm not working in a place like this all the time like they are. I may have to deal with egotistical dumbnuts sometimes, but at least I'm not cooped up in a gilded cage.

"May I help you?" asks the young girl at the desk. She has her dark brown hair up in a sophisticated chignon, and she's wearing chic, librarian-like, black-rimmed glasses.

"I'm here to see Nick Galanos. We have an appointment. My name is Scarlett Barnes."

She smiles. "Yes, he's expecting you. Please have a seat and I'll let him know you're here." She picks up her phone handset and presses some buttons as I turn away.

I wander over to a rack of booklets. The one at eye-level mentions estate planning. Just from the literature available and the office space alone, I can tell this is a big firm that positions itself to handle all the legal needs of its wealthy clients. It's a one-stop shop where the rich and famous can happily unload buckets of their hard-earned cash for estate planning, contract negotiation, divorce, and criminal defense.

"Ms. Barnes?"

I turn around to face the male voice coming from behind me. I'm a little shocked at first by what I find there, having had no idea that I'd be meeting with a Greek god today. I should have known by his name. *Nick Galanos. The Greek god of sexy. God of handsome. God of thrumming pulses…*

He holds out his hand and smiles. I catch a glimpse of perfectly manicured fingernails and cuticles as it comes towards me. Of course his teeth are perfectly straight and white. *Veneers. Don't be too impressed. Relax.* His hair is thick and wavy, maybe a little longer than most lawyers would wear; but of course, he tends to the legal needs of celebrities, so a little bit of bolder fashion goes a long way. His suit is classic in style, tailored to make the most of his broad shoulders and trim waist. As his hands stretches forward to take mine, his jacket slides up a little and diamond-encrusted cufflinks twinkle under the fluorescent lights. He is the total package. I'm willing to bet he's either gay or a total prick to women.

"Nice to meet you," I say, meaning it with every ounce of my being. His refinement is a perfect balm for my nerves right now, regardless of the fact that he's not dating material in my mind. Rowdy lunatic fans and Tarin's careless treatment of both them and me has me ragged. Holding Nick's smooth palm in mine, I feel as though I'm getting ready to have a spa day. A hot oil massage followed by a warm relaxing jacuzzi spell, and then perhaps a pedicure…

My euphoric fantasy is rudely yanked away moments after the elevator doors open. High pitched and breathy giggles rake against my eardrums, making me cringe. I don't want to turn around because I know the nightmare that awaits.

Nick's hand slides away from mine, reluctantly perhaps. He looks at me thoughtfully for a couple seconds before turning to face the ruckus at the elevator.

"Tarin. Nice to see you." He walks over and holds out his hand first to Tarin, then to Ricky and Scott, and finally to Posey.

My heart drops into my stomach as I take in the scene. I feel physically ill. Tarin has his arm looped over the young girl's shoulders, and she's having what looks like happiness seizures as she clings to him with both arms. He's in a fan straightjacket. My expression goes murderous, and Scott sees it. He rolls his eyes in commiseration.

"What's up, Nick?" Tarin detaches an arm from Posey's arm-clamps and shakes his lawyer's hand.

"Not much, not much. Keeping busy. How about you?"

Tarin shrugs. "You know me. Busy having fun." He looks down at the cling-on stuck to his side, and she bursts into more giggles. It's positively nauseating.

"Is she going to wait out here or …" Nick's meaning is clear, and anyone with a brain would answer *yes* to his question.

"Nah, she's with us." Tarin looks down at her once more and squeezes her closer. Then he looks up at me with a smug smile.

There's nothing I want more right now than to walk over and slap his expression right off his stupid face. I make a mental note to give him a good sock in the kisser when we're in the ring next time. I'm so going to make him eat a knuckle sandwich. That thought, that delicious little promise to myself, is the only thing keeping me sane right now.

Scott gets a slightly panicked expression on his face as he watches me make my way over. I go slowly, keeping my eyes on Tarin's until I'm standing right in front of him and his leech. We're just two feet apart. Then I look directly at Posey, using the sweetest voice I'm capable of conjuring at this point.

"I'm sorry, Posey, but you're not invited to this meeting. You can wait downstairs where Tarin will be happy to say goodbye to you." My voice goes harsh. "But just so we're clear … you're not going to be hanging out with Tarin, going to meetings with Tarin, partying with Tarin, or having sex with Tarin, okay? None of that is going to happen. Not now, not ever. Just get it out of your mind and move on."

Her nostrils flare and her lips thin. "Who the hell are you, his mother?"

"If that makes it easier for you, sure. I'm his mother."

"She ain't my mother," says Tarin. He's probably glaring at me, but I don't even spare him a glance. I have zero respect for him right now. He's just a project to me, something that is broken that must be fixed. This game he's playing with this stupid girl is wrong on so many levels I don't even want to think about it. She just needs to be gone so I don't hurt him or her.

"Ricky, please escort her out of the building," I say calmly.

Nick places his hand gently on my upper arm to get my attention. "Would you like me to call security?"

I nod and his hand disappears. He whispers to the receptionist and then I hear the phone coming off the hook.

Posey detaches herself from Tarin's side and reaches up with jerky motions to adjust her hair, obviously uncomfortable but still determined to see this mess through.

"Tarin invited me up here, which means Tarin *wants* me here, so you can just get the hell out of my way because nobody and nothing is going to stop me from being with him." She looks at Tarin, and seeing no argument coming from him, becomes even bolder. "You're just jealous because he doesn't go for sloppy skanks like you, and you struck out. But it's not my problem that you shop at Goodwill and don't appreciate him like I do, so I advise you to just get out of the way before you get trampled."

She reaches out to push me aside, and I grab her wrist.

That's all I need to do to stop the foolishness. This girl is obviously no fighter. She cringes with the pain. Gripping it tightly, I step closer. "Don't be stupid, Posey. Touch me again and I'll bust open that plastic nose of yours and make you so ugly your own friends won't claim you."

She tries to yank her hand away, looking desperately at Tarin. "Tell her, Tarin! Ow! She's hurting me. Tell her!"

Tarin has the decency to look embarrassed. "Aw, man, come on, Scarlett. Let her go. We were just playing around."

I throw her hand down and away from me while I stare at him. "Was it fun?"

"What?" he asks stupidly, pretending he doesn't know what I'm talking about.

Coward. I deliver up every ounce of disappointment I have in him with my expression. He has the decency to look slightly ill.

A crowd of people has gathered in the reception area. I can see secretaries and a few lawyers standing in the field of my peripheral vision.

I'm not done with Tarin, though. He's pushed me too far this time. "Was it fun playing with this young girl's emotions and making a fool of her in front of all these people?"

Tarin says nothing, but his face goes white.

I probably should stop, but I can't. I'm overwhelmed with disappointment and sadness. I feel his happy future slipping away from me. "Was it fun leading her on? Making her think she's special to you … that she's going to be in your life now?"

"Tarin?" says Posey, her voice full of the tears that are staring to fall. "Tell her."

"Is it fun making her cry? Breaking her heart in front of an audience? Treating her like she means nothing, like she's not a human being with feelings?" I'm on a roll now. Even Scott's hand squeezing gently on my arm is having no effect. "Does this make you feel important? … Doing these hateful things to people who are guilty of nothing but loving your music, loving how your creations make them feel inside?"

"That's enough, Scar," says Scott gently.

It's then that I feel the pain I'm causing him too, and realize it is enough. Tarin's heard all I have to say to him right now. Maybe ever.

Ricky takes Posey by the shoulders and turns her around to face the elevator. She stumbles forward, bawling loudly the whole time.

When she reaches the elevator doors, she looks over her shoulder. "I love you, Tarin! I love you! Please don't make me go!"

My heart cracks for the poor girl. Her face is a mess of bleeding mascara, saltwater tears, and snot. She reaches for him and barely touches his arm with her fingers, but he yanks himself away and takes a step forward to get farther from her. She cries louder.

The doors to the elevator open up and Ricky steps inside, pulling Posey in with him and putting his arm around her; it looks like it's there for the dual purpose of supporting her and keeping her from running out after her man.

"Turn around and say goodbye," I grind out, my voice low enough only for him to hear.

"Fuck you," Tarin says back.

"Do it. You owe her a goodbye at least."

His chin juts out and he hesitates, but eventually he turns to face her.

As soon as she sees him, she reaches out and screams. "Tarin!"

"Goodbye, Posey," he says. It comes out more as a growl than real words, but it does the trick.

The expression of sheer pain and disillusionment on the girl's face is physically painful to see. It's the last vision we have of her before the doors press closed.

As soon as I turn around, the onlookers scatter, pretending they were just passing through and not noticing a thing.

Scott takes me by the hand and laces his fingers through mine, and I don't fight him on it. Right now, I need my best friend to be this close. He and I have been through this shit before, and it never stops being painful and it never becomes easier. Every time we witness an innocent heart being broken, ours break just a little bit too. I'm surprised either of us even has a heart left to break at this point.

"Well, that fucking sucked," says Tarin flippantly.

I give him a tight smile, but Scott responds out loud.

"Yeah, it sure did. Well done, asshole. Way to break a young girl's soul. You're such a fucking stand-up guy, you know? No wonder Austin hated your ass. Big mystery there."

This shocks me so much I can't hide my reaction. My mouth drops open. I turn to look at Scott and catch Tarin's expression.

Tarin doesn't seem nearly as surprised as I expect him to be. In fact, if I'm not completely lost, I'd say he looks ... guilty.

"What the hell, Scott?" I whisper loudly.

He lifts my hand up and gives it a quick kiss on the back, just above my watch. "Sorry. Slipped out." He's looking at the ground when Nick interrupts.

"The ... um ... conference room is ready whenever you are."

I let go of Scott's hand and leave him behind with Tarin. "Thanks, Nick. Lead the way." My voice is strained, but at least it's working. I half expected it to break mid-sentence, my throat is hurting so much. Unshed tears can be very painful sometimes.

I walk behind Nick, my mind swirling with images of Tarin and Scott, memories of things they've both said getting tangled in my brain and making me think that there are things happening here that I'm not completely aware of. Things they know that I don't.

We reach the conference room before I can make heads or tails of anything. My focus shifts to lawsuits pending against my dickhead client, and I pretty much forget what it was that was bothering me. Only one word remains floating around in my head for the hour that Tarin stares across the conference room table at me, silently brooding, his dark good looks threatening in the way they almost consume my ability to think of anything else.

Guilty.

Nick and I make plans for dealing with all the vultures looking for legal settlements from Tarin. We review the legal documents that will need to be signed and filed to manage some investments he's made. We discuss Tarin's future legal dealings and contractual commitments he's made, ensuring he knows what to do to follow through on his promises.

Yet all the while this is going on, even though we're knee-deep in legaleze and intricate business dealings, that one word never leaves me. It hovers. It haunts. It floats in the ether, on the outside edges of my consciousness, and eventually takes shape in the form of a tattoo I saw earlier today.

Guilty.

CHAPTER
TWENTY-ONE

I SEND TARIN ON A two-mile run with his bodyguards when
we get home. I can't even stand to look at him, and beg off par-
ticipating with excuses of having to call my office and deal with
messages. Half hour after they're gone, Scott and I are sitting in
the family room, on the couch by the video game Taj Mahal. My
feet are hanging off the edge and my back is wedged up against
one of the arms with a pillow behind it.

"So …," Scott says, fiddling with a game console absently. The
television isn't on. "That was pretty ugly, huh?"

I nod, staring at a stack of books on the coffee table. I pick
one up and page through it, not paying much attention to the
photographs within. "Yeah. Ugly as hell. Let's not do that
again."

"I'm worried."

I look up at Scott, the weird tone in his voice catching my attention. "What about?"

"You."

I snort. "Why me? I'm not the one with the problem."

"No, you don't have a problem, but you're letting him affect you way more than you should."

I frown. "I don't know what you're talking about."

"Yes, you do. Don't play games with me, okay? It's just me here."

I sigh, going back to paging through the book. "It's no big deal. I'll get over it."

"I don't think so."

I slap the book shut. "So what's the deal with *you?* You've got some kind of secret I don't know about, apparently. Don't think I didn't pick up on that. Since you're in such a mood to share, why don't we start with that?"

He raises his eyebrows at me. "Bitchy much?"

I've completely failed to intimidate him and that pisses me off. I kick him with my foot. "Shut up. Stop trying to deflect. I'm not going to let this go until you tell me what it is."

He tosses the controller onto the nearby chair. "Shuh… Don't I know it. Talk about a dog with a bone." He picks up my foot and puts it in his lap, wigging my toes one at a time, staring with the biggest one. "This little piggy went to market…"

I lift my foot to put my big toe closer to his face. "This little piggy is going to be up your ass in a second if you don't start talking."

He wiggles my toe again, talking right to it, his eyes crossing it's so close. "This little piggy is *not* going to be up my ass. This little piggy is going to shut up and just relax before I bite it." He gives it a good snarl for effect. The combination of his crossed eyes, his goofy declaration, and his vampire teeth make me giggle uncontrollably.

A voice comes from the doorway, laugher barely veiled. "Sorry to interrupt the love fest in here, but dinner's almost ready. Where should I serve?" Josh is standing there, his coat buttoned up and bright white, showing no signs that he's just whipped up a gourmet, healthy meal for eight. I have no idea how he stays so neat all the time.

"Let's eat outside," I suggest, looking to Scott for his preference. He's too busy trying to fold my toes over on each other to pay attention.

"Got it. What time?" Josh asks.

I look at my watch. "Seven? Tarin should be back any minute, and he'll want to shower first."

"That works. It'll be ready then. Just let me know if there's going to be any delay." Josh is used to the fickle moods of our clients and has on more than one occasion had to make changes on the fly. It never pisses him off or causes him to ruin the food, so in my book, that makes him a superhero. The worst thing in the world I can do with a cranky celebrity who's coming down out of the clouds is feed him bad food.

As if on cue, the front door opens and voices fill the foyer. When it slams shut, I throw the book back onto the table and pull my feet out of Scott's lap, sliding them back into my sandals. Zach walks in moments later, covered in sweat.

"How'd it go?" I ask.

"Good, if you skip the part about being chased down by lunatics." He walks over and drops into the armchair on my left.

Scott's smirking, looking at Zach's sweat-stained shirt and dripping face. "They must have been fast lunatics."

Zach leans his head back on the seat and closes his eyes. "Never underestimate the adrenaline levels of a horny teenager."

"Teenager?" I ask, trading a worried glance with Scott.

"Yeah. Posey and the Pussycats, actually. Fucking nutcases, all three of them, but that Posey chick is the worst."

I stand up, my nerves going back to frazzled with just those few words. "Are you serious? It was really them again?"

"Again?" Zach asks, sitting up. He looks worried for the first time.

"Yes, *again*. They caused a huge scene at the lawyer's office today. Didn't Tarin tell you?" My quiet zen moment with Scott dissipates like steam into the air around me.

"No, he didn't. He just ran the entire time with his mouth shut."

"Is that normal? For him, I mean," asks Scott.

"Yeah, right. First of all, normal for him does not include running. So maybe after he's in shape we'll know what's normal in the talking department, but at this point, I think he was just focusing on breathing. Talking would have been too difficult. All that partying he's been doing for the past two years has messed him up."

I move to the doorway. "I need to go talk to him."

"Did he engage?" asks Scott. "Did he mess with that Posey girl again?"

I hear Zach's answer as I leave the room. "Mess with her? What do you mean, mess with her?"

He better not have messed with her. I stride down the hall and into the foyer. Leonard is there by himself doing stretches. He's covered in sweat too.

"Where's Tarin?" I ask, looking around.

"Upstairs. Taking a shower, I think."

"Thanks." I take the steps at a jog, stopping at the top to look around. I realize I have no idea where his room is. Looking down over the railing I meet Leonard's eyes. He doesn't say a word, he just points off to my right.

"Thanks." I walk down the hall and push open doors as I go. I pass bedroom after bedroom, then a laundry room, a bathroom, a storage closet and finally a closed door at the end of the hall. Tapping on it, I listen for sounds telling me Tarin might be inside. No one answers.

"Tarin? Are you in here?"

"Not yet." The responding voice comes from so close behind me, it makes me jump and squeak with fright.

"Holy *shit*, Tarin!" I spin around and back into the corner of the hallway. "*Don't* sneak up on me like that!" My heart is pounding so hard in my chest I can feel it from inside. My hands are gripping the wall and door, as if I'm going to do a Spiderman move and crawl up to the ceiling backwards using sticky-fingers.

He's smiling, obviously very proud of himself. "What's up? Come to join me in the shower?"

"Ew. No." I grimace at the idea, stepping away from the wall and letting my hands drop to smooth my hair and shirt. He's covered in sweat, and all I can picture is him running deliberately slow so Posey and her goofy friends could catch up to him and fawn all over him. He's nothing but a tease and a mean-boy in my eyes right now.

His smile drops away to replaced by a hurt expression. *"Ew? Seriously? Man, talk about a shot to the ego."* He leans in really close, his chest almost touching mine as he puts his hand on the door handle and turns it. "Sure you don't want to join me?"

The musky smell of his sweat mixed with cologne or deodorant or something woodsy filters up into my nose. His smile is so close I can see his individual teeth and the way his eyes crinkle up in the corners a little. I want to say something sharp and quick, cut him down to size, but the words won't come.

"I need to talk to you," is all I can manage.

The door pushes in and he walks past me, pulling his sweaty shirt off and letting it drop to the floor. "So talk." He moves towards the bathroom that's connected to his bedroom.

I stare at his tattooed, lean and muscled back as he moves away, trying to correlate the feelings of anger I have towards him because of what he did today with the feelings of desire his semi-naked body creates in me as I stare at him. It makes no sense how I can hate him and want to see more of him at the same time. It infuriates me, making me want to blame him for something I'm sure he doesn't even know he's doing.

Once he's out of sight, I step into his room, remaining near the door. If he decides to do something stupid, I can always run out easily. Not that I expect him to do anything I should be worried about. He flirts like this all the time with every girl he meets, I'm sure. I'm no one special to Tarin Kilgour.

"I want to talk about Posey and her friends," I say somewhat loudly so he can hear me in the next room.

His voice is tiny, like he's far away or maybe in a closet. "I don't."

"Too bad." It's easy to be bold when I can't see his half-naked body.

The shower goes on, so I move farther into the room. "I think she's a bigger problem that we anticipated."

"She's harmless," he says. "Let's talk about you instead. I'd rather talk about that than Posey."

I sigh. He's being frustrating on purpose, trying to scare me away from pushing him, but I'm not falling for it.

"How often do you see her?" I wander over to his dresser and pick up a framed photo. It's him and the other guys in the band a couple years ago. They look so much younger. My heart skips a beat when I realizes the scruffy guy in the back, standing just behind Stick is Austin. I pull the photo closer, trying to pull in more detail. Tarin is shirtless. Everyone is sweaty, making me think they just finished a show. Something about Tarin is different, other than the fact that he looks so much younger. *What is it?* My finger traces over the outline of his body. When I get near the bottom of the skin he's showing, I realize what it is. That tattoo is missing. The one that declares him *Guilty.*

"Oh, I don't know. Maybe I see her a couple times a week? More if she's on break from school."

"Couple times a week?" I whisper mostly to myself. *Crazy bitch.* "That's a lot," I say louder.

"She's definitely one of the more dedicated ones."

I shake my head, putting the picture down again. For some reason I don't like the idea of it being that close to me anymore. All my pictures of Austin are put away. Scott and I decided a couple months after his death that seeing him so alive like that was just too painful.

"That's not dedication," I say loudly. "That's stalking. Is she stalking you on social media too?"

"I don't know. I don't handle that stuff. My publicist does."

"Maybe you should be more in touch with what's going on in your life," I say, moving around the room some more, my gaze drawn to his bed. I try not to look, but it's impossible. I stare at it, wondering how many poor girls looking for love and acceptance have had their hearts broken there.

"Why? That's what I pay other people to do. It's supposed to leave me time to create." He says it bitterly like it's a joke.

"I guess if you were creating something, that would make sense." I can't help delivering the barb. I'm still pissed at him for what he did today, and that picture of him with Austin has me unnerved.

He sticks a wet and soapy head out of the doorway, thankfully keeping the rest of his naked body behind the wall. "This would be a lot more interesting if you were in here with me, you know."

I turn my back on him and his slippery charm. "Tarin, the day I'm in a shower with you, naked, will be the day Hell freezes over, okay? Just get it out of your head."

"Most girls think I'm irresistible." He sounds confused.

"Most girls obviously don't know the real you," I say, moving towards the bedroom door.

"Damn, girl. That was cold." He hesitates. "Wait … where are you going?"

"Downstairs. Dinner will be ready in fifteen minutes. Don't be late or you'll be eating cereal."

Now he's mad again. "Jesus Christ, Scar … you're harsh, you know that? Anyone ever tell you that you can catch more flies with honey?"

"Nope," I say as I walk out the door. "And don't call me Scar."

"Well I'm telling you …!"

I shut the door before his last word makes it out.

CHAPTER
TWENTY-TWO

THE DOORBELL RINGS AS I'M walking towards the kitchen. I hesitate in the hallway and listen as Ricky greets the arrival. The second her bubbly, fake-happy voice reaches my ears I cringe. *Jelly*. I'm not sure how I'm going to get through dinner tonight without choking someone. I take a deep breath and continue on my mission.

Walking into the kitchen, I see Josh plating-up the food. The display on the dish nearest me looks like a work of art with its bright colors and interesting, varied textures. The smell coming from the stove is mouth-watering good.

I know which is Tarin's plate by the portion sizes. He's supposed to be bulking up, so he'll eat about twice as much as the rest of us will. The mound of meat and the sweet potato puree next to it makes my stomach growl in anticipation. Josh is so good at mixing savory, salty, and sweet flavors. It's almost like a symphony of food. I feel cheated whenever one of our jobs is done and I have to go back to eating my own boring meals. He calls me a closet gourmande.

"All set?" I ask, walking over to stand by him. He smells like the food he's been preparing for the past couple of hours. It's comforting, with Jelly so close in the other room. I need comforting in order to deal with her; I have a feeling she's going to make a scene. Josh is all about creating meals, and Jelly is all about creating drama.

"Yep, almost done. Just have to garnish these last few plates and we'll be ready." He picks up a frilly little piece of purple and green kale and puts an artfully carved radish and carrot sculpture inside its curved interior. I want to take a picture of it, it's so dainty, colorful, and pretty.

"Can I carry some of them out now for you?"

"Sure." Josh picks up a white kitchen towel and wipes off some brown sauce that dripped onto the edge of the white china plate. I tell him all the time that little drips won't change the way things taste, but he insists on perfection for his employers and their friends and family. "Start on your end there," he instructs, pointing at the plate nearest me. "By the time you're back I'll be done and you can take the rest."

I carry dishes covered in delicious healthy food in several colors out to the back patio where a table is set with crystal and candlesticks. Someone made sure Tarin has pretty things that he hasn't yet managed to destroy, and I silently thank whoever it was, glad to not be drinking out of plastic cups. That had been the case for the first few nights at Jack's place, almost year ago, before Scott had managed to get new glassware delivered.

Jack was notorious for his glass-shattering temper tantrums before I met him. I smile with the memory. Seeing him now being so relaxed and in control makes me feel like a million bucks. I'm so happy that I'll be seeing him tonight. I need a reminder of the good I can do; it will help smooth over the feelings of failure and frustration I'm suffering right now with Tarin.

"Looks delicious," says Zach, appearing on my left as I put down the first two plates.

"I know, right? Josh is a wizard in the kitchen."

Zach helps me bring the rest of the plates out, and by the time we're done, the remaining members of our dinner party arrive. The only one missing is Tarin.

Jelly has been escorted through the house by Ricky and is standing across the table from me, the space beside her at the table empty. Randy, Dave, Leonard, and Scott sitting on my right, take up the remaining places. They're all exchanging small talk, oblivious to the tension between Jelly and me.

I do my best to smile and be polite. "I like your dress, Jelly." It's black and short, but at least it's not as tight as she normally wears them. Her clunky platform stilettos make her almost six feet tall, so I have a good view of her thighs above the table. Her makeup is overdone, as usual. It makes me wish we had the kind of relationship where I could tell her that she'd be prettier with less of it. She really is a beautiful girl. Why she works so hard to look plastic is a mystery to me. Tarin might be all Hollywood now, but I have to believe that he appreciates a fresh-faced girl, being from the mid-west himself.

"Thank you," she says, a fake smile plastered on her face, making it look a little twisted. "I didn't realize this was such a casual dinner." She looks me up and down with disdain.

I glance down at my t-shirt and jeans before shrugging. "I'm still on the clock. I'll get dressed up later." I pull out my chair and maneuver to get in front of it.

She follows my lead and sits down in her seat. "Later? Are you going somewhere? Like out?"

I want to smack myself in the forehead for being so stupid. "Maybe. Not sure yet."

She keeps her hands in her lap and tilts her head a little, acting like she gives a flying hoot about my life. "Where are you going? Anywhere fun?"

"Nowhere special." I shrug again, trying to put her off. No way do I want Jelly showing up to rain on my parade. Pulling my linen napkin out from under my silverware, I feign great interest in the food on my plate. I nudge Scott at my right. "Delish, right?"

Scott nods enthusiastically. "Oh, yeah. I love duck. It's one of my faves."

Jelly frowns at her plate, a look of disgust replacing her fake smile. "This is *duck?* Who eats *duck?* That's like ... cannibalism."

"We do," says Scott. "And since I'm not Daffy or Donald, it's definitely not cannibalism." He quacks a couple times for good measure, maybe to confuse her, I'm not sure. Whatever the reason, it's bound to piss her off, and I'm pretty sure that's the whole point. I elbow him in the ribs.

Trying to diffuse the situation, I say, "If you don't want to eat it, I'm sure there are more of the side dishes in the kitchen you could fill up on."

She leans back in her chair, not looking appeased at all. "No thanks. I'll have something different. Where's that cook guy?" She looks over my shoulder, squinting in the direction of the kitchen.

I grit my teeth together to keep from saying something I'll regret. Luckily for all of us, Tarin makes it easier for me to control myself by choosing that moment to appear on the patio. His hair is wet and flopped around his head carelessly, and he's wearing jeans and a t-shirt like me. All the heads around the dinner table swivel in his direction.

Ricky breathes a sigh of either relief or stress at his employer's arrival. It could easily be either. Our gazes meet and we exchange a couple of rueful smiles.

Jelly jumps up and runs over to her Tarin. "Tarin, baby!" She throws herself against him, chest first, wrapping her arms around his neck and effectively smothering him in boobs and big hair.

Scott snickers but quits immediately when I turn and glare at him.

Tarin puts his hands on her waist and pushes her away. "Easy, Jelly. Let a guy breathe, would ya?"

"What's the matter, baby? Are you okay?" Her baby-talk simpering is curdling the creme in my puree. I pick up my fork and poke at it, waiting for this awkward moment to be over and hoping I'll get to eat my duck before it gets too cold. It's one of my favorites too.

"Just a little sore from my workout." He holds his arm out to keep her from rushing him again. "I just need a little space to breathe, okay? Go ahead and sit down so we can eat. I'm starving." I get the impression he's annoyed but trying to act like he's not.

I have to give him points for being somewhat nice to the alleged mother of his alleged child when it appears he'd rather she not be here. Or maybe I'm just imagining that. *Wishful thinking.* I'm instantly irritated with myself for giving a crap about them as a couple. *They deserve each other. Two self-centered jerks. Their baby's going to be born with the biggest head ever recorded.*

"I would love to sit down, but I can't," Jelly says, pouting.

Tarin walks over to his seat and pulls it out, saying nothing in response to her obvious open invitation.

"Wow, this looks great," Tarin says, picking up his fork. He's ready to stab some thinly sliced meat when he realizes the entire table is silent, waiting for him to catch on.

He looks up. "What?" He scans the faces at the table, and finally stops when he gets to me.

I look at him first and then behind him at the angry girlfriend huffing out her frustration at the back of his head.

Tarin rolls his eyes and turns around. "What's your problem?"

"I can't eat that … poison." She pokes her acrylic nail at her plate.

Tarin turns back to his plate and frowns. Then he looks at her plate. "Poison?" He scoops some sweet potatoes up on his fork and puts them in his mouth. He nods and swallows. "Delicious. What's this?" he asks me, poking his meat.

I answer, keeping my tone even. "Duck. Otherwise known in certain circles as poison."

He winks at me, and my heart flips. Stabbing several slices onto his fork together in a stack, he grins as he lifts it to his mouth. "Looks amazing." He shoves it with zero finesse, making his cheeks bulge out with the effort of keeping it all in. After a few chews he moans and his eyes roll to the sky. "Mmmm, my Gob." He still has a mouthful when he speaks again. "Viff iv ah-may-ving." He points at the plate with his fork over and over before waving it at the people around the table. Finally swallowing, he's able to speak like a normal human again. "Eat, eat! Don't let it get cold … Jesus." He eats a forkful of sweet potatoes and spears some more duck for his next go-around, but only has it halfway to his mouth when he's bapped upside the head by his angry girlfriend.

He drops his fork and twists in his seat. "Did you just fucking *hit* me?" Some sweet potato falls out onto his lip and he swipes it off absently with his napkin, waiting for her to explain herself.

She backs up a step, her anger shifting to misapprehension at his tone. "I told you I can't eat that poison, Tare. I want something different."

I raise an eyebrow as he turns to face me. "Help me out here, would ya?"

I shrug. "I already told her. If she doesn't want to eat the duck, there's probably more side dishes in there to help fill her up. This isn't a restaurant. Josh has already cooked for us, and he's not going to cook anything else. His crew handles the dessert which is already done, and now he's off for the night."

Could I get Jelly something else for dinner? Sure. There's probably a ham sandwich or something like that in there. But if I cave and give in to her demands, then the toddler tantrums and the bullshit will continue. Better they all learn now that homey don't play dat game. I smile inwardly over my internal dialogue. I wonder if anyone would pick up on the old school Mad TV reference if I said it out loud.

Scott nudges me, whispering, "Stop smiling," out of the corner of his mouth as he stabs an asparagus spear on his plate.

I school my features to look bland, but not before Jelly catches me being too happy.

"You think this is funny don't you?" She puts her hand on her lower abdomen protectively and lends some tears to her voice. "What kind of person denies a pregnant woman a nutritious dinner in her fiance's home?"

I nearly choke on the word.

Fiancé?

I look at Tarin, my expression one of disbelief and possibly even hurt. I know we're not even really friends, but considering what I'm trying to do here in his life, I would have thought he'd share that little detail with me.

"What the fuck?" Tarin drops his fork to his plate and stands awkwardly, his chair legs getting caught in the patio tiles. He reaches around and grabs the back of the chair, forcibly jerking it back so he can get up properly.

Jelly steps back farther, a wavering, cautious smile on her face. "What's the matter, baby?" She holds up her hands like she's going to put them on his chest or shoulder.

He backs away to avoid touching her, bumping into the chair next to him. Leonard looks up with a bland expression. He doesn't stop chewing as he watches the spectacle unfold behind him.

"Fiancé? Where do you come *up* with this shit, Jelly?" Tarin is mad. He looks at all of us around the table. "She's nuts. This is not happening." His gaze stops when it reaches me. "I swear to God, I did not ask this crazy bitch to marry me."

My heart soars for a brief moment before I realize how messed up it is that I'd be happy about what he said or how he said it. Jelly *is* a crazy bitch, but even she doesn't deserve to be called that in front of all these people.

Apparently she agrees, because she starts waling on him, slapping him with her open hands for all she's worth.

He hides behind his upraised forearms, trying to avoid the worst of it. He manages to find his voice after about the twentieth slap. "Fuck, Jelly, back the hell off, would ya?" His arms have to be stinging with the abuse they're getting, and yet he does nothing to fight back. I'm impressed with him sticking to his code of not hitting girls. If it were me over there, I would have definitely hit her by now.

I exchange looks with Zach and he stands up, moving around the table with Ricky towards the mess that is Jelly-drama. Leonard is trapped in his seat with Tarin up against the back of it so he remains where he is, but his fork is down and he's ready to get up as soon as the opportunity presents itself.

I cringe with every slap and smacking sound. Jelly is on fire, her face an ugly red and her words spewing out like venom from a spitting cobra.

"Don't you *dare* call…me…that…word!" She punctuates her slaps with the words of outrage. "You sonofabitch, liar, soul-sucking bastard, cheater, *asshole!*"

"Jesus Christ, Jelly, I never lied to you! And how can I be cheating on you when you're not even my girlfriend?"

She shrieks in frustration. "Not your girlfriend?! Not your *girlfriend?!*"

Zach grabs Jelly and pulls her away, suffering a few slaps to the face himself. He just blinks and shakes it off as he half drags, half carries her out onto the back lawn. She screeches the entire way.

Tarin drops his arms and stands up straight as I come around to join him. We both watch Jelly alternately struggle to escape and collapse in tears, clinging to Zach. She's a complete mess, clearly not sure whether she should be strangling someone or crying herself to sleep.

"I swear on my life I did *not* ask her to marry me," says Tarin, quietly so only I hear him. He's shaken up, and I'm not surprised. Being forcibly married to Jelly would freak me out too. He shakes his head. "Not even wasted out of my gourd would I have done something *that* insane."

"I believe you. But she is pregnant with your baby, so…"

He looks at me, running the fingers of one hand through his still-wet hair. "Are you saying just because she's supposedly pregnant, I'm required to marry her?" He puts his hand loosely on his hip. "Because that's bullshit, Scarlett, you know it is." He sounds like he's pleading with me.

I search his face for clues of his real feelings. He seems desperate, and it makes me think he really believes I would force him to marry her. I frown. He must think I'm a monster bitch.

"I didn't say anything like that, Tarin. Why are you so worried all of a sudden?"

He huffs out a short laugh of relief. It sounds a touch bitter. "Because. I was afraid you were going to make me do it."

I laugh too. I'm amused that he feels that compelled to do what I say. I'm controlling, yes, but I'm not a monster. Not most of the time, anyway. "As if I could make you do *that*."

His expression is one-hundred-percent dead serious, and that's what makes his words blow me away. "You could. With that shit you hold over my head … you could make me do anything."

I'm taken aback. Until now, I had no idea that Tarin was taking our contractual agreement this seriously. I'm happy but a little freaked out at the same time. "Listen, Tarin … I want a willing participant in this process, of course … but that doesn't mean I want a mindless slave who'll sacrifice his entire life on my orders."

He shrugs, looking over at Jelly. "I'll do whatever you say. Anything. It's the least I can do."

My mouth drops open. He's making absolutely no sense, until it hits me. I'm instantly pissed. "Did you take anything after your shower?" I so want to put boxing gloves on now and mangle his face. I can totally appreciate Jelly's physical response to his idiocy.

"Take anything?" He looks at me, confusion marring his features.

"Yes. *Anything.*" I press my lips together, waiting to hear his excuse. I know it'll be lame and make me want to quit this job. I steel myself for the bad news.

"Like drugs?"

"Yes, like drugs. Stop acting stupid."

He's genuinely surprised. "No … No! Of course I didn't take anything. I'm clean, I swear it." He places his hand over his heart and for some ridiculous reason, it makes his claim more believable.

I'm so frigging easy it's not even funny. Now I'm just mad at myself for jumping to the wrong conclusion so quickly. He really is trying. The relief that washes over me is way too much for such a simple thing. I don't know why Tarin staying the path is so over-the-top important to me. I've never been this attached to a client ever. It makes me really nervous, like there's a lot more riding on this job than normal.

Jelly interrupts our conversation with a scream. "Tarin! Tell him to let me go!"

"You need to handle this," I say, folding my arms, readying myself for the entertainment and glad for the distraction. Our conversation is getting way too heavy for comfort, especially with all these people sitting there watching. I'm afraid they're reading my mind or my body language and seeing that I'm too attached. I need to work on remaining professional and ignoring these out of control reactions I keep having.

"What should I do?" Tarin asks.

"Do the right thing by her and you."

"Marry her?" he asks, sounding in pain.

I drop my arms and and shake my head. I want to scream right along with Jelly. "No!... Shit, Tarin... don't you listen to anything I say?"

He runs his fingers through his wet hair, making it stand on end. "Fuck! ... Yes! I'm listening to every single word, but it's not making sense! Do you want me to marry her or not?"

I want to punch him in the face, he's frustrating me so much. "The question is not what *I* want, but what *you* want, idiot. Do you want to have this woman in your life as your wife for all of eternity?"

He looks like he's going to vomit. "Please don't make me," he whispers. "I'll end up killing us both."

All the wind goes out of my sails and my anger collapses. "Then don't." I put my hand up and squeeze his bicep. I resist the urge to stroke its hard, warm surface. He's a client and I don't touch clients that way. Or I shouldn't. I hate that I keep thinking about breaking the rules with him. "If she's pregnant, we'll deal with that. But whatever you do, don't let a temporary situation determine the entire rest of your life."

I expect him to remain pensive as he thinks through his options, but he does pretty much the opposite. He grabs me on either side of my head, and before I even realize what he's going to do, he smashes his lips against mine. For the brief moment that our lips are touching, I'm closer to this man than I've been to another human in years.

My heart stops beating and the world spins. I step outside myself and a piece of me flies away into the night, carried away on some magic carpet ride into the darkness. It's just him and me and that kiss. I think I'm going to faint. He's a client and this shouldn't be happening and I shouldn't be feeling this way about it, but it is and I do and there's nothing I can do about it now.

And then just as quickly as he was there, he's gone. He pulls away and drops his hands from my cheeks. His face is flushed and he's grinning like a madman. "Thanks. Thanks a lot. You're cool, you know that? And cute too when you're getting all passionate and shit." He spins around and walks over to where Jelly and Zach are waiting.

I can't hear what they're saying, probably because the buzzing in my ears is so loud. I'm cool. He kissed me and I'm cool and I'm cute. And everyone at the table saw him do it. Apparently, so did Jelly.

Jelly's reaction comes across loud and clear when she slaps Tarin right across the face and storms into the house, Zach following closely on her heels. As she reaches the back door, she stops and sends us her parting message, Zach at her shoulder and ready to help her to the front door if she decides to change her mind about leaving.

"You'll be hearing from my lawyer, Tarin! And the rest of you … you … you can just *suck it!*" She storms into the house, and the sound of her rapidly clicking heels fades into the distance.

The entire dinner table is dead silent for about three seconds before Scott speaks up.

"Holy loudmouth. Can I have her duck? Pass the salt, Leonard."

Dave snorts and Leonard smiles along with Ricky. Tarin walks over to stand in front of me again, a red handprint on his face. I'm still too stunned to move.

"How'd I do?" he asks, grinning awkwardly. He reminds me a of a little kid, and it's endearing and scary at the same time. He makes me feel too many conflicting emotions at once and it rattles me badly. My calm and cool demeanor is nowhere to be found. I hook my thumbs into my front pockets and shrug.

"I'm not even sure what you did, to be honest." My hearing is now only just fully restored, the ringing his kiss started finally quieted down.

"I told her that we aren't engaged, that I don't see her as a girlfriend, and that I want a paternity test done to prove I'm the father."

I swallow with difficulty. "Wow. You really laid it on the line didn't you?" This feels like a really big deal. It *is* a really big deal, but on more levels than I care to think about.

"You said to be honest. That's what I'm doing."

I nod, afraid of what he might say next. "Good for you." I look at the table. "Ready to eat?"

"Yep. I like that duck."

"Good. Me too." This conversation is awkward. He's not a rock star anymore. In this moment, he's just a guy, trying to think of something to say to me, and I'm just a girl, torn between wanting to hear whatever it is he's thinking, and wanting to run and run and run and never look back.

"Better eat now before it gets cold," says Scott loud enough for everyone to hear.

I brush my hair away from my face and smile, breaking away from Tarin to go to my spot at the table. *Thank heaven for Scott.* "How is it?" I ask everyone at the table as I take my seat, trying to smooth over the weird mood that has settled on us.

Everyone chimes in with platitudes for Josh and his skill in the kitchen, warming the atmosphere and turning it from surreal to real again. As I settle into my chair, Scott nudges me and leans in.

"What was going on over there? Do I sense some possible future hanky panky yanky his wanky?"

"*Shut* up and *don't* ask and just *ew*, Scott. *Ew.* How do you expect me to eat now?" I act busy with my silverware and try not to look at the gorgeous mean-boy across the table from me. Tarin's not quite as mean-boy now as he was just a few hours ago, and it makes me really, really nervous. I'm afraid of how my body is reacting to him and the fact that I'm losing control whenever he's around.

"Yeah, right," snorts Scott.

I elbow him, but he keeps on smiling. I feel like he's managed to crawl into my head somehow.

CHAPTER
TWENTY-THREE

THIS IS ONE OF THOSE times that I'm happy to take the star-treatment and use it to my advantage. As soon as Tarin steps out onto the curb, a man in a suit comes out to usher us into the club ahead of a huge line of people standing outside. Only a few flashbulbs go off in our faces as we make our way through the front door, cocooned by Tarin's bodyguards and people manning the door.

A gorgeous, heavily-muscled and tattooed doorman nods at us as we go in, his biceps bulging out from the sleeves of his t-shirt. When I have to squeeze past him to fit through the door with Scott at my side, I feel like I've just brushed up against someone in the Russian mafia. I can't imagine anyone causing trouble in this place with a guy like him nearby. He nods at me once without even the slightest adjustment to his expression, strengthening my impression even more.

"Man, it's been too long since I've been to a club just to hang out," says Tarin, his face lit up with excitement. He rubs his hands together and does a little dance move forward instead of just walking. Something tells me he can dance his ass off, the way his hips are moving. I feel arousal making its way through me as I picture us dancing close and rubbing our bodies together on the hot mess of a dance floor. I jerk my gaze away from his gyrating form and focus on Scott, trying to get a handle on my runaway thoughts. He's looking around the room like he's not that impressed.

I'm styled for clubbing, my black form-fitting dress much higher on the thigh than I'd ever wear in the daytime. I opted for shorter heels than most of the women are wearing here, knowing I have to be prepared for just about anything when celebrities and alcohol are involved. Tarin worked out a deal with me on the way here. He can have two near-beers in exchange for an extra hour of working out. He's going to be really sorry he made that deal, but I don't tell him that. I'll let him see for himself in the gym tomorrow.

The beat from the DJ's mix makes it difficult to hear. Tarin comes over and leans in close to my ear. "Want a drink?" He places his hand on my lower back, and I'm torn between leaning in closer to him and stepping away. I choose the neutral path and do nothing. A little thrill rushes through me when his hand moves in tighter, giving his palm more contact with my back as it presses against my clothing. I wonder if it means anything special to him or if I'm just living in a fan-girl fantasy world. I try not to hate myself too much over it.

"I'll take some fuzzy water!" I practically yell, even though his face is really close. I can smell his cologne, and it's intoxicating. I want to snuggle up against him and then just as quickly consider running out of the club and going home. I don't like how he's affecting me *at all*. I'm a traitor in my own skin.

"What?!" he yells, getting even closer.

"Fuzzy! Water!" I repeat.

"Do you mean *fizzy?!*" He turns his face to look at me, confused. Our noses are practically touching.

I could kiss him if I just leaned forward two inches, but I back my face up, removing the temptation. His hand slides away from my back, leaving me feeling sad over it. "Fizzy ... fuzzy ... same diff." I shrug, my body swaying a little to the beat. I'm playing off the weirdly intimate moment like I don't even notice it happened. I'm sure I'm pulling it off too, because it's hard for anyone to remain still when the bass is pounding like this. Every single person in the place is moving, except for that Russian guy.

Tarin's lip quirks up in a half-smile. "Okay … one fuzzy water, coming right up." He leaves my side and heads to the bar. Before he gets three paces away, two girls glom onto him like bugs on flypaper.

I sigh. "So much for my fuzzy water, I guess." I turn to find Scott on my other side. He's staring off into the crowd.

"See anything interesting?" I yell at the side of his face.

"Nah." He doesn't even look at me. "Same old same old, you know? I keep wondering if I'm missing out on something, but then I come to places like this and realize I'm not."

I nod. "I know what you mean." I check the place out as the beat fills my entire body, making me wonder if the music is becoming a pacemaker for my heart. I hope not; it's going way too fast.

The space is huge, a warehouse that was converted into a dance club several months ago. It has a DJ booth on one side of the big open floor and a small stage towards the very back of the building. The dark steel and wood structure is elevated, its surface above all the gyrating bodies on the dance floor, and I can see a drum set and some amps already set up on it. Black, spray-painted walls block the view of the back stage area from people down at our level.

The graffiti that decorates the entire place is amazing. Someone with a lot of talent spent weeks in here and probably went through hundreds of cans of spray paint. I imagine I can still smell vestiges of the fumes.

"Fuzzy water!" yells Tarin, appearing out of a sea of bodies to hand me an ice-cold glass of clear bubbly liquid.

I look around casually as I take it from him, searching for his newest cling-ons. I'm *so* not in the mood to play nicey-nice with bimbots tonight, but I don't see them.

"What happened to your girlfriends?" Scott asks, taking the beer Tarin hands him. Scott's isn't alcohol-free, but Tarin's is. I make sure of it before turning my attention elsewhere.

"I told them I was here with someone." He doesn't look at me when he says it, but my face catches fire anyway. I focus on sipping tonic through my straw and pretending to be interested in what's going on around us. Of course he didn't mean he's here with *me*, but that doesn't stop my body from reacting like he did.

I feel someone's hands slip around my waist from behind and my first instinct is to toss my drink into the unseen molester's face, but when Jack's voice tickles my ear in the next second, I stop myself.

I glance over my shoulder, giving him my best scolding look. "You almost got a cold shower doing that, you big dummy." I turn around, effectively removing his hands from my body as I face him.

He leans in for a kiss on the cheek and I indulge him, even though I still feel like giving him a smack. For some stupid reason I can't look at Tarin right now. I don't want to know if he saw Jack touching me, and I don't want to know what he thinks about it if he did.

"I'm so glad you came," Jack says, a grin splitting his face. "We're going on in about ten minutes." He looks at Scott. "You ready?"

Scott nods.

I look from Scott to Jack. Their expressions are unreadable. "What's going on here?" I ask.

Neither of them answers me. Scott shrugs absently and stares off into the crowd as he takes another sip of his beer. He seems worried about something, and I should probably grill him until he caves, but my head is going in too many directions right now. I promise myself I'll harass him later when we're alone, and then focus on my molester.

I punch Jack lightly on the shoulder. "Come on, confess. It's good for the soul. Tell me what kind of trouble you're brewing up."

He leans in for another quick kiss on my cheek managing to steal one; I back away too slowly to stop it from happening.

"You'll just have to be patient for once in your life," he says, walking away and leaving me standing there to yell at a sea of strangers.

He probably can't hear me, but I shout it out anyway. "I'm always patient, Jack! And good thing too, or you'd be dead!" A swarm of fans follow behind him once they realize who he is and he disappears in the crowd.

Jack may have toned down his rock-and-roll persona, but that doesn't mean he's lost a single admirer or a drop of talent. He is, was, and always will be a superstar, even when he deigns to play in small venues like this place.

Working together last year, we discovered that doing things like this - getting close to his fans and performing smaller, more intimate gigs - is something his creative genius needs. I'm proud of him, that he's kept it up, even though it makes his manager and agent nuts sometimes. He makes practically no money at it and it pulls him away from other projects, but it feeds his muse. I told him to ignore the suits and do what makes him happy. He rocks out and then donates the money to charity. It's a win, win, win.

Jack sure did push my buttons when we were working together, though. Despite his insistence tonight that I be patient for once in my life, I'm sure he remembers the trials he put me through and how I was the patron saint of patience when I spent my thirty days with him. My first, middle, and last names were Patient. After dealing with him, I thought anything would be a piece of cake. *And then there was Tarin…*

"What's that all about?" asks The Devil Himself, pulling me out of my mini-outrage and reminiscing, startling me with his nearness.

"What's what about?" I sip my fuzzy drink again, wishing I'd asked for vodka instead. This place is getting on my nerves. There are too many people and too much noise, and it'll only be a matter of time before more people recognize Tarin and start giving us a hard time. I look over my shoulder for the muscled doorman and see him not that far from us. It gives me a small sense of security, reasonable or not.

"Are you guys dating or together somehow?" asks Tarin.

For a split second I think he's talking about the doorman, but when I see Tarin glance towards the stage I realize it's Jack he's referring to. "No, don't be ridiculous." I chew on my straw as I stare at him. I can't tell what he's thinking, but I'm too curious to look away from my attempted mind-reading.

"Why is that ridiculous?" Tarin asks. It seems like he really wants to know.

"Because … I don't date guys like him."

Tarin takes a pull of his fake beer and winces as he swallows it. He's staring out into the crowd when he asks his next question. "What do you mean by 'guys like him'?"

I don't want to say it. Something's holding me back from doing the thing I know I have to do. It's stupid and dangerous to play games with Tarin right now, so the smart thing to do is nip this noxious weed in the bud before it grows up and strangles us both. *Or maybe I can let it grow…*

"She doesn't date rock stars," says Scott, handing me his empty bottle. He's rescuing me from making a really big mistake; I know this, and yet I wish he'd kept his damn mouth shut.

"I gotta go. See you in a few." Scott leans in and kisses me on the cheek before pushing his way into the sea of bodies.

"Where the hell is he going?" I ask, standing there like a dope with the empty bottle hanging from my fingers.

Tarin takes it from me. "I think he's getting on stage."

"What?" This doesn't compute. Scott doesn't get on stage. Not for Jack, not for anyone.

"Look." Tarin gestures to the side of the stage where Scott is climbing some rickety-looking stairs. The burly Russian-looking guy from the front door is there making sure no one else goes up with him. Jack comes out from behind one of the black walls and joins Scott on stage.

The DJ's music is still pumping away, but people on the dance floor are turning together to face the stage as they realize something's about to happen. Cheers rise up and drown out most of the other sounds in the room. The only thing I can hear over their voices is the bass.

"Let's get closer," Tarin says, taking me by the elbow.

I chug down the rest of my drink and put my empty glass down on a tabletop as we walk by. Tarin leans behind me and puts the beer bottles there too. His hand moves to my lower back as he guides me onto the dance floor.

It's too dark for anyone to recognize him out here. For the first time since we're together, he's anonymous to the outside world. The music is so loud and the lights so flashy, we should probably feel completely disoriented, but it's having the opposite effect.

Tarin turns to me, and it's like we're in our own little world. We both start moving to the beat as we look into each other's eyes. To stand still would have been awkward.

My earlier daydream is coming true. I'm dancing with Tarin and my blood pressure is ready to go through the roof over it. *Be cool! It's not a big deal!* I'm trying to listen to my own counsel, but it has zero effect. I'm freaking out.

"You like the music?" he asks, his hands moving to my elbows. People are pushing us together and our bodies are touching at our thighs. I never meant for this to happen when I agreed to come here and bring him with me. There's a storm brewing inside my heart and mind, and the temperature between us is rising to dangerous levels. I don't know whether to be distressed or thrilled, so I settle for a mixture of the two conflicting emotions.

"I'm not big on raves," I say, looking around us, playing it as cool as possible considering I'm about to explode with pent up sexual frustration. The spaced-out happy smiles on a few of the faces around us and some exaggerated dirty dancing by others tells me some of them took some X recently.

"You like my music better than this techno bullshit," he says, giving me one of his devilish grins.

I nod, because there's no point in lying. "Much."

"What about Jack's music? Do you like his better than mine?"

He's serious. The playful smile has left his face. I get the impression that the answer is important to him too and that he doesn't just want platitudes from me.

The problem is, I don't know whether it's music that he's talking about or something else. I feel like I'm about to cross the line and tell him something about not just his music but things between *us*, but I don't care enough to hold back completely. I let some of my abandon slip through and guide me.

"What difference does it make?" I ask, my body moving in perfect rhythm to his. We're good together on the dance floor. It's like each of us knows what the other will do and responds without thinking. It makes me wonder what else we'd be good at together, and I picture us naked in bed before I can stop my runaway train brain. *So, so, so not professional.* I wish I felt worse about the fact that my rules about not getting involved are becoming less and less important to me, but I don't. Something about Tarin makes me re-evaluate my carefully crafted life and find it wanting.

"I just want to know." He pulls me closer. I can feel almost all of him. Smell him. We're sweating together. The hardness of his body is intoxicating.

"You just want to know what?" I'm playing games. Stalling. Not sure how far I should let this go. My heart is racing, and I know now that it's not the music setting its pace. It's Tarin.

He answers me, but I don't hear him.

"What?!" I yell, leaning in closer. Now our chests are touching too.

He puts his hands on my upper arms and pulls me into him. We're almost embracing when his voice finally comes to my ear. "I want to know what my competition is." His breath tickles my neck and sends shivers down my spine.

I pull back, quickly putting space between us. I can't control the flush coming over my body or how I'm responding to his touch, but I can keep this from going any farther. I shouldn't have led him on. It was stupid and thoughtless and selfish, not to mention beyond dangerous. "There is no competition, Tarin."

He goes from playful to angry in the space of two seconds. He doesn't say anything, he just lets me go and turns a little towards the stage.

He's still dancing, but his moves become more fluid, more obvious. A girl standing nearby starts moving with him, and I get pushed off to the side by their swaying bodies. He lifts his arms above their heads and really starts moving his hips with purpose.

She takes the clue and backs up into him, giving him what he's obviously looking for.

I turn away, unable to look at them anymore. My heart feels like it's being torn in half and I'm instantly sick to my stomach. Such a simple, stupid thing ... him dancing with a stranger ... and I'm ready to cry. *Jesus, what is wrong with me?*

I try to leave the dance floor, but there are too many people in my way. I'm trapped, but the idea of standing there next to Tarin like a sad, dumped loser is so unappealing, I dance. I act like I don't care that his emotions come and go like the tides, that he can look at me and slay me with a single smile, or that seeing him having fun with another nameless bimbot is killing me.

Doing my best to feel the beat and move with it, I act like I'm completely cool with Tarin's games because they don't affect me. I think I'm doing pretty well at pulling it off too, and then someone up on stage strums a guitar and I spin around, instantly forgetting the game I'm playing as I get lost in the vision before me.

Scott?

I stop dancing as the music fades into nothing and a man steps up to the microphone. It's the DJ and he's standing next to Scott.

"Yo, yo, yo!! What's up!" He's still wearing headphones, only now they're around his neck. "Party people in the houuuse tonight!"

The cheer that rises up in response is deafening.

"That's what I'm talkin' about! Who's ready to rock this party?"

More cheers blow out my eardrums. It has the miraculous effect of drowning out my misgivings temporarily, picking me up and carrying me along on a wave of abandon. I can't help but let go of my frustration and join in the fun. It's easing the sting of Tarin's rejection to be a part of such an excited group of people, and I'll be damned if I'm going to sit around and feel sorry over something that can never be.

I can tell by people's expressions that some of Jack's most die-hard fans are in attendance. I wouldn't be surprised to find out that some of them traveled from other states to be here. Many are chanting his name.

"That's good, that's good …," says the DJ, "…because we have something special going on for you tonight. I'm not playin', y'all, this is the first time … ever … that you are gonna see somethin' like this. Give uuuuup! Give it up for Austin Betzer's little brother Scott Betzer…!"

He turns sideways to give us a view of the stage, the performers there but too bathed in shadows to see clearly. He waits for the insane screaming that ensues to die down a little before he finishes, "… And of course our very own … Jack Oooo'Leary!"

The fans go bananas. I'm jumping up and down, and I don't even have to move a muscle to make it happen; the crowd is carrying me with it. I lose Tarin in the mess while I'm getting elbowed and dry humped and spilled on, but I don't care. The energy is palpable and electrifying. Multi-colored lights are beaming and flashing all over the place. I'm not even sure at this point that the band has to play anything to keep these people happy; they're high on just the idea of it.

A spotlight goes on and suddenly Scott is visible on stage. He has a guitar strapped to the front of him and he's staring at the neck of it.

Tears leap to my eyes and my throat closes up. He's the picture of his brother standing there like that, and I know I'm not the only one who notices. Girls around me start shrieking like it's the nineteen-seventies and they've just seen a Beatle. A couple of them are crying.

"Oh my god!! It's Austin!!" someone near me screams. I want to slap whoever it is, the bile rising up in my throat to choke me. Scott is *not* Austin. I'd never ever let that happen.

Another spotlight goes on, distracting me from my anger. Jack is suddenly visible under its glare. The crowd goes nuts all over again. My eardrums will suffer for the rest of the night for this, but I don't care. He really is frigging amazing. Not only is his music pure rock-and-roll perfection, but he strikes the most elegant rocker pose without even trying.

His long arms hold the guitar in his hands, his fingers casually resting on the strings like it's no big deal. His hair is a crazy mess and his eyes are lined in smudged black. He smiles and every girl around me swoons. He's like a cross between Billie Idol and Elvis - purely intoxicating on a visual level, and then his music … that's where he hits you on the emotional level. He's the real deal, and a small piece of me wishes that I don't have a rule about not falling for rockers. He'll make a great husband for someone someday, but that's not in the cards for me now or ever.

Jack steps up to the microphone and lays his hand over the top of it in a loose grip, the bulky silver rings on his fingers obvious in profile. As he leans forward and speaks to the crowd, I'm overwhelmed by the memories that come flooding back, seeing the two of them there. Jack and Austin. *No, Jack and Scott.* It's not Austin … it *isn't.* My vision blurs and Scott's face merges in and out with a memory of Austin's.

My earlier euphoria is replaced by stark fear. *Panic mode level ten. Run away! Run away now!* I spin around, looking for a way out. I can't take it. I have to leave. I have to get out of here before I throw up on someone.

Strong arms wrap around me from the side. I immediately start fighting whoever it is, throwing up a punch without even aiming.

"Ooooph!" yells Tarin, bending over and forcing me to go with him. His arms are like steel bands around me. "Shit, Scarlett," he grunts out as he tries to catch his breath. I got him right in the solar plexus.

"What the hell are you doing?" I yell, pushing on his chest to get him to stand up. My words come out more like I'm crying than angry.

"Don't go," he says, fighting to get his breath back. "Stay with me."

"I can't! I don't want to!" My fight or flight instinct has kicked in and I've chosen *flight* … big time, flight. I want to sprout wings and soar over all these heads and out the door into the night.

"I'm sorry I danced with her, okay! I'm sorry!"

His apology catches me by surprise, so I forget to struggle. "What?" I stand up straight too and now we're facing each other. The first few chords of the guitar being played by Scott come out of the big speakers.

"I said I'm sorry I danced with that girl. I was jealous."

Suddenly we're alone again, in our own world. All the strangers in the room become ghosts just dancing around us but not intruding on our drama. I forget what I was running from. "Jealous of what?"

"I don't know!" He runs the fingers of one hand through his hair while the other hand holds my waist. "Of Jack, I guess."

I frown at him. "That's just … stupid."

"I know it is, I know! I don't need you to tell me that." He's mad, but not at me. I think he's upset with himself.

"I don't feel that way about Jack."

He stares at me. "You don't?"

"No, of course not. He's a former client."

"So?" He's asking for more explanation and I almost don't want to give it. But it's for the best. It would be a mistake to let this go anywhere.

"I don't get involved with clients, Tarin."

"Why?"

"Because. I just don't." I can't tell him why … that it's because I'm afraid of being destroyed all over again. I know that the minute I give him the key to my world, he'll use it to unlock the door and force his way in. I'm a challenge to him, that's it; and I know Tarin well enough to know he loves a challenge.

His mouth moves around like he's about to say something, but he doesn't. He just turns and faces the music. I expect him to take off again and start grinding on the nearest ass, but he doesn't. He just slides his hand down my arm and weaves his fingers in with mine. We stand side by side and listen to the music together.

CHAPTER
TWENTY-FOUR

SCOTT AND JACK HAVE OBVIOUSLY been practicing for a while. They've made music together - haunting, sad, emotion-packed songs that tear my heart out and shred it. I'm angry and happy at the same time. I wish Scott had told me what he was up to, but I'm so excited that he's actually writing music, I forgive him. He'd started doing it when he was just fourteen with Austin, but had given up when Austin pulled away from us. This is the first I know of him getting back to it. He'd always told me that his music died with his brother.

Tears run silently down my face the entire time they perform as I sway to the rhythm and the haunting melodies, but I actually cry like a stupid baby when the lyrics to the fourth and last song come across the space between them on the stage and me out in the crowd.

Before they start, Jack steps up to the microphone as the drummer behind him beats out a few random hits on his snare. "This one is for a very special girl." He turns around to shush the drummer before continuing. "I wish I could convince her of some things, but she's making it really hard for me." He strums one chord to emphasize his words and then speaks again. "But that doesn't mean I'm going to stop trying." He puts his hand over his eyebrows to block the spotlights and scans the crowd. He stops when his eyes land on me. "This one's for you, Scar."

People nearby look around to see who he's talking about. I don't make eye contact with any of them. I don't want them knowing that I have a connection to Jack or to anyone on that stage. My work requires that I be invisible to the world. My heart requires that I remain alone.

My throat closes up over what's about to happen. I can't breathe. I don't want to hear what he's going to sing, what he's going to play. I know it's going to cut me like a knife and make me bleed all over this floor.

I turn to leave, but Tarin stops me. He grabs me by the shoulders and turns me around, stepping up to stand behind me. He wraps his arms around me, trapping me in front of him as the first chords come out of the speakers. He makes me feel safe and warm, like maybe I'll be able to handle what happens next. It's stupid and weak and it shouldn't be this way, but it is. I hate that I can't create my own reality, that it keeps getting created for me by this guy I shouldn't want to be with. *Tarin.* He has too much power over me, and that kind of thing is never good. Especially when it's my job to get him back on track.

Jack and Scott are nodding to each other as the music from the two guitars becomes entwined, making it impossible for me to tell who is playing what. It pulls me out of the moment with Tarin and shoves me into one with Jack. Talk about emotional whiplash.

Jack's raspy voice goes into the mic and out through the speakers, driving the words he sings into my heart. His eyes are closed as he feels the lyrics he's singing and the music he's playing.

> *Oh, you've got it bad, girl,*
> *Those eyes, gray eyes still sad, girl,*
> *Let me be the one to show you*
> *It's time to let it all go now.*

I can't listen to anymore of this. It's too much. He should never have written this goddamned song. I'm sad and angry and feeling more than a little bit violated. Some lines should just never be crossed, and the ones that lead to the memories of Austin are on the top of the list.

I turn around in Tarin's arms and look up at him, pleading for my release. I sound weak and pitiful, but I can't help it. "I have to go, Tarin. I can't stay and listen to this."

He nods, his expression showing concern for me. "Fine. Come on." His arms slide away and his hand slips into mine. He turns and begins forcing his way through the crowd. People ignore us, too drawn in to the music to care that they're being pushed around.

Jack's voice slips into my head along with the music again, the haunting melody following me off the dance floor.

> *I know it had to be that way before,*
> *But things have changed for both of us,*
> *You've gotta trust me girl when I say this,*
> *It's time to start all over now,*
> *It's time to trust another now…*

We make it to the edge of the crowd and Tarin's bodyguards close in on us. I focus on them so I can block out the next part of the song. I don't think I can take any more. My chest feels like it's going to explode with anxiety.

"What's up?" asks Zach.

"We're outta here," says Tarin. "Stay here and take care of Scott, would ya?"

"Whatever you say, Tare." Zach looks at me. "We good?"

I nod, trying to keep the tears from falling. "Yeah."

He puts his hand on my shoulder and gives me a sad smile. "Be careful."

I don't know what he means, but I nod anyway, unable to speak.

Zach makes his way towards the stage through the crowd behind us; I assume his destination is the stairs. I'm glad to know that Scott has protection now, and even happier to know Tarin made sure of it. My idea of him being a mean-guy is slipping away with every minute that goes by.

Leonard walks with us to the door. I nod at the Russian guy who's once more at the entrance to the club.

"Need a cab?" he asks me.

I'm startled by his deep and unaccented voice. *I guess he's not Russian after all.* "No thanks. We have a car."

"You want me with you or with Zach?" asks Leonard.

Tarin looks at me as I jerk my head towards the stage. He takes my hint. "Go with Zach. Help him with Scott. I have a feeling he's going to be mobbed." He pulls his cell phone out of his pocket and puts it to his ear.

Leonard leaves us there with the doorman.

Tarin says a few words into his phone and then hangs it up. "Ricky's on his way." He rubs my back, trying to make me feel better, I know, but all it does is ramp up my emotions.

I look at the floor trying to get a grip on myself, trying to keep myself from moving up against him. It's every kind of wrong, but I want his arms around me again. I feel so vulnerable right now, it's beyond ridiculous. Tarin's a lot stronger than I gave him credit before. As I fall apart at his feet, he stands there like a rock. A dependable rock of a man.

I'm going a little nuts. That's the only explanation for my next thought. It strikes me that Jelly could very possibly be the luckiest girl alive. Maybe he doesn't want to have her around as a girlfriend, but if she has his kid, she'll see him plenty for the next twenty years or so. But I won't. After three more weeks, I'll be gone and I'll never see him again except for on the television or online news articles. Tonight's fiasco with Jack has taught me that keeping in contact with old clients can be too risky, too painful. I can picture Tarin playing me a song like that and know without a doubt that it would be my complete undoing. Tarin is not like anyone else. He's not just a rocker, here one day to party it up and then gone the next. My heart aches with how much he reminds me of Austin in that way.

"Have a good night."

I raise my eyes to the man with the deep voice. The not-Russian guy is looking at Tarin and nodding slightly.

"Hey, don't I know you from somewhere?" Tarin asks, frowning at the guy, his head tilted.

The doorman shrugs. "Maybe."

"You don't work just here, do you? You work somewhere else, too."

The man nods. "No, I don't work just here. I have a garage."

Tarin smiles and points at him. "That's riiiight. Muscle cars, right?"

The guys smiles back, and I'm stunned with how it transforms his face. He goes from stoic and unapproachable to gorgeous in half a second. The smile lasts only that long before it's gone again. "Yep." He's a man of few words, apparently.

Tarin goes from slightly aloof celebrity to fan-boy in an instant. "Dude, your shit is *seriously* sick. I've been wanting to stop by, you know, but life's been crazy." He glances down at me.

The guy gets the wrong idea, following Tarin's gaze and nodding. "I get it."

"Oh, no … we're not…" I want to straighten out the misunderstanding but Tarin interrupts me, agreeing with the guy.

"Yeah, right? So are you open this weekend? I'd love to stop by and check out what you're working on." He pauses and looks down at me. "If that's all right with you."

I shrug. "Whatever. I can work around it." I give up on dissuading this guy from thinking Tarin and I are together. It makes no difference in the scheme of things what a stranger might think, and the story's too complicated to explain right now anyway. I'm not even sure I know what my job is anymore.

The guy pulls a business card out of his wallet and hands it to Tarin. "Just give me a call. Shop's open pretty much all the time."

"Cool, man. Thanks." Tarin looks at the card for a few seconds. "That's your name? Rebel?"

"Yep."

Tarin looks the guy's tattoos and muscles over, grinning. "My kind of guy."

Rebel shrugs and then holds out his hand. "Nice to meet you."

Tarin shakes his hand. "My name's Tarin by the way. Tarin Kilgour."

The guy's expression doesn't change. "Yeah, I know who you are."

Tarin nods and takes me by the hand. His fingers are warm and dry to my cold and clammy mess. Ricky has just pulled up. "See you soon, man," he says to Rebel.

I give Rebel a small wave goodbye, not trusting myself to speak right now. Tarin leads me out of the entrance and down the sidewalk, and I'm happy to just follow along. It's easier to not think and just do what he wants, at least until my head is back on straight. Ricky wasn't able to park close enough to the front for us to rush right in, so we have to battle some people hanging out by the line of wanna-be clubbers to get to him.

We're almost there when someone jumps in our way. "Tarin!" the vision-in-pink squeals.

"What the fuck … *Posey?* What are you doing here?" Tarin says, pulling on my hand to force me behind him. I take it as a protective gesture, but I fight his good intentions, jerking my hand away and going back to his side.

"I came to be with you, of course!" She's grinning like the lunatic she is. "I heard you were here, so I came right over."

Her friends join our little meet-up, standing just behind her. One of them has the decency to look embarrassed about her painfully misguided friend.

"I'm outta here," says Tarin, stepping to go around her. "Have a good night." He's angry but holding back, I think to be nice. He's much more calm about it than I am. I should probably feel bad about the fact that he's holding it together better than I am right now, but I don't; I'm too emotional to think straight. I just need to get away from here so I can fix things.

She reaches out and grabs his arm. "But Tarin … wait! I need to talk to you."

He yanks his arm out of her grasp. "Not now, Posey, I have to go."

A flash goes off and I turn my head in surprise, noticing for the first time that there's a guy with a big camera getting several pictures a second. His automatic shutter is going off like a machine gun.

Chick-eh, chick-eh, chick-eh.

Posey finally notices me standing there. I haven't moved, so Tarin is no longer at my side. Ricky's out of the car now and coming around to open the passenger door. A moment later, when Tarin realizes he's left me behind, he turns back and reaches for my hand, looking up just in time to get a flashbulb light to the face.

He growls, putting his hand up to block any more shots. "Fucking paparazzi … get outta here, would you please?!"

"What are you doing here?" asks Posey, practically spitting the words at me. She's oblivious to the camera or Tarin's annoyance.

"Posey, you really need to stop following Tarin around, okay?" I say, using my reasonable, professional tone. Thank God my work-brain has kicked in; I'm pretty sure crying on her shoes wouldn't be very convincing. "At this point, your behavior's coming dangerously close to stalking."

The cameraman moves to the curb to grab some shots of us in profile. Tarin moves to put his back to the camera and block the guy from getting me in the frame.

"It's not stalking if he wants me to do it!" she screams, stepping forward to get closer to me. Her hands are balled into fists and her small beaded handbag is swinging out in front of her.

More flashes go off.

Chick-eh, chick-eh, chick-eh.

Tarin gives up on trying to grab a hold of my evasive hand and takes me by the wrist, pulling me towards the car. "Come on, Scarlett, just leave her be."

The cameraman is going bananas, probably already seeing dollar signs for the two thousand actions shots he's taken.

"Yeah, Scarlett, just leave us alone." Posey shoves the back of my shoulder as I walk away.

I halt in my tracks, spinning to face her. My reasonable, rational voice is gone, and now I'm just mad. "Touch me again and I'll lay you out, right here on this sidewalk, you lunatic bimbot."

"I dare you!" she shrieks. She's clearly lost her mind, thinking she's fighting for her man or something. She's no match for me in her stupid heels and tight dress. One punch and she'll be toast.

I take a step forward. Once again, I've lost my ability to think rationally. All I want to do is make her shut up, go away, and never come back again to bother Tarin. He deserves some peace; he's a good person.

Ricky comes between us. "No, no, no … nobody's laying anyone out anywhere tonight. 'Least not here in public." He puts his hand up to stop Posey from going anywhere, but she's not interested in being tamed.

She pushes on Ricky's chest, grunting with the effort of trying to move him. "Get out of my way, you stupid chauffeur!"

Rebel the doorman appears out of nowhere. He pushes the cameraman firmly down the sidewalk away from us, giving him a warning with a pointed finger before coming back over. He's like a mountain of muscle, and it calms my racing heart down to half its frantic pace just to have him there. I'm glad I won't have to beat up a lust-crazed teenager tonight.

"Listen," Rebel says to Posey in a totally cool and calm voice, "if you don't calm down, I'm going to call the cops and ban you from the club, too."

"Who cares about your stupid club, you big gorilla. I don't even *want* to go into your club. I'm here for Tarin." She tries to look around Ricky's large frame. "Tell him, Tarin. Tell him to let me in the car with you. And leave *her* out." Her eyes are shooting daggers at me, and her way-too-long fake eyelashes make it almost comical. It's like getting a stare-down from a camel … *so* not intimidating.

"Posey, go home," Tarin says. He sounds tired.

"But … Tarin!" she wails as he pulls me towards the car again. He opens the back door so I can go in first. I hesitate.

Posey's tone is helpful now, concerned and overly sweet. "What's the matter, Tarin? Are you feeling okay? Are you sick? Do you need me to take care of you?" She's doing her best to yell around Ricky, but he dodges left and right to block her.

"Please, let's just go," Tarin begs me. "I'm so fucking sick of this shit."

"I'll go if you go with me."

He takes my hand and squeezes it gently. "Deal."

We're in the car when Tarin rolls down his window and yells over to the doorman who's now alone in the controlling-Posey business. "Thanks, Rebel! I owe you one!"

Rebel doesn't respond to the statement, focused on restraining a very upset Posey. She's bucking around, hitting and yelling, her dress going sideways and her hair turning into a tangle with her efforts to get to our car.

Ricky jogs over to the driver's side and gets in, shifting the vehicle into drive before he even has his seatbelt on. He battles to put it on as he spins the wheel of the SUV with one hand and we move away from the curb.

As we merge into the small amount of traffic on the road, Posey manages to get loose. She runs next to us in the street, screaming something I can't understand. Her clunky heels are clocking against the asphalt in fast-forward-time, and her screeches sound deranged. The last thing I see before we're going too fast for her to keep up is her little purse, swinging out and coming into Tarin's window.

He shouts out in pain and bends over, holding his eye. Posey's purse falls to the floor at our feet as we leave her and her friends behind.

"Holy fuck! That bitch hit me in the eye!" he yells.

I slide over the bench seat quickly and put my hand on his back, leaning over to look at his face. "Are you okay? Sit up and let me see."

He's breathing in and out sharply, the pain he's suffering obvious.

"Come on, Tarin," I cajole. "Please? Let me see." I pray he hasn't suffered any damage to his cornea.

I keep my hand on his back as he sits up, then move it to his shoulder as he twists sideways. I put my hand on his and gently pry it away from his face.

Tears are streaming out of his eye and I can tell he can't open it. When his hand is fully away, I hiss inward. "Ricky? Better take us to the hospital." I can't see everything with his eyelid in the way, but there's a cut and some blood near the outside corner of his eye, and it's all way too close for comfort. The whole area is already swollen.

Ricky makes a giant u-turn in the middle of the road and speeds off in the opposite direction of Tarin's house. Posey sees us coming back and tries to head us off, but Rebel grabs her and drags her back to the curb. The cameraman is there, his flash going off over and over.

Tarin puts his hand back over his eye as he smiles at me, the club disappearing behind us.

"I'm gonna have a scar," he says.

"Probably. I don't know why you look so happy about it." I'm worried about him and it's making me cranky.

"Scars are sexy. Chicks like scars. It's gonna make me look dangerous. Chicks like bad boys, haven't you heard?"

I laugh, relieved that he's at least okay enough to joke about it. "You're ridiculous, you know that?" I sit back, sliding over to the far side of the seat. I have to get away from him; even injured he's too charming for his own good. Or for mine.

He sits back too, but his hand slides across the back seat and settles over mine. "You like me like that. You like ridiculous."

I don't argue. There's really no point in denying the obvious. Dangerous? Bad boy? Scarred? Yes, to all the above. Tarin has way too much going for him, and I don't have strong enough walls to keep him out. The risks are piling up.

What in the hell am I doing?

CHAPTER
TWENTY-FIVE

AFTER AN HOUR IN THE hospital with a plastic surgeon who was only too eager to come in immediately and put a couple stitches in the famous Tarin Kilgour, we make it back to the house. Ricky leaves us alone at the front door, claiming fatigue and a need to get a good night's sleep for tomorrow's workout. We watch as he disappears around the side of the house, headed to his small cottage located on the grounds just beyond the pool area.

Tarin opens the front door for me, allowing me to go in first. I stand in the foyer, not really wanting to go to my room, but also not wanting to invite more trouble into my life. The smart thing would be to go to bed. I know this.

"Want to have a drink with me?"

"Sure."

I roll my eyes at my eager response as I walk behind him to the family room. *Could I be more of a fool? No, I don't think so.* The whole time I'm walking down the hall, I know I'm going to regret this, but I can't seem to stop myself. Headlong into self-destruction; I've taken a page out of Austin's book. Whatever lessons I've learned about running my business over the past two years don't seem to apply here; or they apply, but I'm ignoring them. I can plainly see myself headed into a dangerous position, but I just keep going there anyway. I've never been so irresponsible in my entire life, and I cannot figure out what it is about Tarin that inspires this in me. No one before ever has, not even Austin.

Tarin seems completely cool with everything, especially considering his injury. He walks around the wet bar in the corner of the room and bends down, getting a bottle from under the counter.

"How can you be so calm after all that happened?" I ask.

He shrugs as he pours some amber liquid into a tumbler. "Just another day in the life, I guess."

"I get the stalker thing, but the slingshot ninja purse? Not so much." I look at the small bandage at the outside corner of his swollen eye and feel terrible all over again. I'm partially responsible since I'm the one who got Posey the purse-ninja-bimbot all worked up. If I'd stayed out of the picture, they'd be making out on this couch right now, and without the stitches.

He smiles, reaching under the counter again. The fridge is open and he's sliding something out of it. "Yeah, the ninja purse was a new twist, but it's not the first time I've had something thrown at me. Not by a long shot. I've ducked beer bottles, food, bras, panties, condoms ... thank God they weren't used."

"That's so not cool," I say, disappointed in the entire human race. "You write songs that make the whole world sing. No one should be throwing anything at you."

He looks up at me and grins. "You didn't just say that, did you?"

I grimace at my retro seventies humor. "I may have. Can we pretend I didn't?"

"Sure." He goes back to focusing on his task. He's pouring a little bit of brown soda, adding it to the alcohol he already put in the crystal glass. Swirling and then sipping the concoction, he frowns at first, then he nods his head. "Not bad. Tarin's bubble gum special is ready for ingestion."

I walk over, intrigued by his madness. "I have no idea what you're talking about, but it sounds interesting." I'm totally ready to drown out the memories of the last couple of hours with alcohol. *Sure. Why not?* I mean, yeah, it's a terrible idea, I know this. But it's the best one I can come up with when lying in bed and torturing myself with flashbacks is not an option. Tonight I want to spare my heart that extra dose of awful.

He walks over and hands me a glass. He holds up a bottled soda and waits for me to respond in kind.

We touch our drinks together with a slight *clink.*

"Cheers," I say. "I'm glad you're not drinking a real drink. That would be a violation of the rules."

"Cheers. Here's to rock and roll. I guess rule violations are a real no-no with you, huh?"

I raise my glass again. "To rock and roll," I repeat, "and yes … rules are not made to be broken. They're made to be followed to the letter." *Except for the one saying I don't get involved with clients. Apparently, that one isn't nearly as strict as I thought it was.*

"If you say so." He winks as me as he takes a sip of his soda.

I take a big swig of the drink he made me, nearly gagging when the taste finally hits me. I can't remember what he calls this drink but if it were me doing the naming, I'd call it Frankenstein. *Holy ugly monster of a cocktail. Give me more.*

He grins at my reaction. "What do you think?"

When my voice is working again, I say, "It's interesting…"

"Sip it, don't gulp. Tell me that doesn't taste like bubble gum, like the kind you can get with baseball card packets."

All I tasted on my first try was overly sweet firewater, but I'm willing to give it another shot. I convince myself I can already feel its warming effects. Taking a small sip, I concentrate on the flavors more closely.

"What happened to the soda?" I ask, swirling the liquid around as I stare it, wondering why there aren't any bubbles of carbonation.

"It's there, it's just flat."

"Flat?"

"Yeah. That's the secret. Flat soda." He holds his bottle up to his mouth, placing his index finger against his lips. "Shhh, don't tell anyone."

"Or you'll have to kill me?" I say. Why busting out the most over-worked joke on the planet seems like a good idea, I don't know.

He lifts an eyebrow. "Kill you? No. But other things, maybe."

My heart is instantly racing. He's got promises behind those eyes and I'm so very tempted to find out what they are. *Stupid, stupid, stupid! Run away! Go to bed! Stop drinking Frankenstein concoctions! Remember what you're here for!*

A smile moves across my face as I recklessly ignore my common sense. I try to save myself and whatever pride I have left by moving away from the bar. Turning my back on Tarin, I go over to the big couch that faces the television and video game closet.

He joins me, dropping down in the middle before I can sit. I'm forced into the corner to put some distance between us. I look over at him as I take another sip of my drink, wondering if he sat there intentionally to make sure we'd be close.

"So ... truth or dare?" he asks.

I have to force the liquid down my throat. My first instinct is to cough and spray it out everywhere.

"Say what?" I finally ask. My pulse is so out of control, I'm convinced he'll see my artery pumping in my neck if he looks too closely.

"Truth or dare. You know how it works, right?" He winks at me.

He's winking at me! Why does he have to be so freaking hot all the time, dammit! And he was right earlier in the car ... Injury = bad boy = sexy. I feel like a cavewoman, my internal dialogue completely devoid of intellectual thought. It crosses my mind that I'm having a walking, talking functional breakdown of sorts. I can act like everything is normal on the outside, but inside my life is falling apart. The rules are crumbling along with the walls that separate my heart from my work.

"Yeah, I know how truth or dare works," I say, trying to act cooler than I feel, "but I haven't ever actually played it before."

"Oooh, good. I have a virgin on my hands."

I know he doesn't mean it the way I'm taking it, but his thrill at getting a crack at a virgin 'like me' is exhilaratingly hot. I'm no virgin, but he's making me feel like one as I blush and stammer my way around a response.

"That's … funny … ha, ha … virgin…"

"You want to start? Cause if you do, fair warning, I prefer dares."

The smile won't stay off my face. It easily betrays my interest in his silly games and loaded words. He *so* has me in his trap. I feel stupid, like the worst kind of bimbot. I wonder how many girls have fallen into this mess of sexy before me. Now at least I know what drives them to the flame. We're all just a bunch of moths eager to get set on fire. I've been around celebrities for most of my adult life, and this is the first time I feel like I'm out of my league. I cannot let him know that or this whole gig will be over before it starts.

Even the simple act of him raising his soda bottle to his lips has me wanting to do and say stupid, stupid things. His fingers with tattooed letters on the backs of them, the way his muscles pulse under the ink on his forearms, how his strong jaw moves as he lets the liquid slide down this throat… He could have anyone, be anywhere … but he's here with me. At least, that's what I'm telling myself, because tonight, I have no brain.

"Fine. I'll go first," I say, pausing to gulp some more whatever he calls this mess of a drink. *Frankensteins brew.* "Truth or dare?" I ask, grateful for the buzz that's taking hold. I'm a complete lightweight and the cocktail is working it's magic. *Thank God.*

"Dare, of course." He takes a sip of his drink. There's twice as much liquid in his bottle as I have in my glass.

"I dare you …" I can't think of anything that doesn't involve him getting naked. I'm freaking out like a fan-girl on Tarin-crack. I blurt out the first non-sexual thing I can think of. "…I dare you to write a song about hot dogs!"

I cringe at my total and utter lameness. *Hotdogs? Are you serious? What are you … ten?*

He stares at me for several seconds with no expression on his face.

"Hot dogs," he finally says.

My face is on fire. I'm so embarrassed I want to run from the room and never look at him again. "Never mind."

He jumps up, putting his drink down on the table. "No, no, that's fine. You want a song about hot dogs, I'll give you a song about hot dogs." He sounds way too happy as he strides over to the far side of the room and takes an acoustic guitar from a stand. Bringing it back over to the couch, he swings it up to land in his lap as he sits. The fingers of his left hand settle under the neck and over the strings while his other hand hovers with a pick, ready to strum out a chord.

Tarin clears his throat and winks at me before starting. "An ode to the hot dog…" *Strum, strum, strum…*

He begins to sing in his gorgeous, raspy voice. "She looked at meee … and she said to meee … oh Tarin pleeeeasse … would you let me seeeee … your *hot dog…*" *Strum, strum…*

He waits for my reaction.

I want to crawl under a giant rock and die. I'd even welcome a painful death at this point. *Just put me out of my misery, please!*

He smiles and strums another chord before picking up the singing again. "I looked at herrrr … and I said to herrrr … oh Scarlett pleeeasse … I'll let you seeeee … my *hot dog* …"

And then he picks up the pace.

"…But only if you promise, to show me, to show me, those glorious buns you got! You got! And only, if you promise, to show me, to show me, what you'll do with those buns … you got … you got … those buns … you got…" He pauses for a few more chords and finishes it off. "Please, baby, I'll show you mine if you show me yours, and together we could have a hell of a cookout, yeaaaahhh…"

He finishes off with some hardcore licks that I might have seen Eddie Van Halen do on stage once, and then he stops, swinging the guitar off his lap and against the edge of the couch where it leans there mocking me.

Tarin grins like a maniac and then takes a big swig of his soda, burping when he can breathe again. "Didn't think I could do it, did ya?" He says, very happy with himself.

My mouth opens but no words will come out. I wet my whistle with the rest of my drink to get my vocal chords working again. "Um, I guess I didn't know what to think. That has to be the lamest dare that has ever been issued in the history of truth or dare and you followed it up with the lamest piece of music that was ever created. I'm pretty sure Jim Morrison just rolled over in his grave."

"Maybe. But it's the mark of a true master, to take a lame dare and make it special, right?" He lifts an eyebrow at me and nods encouragingly. "Right?"

I nod. "Yes. You are a true master."

He gets a devilish look on his face. "A true master? Oh, baby, say that again." He slides over closer to me.

I panic and giggle at the same time. *Bimbot alert.* "What are you doing? Go away!" I squeeze into the corner of the couch and hold my drink with two hands at my chest.

"What? No hotdog? No buns?"

I laugh. "No! No hotdog and no buns. Stay over there." I kick him a few times, but not hard. A thrill races through me when he grabs my foot and puts it in his lap. Scott does this to me sometimes, but it never feels like this when he does it.

Tarin's staring at the TV in mock contemplation. "Okay fine. I get it. You don't appreciate musical genius." He pauses and then turns to me. "But it's my turn now … truth or dare?"

I swallow with effort, holding out my glass. "Fill me up first?"

He takes the glass from me, hesitating just a few seconds as our fingers touch before sliding it away from me. "Do you believe in Freudian slips?"

I realize what I said as soon as he brings up the psychology. "No. Not at all. That's total bullshit." I'm lying, but he doesn't know that. I think people accidentally reveal their inner thoughts all the time, me included, and right now my inner thoughts are on one track: the people getting naked one.

"Liar." He stands, letting my foot drop to the couch. "Another Tarin's bubble gum special coming up."

I snort, enjoying my buzz, letting the fact that he's reading my mind disappear from my brain. "That's a stupid name for a drink."

"Shun the drink and you'll get stuck with beer."

"Love that name. Love it. Best name eh-var."

"That's what I thought."

He sounds so satisfied, I want to go over there and put him in a headlock. But I don't, because I know that would be a Freudian slip of another kind.

He comes back and hands me the drink. "Truth or dare. Don't play games now, this is serious." He *looks* serious too.

"I thought it was just a game," I say, stalling for time. I'm both afraid and excited about what he's going to make me do or have me tell him. Truth or dare is a dangerous game for amateurs like me to play.

He drops his head back on the couch and talks to the ceiling. "God spare me from girls who cannot handle the pressure of going head to head with The Tarin."

I kick him, harder this time. *The Tarin my ass.*

He traps my foot with his hand and clamps it to his side. The warmth coming through his t-shirt goes into my foot and makes its way up my leg.

"Fine. Just do it," I say, rising to his challenge. Screw not taking risks. It's just one game. "Ask me again."

He rolls his head sideways. "Truth or dare, Scarlett. Don't be chicken."

"Chicken?"

"Bawk! Bawk!"

"Fine! Truth!"

He rolls his eyes. "I knew it." He sits up, suddenly way too happy for my comfort. He puts his drink down again and turns slightly to face me. "Truth, huh? You probably thought that was a safe bet, right? That if you chose dare, you'd end up naked or something, right?"

I say nothing. He's reading my mind *again*, and the only thing worse than him reading my mind is him knowing he's doing it.

He smiles with the devil in his eyes again. "You so don't know how to play this game."

CHAPTER
TWENTY-SIX

HE SHIFTS POSITION ON THE couch so he can put both of my feet right at his crotch. He's facing me completely, close enough that I could reach over and touch his chest. His nearness is making me sweat. It's making me completely disregard my work, my policy about not getting personally involved, and the danger that a rock star can bring to a heart like mine.

"Truth, Scarlett. Do you like me?"

I burst out laughing. I was so not expecting that question.

He squeezes my feet, a confused half-smile coming out to tweak my heartbeat. "This isn't a joke. Why are you laughing?"

When I can finally speak again, I shrug. "I don't know … I guess because I was expecting something so devastating that I'd have to run from the room crying. Instead I'm getting one of those 'check yes or no' notes I used to get in second grade."

"That's not a big deal to you? Whether you like me or not?"

He looks hurt. I'm so touched by the little boy who's hiding somewhere inside Tarin that I lean forward and give him my best play-frown. "Oh, I'm sorry. I didn't mean it like that. Of course it's important."

He captures my hand - the one I'm petting his face with - and holds it against his cheek. "Okay then ... answer the question. Do you like me?"

He's dead serious and staring into my eyes as he challenges me. All the humor of the question disappears, and I see this as the trap it is. He's way, way, way too good at this game, and I've had way, way, way too much of that stupid drink.

"Uh ... okay ... the answer is ... yes. I like you." I try to pull my hand away, but he won't let me. He lets it come off his face, but then laces our fingers together. He's so close I can see the beard stubble growing in on his chin. It darkens his face and makes him seem sinister, but that only accentuates the bad boy image that's turning my insides to jelly. He looks like a gangster, even while I know he's an artist; it's an intoxicating combination.

"You have to give complete answers or you're not playing fair," he says. "I wrote a whole song with a kickass guitar solo at the end. Don't let me down, Scarlett. Give me your complete answer. None of this halfway bullshit."

I smile, but I'm so nervous my lips spasm in the middle of it, making me look like I'm having an attack. I let it drop away. "That is all of it," I respond lamely.

"Bullshit." He squeezes my foot. "I'm going to ask again, and if you don't answer completely, you have to pay the forfeit." He shakes his head slowly, as if he pities me.

"Pay the forfeit?" I take a big drink of my new cocktail. This one is stronger than the last one, and I'm glad for it. I take a second swig, this one just as big. The glass is half empty. Or maybe it's half full. I can't tell.

"The forfeit is ... you have to be my slave for an entire day."

I snort. "You just made that up."

"Nope, it's in the rule book. Look it up."

I don't want to look it up. The damaged, tortured part of me wants to be forced to be honest. It's the only way I can do it. I'm such a jerk.

"Fine. Ask again." I slam the rest of the drink down and put the glass on the table, wincing at the fire that travels down my throat and into my stomach. It churns and burns down there like lava in a volcano. I pray it doesn't erupt.

"Do. You. Like. Me? It's so simple. Just answer the question."

I take a deep breath and let it out loudly.

He takes my other hand and scoots closer so we're just a foot apart.

"This is stupid."

"Answer the question."

"It's totally juvenile. We're adults."

"Answer the question, Scarlett."

"We have a business relationship."

"You will be my slave. And I have to warn you … I'm getting really attached to the idea of ordering you around for a day."

I think about him doing that, and if there weren't going to be witnesses to my shame, it might actually be fun. But to imagine his group of bandmates, employees, and Scott as onlookers is to realize … no way in hell will that ever happen. And I might be a wimp and a freak sometimes, but I'm no one to back out of a bet, agreement, or any other kind of challenge.

"Yes. I like you. I like you a lot, okay? I wish I didn't like you, because it's really bad for business and really bad for *me*, but I do." I sigh loudly. "There. I said it. Is it my turn yet?"

"No, because you haven't given me everything. Let me help you." He shifts even closer, staring into my eyes. "What kind of *like* are we talking here?"

"You already asked your question," I say. My voice comes out a little weak because I'm getting lost in the dark green of his eyes. His eyeliner is smudged and it makes his irises glow with color.

"This is the same question, I'm just helping you answer completely. I'm doing you a favor since you find the idea of being my slave so unappealing."

"What's the question again?" I'm dizzy from the drinks, happy to think I might forget some of this by morning. I'd *better* forget this crap by morning or I'm going to have to get my money back on this alcohol.

"What kind of *like* are we talking here?" he says again.

I swallow, the sound so loud I'm sure he hears it. "The kind that is really stupid and dangerous and not allowed."

"Explain."

My nostrils flare. I'm afraid. He's pushing me to say things I don't want to say. "I can't."

"Let's talk slavery, then. We'll start with you giving me an ass massage at nine a.m. Have I told you how much I like ass massages? Deep tissue all the way, baby, none of that feather touch stuff. And I have a hairy ass, too, let me tell you."

"Fine, I'll explain. Please don't tell me about your hairy ass." I'm barely holding back the laughter. My emotions are a mess. I'm ready to laugh, cry, and yell, all at the same time. There could also be vomiting involved.

I blink a few times, trying to just put on my professional face and get this over with. What a terrible idea this game was. "Okay, here's the thing … I don't get involved with clients. It's bad business first of all, and second … I just don't. Austin was my first love and my only love. Being with him … it just … messed me up, okay? I got seriously messed up being with him and I can't do that to myself again. I almost didn't make it out on the other side."

He's rubbing his thumbs on the tops of my hands. It's strangely soothing, despite the fact that I'm saying things to him that I've never said to another human being. I'm not even sure I've said them to myself. And now that I've started, I can't seem to stop.

"He was my everything. I fell in love with him in junior high. I was there when he picked up his first guitar. Every song he wrote was pretty much about our life together. We were kids, but we loved hard and we loved deep. And there was Scott in the middle of all of it, and he became like my little brother …" I shake my head with the memories, dropping my gaze to our linked hands. "When Austin came into the fame-and-fortune part of the business, I was there. I saw and felt him slipping away, but I didn't realize how seriously bad it was until it was too late. He wouldn't listen to me anymore or let me have any influence in his life. His new friends blew me off. His agent acted like I was nothing and encouraged Austin to keep us apart." I'm upset at myself now. This is the worst part of my memories. "But I just didn't try hard enough. I should have forced him to listen to me, to do what I knew was right. I should have punched that agent right in the fucking face and told him what I knew was going to happen."

"You knew." Tarin says it with a soft voice that breaks at the last word.

I look up at him, wanting him to feel the pain in my heart right now, hoping it will help him see what I'm trying to do for him. "Yes. I knew. I saw him going downhill fast - lost in the drugs and the attention, and the bimbots and all those other bad influences - and I just stood off to the side feeling sorry for myself and for Scott. I didn't fight hard enough for him and I lost him. Scott lost him. The whole world lost him that night in Chicago, and I can never get that back."

"You have his music."

I shake my head. "No, I don't. I can't listen to it anymore. It breaks my heart all over again. I haven't listened to it since he died two years ago."

Tarin drops my hands, and I think for a second he's going to get up and leave me there. It's what I deserve. I let one of the greatest musicians of our time fade away to nothing.

But he surprises me, standing and grabbing my hands, pulling on them. "Stand up," he says.

I do what he orders because I really don't have any choice. He's a lot stronger than he looks.

He does the last thing I expect of him; he envelopes me in a hug and I stand there, too startled for a few seconds to react. My arms hang limply at my sides.

He speaks over my head. "What happened to Austin is a real shame, but it's not your fault." His arms go tighter. "You hear me? It's not your fault." His voice goes rough. "Maybe it's other people's fault, but not yours. You're not guilty of anything but loving him."

My body relaxes a little at a time. He's giving me understanding and comfort. Forgiveness in a way. I wish it was enough. "That's easy for you to say."

He's holding me so tight now I feel like I'm in a straightjacket, but I don't complain because I like it. It's as if my sins aren't sins in his eyes and absolution is more intoxicating than those cocktails I just drank.

"It's *not* easy for me to say. You have no idea how difficult this is for me." His words are loaded with meaning that I don't understand. I can feel their weight.

"What do you mean?"

He just hugs me more, moving his arms up and down my back, making the friction build between us, both under his hands and where the fronts of our bodies are practically melded together.

"Tell me, Tarin." My arms come up, and I place my hands gently on his back. I love the feel of his lean muscles beneath his shirt. My hands move up of their own accord, gliding over the soft cotton, feeling the heat of the skin I cannot touch. If I do, I'll be lost, and I cannot get lost in Tarin.

"I wish I could tell you. I really wish I could." His face moves to my neck and his breath gives me chills.

My nipples go hard under my bra and I press against him without even realizing what I'm doing. I just need him to do something with this feeling that's coming over me. There's an urgency inside me that's too strong for me to ignore or stop. I don't know what it is or where it's coming from, only that it's making me hot and jittery and wanting to see him with a lot less clothes on. The alcohol is doing what it does best - making my inhibitions fade to black.

"Truth or dare," I whisper as his lips touch the sensitive skin of my neck.

"Dare," he says back, his voice deeper and raspy.

I say the first thing that comes to my mind as my fingers dig slightly into his back. "I dare you to take your shirt off."

He pulls away without a sound or complaint and yanks his shirt off. One second he's standing there in a Quicksilver surf shirt and the next, he's half-naked tattooed perfection just inches away from me.

I'm fascinated by his skin. He steps closer and my finger comes up to touch his chest where there's a tattoo of a dragon wrapped around a skull. I follow the beast's tail down to Tarin's stomach and stop at the word *Guilty*, tracing each letter with my finger.

He grabs my hand and holds it in a firm grip, pulling it away from his abdomen.

I look up and his jaw is clamped shut. He looks angry.

Cold sweats come over me as embarrassment takes hold. "Are you mad?" I ask softly, worried I've totally misconstrued every signal he's ever sent. And now I've made him take his shirt off. My complete lack of finesse or professionalism makes my face and neck burn with shame. I'm a joke. A walking, talking, bull-shitting joke.

"No," he says, his voice still rough. "I'm fucking turned on way too much, so unless you want to be naked on that couch in about two seconds, better look but not touch."

He releases my hand and it floats there in the space between us. It takes me less than a second to make my decision.

.

CHAPTER
TWENTY-SEVEN

I STEP BACK, PUTTING SPACE between us. I turn to go. "I'm sorry, I shouldn't have ..."

His hand is on my arm and I'm spun around before I can get the rest of my sentence out.

"Bullshit. You wanted to touch me." He's gripping my wrist between us. His eyes carry the biggest challenge I've ever seen. He speaks in a completely relaxed tone of voice, with just a slight edge of sexual confidence. "Touch me. Don't be afraid. You know you want to."

I'm breathing so hard it could almost be called panting at this point. I don't know what to say. His anger looks so good on him, arousing me more than I ever have been before. The sexual energy I felt with Austin was always an eagerness coated with the candy floss of young love. Tarin is making something entirely different come over me. Something way more adult and way more hot.

"I can't," I whisper between breaths.

"Scarlett, don't do this to us." He's begging at the same time he's angry at me.

"Us?"

He yanks me closer and I go without a fight. Putting his free hand behind my neck, he pulls my face closer to his, speaking in a soft voice. "I'm going ninety percent here. This isn't me forcing you. All you gotta do is ten percent. That's it. Ten percent and then you get all of me."

He draws me to him. Closer and closer my mouth gets to his. I've never wanted a man more in my life than I want him right now. He stops pulling me when our lips are an inch apart.

"Here's where you decide," he whispers, his sweet soda breath puffing in my face. "I did the ninety, you do the ten."

Visions are racing through my mind as if I'm dying and I'm seeing my life in review. I see my first kiss with Austin, us laughing in bed together, seeing him on stage and then drugged out on a couch backstage in some city I can't remember the name of, his face in the coffin, Scott's tear-stained cheeks, and then Tarin, angry at me, drunk, scared, laughing, his tattooes, his efforts to be kind … it all adds up to me being stupid and careless and too drunk to do the right thing.

I ante up the ten percent and close the distance between us.

Our lips meet and Tarin doesn't hesitate to go deep with his tongue. The tide of sexual energy flows in and washes over my reticence, pulling it away and drowning it in my deepest desires. To feel him against me, to have his hands on my body, to know that just for a moment, this messed up man who can make music that breaks my heart wants to be with me and be a part of my world, it blows my mind. I don't know who I am anymore. I'm not The Normalizer anymore. I'm just a girl. A really horny one.

His hands are everywhere, pulling off my clothes. My shoes go flying, my dress gets unzipped, and in the middle of it all, our mouths are roaming everywhere. First he's kissing me on the lips and then the shoulder of my dress is down and he's at my breast, sucking and pulling at my nipple. The pain is erotic and it makes me moan loudly as I pant with anticipation over what's to come. He squeezes my breast hard as he sucks some more.

I can't find a good place to put my hands. All I can reach is his back and head. I want to touch him everywhere, somewhere that will make him feel the electric shocks like he's giving me right now.

He moves to my other breast, pushing my dress down to my waist and unsnapping my bra with one hand. I'm naked from the hips up, and the cool air conditioning mixed with the licking saliva he leaves behind gives me hot and cold chills. I moan with the suction he puts to my nipple again. His other hand is busy massaging the one he's already teased, and I'm beginning to feel like I'm going to have an orgasm before he's even really started. I never knew my breasts could be this sensitive.

"Tarin," I gasp, quickly becoming overwhelmed by the sensations. "I can't … I can't…" I mean to say that I can't handle the feelings, but he reacts like I mean I can't be with him and he's having none of that second-guessing crap.

He growls and pushes my dress the rest of the way down to my feet.

His pants are next; he somehow manages to get them off while never taking his lips off my body. "Fuck that," he says between kissing and sucking and licking, "this is on. This is *so* on right now. Don't say no to me or it'll fucking kill me. I'm not kidding, Scarlett, I need you."

He needs me. I know he needs me. But I also know he doesn't need *this* from me. I'm a selfish bitch though, because I put my hands on his cock and run my fingers along the length of it. If I'm going to fuck this job up, I'm going to fuck it up all the way.

"I need you too, Tarin," I say, sliding a leg up his thigh. It's been so, so long since I've had sex. Years now. I haven't wanted to until this moment with this man.

He roars and picks me up by my hiked-up thigh, flipping me around to throw me down on my back on the couch. He leans over and grabs the edge of my panties and yanks them down. The thin wisp of fabric disappears over his shoulder as he lowers himself down to me.

He kneels on the edge of the cushions with one knee while he gets a condom out of his wallet from the ground. It's on and he's ready so fast, I don't have time to cool down at all before his cock is pressing against my opening.

"No more foreplay?" I say as a lame joke, trying to pretend this isn't as serious as it is.

"Fuck foreplay. I'll give it to you after if you still want it." And then he's inside me, buried to the hilt.

I arch up and shout with the shock and pressure. It's not unpleasant ... anything but. I've just never been taken so fully and so abruptly in all my life. And I don't ever want to go back to soft and meticulous lovemaking again. My other sexual experiences suddenly seem like fumbling in the dark compared to this.

He's pumping into me with everything he's got, showing no mercy. Sweat drips down off his face and lands on mine, mingling with my own saltiness. In the full light of the nearby lamp I can see his face perfectly. He's staring at me, and he looks furious.

"Tarin," I say, barely able to get the word out. Feelings are coming over me that are alien to my world. I want to feel him deeper. Harder. I don't know what's happening. I cling to his back, my nails digging in for purchase, and my legs are wrapped around his. I meet him with every thrust, practically throwing myself up at him and gasping with pleasure when the pain of our sharp impacts become pleasure of a sort I've never known. It's so savage, but I want nothing more than to disappear in the wildness he brings.

"Scarlett," he growls in response, still staring at me, and my heart flips over and over. He's possessing me, mind, body, and soul. In this brief moment in time, I'm gone. I've answered his Truth question and yet I'm paying the forfeit too. I am his slave; I'll do anything he wants just so long as I can keep feeling this.

He puts his hand under my ass and squeezes my cheek, effectively spreading my folds from behind and making his cock hit deeper into them. He's pushing against my clit and it's causing something to happen inside me. *Heat. It's coming for me.*

He's too intense. His body on me, his cock invading my very essence, his expression. He's consuming me. Overwhelming me. I feel myself falling away.

"What are you doing?" I sound like I'm crying.

"I'm fucking you, Scarlett." He says it so calmly and matter-of-factly it sends a bolt of sensuality into my center, and I scream with the thrill of it. I'm a sorry mess and he's in complete control. Oh, how the tables have turned.

"That's right, babe, let it out," he says while he strokes in and out of me, going a little easier now. Here is the finesse I thought I didn't want anymore, and oh god, he's so good at that part too. "You know you like it," he says, and there's no way I could even hope to convince him of the lie that I don't.

I do exactly as he wants; I let my emotions out and fuck him back with abandon. As I meet him thrust for thrust, I yell with every bit of passion I'm feeling. I'm someone else tonight. A slut. A loud slut. Someone who has zero regrets over the silly, stupid, careless things she does.

"Oh, God, you feel so good," he moans, his cool slipping a little. "Do you feel that?" He's lost too now. His eyes are closed and his expression reveals surprise, pain maybe. I feel strong and in control, no longer the weepy woman swept away by the beast of a man. I'm doing this to him. My body and my voice are making him come to heel.

"Yes," I whisper. It's all I can do. More moans come from my throat.

"I can't hold back much longer, babe. You gotta meet me there."

He called me *babe*. He's waiting for me. The idea that this selfish, big headed jerk is doing this for me when he doesn't have to is all I need. I have power over him. I am both his slave and his master. It brings a wave of pleasure that has me clinging to him and screaming with ecstasy.

He shouts too as his jerky movements bring his pleasure too.

CHAPTER
TWENTY-EIGHT

FOR A LONG TIME AFTER it's over we lay on the couch, clinging to one another. When we're both too sensitive and wiped out to move, he rolls off me and lands on his back on the floor.

"Ow."

I giggle, turning on my side to look down at him.

"Do you have any idea how bad I want a cigarette now?" he moans.

"Too bad. No smokes and no pity from me, either."

His bandage is hanging off the side of his eye and his face is screwed up with pain.

I reach down and press the bandaid gently back into place. "Sorry about that."

He grabs my hand and kissing my finger. "Don't apologize for the best sex of your life."

"My life?" I try to pull my hand away but he won't let me go.

"Yeah, your life. It was, wasn't it?"

I scowl at him. "Shut up, you idiot. That's so not sexy you know … to brag when a condom is still hanging off your dick."

He yanks on my hand, pulling me almost off the couch.

"Let go!" I screech, pretending to be angry.

"Get over here, slave," he says, pulling me the rest of the way down. I'm on top of him now, the floppy used condom between us.

I hesitate. "What'd you just call me?"

"You heard me. *Slave*."

"Oh, no freaking way am I your slave. I answered the question."

"Apparently, you didn't. See … you said you didn't like me that way. But since you just fucked my brains out, you were obviously lying. You *do* like me that way, ergo, you are my slave starting tomorrow at nine a.m. with ass massages. Make sure the oil is warm, by the way. I don't want to cramp up."

I try to slap him but he catches my hands and traps them, stealing a kiss when I'm not paying attention.

I try to fight the idea of ass massages, using logic as my weapon. I don't let the fact that truth or dare could never be logical stop me. "First of all, the game is over. No going back. And second, sex is not necessarily anything. Sex can be just sex."

He goes quiet and still. Staring up at me, he says, "Are you trying to tell me that was just sex? That this is all it was for you?"

I bite my lip to keep the lie from slipping through. I can't say anything or I'm sunk. I struggle to get up and he lets me. As soon as I'm free of him, I grab my dress and panties out from under his legs and put them on.

While I put myself together he takes the condom off and wraps it up in a tissue, depositing it in a trashcan by the wet bar before pulling on his jeans.

The silence is awful. Painful, even.

When I'm dressed I stand up straight and face him. He's there in his jeans just staring at me. I cannot read his expression, it's so guarded.

"I'm sorry. I didn't mean to hurt your feelings," I finally say.

"Feelings? Who's got feelings?" He shrugs like he doesn't have a care in the world.

His words are like a knife cutting me deep. My soul is bleeding, I know it is. But I soldier on, because that's what I do best.

"Okay, good. I'm just saying … I know this was a mistake, one we won't be repeating, but thanks. I mean … yeah. Thanks." I am so lame, I can't even stand myself. Who thanks a guy for banging her on his couch?

"No, thank *you*," he says, his voice sarcastic but distinctly joyful at the same time. "I'm really looking forward to having you at my beck and call tomorrow. It's going to be fun."

I sigh. "Tarin, we're not doing that."

"Double or nothing."

I cross my arms. "No."

"Yes. Double or nothing or I shall call you Petula."

"Petula?" I'm trying not to laugh.

"That's a slave name. I read it somewhere."

"No. I'm not going to be Petula."

"Double or nothing or I tell my agent I can't work with you because I slept with you."

I gasp with outrage. "You wouldn't! You can't! That's not fair! You did this too!"

He shrugs. "All's fair in love and war … and since you keep trying to convince yourself you don't even like me, I guess that makes this *war*. Double or nothing." He takes a step closer.

I tap my foot. He has me over a barrel and he knows it. My Frankenstein cocktail buzzing brain cannot compute a way out of this mess except by taking his challenge. Maybe it doesn't want to not figure out the smart answer. *I can do this. I can tell the truth or take a dare and get it over with. I just can't tell him I like him or how I really feel.*

"Fine. Truth or dare, but you can't ask the same question."

A very satisfied smile comes over his face as he moves closer.

I'm nervous again. My heart is racing. He's staring at me, the smudged eyeliner, scruffy beard, and tattoos making him look like a rocker demon about to possess my soul. I feel like letting him do it too, which is the scariest part of this scenario.

"Truth or dare, little girl," he asks in a low growl.

"Truth," I whisper, afraid if I say dare he'll make me touch him again, and I know if I do that there will be no going back.

He closes the space between us and stops just in front of me. "Okay … tell the truth … if I were to get down on my knees right here in front of you, and put my tongue between your legs and lick your clit until you come screaming, would you stop me? Or would you let me do it?"

I nearly faint at his words. My jaw drops open. I stare at him and in that moment, I know he's dead serious. He will do this to me if I *just don't say no.*

I practically come in my underwear just looking at him. Two licks. That's all it will take. *Wham, bam, thank you ma'am.*

My mouth moves around in imitation of speaking, but again, words escape me.

He reaches up and puts his hand over my breast, squeezing it and pinching the nipple through my dress. He's so bold and so uncouth, and I wouldn't change that about him for all the money in the world.

I moan. "Tarin … this is so unfair…"

Voices come from the hallway. A split second after I move away from Tarin, the door bursts open and Scott walks in. It's like a cold shower, but with people watching me take it. Horrible doesn't begin to describe how it feels.

"Yo, yo, yo! Don't all you rock-n-roll fans rush me at once. I don't want you mess up my new threads."

I turn around, my face frozen in shock and horror at what might have just happened.

"What?" Scott looks at me, his expression going from pleased to confused. He looks down at himself. "You don't like it do you? Dammit, I knew it was too much. Why didn't you say anything before I got up on stage?"

I shake my head, unable to respond.

"Dude, it's good. You're all good." Tarin walks past me like we weren't about to lick each other from head to toe in the middle of his family room and shakes Scott's hand. "Congrats, man. You got skills. If you want, we can hit the studio tomorrow."

"Yeah, sure, that'd be awesome." Scott's back to being thrilled with himself and I'm working on recovering from sexual shock.

I walk slowly around to the couch and pick up my shoes that are next to the coffee table.

"I'm going to bed," I say, my voice not my own. I shove my bra under the couch with my foot. I'll get it later.

"But I just got here," whines Scott. "Don't you want to celebrate my awesome self?"

I kiss him on the cheek as I walk by. "Tomorrow. When I'm not as exhausted. You are awesome, though. I am your biggest fan of all time."

"Jack wants you to call him," Scott says as I walk out the door.

I'm able to remain silent until I pass through the door. Then I scream at the top of my lungs when I get out into the hallway, no longer able to manage the pressure. The frustration echoes around my head, banging into my skull and making me wish I'd just held it all in. *Holy headache.*

"What's her problem?" asks Scott.

"She's just frustrated. She has to give me an ass massage tomorrow."

I shut the door to the family room behind me to keep from hearing anymore of Tarin's nonsense. There is no way in hell I'm touching his ass, even though I now know it's not really as hairy as he made it out to be.

I trudge up the stairs and go into my bathroom. The shower removes every last trace of Tarin off my body, but it can't erase the feelings that still plague my system and the memories of his face and body that are burned into my brain.

Still wearing a damp bathrobe, I collapse into bed and fall into a restless sleep. I dream all night of Austin, a ghost standing just out of my reach. He just floats there and stares at me, saying nothing. I beg him for his forgiveness, but it doesn't come for me. The only thing I can feel is pain, and the worst part is that I don't know if it's his or mine.

CHAPTER TWENTY-NINE

I'M AWAKENED BY SOMEONE TAPPING on my door. I slide off the bed, knowing before my feet even hit the floor that today is going to be a major chore. I have a headache, either from the terrible cocktails or the self-loathing that has taken me over, and my tongue tastes like I've been licking cat butts all night. The clock says it's seven o'clock in the morning.

I crack the door open, fully expecting to see Scott there. My heart drops to the floor when I realize it's not him.

"Time to work out, sunshine. Why aren't you dressed yet?" Tarin's looking me in the eye like nothing happened last night. He's freshly shaved and showered, the bastard.

I put my hand over my mouth so my breath doesn't leak out into the hallway. "I overslept. I'll be out in a few minutes."

"Are you sick?"

"No. Just a little hungover."

"Mmm…" He nods his head. "I hear great sex'll do that to ya."

"Shut up." I close the door in his face. He walks away laughing, and I rest my head against the wood frame, a long sigh breezing out of my lungs. *I am so going to wish last night never happened.*

I slog through the tasks of showering and dressing for our morning workout. I put on my navy blue running shorts, a white jog bra, a hot pink tank top, and light green running shoes. It looks like a toy store vomited on me, but I don't care enough to try and match anything; I'm too hungover with regret.

Everyone is down in the foyer waiting for me thirty minutes after my wake-up call, dressed in workout gear that's way less obnoxious than mine. Except for Scott of course. His shoes amp my headache up another couple notches with their horrible orange fluorescence. He has a collection of truly awful footwear, but today he's outdone himself.

Scott smiles up at me. "Ready for a run?"

I shake my head, trying not to smile back. "You're enjoying this torture way too much." I hold up my hand to block the view of his feet. "Could you please turn off your shoes? They're giving me a migraine."

"That's just the booze talking," he says, stepping outside ahead of me.

As I walk through the front door, Ricky says, "Tarin made you one of those nasty bubble gum drinks, didn't he?"

"Two of them actually," I said.

"Damn, that ain't right," he says to Tarin. "Taking advantage of the boss like that."

"Hey, I didn't force her." Tarin's pretending to be all put-out when I know very well he's totally proud of himself. He's a giant, walking penis throbbing with testosterone right now. "She did everything she did last night without any encouragement from me."

I snort loudly but say nothing as we jog down the driveway en masse. My heart-rate is already elevated now, thanks to Tarin, and I haven't even left the property. Damn him and his casual sexy grins and attitude. I hate that this mean-boy gone nice is affecting me like this.

We get to the sidewalk and Zach is in the lead followed by Tarin. Scott and I are last, jogging side-by-side. Leonard must have stayed at the house because I haven't seen him at all this morning. I'm glad Tarin's in front of me and not behind me watching my butt, or next to me making me all hot and bothered. It's bad enough I have to watch his back, ass, and legs and know that I was under him on his couch just a few short hours ago. The memories make me blush.

Guilty. So, so guilty.

"So, d'ya like the show last night?" asks Scott. He's playing it casual, but I know my answer's important to him.

"You were awesome. I'm sorry I took off, I just couldn't listen to that last song." The memory of the lyrics tries to bust into my conscious mind, but I beat it back.

"I know. Sorry about that. I tried to tell Jack not to do it but he wouldn't listen."

"I wish he wouldn't push me into a corner like that." I'm getting stressed just thinking about it. He should have known better.

"I told him you don't react well to pressure, but he's doing his own thing. He said …" Scott cuts off in the middle of his sentence, and all I hear now is the pounding of our feet on the sidewalk.

Row hedges and trees go by in a blur as we eat up the pavement with our group stride. Sweat is running down my back and my heavy breathing belies the pain I'm in running hungover like I am, but this conversation is not over.

Scott continues. "Anyway, I'm happy with how it went. We're going to do another one in a couple weeks."

"What did Jack say?" I ask. Maybe I don't want to know the answer, but I'm not thrilled with the idea of him and Scott talking about me behind my back.

"I think I'd like to plead the fifth on this one." Scott tries to speed up, but I grab his shirt and pull him back.

"Not happening, but nice try. Tell me or else."

"Or else what? You'll make me run before nine in the morning in the eighty-five degree heat? Oh … wait … already suffering that torture. Try again."

I lower my voice so Tarin won't hear me. "Just shut up and tell me or you're going to be giving His Highness an ass massage after this run."

"Was he serious about that slave stuff?" Scott asks, sounding way too happy about it.

I punch him in the arm. "Seriously ... shut up and tell me."

"Fine. But don't shit on the messenger, okay? I was just there listening. I didn't contribute to the madness."

"Still waiting..."

"He said he thinks that he needs to do you a solid. Help you like you helped him."

I frown, confused. "What?"

"I know, right? The guy's wishin' and fishin'. That's what I told him, but he's convinced."

"Convinced of *what?*"

"That you need him. That you need help."

My brain tries to put that together. "That makes no sense at all."

"According to him it does. And since he's helping me write some great stuff, I didn't argue too hard. But I swear, I did try to get him not to play that song." He runs for a few more pavement squares before he finishes. "You know, though, if you remove the part where he's throwing his heart out there on the street for you to run over with your car, the song's good. I mean, the melody's solid, the lyrics are rip-your-heart-out amazing, and the crowd loved it. It was a five-panty hit. I swear, a pair of red lace ones landed right on my face after the first chorus, like it was shot from a panty cannon or something. They smelled good too, like bubble gum. Weird right? Who puts bubble gum in their underwear? Anyway, he's going to release it as a single."

I feel like I've been bashed in the chest with a baseball bat, the way my heart is caving in on itself. "Like *hell* he is," I growl, taking a sharp right turn out into the road. I yell over my shoulder as the group of guys slows down, each of them looking over their shoulders at me in confusion. "Go ahead! I'll meet you back at the house, keep going without me!"

Scott takes off first, running on his toes. The little wanker is more than happy not to get in the middle of the shit storm he just conjured up for me. Tarin is the last to continue on, but he does it, turning around to jog backwards. He lifts his hands up, as if to ask what the hell I'm doing. I just wave him off and continue back towards the house.

I need to find my cell and call Jack right away before he goes too far down that road. No frigging way do I want to see that song about my life and my issues going public. Anyone who knows him and what we went through will realize the song's about me and my personal business. Word will spread and then the whole world will know. He needs to be perfectly clear about what it will mean to me before he makes that decision. I pray our friendship is more valuable to him than the money.

CHAPTER
THIRTY

AROUND THE LAST BEND on the trip back and see Tarin's driveway ahead of me. There's a gate that connects the high fence circling the property. It should be locked up tight, but for some reason it's open. I could swear I remember hearing it swing slowly closed as we were leaving, but maybe I'm just thinking about another time that happened or another gate from my past. There have been so many.

I slow down to a jog and go through, stopping only to press in a code on the keypad that will shut the gate behind me. Once I'm sure it's closed all the way and not opening back up, I run up the driveway to the front of the house and go to the front door. I try the front handle, even though I'm almost positive it will be locked. It swings open easily.

Frowning in confusion, I hesitate before going inside. *That's weird. Why didn't Ricky or Zach lock it up behind us?* This door has a keypad too, but when I glance over at it, the light is green. No alarm is set and everything looks normal. The door and keypad should only be like this when one of us inside. *What the hell?*

I walk into the foyer. "Leonard? Are you in here?" I had assumed he was in his place behind the main house, but I guess not. He must be inside, maybe having breakfast.

No one answers my call.

I walk swiftly to the kitchen but find it empty. There are half-filled coffee cups on the counter, but no Leonard.

I turn towards the hallway again, yelling, "Marta?!" The housekeeper who's here most afternoons might have come early. I hope it's her and not just us being really careless and leaving things open like this.

Still no answer.

Walking out into the foyer again, I hear a noise upstairs.

The hairs on my neck stand up. Leonard has no reason to be upstairs when we're not home, and Marta *always* starts in the kitchen. Josh told me yesterday that it's some weird superstition she has about always cleaning the house in the same order: first kitchen, then bathrooms, laundry, and bedrooms, and everything else last. Coffee cups on the counter means she isn't here yet.

I take the stairs two at a time, first stopping in my room to get my phone. It's sitting on the bedside table where I left it. I open it up and just for the hell of it and press in the numbers 9-1-1. I don't hit the dial button, but I'm prepared to if necessary.

Leaving my room, I take a left, going in the direction I know Tarin's room to be. If someone has broken in, it's either a thief or a nutty fan, and that's where they'll be. Guest rooms are for amateurs.

I walk down the carpeted hallway quietly, my thumb hovering over the green button on my cell. The door to Tarin's room is slightly ajar and there are muffled noises coming from inside.

My heart is beating like mad. I want to call the cops and run, but if it's not an intruder and I call in the troops, there will be all kinds of crap press to deal with, and I don't want that kind of attention on Tarin right now; things are going too well. All we need to do is alert the crazies that his house is easy to get into, and we'll be up to our assholes in the need for massive security. A fence, gate, locks and alarms along with a couple of bodyguards should be enough in theory. Unfortunately, nutbags don't need much to construe an invitation; it's almost as if one person gets in they feel like they're all welcome to visit.

I push open the door. It swings in slowly, just a whisper coming from the soft carpet being brushed by the wood.

There's a tall girl in shorts, a t-shirt, and white cheer sneakers standing in front of Tarin's dresser and one of the drawers is open.

"Posey?" I say, my eyes practically bugging out of my head.

She whips around, one of Tarin's t-shirts in her hands as she holds it up to her chest.

She screams in surprise for a few seconds and then stops to yell at me. "What are *you* doing here?" She actually has the nerve to sound annoyed with me.

My heart is pounding almost painfully in my chest. This girl's just gone from crazed fan to criminal stalker in my mind, and I'm alone with her. *Holy bad luck.* "The better question is what the fuck are you doing here?" I look at my phone and press the green button. *Fucking lunatic. Way to blow everything I've been working on.* I quickly add up the cost and hassle of all the extra security we're going to need to bring in.

"Who are you calling?" she demands to know, flinging her arms down to her sides. The t-shirt dangles near her knee. "Are you calling Tarin? Because *good*. I hope you are. I need to talk to him."

"No, Posey, I'm not calling Tarin. I'm call the police."

I'm completely unprepared for her reaction. She bum-rushes me and rams into my torso like I'm some kind of football tackle dummy. Her boney shoulder hits me full in the chest, taking me down in a big way. Tarin's t-shirt goes up to cover my face as I'm slammed into the open door behind me. I hit it hard enough to lose my breath and fall to the floor gasping for air.

Posey's still on her feet, and her pointy shoes dig into my face and ribs as she kicks me over and over. "You bitch! You horrible ugly, sweaty bitch! You're ruining *everything!* You don't belong here! You don't belong *anywhere!*"

I curl into a fetal position to protect my soft parts, still not able to catch enough of my breath to fight back. I hate that I'm so vulnerable to this bimbot's attack, but until my lungs cooperate, I'm a sitting duck. Or a lying down one. The pain is relentless.

Posey's voice has entered a new, higher octave. "I hate you! I hate you! You're nobody to Tarin, *nobody!* No one loves him like I do, do you hear me? Do you hear me?"

I'm finally able to pull the shirt off my face, and I catch a glimpse of her red-mottled face before her sneaker catches me in the chin.

I reach out and grab the closest thing I can find as bright specks of light swim before my eyes. A baby song trickles into my head … *Twinkle, twinkle little star…*

Her ankle is suddenly in my grasp, and I hang on for dear life. As the flow of air re-establishes itself inside my lungs and the stars fade away my strength comes back and I yank on her with everything I've got. She stumbles and then goes down next to me on the floor.

Spinning partway around on my back while still holding onto her ankle, I use my feet to defend myself. My ribs are aching too much to throw a punch, so I kick the ever-loving shit out of her thighs and crotch and don't stop, even when a voice finally comes over my cell phone.

"Nine-one-one … what is your emergency?"

I don't know exactly where my phone is, but it's near my head somewhere, so I just start yelling.

"Intruder in the house! Tarin Kilgour's residence! The musician from the band *By Degrees!* Beverly Hills!" I can't for the life of me remember his address. I hope I've given her enough information to find me.

"I need your name and a description of the intruder, ma'am."

"Fuck you!" yells Posey. "Give me that goddamn phone, dammit!" She struggles to sit up and reach for my cell, but I give her a running shoe to the face, making her fall back again.

I keep kicking, but her foot slips out of my sweaty grip. She's crawled out of my way, but I can tell by the way she's eyeing my pin-wheeling legs, she doesn't want to eat any more of my sneakers than she already has. All those hours on the stationary bike are paying off.

I yell again, hoping the operator can hear me. "My name is Scarlett Barnes and I work with Tarin Kilgour! The intruder's name is …" I'm cut off by her struggle for my phone. When I kick her away, I continue. "She's an unwelcome fan of Tarin's! She broke into the house while he was out and she's in the process of taking some of his things!"

"I was not taking anything!" she screeches as she stands somewhat unsteadily on her feet. She sways there, out of her mind with anger. "And I'm not an intruder! Tarin loves me and I love him!"

"Get over it, freak!" I yell at her. I've officially lost my cool and I don't care about her delicate psyche anymore or the fact that all of this will be on the operator's recording. "You're just another bimbot deluded fan! He doesn't give a shit about you!"

She freezes in place, hunched over, her make-up starting to smear a little and her hair a crazy mess. Backing up, she points a shaking finger at me. "You don't know anything about Tarin and me." Her voice is quavering.

The operator speaks again and I can barely hear her. I look over and see my phone turned upside down, the speakers facing the carpet. I pick it up in time to hear her say, "We're sending someone to the house now. My advice is to not engage with this intruder and just leave the premises until she can be apprehended."

"Yeah, sounds like a good idea," I say, attempting to stand. My ribs are aching, and as get more upright, I shift to the side a little. A sharp, stabbing pain sears into my guts and makes my breath catch in my throat. "Fuck," I grunt out, bending towards the pain, trying to make it stop. "You fucking broke my ribs, you freak." I look up in time to see her nostrils flare.

"You broke your own ribs, coming after me like that."

"Coming after you? After *you*? Are you fucking kidding me? How deluded can a person possibly be?"

"Ms. Barnes, I suggest you leave the premises," says the voice over the phone.

"Yeah, well it's not that easy, actually."

"I'm not deluded," says the freak, lifting her chin, "I'm in love. Love can make you do crazy things, but that doesn't mean it's wrong."

"Yes, actually, it does. What you're doing is wrong. You need therapy and medication." I resort to begging. The pain is bad. I can't move enough to escape. "Please just get out of here."

She starts crying. "Tarin loves me."

I shake my head, backing up until I'm leaning against the wall. "No, he doesn't. He doesn't love anyone but himself."

"No!"

I nod. "Yes."

She moves around the side of his bed, never taking her eyes off me. "You don't know about love. You're empty inside. I can see it."

"Wrong." I slide down the wall a little, my legs apparently deciding that injured ribs are too heavy.

She stops when she's in front of Tarin's nightstand. "You want Tarin for yourself, don't you?"

I shake my head. "God, somebody shoot me." Her words combined with the pain make me nauseated. I'm afraid I'm going to barf right here on Tarin's silk carpeting. With my luck I'll probably fall in it too, making the thought of it doubly awful.

Her eyes flash anger, and her color goes up again. "Oh my god! That's it! You want Tarin for yourself. That's what this is all about! This isn't about him not loving me or me having problems … this is about you and your sick little infatuation with Tarin!"

My butt hits the ground, and I drop my face into my hand, using my other to prop myself up. I half whisper, half moan, "Jesus Christ save me from delusional nutbags." I swallow over and over to keep my stomach contents where they belong.

I hear a drawer open and lift my eyes in time to see her pulling a handgun from the nightstand.

My heart stops beating for what seems like forever. My salivary glands go into overdrive. The vomiting is near.

The gun comes up and she stares at it, almost mystified. And then a big grin comes over her face as she looks at me. "Tarin keeps a gun in our bedroom to protect us from people like you."

"Jesus fucking Christ." I lift the phone to my ear with monumental effort. It jitters against my head, I'm shaking so bad. My heart starts beating again, only now it's going a mile a minute. "She's got a gun," I say to the operator. My voice is all over the place. "I'm pretty sure she's going to shoot me."

CHAPTER
THIRTY-ONE

GOD, IF YOU'RE OUT THERE *listening, I seriously did not mean it when I said I wanted someone to shoot me. If you get me out of this, I swear I'll never be sarcastic again.* I hate the Fates for allowing my sarcasm to raise its ugly head at exactly the wrong moment, just when the universe was willing to grant me one wish. I hope God doesn't take my request itself as sarcastic and allow a bullet to enter my brain as a lesson in humility.

Everything takes on a surreal quality. The details of the room fade except for two things: Posey and the gun she's pointing at me. Their focus is so sharp for me, I can see the nubbed texture on the grip of the weapon and the way her finger is hovering just in front of the trigger. It's like I'm in a movie, and I'm so into my role, it feels real. But not real. I'm so confused.

This can't be real. I'm just here so I can call someone on the phone. I can't remember who it is or why I was calling him. I'm wearing jogging clothes. Am I going jogging? There's a high-pitched ringing in my ears and it's getting louder and louder. *Beeeeeeeeeeeeeee…*

The gun looks heavier than Posey expected it to be. She goes from one-handing the weapon to using both hands. She walks around the bed and stops at the far corner of it. There's still a lot of bedroom between us, but I'm a big enough target that I don't think she'll miss.

I hate the idea that I'm going to be killed by someone so stupid; it's like an insult to my own intelligence or something. Outrage over the unfairness of it clears my mind just a bit. *Why can't it be a smart person about to murder me right now, dammit!*

The ringing in my ears stops just in time for her words to come across loud and clear.

"I think I *am* going to shoot you," she says, smiling like I just gave her the best idea she's heard all year. She reminds me of that guy in The Shining with her maniacal grin. "Tarin will thank me. He'll be glad I stopped you from messing up his life. What are you doing in here anyway? Are you stalking him? He's not going to appreciate that. He'll totally thank me for shooting you and stopping you in your tracks. This is totally self-defense." She points the gun higher, aiming it at my face.

"Tarin will *not* thank you. Tarin will hate you until his dying day if you kill me, since I'm his … sister." I have no idea where that BS came from, but I feel inspired, like there's a guardian angel watching over me and whispering in my ear. And then I actually *hear* Austin's voice in my head. *Easy, now, babe. You can do this.*

Tears leap to my eyes and my heart spasms painfully. "Oh, God, Austin … are you here?"

Posey backs her head up, genuinely thrown off. "Austin? His sister? What are you talking about? Tarin doesn't have a sister, he's an only child."

I shake my head, my hair turning into knots against the wall as it rubs. "No, he has a sister. Half-sister. It's me. He's my brother. We're totally close. If you kill me it'll break his heart." *Please let her buy my bullshit!*

She slowly lowers the gun. Her self-satisfied smile wavers. "I don't remember reading about you online. Wikipedia doesn't say anything about him having a sister. Neither does his website."

I try to smile reassuringly at her. She's almost falling for my stupid story, and even though I have no idea where to go from here, I have to keep it up. Fighting the tears that want to wash me away, I open my mouth, hoping the ghost of Austin will put words in there for me.

He doesn't.

"What's wrong with you?" she asks, finally lowering her hand to her side. Then her face brightens. "Ooooohhh, I get it…." She smiles at me like I'm a little infant or something. "He keeps you hidden because you're *special*."

She looks pointedly at my clothing and my open-mouthed silent scream.

Do it! Do the crazy eyes! Austin's whispering in my head again.

I nod my head slowly at Posey, crossing my eyes for effect. It makes Scott crazy when I do this; only one eye goes in and the other goes off to the side a little. He says it makes him queasy. Austin always thought it was hilarious.

"Oh my god … are you like, *retarded* or something?"

I try to drool for extra effect, but my mouth's gone dry.

She giggles. "Holy shit … I can't believe I almost shot Tarin's retarded sister."

I straighten my eyes back out and watch her walk over to the nightstand and put the gun away. She comes back towards me, and I try to get my legs going again, but my ribs hurt too much.

"Come on, let me help you up, sweetie," she says, bending down to grab my hand. She sounds deliriously happy.

I hear the front door open and slam closed. Voices make their way up the stairs.

Screams come bubbling up from my throat as she yanks on me.

"Get up, silly," she says, completely ignoring my distress. "I don't want Tarin to find you on the floor. He'll think the wrong thing probably and get upset."

"My ribs," I moan, trying to hold them with one hand, praying there are no jagged edges in there to puncture a lung. My other hand is still trapped in her psycho grip, so I spin sideways, falling at her feet on my side. I scream with the waves pain that flow through me. I'm huffing and puffing as I try to speak. "Fuck … off … you crazy bitch! … Let me go!"

Feet pound up the stairs.

She kicks me once, catching me in the head with the toe of her shoe. "Get up, dummy! Get up!"

I'm crying now. I can't hold it in any longer. "Posey," I manage between tears, "you better get the fuck away from me and run very, very far, … because when I catch you … I'm going to strangle you with my bare hands."

She kicks me once more, this time in the ear. "I thought retards were *nice*." She jerks on my wrist. "You're not very nice at all, are you?"

My vision goes a little gray, but when it comes back, all I can see is a horrible bright orange color.

Sneakers. *Thank God, it's sneakers.*

"Scarlett?" Scott sounds confused. Unsure. Like maybe he thinks his eyes are deceiving him.

"Get that crazy bitch!" I gasp out.

Scott's shoved to the side by someone wearing cowboy boots. My hand is jerked sharply backwards as the mystery cowboy takes Posey down in a flying tackle onto the bed.

She screams.

I scream.

Orange shoes are in my face again. I smell cat pee. It makes the nausea worse.

"What the fuck is going on in here!" yells Tarin.

Scott's breath washes over my nose.

Oh fuck me, it's stale beer.

Scott's concerned expression and his chocolate brown eyes appear about three inches away from my face. "Are you okay?"

My face crumbles as I start to sob. "No, I'm most definitely not okay."

And then I throw up on Tarin's silk carpet.

CHAPTER THIRTY-TWO

EVERYTHING GOES HAZY FOR A while. Someone's scream-ing. Guys are yelling. There's pounding on the stairs and hallway floor again.

Police.

A man with a white shirt looming over me.

"Who are you?" I finally think to ask. I'm so out of it. The pain is awful.

"My name is Louis. I'm an EMT. I'm just going to put you on a board so we can get you into the ambulance." Something goes around my neck and doesn't quite choke me, but it's not the most comfortable thing I've ever worn.

I cry out when I'm rocked sideways and back again. Suddenly the ceiling is closer and I'm moving. Louis is somewhere; I can hear him barking out orders for people to get out of the way. Going down the stairs is not fun. Straps hold me to the stiff thing they're carrying me on, keeping me from falling off.

We're outside. The sun hits me in the face and it makes me feel alive. I smile, despite the pain. My carriers put me on a bed with wheels at the back of the ambulance. The bumping makes me cry.

And then Tarin's face is in mine. "What the fuck happened in there?" He looks angry, but I don't think it's at me.

"Your number two fan tried to kick me to death."

A storm crosses his features and then he shouts at the sky. "Fuuuuuck!" Placing his hand on my forehead, he leans in close. "I'm so, so sorry, Scar. I should have listened to you. I shouldn't have led her on like I did. I had no idea ..."

I close my eyes, a tear slipping out. The sense that he's turned a corner in his selfish thought process is making me sad and proud at the same time. "People aren't toys, Tarin. You shouldn't play with them, you know."

"I fucking know, okay. I know that now. I was a dick, and I'm so sorry. I really am. It's so unfair that you're paying for my mistake."

A stranger's voice interrupts our love fest. "Sorry, buddy, but I need you to get out of the way."

Tarin's hand leaves my forehead, but he grips my hand. "I'll see you at the hospital."

"No. Stay here. It's not safe right now. You don't have adequate security ..." My voice fades out with the effort of bossing him around.

Scott appears on the other side of my gurney. "I'll take care of it, sis. I promise, I'll take care of everything." Guilt mars his features.

I reach a hand up with effort. "Good. I know you will. See ya, bro."

"Wait a minute." Tarin's face is hovering above me again. "You said number two fan."

"Yes, I did," I whisper. I don't know what made me say that out loud. This is so not the time to have this conversation.

"Who's number one?"

I don't say anything, and then Tarin's gone again. His protests are ignored as he's pushed out of the ambulance and the doors are shut closed behind him.

"Are you allergic to anything?" Louis asks me.

"No. Just pain."

"Pain meds? Which ones?"

"No, not the meds. Just the pain."

He laughs. "Oh, okay. I'm going to give you something to take the edge off, if you want."

"Please," I say. And that's the last thing I remember before waking up in the hospital.

CHAPTER
THIRTY-THREE

I'M WITH NURSES AND A doctor within minutes of arriving at the emergency room. Apparently it hasn't gone unnoticed that I'm with Tarin Kilgour of *By Degrees*. He has fans here and they give me the star treatment.

Twenty minutes go by, during which I'm examined, cleaned up, and wrapped in bandages. Scott is the first one by my side. We're in my private room, the lights dimmed and the shades drawn.

"They said you can go home in a couple hours. No overnight if you don't want it."

"Hell no. Just get me home."

"Home as in the apartment…?"

I sigh. "You know what I meant. Tarin's place. I may have gotten my ass kicked by a psycho cheerleader, but that doesn't mean the job is over."

"Okay, good. Because I really think this one's on the right track. He's really responding to your methods and the crew seems really on board with everything."

"Plus he has all those video games and the studio," I add.

Scott smiles, knowing he's totally busted. "Yeah, that too."

"Is he out there?" I say, knowing I sound totally pitiful, but unable to stop myself from asking.

Scott takes my hand and stares at me, his eyebrows drawn together in concern. "Yeah. He's just working his way through the fannage. Those nurses are almost as bad as Posey."

"Ugh."

"Listen … are you sure you want to do this?" Scott asks, his voice going lower.

"Do what? Lie here in this hospital? Do I have a choice?"

"Stop playing. You know what I'm talking about. Tarin."

"I'm not *doing* Tarin, so you'll have to be more clear." At least, I'm not doing him *ever again*.

"I *mean* staying at his house, doing this job with him, getting so involved in his life. Are you sure you want to keep doing that? We can just call it a draw and walk away. I have plenty of money and I know you do too. We don't need to do this."

"We've never walked away from a job or a person who needs us, Scott." *Not since Austin, that is.* "Why would we do it now?"

He squeezes my head. "Because this time, it's different. Way different. You and Tarin …" He sighs and drops his gaze to the bed.

"What? Me and Tarin, what?"

Scott looks up again and his expression is just short of tortured. "I think he reminds you of Austin too much. It's messing with your head."

I swallow hard. I hate hearing him say this. "That's not fair."

"I'm not trying to be mean, I promise. I just don't want you to get hurt."

"There's no way for me to get hurt. It's not like that."

Scott reaching up and presses my nose. I think it's the only place on my body that's not bruised, but it still hurts. "Truth," he says, and then he waits.

My heart hurts more than my ribs now. "I don't want to talk truth. It hurts too much right now."

"Too bad for you that I'm all about the tough love. Talk to me."

"Since when are you all about the tough love?"

"Since Austin died."

"Ouch."

He shrugs unapologetically. "Just tell me the truth. That way I know we're both hearing it."

Tears fill my eyes. "When did you get so mean?"

He squeezes my hand so hard it cuts off my circulation. "I'm not being mean. I love you, Scarlett. We may not share the same parents, but you're my sister, and I don't want to see you get destroyed all over again. You almost didn't make it after Austin. Do you know how hard that was for me? To lose him and then almost lose you too? I don't think I could take that. Please just talk to me. Tell me I don't need to worry about you doing anything stupid."

I yank my hand away and then grimace at the pain it causes my ribs. "Fine, you want the truth? I'll tell you the truth. I like him, okay? Probably way too much. Yes … he reminds me of Austin. A lot. But that's not why I like him. He's different in tons of ways. He's wilder. He's darker. He's … Tarin. He's not Austin."

"No, he's no Austin." Scott sounds bitter.

"Don't say it like that. He's not a bad person."

"No. He's just a spoiled asshole."

"Stop. Come on, you know that's not true."

"I just don't like that you like him. That's my truth." He's pouting, lower lip sticking out and everything.

"Oh, I see what this is all about. You want me for yourself." I smile despite the pain, knowing this will gross him out.

"That's just sick. Now I'm picturing you without your clothes on and that's just … wrong." He stands. "I need to go wash my eyeballs off with soap." He disappears into my bathroom and I laugh through the terrible pain my body moving causes me.

The main door opens and Tarin steps partway in. "Mind if I come in?"

"No, I don't mind." I hate that my heart goes soft just seeing him standing there. Maybe it's the fact that I've just faced the wrong end of a gun, but the whole world looks different to me, and he's included in that world. He's the main focus of it.

He mumbles something to someone over his shoulder and then comes in, shutting the door behind him. "How are you feeling?"

"Better. Safer."

Tarin takes the chair Scott just vacated and pulls it closer. His worried face is so close, it makes me both nervous and excited. My pulse picks up its pace and sweat breaks out on my back and forehead.

"I can't believe that shit happened," he says. "I am *so* sorry. I really am. The doctor wasn't supposed to say anything to me, but he told me your ribs are only badly bruised. You're going to be okay. I'm so, so sorry that it happened. God, I feel like such an asshole."

"Yes, I know. And you can stop apologizing. It's not your fault. Not really."

"Don't lie. We both know I'm to blame. I brought her crazy ass up to the lawyer's office for crissake." He drops his head, shaking it slowly. "When will I ever learn? Playing with fire gets you burned every single time."

I hate that the atmosphere is going so dark so fast. I blurt out the first thing that comes to mind. "Tell me about *By Degrees*."

He looks up, confused. "What?"

"Tell me about the band name. Where's it from?" None of Scott's research had uncovered the story behind the name. Now seems as good a time as any to bring it up. I need to distract him from the whole scene I just suffered through with Posey. Just thinking about her makes me want to clobber someone, and Tarin is way too close to be safe from my ire.

Frowning, he opens his mouth, but nothing comes out right away. Then the door to the bathroom opens and Scott comes in, cutting off whatever Tarin was about to say.

"Oh. You're here." Scott sounds very unhappy about the idea.

Tarin turns. "Yeah." He stands and walks over to Scott. "Listen, man … I'm sorry. I know how close you two are, and I just want you to know how sorry I am this happened to her. I'm taking the blame."

"Good, cuz you should. It's your fault."

"Scott!" I struggle to sit up, but give up when the pain makes it too difficult.

"If you hadn't messed around with that chick earlier, she never would have thought it would be okay to go to your house. You practically invited her in. You can't manage fans like that. Too many of them get the wrong idea."

"I know, man, I know that now. I'm sorry, I made a mistake."

Scott scoffs at that. "*A* mistake? As in *one*? Yeah, right. Be honest. It wasn't just one mistake. You keep making them, don't you?" He looks over at me, and I get the distinct impression he considers me one of those mistakes.

"What the hell is wrong with you?" I ask Scott. This temper tantrum is coming out of nowhere. Yeah, I got hurt, but the only one really at fault here is Posey. I don't know why he wants to lay it at Tarin's feet so badly.

"Just take it easy," says Tarin. "I'm going to make sure nothing like this happens again."

"I'm already on that," says Scott, moving past Tarin to get to the door. He looks over at me. "I'm going to make some calls and pull in some more security. Just tell the nurse if you need me. They all have my number. I'll be here in the hospital, and I'm not leaving until you do."

"Thanks, Scott." Now's not the time to rip him the new one I think he's begging for, so I leave it at that. The door clicks shut quietly behind him.

Tarin stares at the door. "He really doesn't like me, does he?"

I sigh heavily. "No, he does. He's just worried about me. I'm pretty much all he's got and he's just freaking out a little."

Tarin comes over and sits down. "I thought he had a dad still alive somewhere."

"He does, but he lives really far away and he's retired … totally not the place Scott wants to be or would be happy in. He likes it out here in L.A., but if I wasn't here, I don't know if he'd stay."

"You guys are tight."

"Yes. Very."

"Maybe he likes you. You know … maybe he's jealous."

"No, that's not it. He's like my brother. But he's got nothing to be jealous of anyway." My heart spasms at my words and the awkward silence that rises up to smother me. I have to focus not to breathe heavily with the stress.

"Yeah." Tarin clears his throat. "So … uh … you wanted to know about the band name?"

"Yes," I say, happy to be on solid ground again, "tell me. Where's it from? Did you come up with it?"

He starts picking at the hospital bracelet on my wrist. "My last name is Kilgour. It's Scottish." The bracelet goes around and around as he spins it and talks. "Every clan in Scotland has a motto, and the one for the Kilgour clan is *By degrees*."

"Oh. That's cool."

"But it's more than that to me."

"Tell me," I say, unable to tear my gaze from his face. He's wide open, laying himself bare to me. I feel as though I'm the only person in the world he's shared this with.

"You know how you see something and you think 'I could never do that' or you think 'That'll never happen to me'?"

"Yeah …"

"It's not true. You have to know that those things aren't true." He pounds my hand gently with his fist to emphasize his words. "Just. Not. True."

I frown, wondering if the pain medication is interfering in my ability to understand what he's saying. "I don't get it."

"By degrees is a way to get past any obstacle. It's also the way things can change in your life and you can become something you would never imagine for yourself. By degrees … little by little."

My throat closes up and gets sore with unshed tears. I can't stop thinking about my past.

"Like Austin," he says, reading my mind and making me feel sick again. "He was the coolest guy, you know? I knew him when his career was just taking off. I was a nobody, but he took time to introduce me to people, to get me gigs, to make sure people listened to me. Even when I was doing things that other people were saying would never work, he believed in me."

"Yeah. He was good like that." I want to cry for the loss of Austin's kindness all over again. But all the tears I had for that are gone and the only thing left is a dull ache.

Tarin continues. "But you know … he started to change. It wasn't abrupt or big things. Just little by little. By degrees. First thing I noticed was him not returning calls. He got too busy for everyone. Then he started being a dick to fans and other new guys coming up on the scene."

"And other people who loved him," I whisper, adding to Austin's list of offenses. It feels wrong to join in, but I do it anyway. He did so many hurtful things before he died. It makes me angry to remember some of them, but saying them out loud is almost like therapy, like maybe if I launch the bad stuff out in the air around me, it can stop eating me up from inside.

"Yeah. He was a dick to the people who loved him. To you and Scott. Then came the drugs and the … well, the other stuff."

"The other girls, you mean. Don't worry … I know about them too."

"Yeah." Tarin drops his gaze again and puts his warm hand over my cold one. "Austin went from being my hero to a being guy I hated, but it didn't happen overnight. It happened by degrees. That's how it always works. Little by little, things fall away. People change. You let things fall away and lose them forever. Yourself, even. People lose themselves, but it never happens quickly enough. It goes so slow, in such small increments, you don't even notice it until it's too late."

I almost can't get the words out, but I know they have to be said. "You went from being a talented musician with a promising future to being a man who reminds me way too much of another."

I hear the loud swallow that nearly chokes Tarin. "I know," he whispers. "I'm a fuck-up. A class-A, number one fuck-up. I don't know why you're wasting your time with me."

I turn my hand over and lace my fingers with his. "You're not a waste of time. We're going to fix this. This is my job. This is what I do, and I'm good at it."

He looks up at me and his expression is nothing less than tortured. "I wasn't talking about your job."

I rewind his words in my head. *I don't know why you're wasting your time with me.*

Tarin lifts my hand and kisses my fingers, wrapping his other hand over ours and enclosing my hand completely inside his. "Is this how it always is for you and your … clients? Do they all just get so wrapped up in what you do that they totally fall for you?"

"What?" His words don't compute. I try to pull my hand away, but he doesn't let it go.

"Jack did. I know he did. That's why he wrote that song. I heard the lyrics. He sent me the mp3 of it last night and I listened to the whole thing. You're his muse."

I finally succeed in yanking my hand away. "No, I'm not. I'm nothing to him. We're just friends. I don't even know what you're talking about." Never mind Jack. The fact that Tarin's confessing something to me, about *feeling* something for me, is freaking me out. It doesn't matter that I was just doing the same thing about him to Scott. I never expected Tarin to go soft on me, to somehow convince himself he was falling for me. It was okay in my mind when it was all one-sided.

"This isn't …" Tarin looks stricken. He scrapes his chair back and stands. Running his fingers through his hair, he stammers through a goodbye. "Okay. So, I … uh … have to go. I've got … stuff to do and a meeting …" He moves backwards to the door. "You coming back to the house?"

"Yes. For now. If that's okay."

He's back to being cool. "Yeah, yeah. That's fine. Stay as long as you want. I'll see you there later." He looks at me quietly for a few seconds. The silence stretches between us until I want to throw the sheet over my face and hide. I can't stand to see all the emotion torturing his mind and reflected in his eyes.

"By degrees, Scarlett. That's how it works." His sad half-smile is the last thing I see of him until I'm back at his house later that evening.

CHAPTER
THIRTY-FOUR

WHO GOT HER INTO THE house?" I ask, resting on Tarin's couch in his family room. My bruised ribs are bound up tight and the last twelve hours of medical attention, a shower, and a nap has made me almost comfortable again. At least now I'm not getting my ass kicked by a psycho Barbie. How humiliating. I guess I shouldn't be surprised that my ribs aren't broken. She had cheer sneaker's on for crissake. Who gets broken ribs from cheer sneakers? Not me, thank you very much.

"Brett Campbell," says Scott, holding up another pillow he wants to put behind my back.

I shake my head no to the extra support. He's mothered me to the point that I'm starting to feel suffocated. "Who's Brett Campbell?" I ask, searching my memory for the name. It's familiar.

"One of the guys on our scratch-off list."

"Ooooh, yeah … the drug guy." I nod, remembering the loser's promise to get me back for kicking him out of Tarin's life. "I thought we told Zack and Leonard to get his keys back and stuff."

"Yes, but we failed to mention that they needed to change all the passcodes on the doors. Major brain fart on my end."

I roll my eyes. "Oh, for shit's sake … we shouldn't even have to say that!"

Scott holds up his hands in surrender. "I know, I know … believe me, everyone feels righteously stupid over it now. I guess at the time they never thought something like this would happen. I mean, who knew Posey would find a way to connect with your worst enemy. Zach and Leonard aren't professional security, okay? They're just friends."

I nod, already tired with dealing with all of this. My pain meds are like sleeping pills, making my eyelids heavy. "I'm not mad at them … I'm just mad at myself. This job has thrown me for a complete loop. I'm losing my edge." I stare off into the distance, hating that I feel so defeated. Hating that I'm falling for a client who also thinks he's falling for me.

"I was meaning to talk to you about that…" Scott sounds worried.

I look over at him, just using my eyes. It hurts to even turn my head. "What? You're not going to give me shit again, are you? Because trust me, I've done enough of that to myself for the both of us and the first time was more than sufficient."

"No, no, it's not that. I'm not going to give you a hard time about this job. I'm just … I'm worried about you. Kind of like Jack is."

"Please, Scott, not now. Not the Jack thing. Don't you have something better to do with your time like writing a panty-tossing song or torching those cat pissery shoes?"

He puts his hand on my arm and looks very sincere, which is weird for him. It puts me on edge. "Don't play that game with me, okay, Scar? Seriously. It's *me* sitting here. No one else is even in the house. You can yell, you can cry, you can slap me … whatever you want. No one's going to judge you. You're safe."

"Are you sure?" I say. I'm feeling really petulant right now. "Maybe there's a nutbag upstairs rifling through Tarin's drawers who'd like to give me a few more kicks to the ribs."

He sighs. "Shut up or you're going to force me to put my running shoe in your face again."

"God, they're so powerful, they're like smelling salts."

"I know." He looks and sounds way too proud of that.

I close my eyes at the memory. "*Why* do they smell like cat pee when you don't even have a cat?"

"Because I sweat, okay? It's normal. Guys have smelly feet."

"Nothing that heinous can possibly be normal. It's like … nuclear awful. Morgue resident awful. Zombie apocalypse awful. You should get that checked out. I pay for medical insurance, so use it, already."

"Stop trying to change the subject. Right now we're talking about *you*, not my feet."

"I don't want to talk about me. And I don't want to talk about your feet either, for that matter. I want to talk about … the weather. What's it like outside?"

"Okay, I get it, you don't want to talk about you. But I do, and for once, I'm putting my smelly cat piss foot down."

"Weather," I insist. "Tell me the temperature."

"You go ahead and talk about the weather while I talk about Scarlett."

I ignore the pain and look towards the back of the room. "I see some sun through the window over there. Looks like a good pool party day. Maybe we should tell Josh to barbecue."

"You're not dealing with Austin's death very well."

"You should go for a swim while the sun's out. Wear that porn horn bathing suit you have … the banana hammock. That's my favorite. I'll stay inside and admire you through the back window."

He snorts, but continues on his mission: Operation Brain Dig. I really hate having people mess around in my head, and he totally knows it.

"I thought you were cool with everything and moving on from Austin, but now I think being around Tarin is fucking with your mind or something."

I swallow the misery that rises up and gets stuck in my throat. My words come out strained. "I wonder what the temperature is. Eighty? Ninety? A hundred?"

"I know Jack's not helping the situation, but he and I talked about it and we both think it's Tarin who's causing you to go off the rails a little."

My temperature is rising from the anger that's rolling around in my belly like hot lava. I power through, refusing to let go of my meteorology. "The humidity must be terrible. I'm glad I'm not going out there today. My hair would frizz out everywhere. I look like Jeff Daniels in *Dumb and Dumber* when that happens."

"And there's something I need to tell you about him. About Tarin. Something I probably should have told you when we first starting talking about getting this job."

For some reason I feel like crying, so instead of bawling like a baby, I get angrier instead. "And I absolutely *hate it* when I look like Jeff Daniels. Hate it. Hate. It. Makes me want to shave my hair off. Jeff Daniels only looks good on Jeff Daniels."

"I know you hear me, Scarlett. I'm going to tell you something about Tarin I haven't told you before. It's about Austin too."

I whip my head around, wincing at the pain it causes my ribs. Tears leap to my eyes but it's not from the physical pain I'm enduring. "Don't, Scott. Just … don't." A giant, black wall comes up between us, and I will not let him scale it.

"You need to know this. I don't want you going into anything with Tarin without knowing the whole story."

I struggle to stand, but it leaves me breathless with pain. "I'm not going into *anything* with Tarin, you stupid *fuckweasel*. Just help me up."

"What's going on in here?" asks Tarin as he walks through the door. He sounds angry. Protective.

Scott twists around, but not before I catch the expression on his face. *Guilty.*

"I was just getting up," I grunt out. I huff out a few sharp breaths, trying to push the pain away. I'm prepared to walk over broken glass to get away from Scott and his stupid attack of the truthies. I hate when he gets all principled on me like that. It doesn't happen often, but when it does, he always unloads a basketful of shit on my head. Last time it was to tell me that he'd caught Austin cheating on me right before he died. That was a fun conversation. I have a feeling this one was going to be a real delight too.

"Let me help you." Tarin rushes over and stands in front of me, holding out his arms like he's going to bend over and pick me up under my arms.

I slap his hands away. "Stop. Go away."

"Want me to help?" asks Scott.

He looks so innocent and sweet it just pisses me off more. He's sitting there acting like he wasn't about to unload a bunch of garbage on me and like I'm not pissing mad at him. He and Jack have been scheming behind my back and I feel like I'm living with a traitor. Not totally a traitor but someone who I need a break from at least for today.

"No, I don't want you to help," I say angrily to Scott. "I think you've done enough, don't you?"

Scott stands abruptly. "Fine. If that's how you feel about it, I'll just leave you with … with …" He scowls at Tarin. "The guy who started this whole bullshit."

He storms off, leaving Tarin and me to stare at his retreating back. The door slams shut behind him.

I look over at Tarin, taking my rage out on the only other person in the room. "What in the hell is he talking about?" Suddenly I want to know the big mystery. I want to hear it from the source, whatever this fuckery is. Painful revelations are like ripping off bandaids for me; get to the source, hear it straight up, and deal with the pain. Wham, bam, thank you, ma'am. "Go ahead, Tarin. Confess your sins. Tell me what I need to know about you and Austin." I don't even know that there *is* anything for me to know about them, but maybe he'll surprise me and let me in on some big secret he and Scott have been keeping from me. I couldn't be any worse than the shit I've already heard about the love of my life. Austin is dead but his ghost will never stop haunting me. Today is just another reminder of that.

Tarin lets out a huge sigh and rolls his eyes as he flops down onto the couch next to me. I don't even feel the pain from him jigging the couch as I listen to the words coming out of his mouth.

"Where do I start?"

CHAPTER THIRTY-FIVE

"HOW ABOUT YOU START AT the beginning?" I suggest, settling into the couch, trying to find a position that doesn't hurt. There isn't one.

"The beginning … the beginning …" Tarin is staring at the coffee table where his foot rests. It's jiggling nervously, his ratty skater boy shoes rocking up and down over and over.

I kick him lightly to get him started.

"Fine. The first time I really saw him and talked to him was the night I met Mel."

"Yeah, I heard that. He got you on stage when Mel was watching."

"Exactly." Tarin starts drumming a thumb on his knee. "Mel was only there for a little while. For that one band we went on instead of. Austin knew Mel was there, knew he wouldn't be staying. He fucked up their equipment so they had to go on later. He liked our sound, he said. He told us he wanted to get us a chance at being heard by a larger audience."

"And you got your agent."

"Yeah. Not just any agent either … Mel fucking Warner. *The* Mel Warner. He took us right to the top."

"It's been a great ride," I say softly.

"Yeah. And no." Tarin sighs.

"Tell me about the no."

He shrugs, the foot jiggling and thumb drumming increasing in speed. "I did some shit I regret. Some little stuff, some big stuff. And one really, *really* big thing. Something I can't ever let myself forget. Couldn't even if I wanted to."

I laugh. "What'd you do, kill someone?" I'm still laughing when he turns his tortured expression my way.

"You could say that," he says.

My laugh cuts off mid-stream. "That's not funny."

"I know. I'm not joking."

Guilty. The tattoo isn't showing, but it's all I can see when I look at him.

"Tell me."

He stands up and begins pacing back and forth in front of the coffee table. He's staring at the ground, one hand on the side of his head. "I was in Chicago two years ago for that big music festival. The one where … Austin … you know."

"The one where he died," I say, my voice devoid of emotion or inflection. I really, really do not like where this is going. I'm sick and I know it's not the pain or the meds. I'm sick over our future, over what he's about to say. But I don't stop him.

Truth.

I need to know the truth.

"It was after the show, and a bunch of us were in the hotel suite together. It was total mayhem. There were girls and drugs and booze … an unlimited supply. Somehow Austin and I ended up in a bedroom together with some girls. One of them - I don't remember her name - she brings out this black zippered case from her purse. She's got H in there and she offers to shoot us up. Me and Austin together."

I look away from him. I can't stand to see his face right now. I stare at the wall where his family's coat of arms is hanging.

"I told her to fuck off. I was scared. I did coke occasionally and weed a lot, but nothing that hard ever. I told 'em, 'That's not me.' I said, 'I don't do that kind of shit.'" He looks up for a second, no longer pacing, a bitter smile passing over his face. "By degrees, right? You say *never* one day and the next ... it's not never any more."

He shifts his focus to the floor again, pacing once again. "They laughed at me. Austin said some shit, I don't remember what exactly, but it made me feel like a total amateur or something. I got pissed at him. He was like my hero, you know, and then he just cut me down in front of those girls. They all were laughing and whatever." Tarin's pissed now, mad at the memories maybe or himself. It doesn't matter.

"I stayed, though. I watched her cook up a rock and pull it into a syringe. She was wasted ... so fucked up. She could barely keep her hands steady. When she was tying off Austin's arm, I asked him. I asked him if he was sure that's what he wanted to do."

I look over at Tarin. The anguish in his voice is palpable.

"You know what he said?" Tarin turns to me, tears in his eyes. "He told me to go fuck myself. He called me fucking pansy loser."

"That doesn't sound like Austin," I say, hurting for Tarin, hurting for myself, but most of all, hurting for Austin. He had completely disappeared by the time that night had come around. The man remaining was only a hollow monster.

"No, it didn't sound like him at all. That's the point. He wasn't himself. I should have punched that bitch in the face and sent that shit flying to the floor to protect him. But I walked out instead." Tarin chokes on the tears and sobs that refuse to be held back any longer. "I walked out as she slid that needle into his vein. I let him go, and somewhere inside, I knew it was going to go bad. I just knew it, but I let him go anyway. And he died that night. From those drugs. Probably minutes after I walked out."

I can see it perfectly in my mind: Austin lying there with two idiot, wasted girls making him feel like a king. Tarin running around at his heels telling him he can do no wrong. And Tarin knew I existed then. He knew about Scott too. He knew Austin was playing with fire.

And he did nothing.

He was there in the last few minutes of Austin's life and he watched it fade to black. He stood to the side and watched Austin burn out. He saw Austin on his last day on earth, his last *minutes* on earth, when neither Scott nor I had the privilege. And he only bothered to tell anyone now.

Guilty.

I struggle to get to my feet. It hurts like crazy, but I manage it. No way in hell am I going to stay in the same room as him. I can't even look at him now.

"Say something, Scarlett," he begs. "Please say something."

Limping to the door, I focus on taking one step, one breath at a time. *One, two, three, four … now I'm almost to the door. Five, six, seven, eight … find a place to store the hate.*

"Where are you going?" he asks.

"Away," I say, as I pull open the door.

CHAPTER THIRTY-SIX

I'M CRYING AND PACKING MY bag when Scott walks in. He stops at my side while I fold clothes and lay them inside.

"What are you doing?"

"Baking a cake." I sniff, and then more tears come. This is so crazy and stupid. All I know is I have to get out of here. I can't think straight surrounded by Tarin's life.

"You can't bake a cake right now."

"Yes I can. Watch me." I throw my running shoes in the bag.

"But we have to finish this … meal first."

"You finish it. I'm going home." Scott can handle this. Or he'll have to. I'm done.

"The apartment's going to be dirty. Don't you want me to send someone to clean it first?"

"I don't mean that home. I mean home, home."

"Chicago? You hate Chicago. Why would you go there?"

"I have to get away. I have to think."

Scott takes me by the shoulders and turns me around gently. "What happened? He said something or did something, didn't he?"

"I don't want to talk about it." I try to twist away but it hurts too much. "Let me go, Scott. I can't do this right now."

"He told you about Austin, didn't he?"

My hand freezes in midair. The shorts I'm holding drop down towards the bag, missing the opening and hitting the side of it. I just stare at it. "What are you talking about?"

"He told you about Austin. About that night. In the hotel room."

I look at Scott, my heart leaping into my throat. "You knew?" My words come out strangled.

He nods. He's scared how I'll take it, I can tell. His face goes very pale. "I knew. I've known for a long time. Mel told me."

"Mel?! How the hell does he know and I don't?!"

Scott looks at the ground. "Remember when they called someone in to identify him? They called me in because I was the closest relative."

"They wouldn't let me in. So?"

"So, afterwards, I guess they had my name on the form and then the cops came to talk to me and told me about this investigation they did into the people who were there at the time. Tarin's name came up. Mel was representing him, so … you know. He heard stuff."

"And yet no one thought to tell me a thing."

Scott puts his hand on my arm, but I shove it off, ignoring the pain slicing through my body.

"Come on, don't be like that, Scar. You didn't want to know that crap. You didn't want to know he died with a slut sucking him off and Tarin in the next room. That wouldn't have helped you get past all of that shit."

I grab my purse off the bed next to my bag. "Fuck it. You can keep my shit." I walk out of the room as fast as my injured ribs will move. What was left of my heart is now destroyed. Even Scott has left me behind.

"Where are you going?" he yells out after me.

I slam the door to the bedroom and don't bother answering.

As I'm going down the stairs, Ricky comes out of the hallway. "What's up? Going somewhere?"

"Airport. Can you take me?"

"Of course." He opens the door ahead of me.

I pass him by and work at controlling my emotions. I want to scream and rail at the world, but now's not the time or the place. Chicago's just going to have to deal with my sorry ass when I get there.

"Don't you have any bags?" he asks, following me out.

"Nope. It's just me."

I get in the back seat and wait for him to start the car. He's sitting in the driver's seat just looking at me in the rearview mirror. "If you don't mind me saying, it's never just you. You're not alone, even if you might think you are. Even if it might feel like you are sometimes."

"I *do* mind you saying, Ricky. Can you please just drive?" I look out the window and let the tears fall silently all the way to LAX.

CHAPTER
THIRTY-SEVEN

HELLO, MEL, THIS IS SCARLETT Barnes. I know it's late, so I'm calling your office voicemail to leave you this message instead of bugging you by calling your cell. I've left Tarin's house and I'm done working with him. Scott's taking over. If you're not okay with that, I'll understand, but I recommend you stay with him. He's worked side-by-side with me for almost two years, and he's pretty much single-handedly managed the whole show from behind the scenes. As you know, he has personal experience in this area, so he knows what your clients are going through. You're probably wondering why I'm quitting. I've never quit before, and I'm not happy that I'm doing it now, but I really feel like I have no choice. I found out that you kept something from me, something I consider pretty much unforgiveable. All of you have. You knew about Tarin and Austin. You knew what Tarin saw and what he didn't do. I can't believe you let me take this job knowing that and also knowing that I was completely in the dark. You probably don't care - I know this is all business to you - but I'm not sure I can ever forgive you for this. Goodbye and good luck with your retirement. Oh ... and of course, don't worry about the fee. I don't expect to be paid anything. I hope if you continue with Scott's services, however, that you will honor the fee and pay it directly to him."

CHAPTER
THIRTY-EIGHT

FOR TWO DAYS I MOPE around the apartment Austin bought a few months before he died, refusing to answer my phone or the twenty-five emails and texts from Scott and Mel. I send away the maid that Scott hired, choosing instead to lose myself in the monotonous task of cleaning up the place. After spending a small fortune on cleaning products and equipment, I turn the two bedroom dust palace into a showroom. The solid surfaces sparkle. The leather gleams. The carpet has geometrically precise vacuum marks. It's like a ghost lives here. Her name is Scarlett.

Once I'm done with the cleaning of areas people can see, I tackle the hidden places. Boxes of Austin's things are stacked in closets and shoved under beds and in a crawl space in a wall. Someone had come in here after he died to erase his presence, to get the place ready to sell, but neither Scott nor I could stand the idea of this piece of his life disappearing too. Since it belongs to us jointly, we both decided to keep it until we could figure out a better plan. This is the first time I've been back since it was first purchased. It's a stranger's house with stranger's furniture in it.

It's not even Austin's style - cold and modern, everything black, white, and chrome. If Austin had been the one to pick the couch, it would have been red. He loved red. It wasn't my favorite color for furniture, but that didn't matter to me at the time. Now I wonder why I didn't get a couch I liked when we shopped for things.

In one of the boxes I find framed pictures. I cry for hours over the stuff in that box with a glass of red wine in my hand the entire time, eventually emptying the bottle as I travel down memory lane. Scott was so little when this whole thing started. I babysat him after his mom died and his father was at loose ends for child care. That's how Austin and I met. After the first night I watched Scott, the three of us were pretty much inseparable. Over our mutual love for his little brother, Austin and I fell for one another, hook, line, and sinker. There is no love like a first love for its intensity and single-mindedness. We were blind to reality when we were looking into each other's eyes.

As I hold one of the frames that holds a photo of just Austin and his favorite Les Paul guitar, I trace his face and body with my finger, thinking back to our time together. We were so young. So naive. We thought we could join this crazy world of rock stars and immerse ourselves in the celebrity lifestyle and yet keep our innocence, keep our wide-eyed excitement over the fantasy and all it had to offer. Little did we know how staring into the bright light of fame can permanently damage your eyesight and make everything take on a dullness that begs to be polished. Spend some money here, travel there, make friends with this person and party until the sun comes up - do anything to make life exciting and new again. It brings new meaning to the term 'burned out'.

It's when I lay the photographs out in sequential order, from the beginning of our love story until the day before he died, that I see what Austin had done. Up until now, I saw him as getting closer and closer to a flame, like a moth unable to resist the lure and willing to disregard his own health just to immerse himself in the brightness of its rays. But now I was seeing something else. Maybe it's Tarin's confession or finally being alone with my thoughts that's doing it, but my vision clears and I see something else defining Austin's last days.

As Austin got closer and closer to the flames, by degrees getting nearer and nearer to the thing that would destroy him, he pushed Scott and me away. He distanced himself from the ones he loved most. At the time I thought he was rejecting us, telling us in a very ineloquent way that we were no longer welcome in his life. But when I look very closely at the pictures of him, when the camera catches him staring at his little brother with longing and a certain sadness, I notice something different. A new emotion comes to the surface and nearly strangles me.

Austin wasn't rejecting us. He was saving us. He was saving us from the thing that he knew would burn him up in the end.

And then I cry some more.

CHAPTER THIRTY-NINE

I WAKE UP THE NEXT morning, and after putting out all the photos, I look at my texts and emails. Scott is to the point of begging me to call, so I wipe the stale tears off my face and press the speed dial.

"Hey," I say. I sound like I'm half asleep, but I'm too disinterested to pep myself up and pretend I'm interested in talking to him or anyone else.

"Oh my god. She's alive! It's a miracle!"

"Shut up."

"Seriously. I'm so glad you didn't jump off a bridge. I have so many questions for you right now."

"Oh, yeah? Like what?"

"Like how many calories should Tarin be eating a day? Josh wants to know. And can he go to Gary Nash's premier or should he decline? Jelly's off the hook. Should I keep her away? And what about Tarin in the studio? Do you think I should force him?"

"I take it Mel was okay with you taking over."

"He wasn't excited about it, but he understood. You must have unloaded a hell of a guilt trip on him. If it was anything like the one you sent me on, I completely get why he signed everything over."

I sigh heavily. "Can I go now?"

"Hell no, you can't go. Answer my questions, woman."

"Fine. Twenty-five hundred, yes to the premier, do what you think about Jelly, and yes to the studio. You should go in there with him."

"Really? You mean that?"

"Yes, I meant all of it."

"Do you still hate me?"

"I could never hate you. I could feel betrayed for a little while, but I'll get over it."

He breathes out a long sigh of relief. "Good. Because I really don't like hanging out in Chicago, but I'm coming back there after finishing with Tarin. Roomies forever, Scar. Or until I find me a lady love, that is."

A big part of me doesn't want to know, but I ask anyway. I can't help it. "How's he doing?"

Silence.

"If you don't want to tell me, just say so. I know I walked away. I don't expect anyone to keep me in the loop. I was just wondering."

"He's having a rough time if you really want to know. He feels guilty."

"Well, he should." I'm angry again.

"Oh, come on. That's total bullshit and you know it."

I'm taken aback by the vehemence of his tone. "How so? He was there, Scott. He was *there*. In Austin's last minutes."

"Yeah. I know. And it just as easily could have been me, all right? I saw Austin do stupid shit like that all the time. We never know when it's going to be too much or going too far, do we?"

His words echo around in my head, bumping into another memory. Tarin said the same thing once, when we first met on the boat, I think. That was the guilt talking.

"So. When you see someone doing that and you know it's going to be bad, you stop them."

"We didn't. We didn't stop him."

I can't answer that. I guess I'm just as guilty as everyone else.

"Goodbye, Scott."

"Wait! I have more questions."

"You don't need me anymore. Figure out the answers on your own. You can do it." I hang up and go back to bed. It's ten in the morning and I'm too exhausted to go on with my day.

CHAPTER FORTY

THE DOORBELL RINGS ANOTHER WEEK into my self-imposed bed rest. I blow it off, knowing that if I ignore the maids and delivery people long enough, they'll go away and leave me alone. But this person is persistent. *Ding dong, ding dong, ding dong* … The pain in the ass is banging on the door with a fist now.

I drag myself out of bed and shuffle to the front door. "Jesus, Mary, and Jerome, I'm coming! Keep your damn pants on." I look through the peephole, and stop breathing for a couple seconds when I see who it is.

"Come on, Scar, let me in. I know you're there."

"Go away, Jack! I don't even know why you came here."

"Of course you know. I'm here to help. Open the door or I'll get someone in maintenance to let me in."

"This isn't an apartment complex, you big jerk. No one has a key but me."

"Fine. I'll just sleep out here in the hallway. Hopefully your neighbors don't mind me singing." He plays an acoustic rendition of *Wild Horses* by the Rolling Stones, his ragged, deep voice seeping through the door and turning my heart into a painful rock in my chest. I should open the door, but the lyrics and his voice bring me to my knees. I stay on the opposite side of the door, weeping onto the marble floor. Alone while ignoring all my responsibilities and the people I've left behind I can manage. Hearing Jack singing those words as I disappoint everyone I care about … this I cannot manage.

I know he's just on the other side of the door from me, sitting with his back against it. I hear his shirt sliding around on the surface. He uses his knuckles and heavy silver rings to tap on the door when he's done. "Wild horses couldn't drag me away, babe. Just open the door. You know you're going to eventually."

"Why can't you just leave me alone, Jack?" I'm crying through the words. That song has always been special but now it means way too much. It's too applicable to my life and I've always thought of it as melancholy.

"Because … you need me. And friends don't leave friends when they're in need like this."

I've left people who needed me before. I torture myself with this knowledge, but I don't share it because I don't want him talking me down off the ledge I'm on. I want to skip and trip along the edge of it until I lose all my remaining strength and plunge into the abyss. I'm beginning to believe that dying could be so much easier than living.

"In the mood for a little Elton John?"

I stand up and open the door as he launches into his *a capella* rendition of *Goodbye Yellow Brick Road*. He falls onto the front entrance floor, flat on his back, smiling up at me. He's left his eyeliner off but his reddish brown hair is still a crazy mess like it always is. He's always what I imagined an Irish guy to look like, with the addition of a full upper body of tattoos.

"What? No Elton John?" He grins big, his blue eyes practically twinkling he's so pleased with himself.

I kick him gently in the side of the head. "No." I leave him for the kitchen and get out a glass. Four gulps of water later and my voice is ready to work again. He hauls his duffle bag and guitar case in the door and then joins me there.

I launch into him, hoping a very cold welcome will get rid of him before he gets too comfortable. "I really don't appreciate you just showing up here. You weren't invited for a reason."

"Actually, Scott invited me. And if you'd bother to pick up your phone once in a while, you'd have gotten my advance notice. I actually hoped you'd pick me up from the airport. I got mauled by a group of chicks at the baggage claim. I almost lost a nipple piercing the painful way." He rubs his chest for emphasis.

I snort. "Yeah, right." I hold out my hand. "Hand me my phone. I'll call you a taxi to take you back."

He picks my cell up off the counter. "Nah. I'm gonna stay in Chicago for a while, I think." He's scrolling through my messages. "Hmmm... Looks like Tarin really wants to talk to you." He looks up at me, his expression all innocence. "Is he your boyfriend or something?"

I jump up and lean far over the counter to snatch it from his hands. I shut the screen off without looking at it and put it back down on the counter. When I'm back on my feet in the kitchen I answer his questions. "No. He's most definitely *not* my boyfriend." I try not to look at the phone, but my eyes keep getting pulled over to it like they're being controlled by the texts there.

"Did you have sex with him?"

My mouth drops open and I sputter. The good news is that I'm finally able to stop fixating on the stupid phone; the bad news is that Jack is so far up into my business he needs a good slapping with my boxing gloves. "What the … Jack! That is none of your business!"

"I'll take that as a yes. I thought you had a rule about not sleeping with clients." He leans on the counter with his forearms, taking up a completely casual stance as he stares into my eyes.

My usual smartass, sharp remarks aren't leaping to mind. All I can do is stare back at him with my ears and cheeks burning.

"I can see how you'd want that rule in place. Sex complicates things. When you and I were working together, trust me, I wanted to sleep with you. There's something very attractive about a heroine. You want to be closer to the person who's there pulling you out of the darkness, you know? But I get it … that you can't do that." He traces patterns in the granite countertop with his fingers, not looking at me anymore. "So what I'm wondering is, why him? I mean, what makes Tarin so special that you'd throw that rule away?" He looks up again and stares at me. There's hurt there in his expression.

Tears come to my eyes. I can't believe I made such a horrible, horrible mistake. And with Tarin of all people. Why hadn't I slept with Jack? He's a much better person. He didn't let Austin die. I can't respond because nothing running through my mind is making sense right now. I would never sleep with Jack. I just don't feel that way about him. That just goes to show how stupid I am.

"Scott thinks you like Tarin because he reminds you of Austin, but I don't see it that way." Jack narrows his eyes in concentration, nodding a little, tapping his finger on the stone. "Nah. He's his own man. Definitely more intense than Austin. And I know the world's seen some of the worst of Tarin lately, but deep down inside, I think he's more careful than Austin was. He doesn't give himself away that easy. When he slept with you, I guarantee it, it was a big deal for him. You're not a groupie. You're the real deal."

"First of all, I didn't admit to sleeping with Tarin. And Austin didn't give himself away easy." I'm angry that he's talking about Austin like this. His attempts at making me feel okay about what Tarin and I did together are falling on deaf ears. I wish he wouldn't waste his time. What's done is done and nothing he says will change the fact that it was a mistake.

But oh, how my heart hurts even just *thinking* those words. I don't want Tarin to have been a mistake. I want … I want … I don't know what I want. *Stupid, traitor heart.* Just once in my life I'd like my heart and my brain to be on the same page.

"Yeah, Austin did give himself away easily. Like candy, man. He fell for you as a kid and gave everything to you for a while. It was intense, I'm sure. Kids always love hard and deep. Then he fell for the life of a star, giving *that* everything he had and leaving you behind. That's how he went so far so fast … focus. Then he fell for about a thousand groupies who stuck their hands in his pants. He was like a puppy running around, distracted by squirrels. Zero focus after he left you behind. Selfish. You deserved much better."

Steam is practically coming out of my ears. "You're really lucky that you're on the other side of this counter from me. You have no right to talk about Austin like that." I consider taking a knife out of the drawer and waving it around but I don't bother because I know I don't have the lady balls to use it against him. He knows me well enough that he'd laugh at me even pretending like I'm going to cut him.

Jack smiles slowly. "What are you gonna do? Beat me up? Show me who's boss?"

I don't dignify his mocking with a response. He keeps talking even while knowing how much he's upsetting me. I totally hate him right now.

"Listen, if you want my opinion…"

"I don't, Jack. I really, really don't." I clamp my teeth together, the fury barely contained.

"…I'd say that Tarin is a better man, comparing the two. When he dedicates himself to something, there's no going back. And he's a grown-up. Austin was a child."

"Tarin is no saint," I spit out at him.

"Oh, no argument from me there. He's a sinner from the word go. But that doesn't mean he's not a good person."

"Yes, actually, it does."

Jack starts moving around the counter separating us.

"Stay away, Jack."

Of course he ignores me. "There's a difference between sins of the body and sins of the soul. Besides, we all sin once in a while. Even you."

"That's just semantics. Sins are sins. I've made my mistakes, I know I'm not perfect." I back up away from him as he rounds the last corner. My butts rams into the handle of the oven, stopping me in my tracks.

He quits walking when he's a foot away, staring me down with those stupid blue eyes of his. His freckles should make him look like a little girl, but he's annoying enough to make them all a part of his sex appeal. I really, really hate him for that right now. I've always had a hard time staying mad at cute guys when they're really persistent. It was Austin's greatest talent - convincing me to love him when I wanted to slap him.

"You can lie to me all day and all night about how you feel about Tarin and Austin. Doesn't matter. I'm still going to love you. But don't lie to *yourself*, okay, babe? You deserve better than that." He reaches up and takes my hands, holding just my fingers. "How come you never let yourself have what you deserve? Why are you always settling for so much less?"

Tears leak out of my eyes despite my best efforts to keep them in. "Jack, I didn't ask you to come here, and I don't *want* you to be here. I don't know what your issue is with me just trying to be alone, but that's what I want. To be alone."

He closes the distance between us and drops my fingers to wrap his arms around me. I struggle to get away, but he holds on.

"Stop fighting me, you wild banshee. I'm just hugging you." He grunts when I punch him in the ribs, but he doesn't let go.

When I realize I'm going to hurt him and he's just going to stand there and let me, I quit fighting. "Why can't you just leave me alone?" My body starts shaking. Sobs are coming up from somewhere deep inside me because I know the answer to my question. He loves me and he wants me to know it. But I don't *want* to know it. I don't want to feel any love in this apartment; I just want the cold, sterile feel of its emptiness to fill and surround me. That's what I've been telling myself for these past two weeks and I keep trying to tell myself now. But then the warmth of his arms seeps into the ice surrounding my heart and a thaw begins. The melted ice comes out as tears. I remember how good it feels to be held and remember that I really don't like living in the cold.

He rests his chin on my head as I soak the front of his shirt with my sorrow. "I know you're hurting, babe. I get it. You need to get through the pain of remembering and realizing not-very-nice things about the guy you loved. But you shouldn't do that alone. Someone really smart about people told me that. No one should hurt alone. Otherwise, you start thinking crazy things like you really *are* alone in the world and then you start wondering whether life is worth living." He pulls away a little to look down at me. "Don't go there, Scar, okay? You mean so much to me, to Scott, to all the other guys you've helped. Do you know what the music industry would look like today without you? So many songs would be missing. So many emotional connections not made. Don't throw that away."

I try to push him off me, but he's not ready to go anywhere. He's stuck like glue.

"I don't *care* about the music industry or any of those people," I say, my voice a raspy mess. "I just want to be left alone." I'm lying. I know I'm lying, but I can't stop. I want to punish myself for failing. Failing Austin, failing Scott, and failing Tarin too.

"Oh, bullshit. Do you see who you're talking to? You saved my life. No sense trying to pretend you didn't, either. You care about music and you care about the people who make it. And I know Tarin's as grateful as I am that you feel that way. You're a good person, Scarlett. It's okay that you fell down. Everyone does once in a while. The important thing is to get back up so you can fight another day. Charlie wouldn't want you staying down on the mat like this."

Thoughts of Charlie make me feel embarrassed about my self-pity. I sag against him, all the fight gone for now. Besides, I'm too tired to keep it up in the face of Jack's complete denial. The idiot thinks I walk on water and can do no wrong. He'll never see the real me - the weak one who fools herself about people and refuses to see what's right in front of her face. I hate that Austin's ghost is still haunting me but now he's turned into a dark specter instead of the vision of light I always saw him as. It makes me feel truly alone for the first time since he died.

"Come on," urges Jack. "Let's sit down on the couch and talk."

"I don't want to talk." My tears have turned into a full-on pout. I want to kick everything near me. The table, the couch, the chair … Jack, maybe.

"Yeah, but let's do it anyway."

He guides me over to the couch and pushes me into a sitting position. He drops down next to me as I stare into my lap. My hands are there, palms up, my fingers mostly open and limp.

"Tell me why you ran."

"I didn't run."

"Tell me why you disappeared without saying anything to anyone and abandoned a job just a few days into it."

I sigh heavily. I really don't want to talk to him or anyone else about this. Avoiding the whole idea of it has done wonders for my ability to sleep.

"Scott says things were going really well. Tarin got on board with minimal fuss, most of the band went on vacation, and the losers got booted out with only one mess-up. Crazy fan attack or whatever. It was your smoothest operation ever."

I shake my head. "Now we know why Tarin got on board right away." I can still picture his face on the boat and his question about bringing lawyers into the mix. "He was worried he was going to be busted for being there when Austin …" *Whatever.* I can't even finish my sentence.

"When Austin killed himself."

My throat closes up with the pain. I've used up all my tears for this today, though. Nothing else will come out. "He didn't kill himself." I know it's a lie as soon as it leaves my lips, but I stubbornly hold onto the idea anyway.

"Yes, he did. Stop kidding yourself. No one does the things he was doing and expects to live."

I was wrong. I do have more tears left for Austin.

"Tarin's still working with Scott and doing really well from what Scott says. He's got the whole healthy living thing going on, and he's even taking cooking lessons from Josh. I guess he didn't really catch on with the painting thing, but Greg says he's great with photography. He's got a web page up with a portfolio already, thanks to Scott. We can check it out later."

I frown, momentarily distracted from wallowing in visions of Austin's last moments. They thankfully disperse into smoke at the idea of Tarin finding something that makes him happy. "What?"

"Yeah, he went in for more painting in the studio and just totally sucked at it, so Greg handed him a camera. I guess Tarin's been taking pictures his whole life, but with a few pointers from Greg it all just gelled for him. Greg says he's the real deal. Like he could go pro if the music gig doesn't work out for him."

I smile faintly. Even though I'm mad at Tarin, I'm proud that he's found another creative outlet. He needed something like that. I know it will help calm and center him to focus through the lens on other things besides his own life and future.

"There's the girl I know. Smiles." He leans over and strokes the side of my face.

I smack his hand away.

"So, what's for dinner?" Jack asks, standing up and walking into the kitchen. He opens up my fridge and cupboards. "Man, what have you been eating? Dust bunnies? That's not very PETA of you." I hear him opening up a drawer and then a big book hitting the counter. Turning around, I see him going through the yellow pages of the phone book.

"I'm not eating dinner with you," I say, turning back to stare at the black television on the wall.

"Sushi? Pizza? Italian? What's your poison?"

"I told you I'm not eating dinner with you," I say louder.

"Italian it is! I can never get decent Italian outside of Chicago for some reason. I think I'm cursed." A few seconds later he's talking to someone and putting in an order for lasagna and spaghetti with meatballs. When he hangs up, he comes over to sit with me again. "Which do you like better? Flat pasta with sauce and cheese or squiqqly pasta with sauce and cheese?"

"I'm not eating with you, you stubborn ass."

"Sounds like spaghetti to me."

My heart is thawing even more with his persistence, much as I'm trying to resist. He's like the waves crashing against the rocks eventually turning them to sand. I hate him and love him at the same time for what he's trying to do. I don't want him doing this to me, but it doesn't diminish the love I know he's sharing. I don't deserve someone this amazing in my life.

He puts his arm behind me and scoots closer until his bent knee is touching my thigh. "So, what's on the boob tube? Anything good? Wanna watch a movie and make out?"

I drop my head back onto his arm and stare at the white ceiling. "Why aren't you listening to anything I'm saying?"

"What are you talking about? I'm listening to every single word."

"I told you to leave."

"No, you told me to stay and never leave."

"I told you I didn't invite you here."

"No, you told me to please come and rescue you from your pain and loneliness."

"I told you I didn't want to eat dinner with you."

"No, you told me that you were starving for love *and* food and that you prefer spaghetti."

I turn my head and look at him, the smile I'm trying to hold back making my mouth twitch unattractively. "You obviously have a hearing problem."

He leans in until his face is resting on the back of the couch right near my face. "Nah. Thing is, I listen with my heart, not my ears. It's a better receiver of the true message being sent."

I roll my eyes to the ceiling once more. "God spare me the company of rocker poets."

"Get over here, you," he says, pulling me into his arms as he lies back against the arm of the couch. I fall against his chest and just stay there. Struggling will take too much effort. "Close your eyes and rest until our food gets here," he says. "I plan on asking you tons of personal questions over dinner. You'll need your strength."

My eyes drift closed at just the thought of a rest. I've done nothing but sleep for a couple weeks, but that doesn't stop me from being exhausted. His fingers slowly stroking my arm only make my eyelids feel heavier. "I told you I'm not eating with you," I mumble as the dark closes in.

"That's not what I heard," he says.

CHAPTER
FORTY-ONE

AFTER A FEW BITES OF spaghetti, I'm done eating. I watch Jack shovel all the lasagna and the rest of the noodles into his mouth like he hasn't had anything to eat in a week.

"Where do you put it all?" I ask.

"I have to feed the machine. All that boxing I do burns off every calorie I can possibly eat."

I smile. "You're still with Charlie?"

"Of course I'm still with Charlie. All your boys are."

I look at the couch, feeling both proud and sad over the idea of 'my boys' continuing on the road to happy lives once I'm gone. I wish the first boy I ever had was on that road with them. I hate that I can't let that thought go, that it's a shadow over everything I do.

"What's the matter?" he asks me, putting his empty plate on the coffee table with all the empty styrofoam boxes. "Why does that make you sad?"

"It doesn't. Well, it does. I don't know." I sigh. "Sorry. My brain just isn't working anymore."

"Tell me what you're thinking. Come on. No judgment here, you know that."

I think for a little while before speaking, trying to figure out what exactly it is that's bothering me. There are too many things swirling around in there, making it hard to get a clear picture in my own head. "I guess I'm angry at Austin. I'm angry at myself. I feel guilty about Scott. I feel guilty about Tarin. I'm mad at Tarin too."

"Whoa. That's a lot of anger and guilt to carry out in that little head of yours."

"I know. How do I get rid of it?" I smile because I know the answer, but I don't really want that answer. I want a different one.

"Slay the beast. Get it out of hiding, confront it, take your sword out and cut its head off."

"Sounds like you've been watching *Lord of the Rings* or something."

"*Once Upon A Time* … TV series, actually. But whatever. It works. Guilt and anger doesn't do anything but hurt the one having the feelings. Don't waste your time with it. Come on. Slay the dragon. Let's start with Austin."

"Why Austin?"

"Because that's where this all started, right?"

I lay back on the couch, resting my head on the arm of the seat. "I'd rather sleep."

"I have a feeling you've slept enough in the last couple weeks to last you the next few months. Talk now, sleep later."

"Doesn't matter," I say, blinking my eyes a few times to keep them from getting teary. "Won't take long anyway. Austin broke my heart. I let him down. Story over."

"Come on, you can do better than that." He takes my foot in his lap and plucks at my toes. It strikes me that everyone who knows me seems to have figured out I'm a sucker for the foot massage. I'm a lucky girl to have this many people willing to touch my smelly feet. Life does not completely suck.

"I used to just worry about how I let Austin and Scott down. Now I'm not sure if I'm more mad at myself or Austin."

"Do you feel like you've wasted a lot of anger on yourself … like maybe it should have been directed elsewhere?"

"Maybe. I guess it's that all this time I thought I knew … that I absolutely *knew* what happened with Austin, what he was doing when he was away from me, what his life was like. But really the only thing I knew was this stupid reality I'd created for myself. And that just makes me the biggest hypocrite on the entire planet. Here I am, being paid hundreds of thousands of dollars to get people to wake up to reality and live in the real world, when the entire time I'm over there in la-la land. I'm a fraud." I throw my forearm over my eyes, too embarrassed to look at Jack anymore. "I'm a fraud. I hate myself for that."

Jack reaches over and pushes my arm back to my side. I turn to look at him.

"Stop that," he demands. "It's me sitting here, okay? And listen … I don't accept that. You're not a fraud. You think you're the only one who creates their own reality? Hell … we all do that. Right now I have this reality that I have a shot with you … that I can come in here, sweep you off your butt and make you fall in love with me. But in the back of my mind, I have a feeling you have a completely different reality where we're concerned." He shrugs, like he didn't just lay out the blueprint for heartache. "That's the way life goes. Sometimes your reality meshes with the person you love, sometimes it doesn't. The key is to realize that we all see the world through our own fucked up lenses, so you need to roll with the punches when those lenses shift and see something that throws off the balance."

"How'd you get so smart?" I ask, my throat rough with emotion.

"I have this amazing friend who helped me see past my own nose so I could wake up to the people around me. I owe her my life. I'd do anything for her, you know." He leans down and kisses my big toe.

"Even kiss her smelly toe?"

"Yeah. I'd suck it too if I thought it would get me anywhere."

I kick him and pull my feet towards my butt. "Stay away from my toes, you perv."

"Seriously, though. Any chance I could get a piece of that action over there? I'm just asking."

I kick him harder this time. "Stop. You know I don't feel that way about you. I'm stupid like that."

"I could kiss you real sexy like and maybe change your mind…" He wiggles his eyebrows at me like a crazy lech.

I cringe. "It would be like kissing my brother. Sorry." I reach out and pat his shoulder. "You know I love you, though, right?"

He sighs and throws his arms over the back of the couch while slumping down in the seat. "Yeah, yeah. Story of my life."

I laugh. He's so good at throwing himself a pity party it's comical. "You could have your pick of ten thousand women five minutes after walking out that door."

He turns his head to look at me over his arm. "The only problem is that you're one in a million. Ten thousand options isn't going to cut it."

Tears come to my eyes. I'm in friend-love with the one guy who would adore me forever and I poured everything I had into the guy who cheated on me and took the easy way out of life. I have to be the stupidest woman to ever walk the earth.

"Don't cry. I'll get over it."

"I'm not crying because of that. I'm crying because it's so unfair that it wasn't someone else realizing this about me … the one person I was born to be with."

Jack rolls his eyes and snorts. "Oh, for shit's sake, Scar, give it a rest would you?"

I'm so shocked by his careless anger, I stop crying. "What?"

He sits up and spins to face me, suddenly full of energy for some reason. "Tough love. Brace yourself." He pauses and then unloads on me, his words coming out in a rush. "Austin was a good guy before he became infected with the fame virus. And guess what? You couldn't have saved him. He was a lost cause from the word go. The word selfish was designed for him. He didn't just leave you behind, he left Scott behind. That kid worshipped him. Hell, he even tried to drag Scott down with him. Bet you didn't realize that, did you? No, Austin was no saint. Did he love you? Sure. In his own way. But the love he had for the fame was stronger. And he didn't like himself at all. Nothing you could have said or done would have changed that. You're a saint, you're a miracle worker, yeah … but you can't change people who don't want to change. He wasn't interested."

I'm too shocked to respond.

"Now don't go all girl-nuts on me, okay? I had to say it so we could move on. Now I'm moving on." He pauses a microsecond and keeps going. "Tarin. This guy … he's fucked up. I mean, you know, he got bit bad by the fame dragon, but he's on his way to figuring this stuff out. You jumpstarted it, but Scott's doing awesome. The kid is strong. So strong. That's you that did that. You've been his mom, his sister, his mentor … but even with all that guidance coming from your end, he knew you had shit going on under the surface. We talked about it. He's been worried for a while."

"What the hell, Jack." I'm more than a little stunned. "The blunt honesty is wearing out its welcome over here."

"Then I'll hurry up and finish. Scott says you need to take some time off and mourn the loss of Austin. You never did. You went from dealing with the aftermath to working to save the lives of the lost boys. Now it's time you find the lost girl and bring her back."

He sits back against the couch cushions. "Phew! There, I'm done. Go ahead and yell at me."

I stand. My heart is too heavy to yell or cry anymore. "I'm going to bed."

"Want company?" he asks as I step over his legs.

I lean down and pinch him before he can roll out of the way. "Goodnight, Jack."

"Goodnight, Scarlett."

I leave him in the family room and close the bedroom door behind me. Resting my head against the frame, I cry the first of ten thousand new tears that come before I fall asleep.

CHAPTER
FORTY-TWO

JACK AND I BATTLE THROUGH my roller coaster emotions for another four days before I finally capitulate to his demands and read the texts and emails from Scott, Tarin, Mel, and several other people, including all my lost boys. Apparently the word is out that I've had some sort of mental breakdown.

From Mel I hear, "… *don't worry about a thing … Scott is taking care of everything. He's really something special. Fair warning, I'm going to try like heck to recruit him away from you. I have a feeling he'll be good at anything he puts his mind to doing…*"

From Scott I hear, "*…old man Warner is up my butt crack every day about coming to work for him. As if. I'm so not into the pinky ring posse. Anyway, your boy is coming along. Bad news for Jelly. That test came up negativo for Tarin as the daddy-o, but he's paying her expenses anyway. He's making her go into rehab too. Smart guy. No one wants a baby born with a third eyeball from all the drugs he knows she's taking. Gold star for him being a nice guy. This photography thing he has going? Holy shit. The dood is so talented. Makes me look like a granny with a flashbulb Kodak. I kind of hate him for that, but then again I forgive him when he snaps* *a few of me and makes me look like a total ladies' man. I'll be on GQ next month, you watch. Anyway, I'm on his back all day, he's doing everything right, and he's on track to meet all his contractual obligations, so we're all good. I'm so going to buy myself that Vespa. And no, it's not going to be pink. I miss you. Come back soon, Pooh Bear."*

From Tarin, I've received no less than twenty texts and emails. I scroll through them, able to picture in my mind the expressions on his face, the way he's standing, and the tone of his voice as I take in the words on the screen. He's proud of himself. It's hard work to make these kinds of changes. He wants to take responsibility for himself and his actions. He's sorry and he misses me.

"...Scarlett, you know how sometimes you just go through life on auto-pilot and you don't stop to take the time to appreciate the little things around you? Well, that's what I did, but I also didn't take the time to stop and appreciate the big things around me either. I guess what I'm saying is I appreciated nothing at all. I took advantage of my friends and the people who care about me. I was and probably still am an asshole. You started me on the road to seeing that, but now I feel like I'm walking it alone. I feel pretty confident that I can do this, but I'd rather do it with company, know what I mean? Scott's a cool guy but not exactly what I have in mind. Would you come back? We could call it work and I'd pay you, or we could just call it friends hanging out with friends. Or maybe even we could call it something more. I'd like to call it something more. What do you say? Are you in or are you out?

I turn off my phone and put it on my nightstand without responding to anyone.

"Everything all good?" asks Jack from my doorway.

"Yeah." I can't muster the strength to say it very loudly. Everyone's doing just fine without me.

"You don't sound very happy about that. How come?"

I shrug, turning to face him. "I guess part of me is super proud and part of me feels useless."

"Did Tarin call you that?"

"No. Actually he said he'd rather that I be there."

"So why not go?" Jack folds his arms and leans against the door frame. "He wants you there, you want to be there ... so go."

"Who says I want to be there?"

"Your face. Your tears. The things you say when you're sleeping."

I frown at him, trying to figure out if he's messing with me or not. "I don't talk in my sleep."

"Oh, yes you do. Loud too. Wakes me up." He breaks into a modernized version of the song by the Romantics, *Talking In Your Sleep*. I'm not amused.

"Bullshit. Your room's on the other side of the apartment."

"Who says I sleep in there?"

I turn and look at my bed, thrown off by the idea that I've had a bed buddy without even realizing it. "You don't sleep in here. I'd know that."

He laughs and pushes off the frame to stand straight. "I'm just messing with you. I sleep on the couch sometimes, though, and I can hear you plain as day. You're always arguing with Tarin. I think you guys have unfinished business."

I take the phone off the nightstand and stare at it. "Maybe we do." I can't believe I just admitted that out loud. "But I'm not ready to go there right now. He needs to finish what he started without me getting in the middle of it."

"Why?"

"I don't know. I think … this thing with Austin … it just … complicates things too much. I don't want him needing me because he feels guilty. Like he has to make something up to me."

"Why do you think he does? Want to do that, I mean?"

"He says he's made mistakes and he's trying to fix them. He's already apologized for the Austin things, so …" I shrug. "I just think getting together based on our mutual situation with Austin is a really bad idea. It'll eventually go down in flames and take me with it."

"Do you care about him?" Jack asks, walking into the room and taking me by the shoulders.

"Of course. I care about all my clients."

"Shut up with the client crap or I'll put my tongue in your ear. Do. You. Care. About. Him?" Jack shakes me for effect.

I sigh in defeat. "Yes. It's totally stupid and awful, though, so I'm going to ignore it."

"You're going to ignore the feelings?"

"Yes. That's what I'm going to do."

"No, you're not." He slides his arm around my shoulders and walks me from the room, snatching my phone out of my hand on the way.

I leap up to try and get it from him in the hallway, but he's way too tall for me, and now thanks to the boxing regime I started him on, he's a wall of solid muscle. His thumb is tapping out a message up near the ceiling.

"Cut it out, Jack!" I yell, panicked about what he might be doing.

"Back off, wild woman, I'm busy sexting your lover."

"You'd better not be!" I scream, doubling my efforts to retrieve my cell. I succeed in messing up his hair, but that's about it.

He hands me back my phone with a very self-satisfied smile. "Here you go. Mission accomplished."

I hurriedly click over to the texts to see what he sent.

The message to Tarin says one thing: "Come see me in Chicago."

"Goddammit, Jack!" I run screaming down the hallway and tackle him over the back of the couch.

CHAPTER FORTY-THREE

JACK AND I ARE WATCHING television that night when Tarin's face suddenly appears on the screen. He's attending a premier of some sort and he's alone.

I've never seen him looking so sharp. We've only been apart for three weeks, but he's a changed person, that much is clear. And I'm not the only one who notices. The girl holding the microphone and hoping to interview him is swept away by it all - the hair, the clothes, his shoulders. *Wow and holy schmokes.* My heart, it be melting. I cannot believe I had sex with that man and left him behind. How stupid am I? *Very stupid. Very, very, very stupid.* I grip the arm of the couch so hard my fingers go white.

"My *god!*" the girl says. "Tarin Kilgour of *By Degrees* is here and he is ... Tarin!" She coaxes him over with her microphone and crazy waving. "Tell us, what the heck happened to you! Are you in love? Did you join a cult? What happened here?" She puts her hand on his upper arm and looks back and forth between Tarin and the camera, her teeth so big and white they're almost too bright to look at. She's rubbing his arm up and down, making me want to reach through the TV to smack her. *Jealousy? Oh my god, I'm jealous. Oh, this isn't good.* I leave off with killing the couch and rub my face a few times, trying to get ahold of myself.

Tarin shrugs, giving her a warm smile while also stepping just a tiny bit to the side, enough to detach her hand from his arm. My heart feels like it's bursting inside my chest cavity, and my face burns with heat. *Oh joy! He doesn't want her to touch him and she's beautiful! Ahhhhh!* This is so not the old Tarin. The old Tarin would have gotten her number and coaxed a blow job from her later.

"Seriously, though, Tarin, how did you do it? You look amazing."

"Well, I made some new friends, cleaned house, started boxing."

She puts her hand to her chest and flutters her eyelashes. "Boxing? Oh my god, be still my heart." She looks at the camera and leans in a little, like she's sharing a secret with the million or so women watching. "As if he wasn't sexy enough, right? … Boxing? Someone bring me a fan." She turns back to him all business. "Tell us who your new friends are, Tarin. Any ladies in the bunch? Anyone special?"

"You could say that." He looks into the camera and winks. He actually winks! My heart stops, spasms painfully, and then one giant *ker-thump!* later, it's back to racing again.

"Man, is he fucking working that camera or what?" asks Jack, smirking. "Do you know how many girls just came in their pants over that one?" He shakes his head slowly. "I gotta hand it to the guy. When he goes clean, he goes all in with the style, know what I'm saying?" Jack looks down at his heavily ringed fingers and scrappy jeans. "Maybe I should buy a suit." He looks over at me, as I sit there dealing with anxiety level nine. "Would I look good in a suit? I know you told me to get one before and I ignored you, but I'm thinkin' maybe I should try one."

I can't peel my eyes from the screen now, trying to catch another glimpse of the most attractive man I've ever seen in my life. *Tarin. Holy shit.*

"Yeah, sure. Get a suit," I say absently. I grab the remote and turn up the sound, trying to catch the mumbled conversation he's having just off camera with someone else. The girl's mic is catching part of it as she prepares to snag the next person coming her way.

"Yeah, I got a lot of things going on right now," he says to someone off-camera. "I'm going out of town soon, so I'm not sure I'll be there next week. Maybe later, though. Call Mel…" That's the last I heard before the girl with the microphone is squealing over her next grab.

"What color should I get?" asks Jack. "Black? Probably black, right? Or maybe I'll swing the other direction and go full-on white…"

"Dark green," I say standing, thinking about Tarin's eyes. They're so, so dark. But on the screen just now, I could see the green. I swear I could see something magic in them. "Go with green."

"Are you serious?" he asks, looking up at me.

"What?" I say, looking over at him, suddenly realizing we're having a conversation. Kind of.

"You want me to wear a green suit?"

"No, I don't want you to wear a green suit. Don't be ridiculous."

"Then why'd you tell me to go with green?"

"Shut up, Jack, I'm trying to think." I rub my temples in circles, trying to make the headache and panic go away.

"What's wrong with you?"

I drop my hands instantly and jump to my feet. "What's wrong with me? What's *wrong* with me? Why are you even asking me that question? You know what's wrong with me." I throw both hands towards the television. "You texted Tarin and now he's coming out here! And he's all dressed up!"

Jack frowns. "I doubt he's going to wear that monkey suit out here. He'll need to get it dry cleaned first."

"Shut *up*, Jack! You know what I mean!"

"Not really." He looks at me like he's worried. "You're kind of wigging out on me right now. Should I go put my bike helmet on just in case?"

I flop down onto the couch. "Don't you get it? You told him to come. He thinks *I* told him to come. He just winked at the camera and sent me a message! He's on his way!"

"Maybe he wasn't talking to you."

I jump-tackle Jack and pound him with a throw pillow. "Of course he was talking to me, you asshole!"

"Okay! Okay!" Jack is laughing hysterically beneath my onslaught. "Relax! Jesus, woman. I have a tour coming up. Don't put me in the hospital. The tabloid's 'll have a field day with that shit. I can read the headlines now ... Jack O'Leary beat nearly to death by crazed wannabe lover."

I calm down in the face of his ridiculousness and go to my corner of the couch to shoot daggers at him with my eyes. "You suck, you know that?"

"You totally love me *and* the fact that I texted Tarin for you. You were too chicken shit to do it, but you wanted it done, so don't play dumb with me." He affects a deep-south accent. "Ain't nobody got time fo' dat."

"I'm going to bed," I say, standing again. "I'm nervous now, thanks to you. I'm going to get a stomach ache too."

"Good. I hope you have lots of sexy dreams too. After the stomach ache." As I get to the bedroom, he yells louder so I'll hear him through the door. "I'll be sleeping on the couch tonight! I hear the secrets that you keep when you're talking in your sleep!"

I lock the door to my bedroom, not convinced he isn't sneaking in to listen to me babble about who knows what. After getting in bed, I lay there listening to the sound of my own breathing and the faint glimmering of voices still coming from the television. All I can think about is seeing Tarin again, and every time I get an image of his face or his hands or his arms in my mind, I think about that time we had sex on the couch and my heart doubles its pace. I'm so not ready to see him again. I don't think I have the strength I know it's going to take to make him go away. Maybe that's why I don't text him back and explain it was all just a misunderstanding.

CHAPTER FORTY-FOUR

THE NEXT MORNING I WAKE up and wander out of my room around ten. I tried to sleep in as long as possible so I could usher the day past as quickly as possible, but this is as far as I got before my eyelids refused to close anymore. I'm ridiculously nervous about Tarin coming, and I know I'm not going to be able to eat a thing until he's come and gone. *Tea. I need some tea. And then some Valium. I wonder where I could score some.*

Shuffling out to the family room, I talk to the back of Jack's head. It's slumped to the side a little and he's wearing a baseball cap, something I've never seen him do, but I write it off as another one of his eccentricities. *Sleeping in a hat. Typical.* I have no idea how he can sleep all night sitting up like that. It's like sleeping on a plane, something I've never been able to do.

I talk loudly to wake him up. "You need to get up and take a shower, Jacky boy. You smell." I smile at myself. There's something evil inside me that makes me want to harass this man from the moment he opens his eyes to a new day until the minute he closes them at night. "You need a haircut too. Go get one, would ya? Hiding your rat's nest under that stupid hat isn't working."

He picks his head up and leans forward. Standing up, he turns to face me as I reach the counter in the kitchen.

I'm looking over my shoulder to laugh at the cranky expression I expect to see there, when I freeze.

Time stands still.

I'm suffocating all of a sudden because I can't breathe correctly. I feel dizzy.

"You're not Jack," I say. I'm whispering because that's all I'm capable of doing. My lungs and voice won't work.

"No. I'm Tarin, actually." He walks over and holds out his hand. "Nice to meet you."

I stare stupidly at his outstretched arm. I know those tattoos. I know those muscles, although they look thicker than I remember them. Looking up, I realize that there's something new about him. I don't know that smile that's lighting up his face. I've never seen anything like it. I feel like a Hershey's Kiss left in a hot car. Sweat breaks out on my upper lip and under my arms. *Attractive.*

"Aren't you going to shake my hand?" he asks. His grin could not possibly be cuter. That hat should make him look like a fool, but all it makes me want to do is dare him to take his shirt off again. *Truth or dare, Tarin. Truth or dare...*

My brain is going haywire. I frown and smile at the same time, and I'm sure I look like I'm having intestinal cramps. They're probably not that far away considering how my guts are churning right now. "No, I'm not going to shake your hand. No way." I scoot to a spot behind the counter so he won't see anymore of my nightgown than he already has. *Ack! How humiliating! I'm wearing my granny gown! Why?! Why did I put this on last night?* It's my comfort-wear. My Wal-Mart Value-of-the-Day that has traveled with me for five years, survived with me through thick and thin. It's heinously ugly, but it helps me sleep. I'm convinced it's magic. Possibly dark magic, but I don't care. At least, I never cared before.

"I hope you don't mind that Jack let me in. He said he was going for donuts but that was like two hours ago."

"When did you get here?" I have nothing to do with my hands so I tap my fingers on the counter. *Tap, tap, tap, tap, tap…*

"In Chicago? I left L.A. last night around ten. I waited a few hours after arriving to show up here, though. I didn't want to interrupt your beauty sleep." He gestures to my nightgown as he smiles and I want to die of shame.

"I didn't tell you to come," I blurt out. I struggle to keep my hand on the counter and not up slapping my face like it wants to. *What a dope. Why did I say that?*

"I got a text…" He's frowning, confused. Maybe a little embarrassed.

"That was Jack. He took my phone from me and did it." I look at the counter, too humiliated to continue. This feels like a really bad high school moment. *Awko taco.*

"You could have changed it, though, huh? … Texted me back and told me that it was Jack. But you didn't."

I look up and he's got that damn smile on again. Its cuteness annoys me because I feel myself falling under its spell. I hate not being in control of my own emotions.

"I guess. But that doesn't matter. I mean, you have places to be and they're not Chicago."

He pauses to take a deep breath and then speaks. "I was hoping I could convince you to come back with me to LA. I chartered a jet just for us."

I shake my head. "I'm not going. I don't belong out there."

"Out there in L.A.? Or with me?"

"Either. Both." My words feel too harsh for both of us, so I soften the next ones. "I don't know. I just don't think it's a good idea."

"What if I do? Doesn't that matter to you?" He tilts his head slightly. I see a vulnerability in his expression that hurts my heart. I despise myself for making him feel this way, for knowing I'm going to keep hurting him.

"Everything matters to me," I say, tears stinging my eyes. "That's the problem. Everything matters too much and it hurts. I'm tired of the hurting." I can't look at him anymore so I stare at the phone book that has been offering Jack and me delivery people laden with boxes of food.

Tarin comes into the kitchen.

"Stay over there," I warn, backing up and pointing towards the couch.

"Why?" he asks. "You're not afraid of me, are you?"

"No, don't be ridiculous."

He takes another step.

"Please, Tarin?" I'm too embarrassed to say any more.

"Just tell me why. I need to hear you say it."

"Say what?"

"You know."

"No, I really don't. What do you want me to say?"

"Tell me you regret ever being with me and I'll go. I just need to hear you say the words so I know the truth. I've almost convinced myself you care and that the reason you left is because you couldn't handle the emotions that were coming up between us, but if I'm wrong, I need to know so I can let you go. Otherwise I know myself … I'm going to be stubborn and keep holding on as long as I think there's a chance."

"I'm not going to say that …" I pause, realizing we're thinking two completely different things. "Tarin, I don't want you coming any closer because I just woke up. I have morning breath like you wouldn't believe, and I'm wearing an eighty-year-old's nightgown."

He pauses and then a sexy smile appears, slowly but surely erasing his worried expression. "I'm kinda liking the old school thing you have going on there." He points at my clothes.

I grab a spatula off the counter, refusing to smile back at him. "Stay back."

He holds up his hands in mock surrender. "No need to get physical. At least not with a spatula."

"Get out of the kitchen and I'll put it down."

He turns to leave and then spins around, leaping to close the distance between us and grab me around the waist. Before I have a chance to whack him away with my dangerous cooking weapon, he throws me up over his shoulder and leaves the kitchen, moving quickly through the apartment.

"Ahhh! Tarin! What are you doing?!" I struggle, hitting his butt over and over with the flat side of the spatula. It's having no effect, and my emotions are exploding inside me. Fear, excitement, worry, embarrassment, anger, and confusion are warring for domination over my brain. None of this makes any sense. He flies across the country to play caveman with me? No way is that happening. "Austin! Put me *down!*" I scream, not realizing what I've said until it's too late.

Tarin stops in his tracks.

I freeze in the middle of hitting him with the spatula and my face starts burning red. Flames of humiliation consume me as my body shifts, my feet moving towards the floor.

He slowly bends over and puts me down. I land in front of him, and as he backs away, I see the hurt I've caused him. Eyes that were twinkling with happiness are now just dull. The smile is gone and a frost has moved in.

Tears come to my eyes and they don't stop there. Soon they're on my cheeks and my lip is quivering.

"You called me Austin," he says, his voice rough. He's sad, that much is clear, and I hate that I caused his pain.

"It was an accident."

"I'm not Austin."

"I know you're not." I can't keep the trembling away. It's like the temperature in the room has dropped twenty degrees the way I'm shaking.

"Are you sure about that?"

I want to assure him. I want to nod and say absolutely, *Yes, I'm sure you're not him, Tarin*. But I'm just not convinced my heart knows what my brain does. And if I know nothing else about myself now, I at least know those two parts of me need to be thinking and working towards the same thing, or my life will always be a mess.

I let out a long, shaky breath. "I'm sorry, Tarin. I know you're Tarin, but sometimes my memories of Austin are really near the surface when you're around. I don't know why."

"Is it because I was there. When he ... you know ... died?"

"No. I thought that was the reason, but no." I shake my head emphatically. I want him to believe me because it's one hundred percent the truth.

"What is it then? You wish I was him, don't you?"

I grab Tarin's biceps and squeeze them, desperate to make him understand, or at least not misunderstand. "No! Don't think that. Please, don't think that. I don't wish you were anyone but you."

"Would you bring Austin back if you could?"

I open my mouth to say, *Yes, of course* ... but the words don't come. I shut my mouth and think about my answer a little longer. *Do I wish he was here? Do I want him in my life? If I could have him here right this second, how would it feel?*

"Well?" he prompts me.

"That's weird," I finally say.

"What's weird?"

My hands drop to my sides and I look at the floor, frowning as I review my confusing thoughts. "I was going to say yes, but then ... I just couldn't." I look up into Tarin's eyes, the revelation hitting me like a ton of bricks. "It felt like a lie."

"Do you think it would have felt like a lie a month ago?"

It only takes me two seconds to find the answer to this question. I shake my head no.

"Can I ask you a really rude question?" he says. His energy is picking up again; I can practically feel it. So is mine. Something big is about to happen to us. I wish I knew what it was so I could prepare myself. I so don't like this flying by the seat of my pants shit.

"Can I stop you from asking it?" I ask, a smile sneaking out.

He smiles back. "No. I'm kind of pushy that way." He puts his hands out between us in a calming gesture. "My question is this ... and don't freak out ... just let me explain ..." He puts his hands on my shoulders. "Scarlett, will you have sex with me? Like, right now?"

I step back away from him so quickly, I forget the wall is behind me and bang my back, head, and heels against it. "Sorry, what?" I sputter out. *Granny gown! Morning breath! Run!*

"Hear me out. I'm not being a total rapist here … there's a method to my madness."

"Oh, I'll bet." I take a side step towards my room, wondering what are the chances that I can get in there where my bathroom and toothpaste are before he catches me. The idea of having sex with him again is not at all distasteful; quite the opposite, in fact. God, how I want to see him naked again. But the idea of him catching a whiff of my morning breath, however? Yeah. Not gonna happen. I had garlic sticks last night. *Fucking Jack and his Italian food.*

"No, seriously," he continues, pressing his case, "see, I was thinking … the last time we were together like that, we'd been drinking and that song Jack wrote was still out there in the air, and you were all wrapped up in the emotions and whatever. I feel like I kind of took advantage of that. Right now, you're all good, right? Totally sober. It's not even night time, so you're not caught up in any music or club atmosphere. And you've had almost a month break from me."

"So?"

"So, if you and I can still connect like we did that last time, then we'll know it was for real."

"What was for real?" He's making no sense at all. I don't know if he's talking about sex or *us* or the price of tea in China at this point.

His shoulders sag. "Aw, come on, Scar. Don't play me like that. You know I wasn't the only one feeling that stuff that night, right?" He reaches out a hand towards me, but when I shrink away as much as possible, he lets it drop back to his side.

"I don't know what to say, Tarin. Mostly because you're confusing the shit out of me right now."

He shrugs, his happiness faded out almost to nothing. "The way I see it is you've got two choices. Either tell me to stay or tell me to go. If I stay, we're doing this. We're going to get naked and get to know each other real well. At least I *hope* we can do this one thing so we can see if it's real or not."

I can't believe how stupid he's being, now that I know what he's actually saying. I stomp my foot. "Sex isn't the litmus test for a relationship, Tarin!"

"No, I know that. But sex like we had? I've never had it like that before!" He starts to reach for me but then thinks better of it and just gestures around wildly. "I know someday when I'm with my forever girl, I want the sex to be like that. Like I had with you. I just need to know if it's *you*. If *you're* the one. Because I already know you have the other things I've been looking for, but the chemistry is important." He smiles at me and shrugs, letting his hands fall to his sides. "What can I say? I like sex." *He's smiling at me! Argh! Why does he have to do that?!*

I swallow with difficulty. "You need to know if I'm the one, you said." I'm tapping my toe super fast, unable to keep still I'm so nervous. "The one for what, Tarin?" I'm not playing games; I'm just not sure I understand what he's saying. I know what I *want* him to mean, but the way we keep misunderstanding each other, I can't trust my assumptions anymore. I cannot imagine anything more humiliating than thinking he wants to be in a real relationship with me when all he's after is a long distance booty call.

He looks me in the eyes and gives me the smile of a young teen boy, still untouched by fame and not yet disillusioned by the world's disappointments. "I need to know if you're my forever girl."

CHAPTER
FORTY-FIVE

I SHOULD DO THE MATURE, adult, responsible thing and tell him to go get a hotel room and stay there. I shouldn't even entertain the idea of sex being an entrance exam for a relationship. I should just lock myself in my room alone until he leaves the apartment. Too bad my sex drive is chauffeuring my life around right now.

"Fine," I say. "On one condition." My body's already tingling with anticipation.

His eyes are practically sparkling. "Name it."

"You give me five minutes to get ready before we start."

"Two minutes," he says stepping closer.

"Three!" I sidestep towards my door. "And you wait out here."

"Done." He looks at his phone. "I just set my timer. Better hurry." He looks up and winks at me and my heart flips over.

I literally run down the hallway and into my bedroom, slamming the door shut behind me.

"Shit, shit,shit!" I dash over to the walk-in closet and want to scream at its empty interior. The only thing in there is a pile of my clothes I haven't bothered to wash since I've arrived. My new line of homeless wear. *That's not going to work.* Wearing anything in that pile would be only effective as a repellant.

I go into the bathroom and squeeze a huge blob of toothpaste onto my toothbrush and work at making my teeth so fresh and shiny that he won't notice I have nothing sexy to wear. My hair is ridiculously awful, since I slept on it wet. A brush and a few clumps of ripped out knots later, and at least it's not sticking out in eight different directions anymore.

I jerk my nightgown over my head and jump in the shower, soaping every crevice on my body, scrubbing my skin until it glows. I'm just shutting off the water when I hear my door shut.

"Tarin are you in here already?" My heart's going triple-time.

"Time's up. Come out, come out, wherever you are."

"Stay in there! I'll be right out, I promise!" *Ohmygod, ohmygod, ohmygod! He's out there and he wants to have sex! Ahhh!*

"You have thirty seconds before I come in after you."

I grab the nearest towel and dry myself off as best I can with shaking hands. I've gone cold with the panic and the air conditioning on my wet body, so now I'm covered in goosebumps. My legs immediately grow stubble all over, even though they were just shaved last night. *Dammit! Cactus legs!*

Wrapping the towel around me and tucking it in near my armpit, I take one last look at myself in the mirror and then go out into the bedroom. Tarin's standing by the bed in only his underwear, a pair of black boxer briefs that leave little to the imagination. His tattoos wind around well-defined muscles that are at least a third bigger than the last time I saw them.

"Whoa," I say, stopping my tracks. He looks fantastic.

"Nice, right?" He's grinning from ear to ear. "Watch this." He gives me a double bicep pose that has my knees going weak, but when he slowly shifts into the Atlas god position, showing not only those biceps again but triceps, back and leg muscles, I'm a mess.

"How in the hell did you do that in such a short period of time?" I'm drawn to him, unable to stop moving forward. I have to touch him to see if he's real. I'm afraid of my emotions, but more afraid of letting him slip away. This seems too good to be true. He came out here to track me down and he wants to give me this? *Merry Christmas and happy birthday Scarlett. Today is your lucky day.*

"How did I do it? With hard work and the help of Josh, Charlie, Zach, and Leonard. Oh, and Scott. Man, he's a pest. But it's all paying off." He stands straight and rubs his hands up and down his chest and six-pack abs. "I just needed to get rid of the padding and build up what was already there." He steps closer so we're just a foot apart. "You like what you see?"

"I like what I see, yes." I'm nodding while my gaze roams all over his body, finally stopping on his face. Everything but his eyes are hard, harsh, tough-looking and dominating. But his eyes … they're soft and vulnerable, and filled with hope, probably just like mine are.

"I liked your other pajamas, but these are nicer," he says, reaching up and hooking a finger in the top of my towel.

I grab onto it, holding it against my body. "It's just a towel." I can't think of anything sexier to say and I cringe inwardly at my complete inability to play bedroom games.

"Sometimes less is more, though." He tugs again, loosening the connection holding the thick material up around me.

He leans in and puts his lips against mine. I'm expecting him to attack me, but he doesn't. Just the gentlest kiss and he's standing away from me again.

I'm breathless with the attraction I'm feeling towards him, already wet for him down there. I'm so easy it's not even funny.

"I missed you, babe," he says. The words make my heart spasm.

"Me too." My voice isn't working properly.

"You sure?" he asks, coming closer and putting his hands on my upper arms. He caresses me, moving his palms up and down over my chilled skin. It sends shivers all over my body.

I nod. "I tried not to, though."

He play-frowns. "Why would you do that?"

"I don't know. I guess I don't want to miss you so much."

"But you can't help yourself," he says smiling, obviously very happy with himself.

"No, I guess I can't." Saying it out loud is almost freeing. I've been denying it for so long, it's a relief to finally stop trying and to give in.

He leans in and kisses me again, another barely-there pressing of the lips that makes me crazy with what it promises but doesn't deliver.

"Take your towel off," he demands. "I want to see you naked."

"You first," I say, grasping at my last bits of modesty. It's so much easier for me to admire his body than to show mine. I don't really have body image issues, but that doesn't mean I'm comfortable running around naked with a guy who makes me think the things he does. The hard shell I built around myself over the last two years feels like it'll come right off with my towel, and I'm afraid to let that happen. I don't do vulnerability well; not since Austin died, anyway.

"You do it," he says.

"Do what?" I ask, as he closes the distance between us. Our bodies are almost touching. We're so close, and yet, far enough from each other that I want to press forward to be nearer to him. He's like a magnet and I can't resist the pull.

"Take my clothes off."

I smile nervously. "You already did almost everything yourself."

"But I left the best part for you." He reaches up a finger and runs it along the edge of the top of my towel, stopping at my cleavage and putting his finger down in it. It makes me think of how he squeezed and sucked my nipples before, and I have to bite my lip to keep from moaning out loud.

He leans in and kisses my neck, then sucks it gently before standing straight again. "I'm waiting." He lifts an eyebrow, and I take a step back, my face going red.

"Fine." The sexy is off the charts right now. I have to get us naked so we can get going on this thing before I have a stroke from holding back.

I get down on my knees, lifting the bottom of the towel so I don't kneel on it. Putting my fingers into the top of his waistband, I slowly peel the stretchy material down, revealing a very swollen cock right in front of my face.

Once released from its silk prison, it stands out straight and proud, practically begging to be touched and licked. As he steps out of his underwear, I can't help but reach up and grasp his hard length. It's hot to the touch and soft like velvet. I run my hand from tip to base and back again, using the softest grip and slowest rhythm possible. My fingers bump over the veins that are bulging out with his need.

He's looking down at me, a storm behind his eyes. "That feels so good," he says quietly. "I love looking down at you and seeing you touch me like that."

He's covered in muscle, but I know I can have him a quivering mess in no time flat, and it emboldens me. I lick him just once and look up for his reaction. His sharp intake of breath tells me all I need to know, but I ask anyway.

"Do you like that?"

He laughs without humor. "Are you kidding me? You're killing me here."

I move in for another taste and then another, wrapping my lips around him. I can tell he's trying to keep still but soon he's no longer in control. Running my free hand up his muscled thigh, I revel in the strong man before me and the idea that even though I'm the one on my knees, he's the one that's at my command. It's such a rush.

With a loud moan he backs away from me, pulling his cock from my hand and mouth and putting some distance between us. "You have to stop," he says, breathing heavily. "I wanted this to be about both of us and you're about to finish me off." He runs his fingers through his hair and stares down at his throbbing length. "Holy shit, babe. Where'd you learn how to do that?"

"Prostitution 101. Took the class in college." I don't know how to tell him seriously that he's teaching me as we go. I'm taking every signal he's sending and letting it guide me. I'm not that experienced in the bedroom, since Austin was my one and only and he wasn't really into foreplay.

"Shut up," he says, taking a big step towards me and helping me to my feet in a hurry. He takes me on both sides of my face and pulls me to him, pressing his mouth to mine and kissing me with abandon. Our lips open and tongues meet, sparking a fire deep inside me. I need him to feed the flames and then put them out. I want it all.

I'm pressing against him and it makes my towel slip, but I let it go. The feel of his skin against mine is like a drug and I need some of it soon or I'll go crazy. The damp terrycloth falls to the floor at our feet and I waste no time making sure every inch of my torso is touching a part of his. He's hard and warm and hairy on his belly. The sensations that rise up in me are taking over.

He pushes me sideways and turns me around so my legs are against the bed. Suddenly I'm falling back and he's on me, both hands on either side of my head as he suspends himself above me. "Scoot back a little," he orders.

I comply, loving the feel of the soft, cool sheets on my naked back. I'm glad I didn't bother making the bed today.

"Can I kiss you down there?" he asks, leaning down to nuzzle my neck. The shivers make my nipples extra hard and goose-bumps sprout up all over me.

I panic at the question, not sure if he means what I think he means. "Down where?" I know it's a stupid question, but I can't help but ask it.

"I'll show you. You tell me to stop if you don't want me to."

He's suddenly gone from view and the weight of his body shifts to my lower legs as he settles himself down there. And then his tongue is on my clit and I spasm with the pleasure the simple touch brings.

"Tarin!" I gasp.

"Yeah," he whispers, moving his tongue around some more. His hands slide up from my knees to where his face is, stroking my inner thighs. The combination of sensations is maddening. I can't stop my hips from moving in a sensual rhythm along with his tongue.

My ability to think rationally quickly disappears in the wake of his touch. I can't even tell what he's doing down there, but whatever it is, it's bringing me closer and closer to something that's going to rock my world. "Tarin! Please stop," I say. I sound almost like I'm crying.

He stops immediately. "Am I hurting you?" His voice is full of concern.

"No," I gasp out. "You're going to make me finish too soon."

He crawls up towards me with a devilish gleam in his eye. "Sorry," I say, feeling bad that I'm ruining such a great time, that I'm such an amateur at this whole thing.

"Sorry? Sorry for what? Sorry I'm so awesome at licking your pussy that you're going to come?"

"Don't say that word," I say, giggling like a schoolgirl.

"What word? Pussy?"

"Stop," I say, still laughing, but now also trying to crawl away from him.

"Why? Does it make you uncomfortable?" He grabs me and forces me back under him.

"It's a dirty word," I say, embarrassed that I've actually said that out loud. Truth is, I don't hate the word. It makes him seem darker when he says it, though. Maybe that should make him less attractive, but it doesn't. It has the opposite effect and now I'm worried that I'm going to fall even more for him than I already have. All for the love of pussy.

"But you like dirty words, don't you? I know I do." He's teasing me now, his eyes crinkling at the corners with his smile.

"Are we still having sex?" I ask, trying to distract him.

He leans to the side a little and then uses a hand to guide the tip of his cock over to my entrance. He moves it around, settling it between my folds before putting his hand on my breast under him.

"I don't know," he says, just before pushing himself into me a little. "Are we?"

A whimper sneaks past my lips and I nod. "Yes, I think we are," I whisper, lifting my legs to give him better access.

"Yeah, I think we are too," he says, pushing in more, reaching under my ass to pull my folds apart and bury himself deeper. "Oh, god, yeah. We're definitely having sex right now. Jesus Christ…"

His eyes close and he's lost in the sensations. The expression on his face tells me he's as bad off as I am in this whole thing. I'd cry with joy if I wasn't so overwhelmed with the heat and wanting to just scream.

"Sex now, cry later," I whisper as I close my eyes.

He stills. "What'd you say?"

I shake my head rapidly, hating that I said that out loud. "Never mind. Just … do this." I pull on his ass, trying to force him in.

"Do what?" he asks.

I open my eyes and he's smiling down at me again. He's evil.

"You know what. Have sex with me."

He pulses in once and then stops. "No, I don't like that word. It's too sterile. Tell me what you want to do."

"Have sex," I say, gasping when he pushes into me hard and fast. My body responds greedily, arching up for more.

"Nope. Not that word. Use another one."

"You're trying to get me to talk dirty, aren't you?" I pull his ass harder and arch into him. We both moan together.

He massages my breast and pinches my nipple between two fingers. "Say it and I'll do it. It's that simple."

I buck underneath him, trying to force him to do what I want from underneath, but I can only get so much satisfaction that way. "Please, Tarin. Don't tease me." I'm sweating from the exertion and anticipation.

"I want to hear you say it." He goes dark on me, all the humor gone to be replaced by pure sexual need. Playtime is over, and maybe it should scare me but all it does is make me want him more. I cannot get enough of the dichotomy that is Tarin, warm and tender one minute, dark and dangerous the next.

"Tell me what you want me to say, and I'll say it," I whisper. Grinding my clit up against the base of his cock is building something in me, and I know it'll only take a little effort on his part to throw me into the abyss. I've only ever been there once before, but now I want to live there. I'll do just about anything he wants at this point, and I think he knows this. Something about the way he's staring down at me tells me he knows he's calling the shots. The tides have turned and the coin has flipped. By degrees, the servant has become the master and the master has become the servant. I never even saw it coming.

"Tell me you want me to fuck you," he says in a menacing tone.

I pause, watching his jaw pulse out with the restraint he's exercising. I know he wants me as much as I want him, but for some reason he needs to make me do this. The old Scarlett, the one who was hired to straighten his life out would have balked. The Scarlett I am now, the one who wants Tarin in a whole other way does not.

"Fuck me, Tarin. I want you to."

He pushes in hard once and growls. "Say it again."

"Fuck me, Tarin, *please.*" I gasp the last word out as the feel of his length sliding into me brings me higher and higher into the clouds.

He pushes in several more times. I feel him growing even harder inside me, his cock getting bigger somehow, stretching me, making me groan with the ecstasy I sense just outside my reach.

"Please … please …" I can't make sense anymore. Words just come out that I have no control over. "Tarin …" Our movements are getting faster, more hurried, both of us rushing towards the end.

But as we get closer and closer to the finish line, I don't want the end to come. It's the journey that is taking me places, the things happening on the way to orgasm that suddenly mean the most. I never want this to be over.

His hands are traveling up and down my body, while kisses rain down around my face and neck. He can't seem to get enough of me as he bucks against me wildly and squeezes and pulls and strokes and shouts. I'm yelling now too and hanging on for dear life. Nails dig into his back as I feel myself falling, falling, falling…

"Scarlett!" he shouts, pulling my hair with a fisted hand and smashing his heavy body into my much smaller one.

"Tarin!" I gasp as I feel myself flying off the cliff. Wave after wave of strong, pulsing, shivering orgasm rock my body. I moan, I shout, I cry, and the two of us turn the bed into a tangle of sheets and legs and arms. The smell of our sex comes up around us and just adds to the sensual atmosphere. One last scream from both of us brings us to the end, and once again, the tears flow from my eyes.

When we finally come down to earth a few minutes later, Tarin is still inside me but lying almost diagonally. I'm spread eagle on the bed, staring at the ceiling as my vision comes back into focus. The only sounds in the room now are our heavy breaths as we try to get oxygen into our lungs.

He reaches over and tries to pet my head, but instead mashes my face a few times. He's talking but his mouth is mushed into the covers so it comes out muffled. "You're so pretty," he says. "And I love your pussy too."

I slap him away and try to roll him off me. "Go away, dirty boy."

He laughs, lifting himself up by his arms and looking over at me. "You like it." His hair is pressed in on one side and he's sweaty. He should probably look ugly to me but I've never seen such a beautiful man in all my life.

I slap his back. "I like you. That's it."

He falls to the side, slipping out of me and lying on his back, his lower body still over my legs. "Man. That was awesome. I'm in love."

I slap him again, this time hard on the arm. "Don't you dare."

He crawls off me and sits on the edge of the bed, taking off the condom and putting it on the wrapper on the nightstand before turning back to lie down by me. "Don't I dare what? Love you?"

"No, stupid. Don't you dare tell me you do like that. It's rude. It's not a casual word and you don't love someone just because you have good sex with them."

He play-frowns. "I'm sorry. You like the romantic stuff, huh? And by the way, it was *great* sex, not just good sex."

"All girls like the romantic stuff, idiot." I'm trying to be offended, but he's so damn cute right now it's impossible. His hair is pure trauma and he's pouting like a little boy. He actually looks worried.

He lifts up his fingers and starts ticking them off. "Okay, so no casual I love yous, no dirty words during sex, and … you like it when I eat your pussy. Did I miss anything?"

I slap his fingers away and press my hand into his face, trying to push him away too. "Go away. You're ruining the moment."

He grabs my hand and pulls me over next to him, forcing me to cuddle up to his side with my head on his chest. My efforts to avoid the forced affection are futile. He's way stronger than he used to be, and I'm really not trying all that hard.

"I'm sorry, babe. Let me try again, okay?" He angles his head to look down at me and I nod.

"Okay. First of all, that sex was magical. I'm going to write a song about it."

"It passed the test?"

"Absolutely. A- plus plus plus. Now I know for sure."

"What do you know for sure?" I'm pretty sure I know what he's going to say but I play stupid just so I can hear it.

"That you're my forever girl. You've got the whole beauty thing going, brains enough for the both of us, athletic skills in the ring - even though you let a teenager kick your ass once, but I'm willing to write that off as a fluke - and you can appreciate the kind of music I make. You're the whole package."

I squeeze him tight to me, more happy than I can express in words.

"Now it's your turn," he says, looking down at me again. "Am I your forever man?"

Some of the happy fades, replaced by worry. For some reason a vision of Austin pops into my head and I worry what he'd think.

"What's the matter?" Tarin asks. "I'm not your forever guy? Dammit, I knew I should have made you come while I was down there."

"Shut up," I say, laughing slightly. "It's not that. I'm just thinking … things I shouldn't be thinking."

"Austin."

I sigh. "How'd you know?"

"It's only natural. You were with him for a long time, he died a tragic death, and I was there. We're all connected. Hell, if it wasn't for him, I wouldn't even be here right now."

The idea of Austin being the reason that we're together is freaky. "What do you mean?"

"He's the one who got me started in my career. Before he intervened, we were playing small clubs and getting ignored along with a million other guys. And he's the one who invited me to that party in Chicago. If I hadn't been there when that whole thing happened, who knows…"

"You agreed to work with me because you felt guilty." I slide off to the side a little and reach down to his tattoo. *Guilty.* I trace it with my finger.

"Yeah. That was part of it. And then there was you."

"Me?"

"Yeah, you." He nudges me. "Don't act like you don't know."

"Don't know what?" My smile is back and it won't go away.

"How sexy you are. You fucking rocked my world the minute you stepped into it. You're like a disease."

"Hmmmm. A disease. Now *that's* sexy."

He pushes me over and climbs on top of me. "Don't make me sex you into submission, woman. Now that you're my girlfriend, we're going to have to lay out some ground rules."

I arch an eyebrow at him. "Getting a little ahead of yourself, aren't you?"

He reaches down and puts his hands on my waist as he lifts himself up higher. "Think so?"

Before I know what's happening, he's flipped me over onto my stomach and he's on top of me, pressing his hard cock into my backside. His lips are so close to my ear as he leans over, the hot air tickles me mercilessly.

"What are you doing?" I say, laughing into the pillow. I'm half suffocating in its softness, pushing up with my arms to arch my back.

He pushes my back down with one hand and positions himself lower to enter my folds from behind.

I moan long and low as he slides into the slippery wetness between my legs. He doesn't have a condom on but I don't care. I know he used them with all the fangirls he was ever with and I'm not going anywhere.

"I told you," he says in a low tone. "I'm sexing you into submission."

Five minutes later with the aching need built up again and the sweat pouring down both of our bodies I submit. "Fine! I'll be your girlfriend." I can barely breathe I'm panting so hard.

"That's what I thought," he says, stroking the orgasm out of me hard and fast. I cling to him to keep from falling into unconsciousness and weep when he's left me completely spent.

CHAPTER
FORTY-SIX

TARIN AND I HAVE BEEN in bed all day and now it's dinner-time. Jack hasn't reappeared and we've decided cereal is the best way to build our strength for another couple days of escape from real life, before he has to go back to L.A. and I have to get on with the business of fixing the damage left behind in the wake of Austin's death. Both of us have a lot of work ahead of us.

Tarin crunches away on his granola. "I've gotta do this European tour. Everyone's counting on me."

"I know. I'll miss you, but you have to do it. You and Scott have worked so hard. You can't let everything fall apart now. It's only four months."

"We *all* worked hard, you included." He nudges me with his elbow and my next bite of dinner goes sloshing back into my bowl. "You could come, you know," he says. "Travel Europe with me. Be backstage for every show." He winks.

I roll my eyes. "As attractive as being your number one groupie sounds, I'm afraid I'm going to have to decline. I have to stay here." I sigh, putting my bowl down on my nightstand.

"I've been thinking about this for a while now, and some things Jack and Scott said are really hitting home for me lately. I think I need therapy."

"What'd they say to make you think that?"

"Actually, it's not just them. It's you too." I cross my legs and sit up straight, plucking at the sheets by my shins. "After Austin died, I just kind of threw myself into rescue mode. I blamed myself for his death, so maybe I thought if I could go out there and prevent it from happening to someone else, it would absolve me of that guilt I was carrying around. But no matter how much good I did, it never did anything to make me feel better about Austin."

"The one who got away."

"Kind of. He slipped away. By degrees, like you said. Maybe if it had happened all of a sudden it would have been so shocking I would have noticed it sooner and thought to do something. But it was like little by little he drew away and got colder, and little by little I let him change me too. Or I changed myself, I don't know." I shake my head, trying to figure it all out. "I just need to talk to a professional to help me work through it."

"There's nothing wrong with asking for help if you need it. I did."

I look sideways at him, raising an eyebrow. "I don't recall you asking."

"People have different ways of asking for help. Some are cool with just walking up and saying, 'Help me.' Others are more like back door people."

"Back door people?"

"Yeah. They ask for help by showing how much they need it."

"You're definitely one of those," I say, picking up my bowl and smiling.

"I don't like asking for anything. That's just who I am. Austin offered to help us out a bunch of times, but I kept turning him down. I didn't want a handout. I wanted to earn it. I guess he knew how much I really wanted the help deep down, so he fucked up that band's equipment and got us the show of a lifetime."

"We both owe Austin a lot," I say softly, watching the lumps of cereal floating around randomly in my bowl. The little lumps kept moving to be by bigger lumps, like they didn't want to be alone.

"Yeah. We do."

The mood has gone suddenly sober, but for some reason, that makes it easier for me to talk about Austin. "It's hard for me to go from being really sad about him, then to angry, then to grateful in such a short period of time, especially when he's not here to talk to about it," I say, giving a voice to the thoughts that have been haunting me night and day for weeks.

"I hear ya. I'm the same with him. Memories of him are like a grab bag. One day I reach in and there's a happy thought. The next time it's one that makes me want to punch him in the face. He was a complicated guy."

I look over at Tarin. "I think you're a complicated guy, too. That's what scares me."

Tarin reaches over and palms my head with his big hand, wiggling my skull a little like he wants to force his words in. "Do not go there, you hear me? I'm not Austin. Never have been, never will be. It's just you and me now. And Scott, okay? I'll adopt him if I have to."

I give him a watery smile, tears coming for about the tenth time today. "You'd do that?"

"Of course. I know you guys are a package deal." He lets go of my head and puts his bowl on the floor. He takes my bowl and puts it there too, pulling me into his arms when his hands are free again. "Come here and give me some more of that love you were offering earlier."

"Who said anything about love?" I say, letting him smooth away my sorrow with his silly talk.

"You don't have to say it. I know you love me. I'm impossible not to love. Ask all my fans."

I try to punch him but he has me wrapped up too tight. "You are so full of yourself."

"No," he says, kissing my head. "I'm full of you. Now go to sleep. Tarin's tired."

"Tarin needs to stop referring to himself in the third person."

"Don't make Tarin upset. He'll have to sex you into submission again."

I smile against his chest. "Oh no. Please. Don't do that."

He rolls me onto my back and we start the game all over again. I can't stop giggling for the life of me.

CHAPTER
FORTY-SEVEN

SAYING GOODBYE TO TARIN IS one of the hardest things I've had to do since losing Austin. Four days, most of it spent talking and playing in bed is enough for me to fall completely and totally in love, apparently. I'm so afraid of what's going to happen next. I really don't do unknowns well at all. I'm a mess by the time he has to leave for L.A.

"You don't have to cry," Tarin says, wiping a tear from my eye at the door.

"I'm sorry," I say, wiping my face with a shaky hand. "I know I'm being overly emotional, but part of me keeps wondering if this is the last time I'm going to see you." I make a lame attempt at a smile. "Stupid, huh?"

"Stop," he says, pulling me close, dropping his bag on the ground at our feet. "I'm healthy, I'm clean, I'm working hard and putting all that shit behind me, and Scott's there. What could possibly go wrong?"

"Your plane could crash." I'm not serious when I say it, but as soon as the words leave my mouth, a new kind of panic sets in. Just what I needed. More anxiety.

"You should be on it with me, then. We could go down together in flames."

I pull away from him and steel myself for the goodbye. "No. I have to stay. I need to do the same thing you're doing but away from L.A. Besides, you're not going to be there much anyway with your tour." I look at the floor, embarrassed a little at the deeply personal things we've talked about that I'm going to bring up again. I just want him to believe me with no reservations that I'm committed to making this work, even though we're going to be apart. "I need to get myself back before I can really have something to offer you. I know this." I reach out and stroke his muscled arm, looking up at him. "Are you mad? I thought you were cool with all of it…"

"No, I get it. I'm just going to miss you, is all." He pulls me into a hug and rests his head against mine. "You do your thing here, I'll do the tour, and then when it's over, I'll come back here to Chicago and we'll figure out our next step. Four months and we're through it. Just four months. It'll fly by."

I nod. "Sounds like a plan." I feel stupid talking like this - like we're entering into some kind of business relationship - but it's the only way I can move past the awkward and into the routine I've planned for myself. While he's gone I'm going to wake up every day, exercise, write in my journal, and see a therapist a few times a week. Dealing with Austin's passing the way I did by throwing myself into my lost-boy rescue work was good for the short term, but it really threw off my long term healing. I'm going to get my crap together so when Tarin is ready for me, I'll be ready for him. I love it when a plan comes together. I just need to focus and work my ass off for *myself* for a change. I can do this. As long as I have Tarin's support, I can do anything.

Jack opens the door from out in the hallway and grins at us. "Ready to go? Car's downstairs."

"Yeah." Tarin picks up his bag and puts his free hand against my cheek. "After the tour."

"After the tour," I say, resting my hand over his for a few seconds as we stare into each other's eyes. I back up before he can think to lean in and kiss me. I'll never let him go if I feel that tongue in my mouth one more time.

I turn my attention to Jack. "Jack, what can I say? You're my hero."

He pushes Tarin out of the way and grabs me in a bear hug. "Damn straight I am. And don't you forget it." After squeezing the life out of me and letting me go, he turns to Tarin. "Drop the ball just one time and see what happens. I gave her away once … I won't do it twice." He leaves, jogging down the hallway and jumping up to hit the light fixture above his head by the elevators. My heart pains me a little over the hurt I sense in him. It shows what an incredibly good friend he is that despite losing me to Tarin, he's still willing to get him to the airport and fly back to L.A. with him.

"I'm not going to drop this ball," Tarin says to me in a quiet tone.

I smile, warmth crawling over my heart and enveloping it in a feeling of security. "Yeah, I know you won't. I believe in you, Tarin. Just believe in yourself and we'll be fine."

"Same goes. Bye, babe." He kisses me quick on the cheek and then he's gone.

I watch his broad shoulders shift as he moves his bag from one hand to the other. The thin cotton of his tight t-shirt leaves nothing to the imagination, and neither do his tight jeans. He has lean muscles everywhere that up until just a couple hours ago were resting naked against my body. I sigh, shutting the door behind him and resting my back against it. My stomach has a whole contingent of butterflies inside it and they're fluttering around like mad. My future is bright and scary and full of all kinds of things I have to get done if this is going to work. And I *so* very much want it to work.

"Time to get busy," I say out into the room. And I smile. For the first time in almost a month, the idea of getting to work sounds like fun, and for the first time *ever* in my life, I'm going to be working on *me*.

CHAPTER FORTY-EIGHT

I DIAL SCOTT'S NUMBER, TRYING not to be nervous. It's pretty much impossible, since my stomach is in knots and I have a cramp in my neck. It's the stress that's killing me right now. The stress of not knowing. The therapist's calming exercises I've mastered over the past three and a half months are not working. Nothing can penetrate the wall of fear that's risen up to block my view of reality.

"Yo, Scar, what's up, my sistah?"

"Hey, Scott. Why are you so damn chipper?"

"I'm not. I'm totally faking it because I know why you're calling. We're at defcon five over here."

I let out a long breath. "Tell me. What's going on? Why hasn't Tarin returned my calls or emails or texts? I haven't heard from him in five days." Tarin and I are almost four months into our long distance relationship and everything was going fine, or so I thought. I'm supposed to pick him up from the airport next month. Two weeks from today, our new life is supposed to start.

"Don't freak, okay?" says Scott. "I don't know a whole lot, just that he was finishing up his last two shows and then he just disappeared. I was there for the one before he left, but I came back to L.A. to work on some projects he has going, so I wasn't there when the doo hit the foo."

"What?! Why am I just hearing this now?!" I run across the apartment with my phone pressed to my head. Still in my sweaty workout gear from my earlier 5k run, I'm not ready to go jump on the plane that I hope Scott has already reserved for me.

"Because, it's happened before and we just thought maybe this would be like the other times. But he's been gone longer than normal, and he missed the Berlin show entirely. He's never missed a show before. Major fucking problems are a-brewin' in Deutschland, let me tell you. Ticket refunds are a fucking mess. Mel's lost all the hair he put into his comb-over. It's very sad."

"Scott, this isn't funny." I'm practically crying with my panic. "What do you mean he's done this before?"

All I get back is silence.

Now I'm crying for real. "Scott, you're my brother and the only family I have left in the world that's worth anything. Please, for the sake of all that's holy, tell me what you know and stop hiding shit from me!"

"First of all, relax. I know that's easy for me to say and impossible for you to do, but do it anyway. I haven't been hiding anything from you. Tarin's helping Jelly. You know that. He told you, you were cool with it, everything was copacetic. Last thing I heard, he was going to visit Jelly. I know his plane landed and he's not shark bait floating on the waves, so don't go flipping out over a plane crash. He's somewhere in L.A."

"Did you book me a flight?"

"Do you really need to ask me that? You leave in three hours. I hope you can get to O'Hare by then."

"I will. What else do you know?"

"She's been having problems. Jelly, I mean. She's not a good pregnant person, apparently."

"What's that supposed to mean?" I put the phone on speaker and leave it on the bathroom counter so I can strip down and jump into the shower.

"Tarin thinks she might be using again."

"What? Why the hell didn't he tell me? Why am I hearing this from you?" I try to think back to the last time we discussed Jelly and realize I haven't asked him about her in probably two months. I'm aware he's helping her financially, but knowing the baby isn't his makes me not care that much about what she has going on. I've been too busy worrying about myself to worry about bimbots. Besides, that's Scott's job now. He's the babysitter, not me.

"You're hearing it from me because I bothered to ask Tarin about it. It's my business to know all, to see all, and to be the omnipotent one."

"Scott, I'm so not in the mood for this right now." I turn on the water and step into the shower before the warmth kicks in. I don't care that I'm now freezing my ass off. I soap myself and shampoo my hair in record time.

"Fine, you want mister businessman? Here you go. I'm mister three-piece suit now." Scott uses his telephone automated message machine voice. "At approximately eleven a.m. Berlin time, Tarin stepped onto a KLM flight out of the Berlin airport, and after transferring at JFK, arrived in L.A. about twenty-two hours later. Ricky the chauffeur picked him up at LAX and drove him to his house in Beverly Hills. Tarin then took the keys to the Chevy SUV and drove off. He hasn't been seen or heard from since."

"How long ago was that? What day?"

"It was four days ago." Scott's back to using his normal voice, so maybe I won't have to slap him when I see him again.

"That's the last time I heard from him," I say, rinsing the soap out of my hair and off my face and body. Shutting the water down, I listen to Scott's response.

"What did he say to you?"

"I can't remember." I climb out and grab my phone. "Hold on, I'm checking. If this thing cuts you off, I'll call you back."

"Holding…" He whistles while he waits. It's the theme from *Snow White* where the dwarves are working. I've changed my mind. I will be slapping him when I see him again.

Looking at my texts, I find the last one from Tarin.

Hey babe. In Germany. Gotta take a quick side trip. No big deal. Talk soon.

After reading it out loud to Scott, I think about Tarin's choice of words. At the time I'd thought he meant some sort of sight-seeing thing. He and the band had been doing that pretty regularly on the tour, so there was no reason for me to question him. Had he been vague on purpose to keep me from asking questions?

"I'm getting a really sick feeling about this," I say, my throat closing up a little at the idea of it.

"He didn't really say much, did he?" asks Scott. "I wonder why."

"Because he didn't want to have to explain himself," I say, getting angrier the more I think about it. "If his plan was to go to L.A. and see Jelly, he should have just put that in the damn text."

"What would your reaction have been?"

"I would have asked why. I would have argued against it."

"Why?"

"Because he's in the middle of a tour! Because she's not his fucking girlfriend anymore and he shouldn't be jumping around and being at her beck and call!" I yank a brush through my hair, taking my anger out on my poor scalp.

"Maybe that's why he didn't say anything."

"What's that supposed to mean?!"

"Wellll, it *might* mean that you're overreacting a little. Or not."

"Honestly, Scott. Do you really think it's overreacting for me to be upset about Tarin leaving in the middle of his European tour to fly halfway around the world to be with a pregnant ex-girl-friend, who would do just about anything to get her claws into him including lying about him impregnating her?"

"I have a better question," he says, completely unruffled by my anger and hysteria. "Do you really think that the guy who's spent the last almost four months living, eating, breathing, and poop-ing Scarlett Barnes, getting his life on track, playing his heart out and filling up stadiums with his enthusiasm for his music, would dump it all for a bimbot dingo like Jelly Summers, a drug-using ho-bag who's about to give birth to some other guy's baby she doesn't even know who? Does that sound like the dude you love so much that you got your shit straightened out for?"

I can't respond for about thirty seconds. When I finally do, I've lost a lot of my steam. "You're such an asshole sometimes. I hate when you do that."

"I know when you say asshole, you mean angel, so thank you. Better get your bags packed or you're not going to make your flight."

"I thought you said I have three hours."

"I lied. It's more like two."

"Scott!"

I shriek as he disconnects the call.

CHAPTER FORTY-NINE

THE HEAT HITS ME FULL in the face as soon as I step outside the air-conditioned baggage claim area of the airport. Ricky's waiting at the curb for me, all smiles. I wish I could return the emotion but I'm too worried and upset to do anything but grimace. The jeans and t-shirt I chose to wear are better-suited to Chicago's cooler air than this muggy awfulness. I'm glad I packed shorts.

"Miss Scarlett! So glad to have you back!" Taking my bag from me, he ushers me to the front of the car, holding the door open for me. I'm glad he's not putting me in the backseat this time. I really need to have my friends closer than that.

"Glad to be back. Kind of. Have you heard from him?"

"No. But Zach has."

My heart skips a beat. I wait until Ricky has the bag loaded and is in the car with me before I grill him further. "Where? When? What'd he say, and what's going on?"

Ricky smiles. "Easy now. I don't know a whole lot, just that Tarin called, he's okay, and he needed Zach to bring him a few things."

"Things?" My voice is coming out too high so I clear my throat and try again. "Things? Like what things?"

"Zach didn't say."

"Holy crap you guys are terrible at this!"

Ricky doesn't even look at me. "Terrible at what? Babysitting a grown man?"

"Yes. Exactly. You should have gotten more details."

"Tarin doesn't need that anymore," he says softly. "He's his own man now. He's on his own two feet, standing proud, making a good life for himself."

Real physical pain hits me from inside. My chest actually aches. "Sounds like you mean he's made a life without me. Is that it? Is that's what's going on?" I look over at Ricky, tears making my eyes yucky, but I can't help it. I feel way too vulnerable right now.

Ricky looks at me with pity. "Hey, now, I didn't say that. Why are you leaping to that conclusion?"

"I don't know," I sigh out. After I think about it for a little while, I answer as honestly as I can, even though it sounds ridiculous. "I guess when things go really good for me, I start wondering when it's going to go bad. This just feels like the answer. This is when things go bad … when Tarin leaves me to go be with Jelly."

"Well … huh…" Ricky seems to be mulling what I said over before he finishes. "I don't know how he can be leaving you, though really, when you weren't even *with* him. Know what I'm sayin'? You were in Chicago, remember?"

There's censure in Ricky's voice, but I ignore it. I've decided I'm not going to speak to him for the rest of the drive. What does he know about my life? He doesn't know that I couldn't be here in L.A. I never bothered to explain to anyone but Tarin that Austin's ghost lives here. That he might have died that night in Chicago, but this is where he lived. This is where *we* lived. Ricky doesn't know that I need to be whole again before I can deal with being in L.A. on a permanent basis. It just figures I'd get here just as Tarin decides he's tired of waiting.

I try not to be mad at Ricky's judgment of me. He isn't in the loop enough to know what my messed up head is thinking and needing. But Tarin is. He's part of that loop I'm in, so the fact that he'd do this tells me things are going very, very wrong. Or I really, really misjudged him and his commitment to us.

"Do you want a suggestion from a friend?" Ricky asks.

"Not really," I say, looking out the window.

"Okay, then." Ricky says nothing else.

I make it about ten blocks before I cave. I hate feeling stress between us. Ricky's such a nice person and has always been a good friend to Tarin. I know I should listen to whatever he has to say. "Fine. What's your advice?"

"Don't jump to conclusions about what's happening. Wait until you talk to him before you decide how to react."

"That would be ever so much easier if he'd just answer my calls, texts, or emails," I say in a bitchy tone. I can't help it. I'm so frustrated right now.

"He told Zach to apologize to everyone for him, that he's just really busy."

I snort bitterly. "Whatever." *Too busy to call me? That must be really, really fucking busy.* I don't even want to know what he'd be doing to be that *busy* with a girl who's almost nine months pregnant.

That's when it hits me.

"Did anyone call the hospital? Where did Zach go when he brought stuff to Tarin?"

"Not the hospital."

The tone of his answer makes me feel sick to my stomach.

"Where did he go, Ricky?"

Ricky sticks his head out, craning his neck a little. "Why don't we just wait until we talk to Tarin to figure this all out?"

"If you know something, just say it, would you? I really hate the idea of people hiding things from me and helping Tarin play games. It's just not worth it, Ricky. Honestly, I thought you knew that."

"It's not like that, Scarlett. Just let it lie for now, all right? Tarin will get this figured out and then fix it all up for you."

I look out the side window again. "I don't think so," I mumble, as the palm trees and carefully manicured bushes flash past.

I'm lost in memories of Austin long since buried. A vision of me sitting with Scott in Austin's big house flits across my mind's eye, the two of us watching television, wondering where Austin is and what he's doing. Everyone but those who loved him the most knew what he was up to. I hated being in the dark then and I hate it twice as much now. I thought Tarin knew better than to do this to me. To us. I hold in the sobs that feel like the undoing of all the hard work I've been through finding myself again.

CHAPTER FIFTY

MY PHONE FINALLY RINGS WITH Tarin's name coming across the screen at ten o'clock that night. He sounds exhausted. I've moved beyond worried and distraught into plain old pissed. He'd better have a hell of an excuse because I'm ready to call it a day. A night. A lifetime. My heart can't take this kind of crap.

"Hi," I say. I don't trust letting any more than that to come out of my mouth right now.

"Hi," he says back. There's caution there, and maybe some guilt. *Please, don't let it be guilt!*

"Where've you been?" I ask. I'm sitting on the edge of the bed in one of the guest rooms. Everyone but Zach is downstairs in the family room playing video games like the world isn't crashing down around our ears. Zach hasn't made it back yet as far as I know. The traitor.

"I'm in L.A."

Some of my anxiety slips out. "Doing what, Tarin? Are you with Jelly?"

"Yes, I am." He sighs heavily. "Where are you right now? Are you still in Chicago?"

"Thanks for asking. Actually, no, I'm in L.A."

"Please don't sound so mad."

My heart is cracking in two because I love him so much and I want to believe he wouldn't hurt me like I think he has. "Kind of hard not to, Tarin." I bite down hard on my lip to keep from screaming. I punch a pillow and burn my knuckles with the friction of doing it several more times.

"I know. But it's not what you think."

"How do you know what I'm thinking? It could be *exactly* what I think."

"I doubt it."

"Are you coming home?"

"Not yet."

A tear slips past the barricades I've tried to erect. I wipe it away angrily and school my features and voice to remain neutral. "When?"

"Maybe tomorrow. I have to get some things worked out. Will you wait?"

"Why don't you tell me what I'm waiting for before I answer that, because at this point, I'm not really sure."

"I want to tell you. I want to tell you everything, but I can't do it over the phone. I need to see you face-to-face."

"Why? What are you worried about?"

He doesn't answer right away. Then he breathes out long and loud. "I guess I'm worried about you hearing the first sentence, hanging up the phone, and then taking a plane somewhere I'll never find you."

"It must be pretty bad."

"It is. But I swear, it's not what you think. I'm not with Jelly that way. I promise you, on my life, I have not been with anyone that way but you since I saw you in Chicago. Hell, since you busted up my life into twenty thousand pieces and put it back together in a different arrangement."

A small sliver of my anger slips away. And then another. "Are you mad about that? About the new arrangement?"

"Hell no. I'm happier than I've ever been in my entire life. For the most part." He sighs again. "There's just the one glitch. Actually, it's more than a glitch, but I think I can handle it. No, I know I can handle it. I just don't know that you can, and that's the part that sucks so bad I can't even fucking breathe." He's crying now. He's actually crying.

And it's then that the thick wall of ice around my heart begins a true thaw, big chunks of unhappiness falling away.

"Why are you so sad? What can it possibly be to make you this upset after all we've been through?"

"You'll see. I'll have Zach pick you up tomorrow, okay? I can't do anything right now. I'm exhausted, I'm completely tied up, and I can't leave to come see you. It's just ... please give me one more night and then you'll see what's going on. I really can't explain over the phone. It's just too much for that."

I close my eyes and try to find a zen place inside my mind. *Deep breath in ... deep breath out.* "Okay, Tarin. I trust you. I'll see you tomorrow."

"Oh thank God. Okay, babe ... shit ... I have to go. I'll see you tomorrow."

"You have to go? Why?"

"I just ... fuck! I do. I have to go. Talk to you soon. Oh! And come alone, okay? No Scott or anyone else." He hangs up and leaves me sitting there in the dimly lit room.

I look down at the disconnected phone. "What the hell?"

CHAPTER FIFTY-ONE

I'M STANDING OUTSIDE ALONE IN denim shorts, an orange cotton top, and orange sandals when Zach pulls into the driveway with the SUV to pick me up. I search his face for answers as I pull open the door and get in to the cold, air conditioned interior.

"Hey, Scarlett," he says. He's completely serious, not a trace of humor or relaxation on his expression anywhere.

I shut the door and buckle up. "Hey, Zach. What's the matter? Are we going to a funeral or what?" I try to laugh it off, but he doesn't join me. My mood goes from hopeful to wary in an instant.

"Not exactly," he says, shifting the car into drive and pulling away. I wave to Scott who's just stepped out of the front door to see me off. I can see him mouthing the words *Good luck* just before the car turns to follow the curving driveway and he's out of my line of vision.

"So you're not going to tell me what's going on either, is that it?"

"Hell no. This isn't my story to tell." He pulls out onto the road that will take us to the main thoroughfare. "Just be patient. We don't have far to go. Twenty minutes."

I nod, trying not to be angry at Zach. He's just doing his job and I'm happy to know his first loyalty is to Tarin. I just hope his loyalty hasn't gone too far.

"Zach, I appreciate whatever it is you're doing or trying to do for Tarin, but just be clear that if you've let him go down a bad path, I'm going to kick your ass. I don't care that you're twice my size, I'll totally do it."

He finally smiles, just a little. "I would expect nothing less. But this path is not my doing."

His hint gives me nothing to work with, and I'm too freaked out over what I could be dealing with that isn't exactly like a funeral to try and guess anymore. I sit back and wait for the ride to be over.

CHAPTER FIFTY-TWO

WE PULL UP TO A small cottage-type house in a neighborhood I know to be very expensive and somewhat exclusive. It's not at all what I would have expected as Tarin's hideout or whatever this place is to him. Zach puts the SUV in park and then looks at me.

"You're not coming?" I say.

He shakes his head no. "It's all you. Just walk up the sidewalk there and go into that red door. Tarin's inside."

"Who else is in there?"

Zach just shakes his head and says nothing.

I un-click my seatbelt and guide it back into its holder. Resting my hand on the door latch, I look at him one last time. "Am I going to regret going through that red door?"

He breaks eye contact and looks towards the house. "I think you'll regret not going through it and never knowing what you didn't know."

I reach over and punch him in the arm. "Thanks for being not helpful at all."

He still doesn't look at me but he smiles. "What are friends for?"

I get out of the car and smooth down my shirt and shorts. I'm so nervous that I'm strongly considering throwing up in the bushes that line the path to the front of the house. Unfortunately, since I haven't eaten anything in twenty-four hours, I'm sure it'll just be painful dry heaves, so I give up on the idea pretty quickly.

The house is up on a small hill and most of it is hidden behind shrubs and small trees. The windows are shut up tight and the hum of an air conditioning unit makes everything seem so benign. The monster I picture waiting for me inside is being very quiet. I see no signs of her.

Will it be Tarin's new girlfriend? An old girlfriend? Is this Jelly's house that he bought her that they live in together? Did he change his mind about wanting to be with me?

None of my guesses make much sense. Why go through all this drama and refuse to tell me anything over the phone, unless the only goal is to humiliate me? And I can't think of a single thing I've done to deserve that from him, so that can't be it.

I put one foot in front of the other, slowly making my way up the front walk. "Might as well get it over with," I say to the lizard that crosses the path in front of me. I take the stairs up, pausing after each one. There's a black metal railing on either side of this part of the walkway, and I hold onto it. It's hot from the late morning sun, the paint chipped and peeling. There is no breeze to cool me down and I'm sweating. The back of my shirt is going to be stuck to me in no time.

I reach the red door and stand there. I want it to fly open immediately, Tarin so anxious to see me that he doesn't wait for me to ring the bell. But that doesn't happen. The door remains shut and there's no sign that anyone's even expecting me. I look for a doorbell and see one to my right, but it has a piece of paper taped over it.

Don't ring bell. Knock softly, it says. I recognize Tarin's handwriting.

I frown as my finger hovers over the paper. "What the hell?" I debate whether to ignore the sign and hit that mother about twenty times. How dare he mess with my head and then tell me not to ring the goddamn doorbell!

But I don't do what my first instinct tells me to do. I lift my hand and knock softly as instructed. Dropping my arm to my side, I take a deep breath and wait for my destiny to unfold.

CHAPTER FIFTY-THREE

THE DOOR CRACKS OPEN AND Tarin's face is in the opening. "You came." He's not smiling.

My heart sinks. *So much for hope.*

"Of course I came." *Because I'm a sucker and I'm stupid and I fell in love with you.* When will I ever learn?

We stand there staring at each other through an eight-inch gap.

"Well?" I finally say, getting more irritated by the second. "Are you going to let me in? Introduce me to your girlfriend?"

He says nothing in response, just opens the door wider and moves back so I can step inside.

So there is another woman. I'm crushed. I knew it. I despise him for forcing me over here to meet her. I hate that he's making me confront the person who's stolen him away from me. My nostrils flare wide as I barely hold back my anger. I'm tempted to punch whoever she is in the face, but maybe I should just thank the bitch for taking him off my hands instead. Better to be wounded by heartache now than killed by it later.

"I really appreciate you coming," he finally says. He shoves his hands in his front pockets and stares at my knees.

"I'm not sure why," I say as he backs up and uses his elbow to close the door softly behind him. "Is this some kind of sick joke? Did you want to gloat or something?" I'm looking around, trying to catch a glimpse of the bimbot. I know she's a dumb blonde fan freak. She has to be. They all are. *Holy shit, it's probably Posey.* I pray it isn't her so I don't have to end up in jail for murder.

"No, it's not a sick joke. Why would you think that?" He's looking at me confused. "Did you talk to Zach?"

"Of course I talked to Zach. Do you think I'd ride all the way over here in complete silence?"

"No. But … never mind. So you know why you're here, then."

"Pretty much. Where is she?" I don't see her in the kitchen or the family room from where I'm standing. She's probably hiding if she knows what's good for her.

"She's in the bedroom."

"Why isn't she out here greeting me with you?" *Figures. Chicken shit.* She knows what she's doing is wrong, that's why she's hiding. *Good.* I hope the guilt follows her around for the rest of her life like the regret will follow me. It's only fair.

He stares at me, a mixture of hurt and confusion marring his handsome features. "She's back there because she's sleeping. Listen … do you want to do this another time? I thought you'd want to do this sooner rather than later, but maybe it was a bad idea."

"Oh, no, please, let's do this now." I snort with disgust. "Let's just get this thing rolling. We'll make it a real good knock down, drag out too, if you want."

"I'd rather not. She kept me up all night and I'm exhausted."

I swallow the hurt and let the anger well up to take control. Hands on my hips, I shake my head at him. "You know, you're really something else. I was so wrong about you. You really had me fooled."

"That sounds like a bad thing," he says cautiously.

I throw my arms up. "What the fuck, Tarin!"

He puts his fingers to his lips, his face a mask of urgency. "Shhhh! Would ya keep it down! She's sleeping!"

This is too much. I cannot believe he's actually doing this. "We'll just see about that," I say, leaving him to go down the hallway, long strides taking me far and fast. "Where is she? I want to meet this bitch."

"What are you doing, Scarlett?" he says coming after me. "You can't call her a bitch, what the hell is your problem?!" He's whisper-screaming at me, making me realize how this person must really have him wrapped around her finger to have him so hyper about disturbing her damn beauty sleep.

The last door on the right is closed. I reach it just as Tarin catches up to me. He yanks me back by my arm and keeps me from grabbing the handle.

"Let me go!" I yell, struggling to get away.

"Scarlett, what's wrong with you? Have you been drinking or something?"

"Oh, right! Because anyone who'd be upset about being two-timed has to be wasted right? What …? You thought I'd be okay about sharing? Well, wake up, asshole. I'm not that kind of girl."

He opens his mouth to respond, but his words are cut off by a very unhappy-sounding wail coming from behind the closed door.

"What the fuck is that?" I whisper, worried he actually has some sort of bobcat or leopard in his back bedroom. Did he want to introduce me to his exotic pet collection? Did I get this completely wrong?

"That's her. Way to go, waking her up," he says, pushing past me and opening the door.

I stare into the room in shock as I watch Tarin walk over to a crib and lift out a tiny baby.

CHAPTER FIFTY-FOUR

MY LOWER JAW IS HANGING down like it's no longer attached. Words are gone. I don't have any that my mouth knows how to use right now. I watch as Tarin pats a tiny bundle on the back and bounces up and down on his toes.

"Shhh, shhhh, shhhh, it's okay. Scarlett's just having a little itty bitty breakdown and she needs a little more sleep before she's allowed to come in your room and say hello, okay baby girl? Shhh, shhhh…"

The cries slow to whimpers, and the volume goes down. My lower jaw finally goes back up where it belongs.

"Shhh, shhh, shhh … Daddy's here. Daddy's here. Go back to sleep. Don't you want to sleep? You've been awake all night and Daddy's tired. I know you're not hungry because you just finished eating."

I feel faint. I take a few steps back until I hit the opposite wall in the hallway. My knees give out and I slide down to the floor.

Tarin comes over, stopping in the doorway with a worried expression on his face. "Are you okay, babe? I know this is a shock. I can explain, I swear."

I nod, still unable to speak. It's taking all my brainpower to process what I'm seeing.

"This is Geneva." He turns her around so I can see her scrunched up bright red face. He keeps bouncing as he cradles her in his arm. "She's Jelly's daughter, and legally my daughter, even though biologically she's not. I'm on the birth certificate."

"Did you…" I try to get my thought out, but my throat's too dry. I struggle to stand, clearing my throat once I'm on my feet again. I use the wall for support because I'm still feeling light headed. "Did you marry Jelly?"

Tarin shakes his head, still rocking the baby back and forth while he responds. "No. But I told her she could put my name on the birth certificate before the baby was born. I didn't want her to be born without a father."

"Where's Jelly?" I look around him as best I can from where I am, but the room looks empty save him, the baby, and about ten grand worth of baby stuff. There's a fancy crib, a changing table, a rocking chair, decorations galore, and about a hundred stuffed animals.

"That's what I wanted to talk to you about. This whole situation is beyond fu… fudged up." He glances at the baby as he puts her back on his shoulder and then he looks at me. "Can you go sit down in the family room and I'll be out in a minute? We can talk as soon as I put her down again."

"Yeah. Sure." I'm too stunned to argue. Retracing my steps back to the family room, I find a spot on the couch and sit down. I can hear him whispering to the baby as I scan the space around me. My brain moves into survival mode, shoving the whacked-out crap in the back room out of my mind in favor of casually observing my surroundings. It's a much less stressful exercise than trying to figure out how Tarin ended up rocking a baby to sleep in a secret bungalow in L.A.

The house is tastefully decorated for the most part. There are no personal mementos around, but there are some hand-made blankets thrown over armchairs and the couch. The television is the older kind, a big box. There's no cable box or remote in sight. Everything is clean, but it's kind of like the place has sat for a long time, unused. There's nothing very modern about anything in this room.

Tarin joins me a couple minutes into my nosing around. He sits on other side of the couch and holds out his hand at me. "Thanks for coming, and for not running out the door and all the way back to Chicago as soon as you saw the baby."

"I still have my running shoes on, Tarin. Don't count any chickens just yet. Tell me what the hell is going on." I'm relieved my voice is back in working order. My heart hasn't decided whether *it* is or not, though.

"About a week ago, Jelly went into the hospital. She wasn't due for another month or so, but she was having problems. I've been paying for her medical care, as you know, and so they keep me updated on what's going on." He plays absently with some yarn on the blanket lying over the back of the couch. "She was supposed to be on bed rest, but she went out partying."

"Who the hell parties with an eight-month-pregnant woman?"

"Plenty of people when I'm paying the bills."

"Ew."

"Yeah. Tell me about it. So anyway, she was using on and off while she was pregnant. Not a lot, because I've had people kind of babysitting her, but this time, she went off the map. Someone dropped her off at the hospital several days ago really out of it. She went into pre-term labor and had the baby almost four weeks early."

"Oh my god, Tarin." I reach out and put my hand on his.

He has a smile for the briefest moment and then it's gone again. "Thanks. So they called me and I came out to just be there for her and mostly for the baby, but before I got to the hospital, she had more problems."

"Who, the baby or Jelly?"

"Jelly. The baby was fine. She spent a couple days in the NICU but after that she was good enough to go home. Jelly had issues with the drugs, though, and with eclampsia, and I don't know what else. Basically her organs just started shutting down. She had a stroke and then her heart gave out and she went into a coma."

My hand flies to my mouth as I picture that poor mess of a girl in such a horrible situation. "Is she okay?" I whisper.

"No." Tarin's voice gets rough. "She died, Scarlett. She died yesterday." Tears come to his eyes and fall down his cheeks. "That's why I've been so busy and out of touch. I was dealing with her and then the funeral home."

I scoot closer to him on the couch and pull him into my arms. "Oh, babe … I'm so sorry. I know she was your friend."

He puts his arms loosely around me. "Yeah, she was kind of a pain in the ass, but underneath it all, she was a good girl. She just liked to party too much. She wasn't treated so well as a kid and it just followed her for her whole life. She could never get away from it."

I can't stop crying now. I said and thought awful things about her. I tried to kick her out of Tarin's life. I feel responsible. Another life lost due to my careless bad judgment. "I'm so sorry, Tarin. I'm so sorry."

"I am too. I feel like I didn't try hard enough."

"But you did!" I pull away and hold his face in my hands. "You were so good to her. You paid for her care and for the baby, you put her in this nice house, you kept her in your life … you aren't to blame."

"I know that. You taught me that. I can only take responsibility for myself, but I still feel like maybe if I had done more, maybe it wouldn't have happened. Now I know what you've gone through, at least on a small scale, with Austin. I keep saying to myself that maybe she wouldn't have needed to party so much if I'd taken over her life and forced her into rehab. Maybe I should have canceled my tour."

"Please don't do that to yourself. I did that to myself for over two years, and I'm still paying for it. You're not to blame. Hell, maybe it's my fault this happened. Everything was fine between you two until I showed up."

Tarin grabs my wrists and squeezes. "No. Don't say that. That's ridiculous. Neither of us is at fault. Come on, we know this. Jelly made her choices and she died because of them." He softens his voice and slows down the pace of his delivery. "And we're left to make our choices about where we go from here."

He drops my wrists and looks me in the eyes, saying nothing.

"What does that mean?" I ask him softly. My heart yearns for him, and it's a physical pain. I want to be closer to him, to feel his arms around me, but there's something between us now. Our lives will be forever changed because of the choices Jelly made for herself and, by default, for Tarin and me.

"I'm Geneva's father. She's my daughter. My life as a single guy living the rock-n-roll life is over."

I don't know what to say to that, so I just listen.

"Before I knew this was going to happen, I was just going to be the friend of the family who paid for Geneva's needs and her school and her music and dance lessons. But now I'm the guy who's going to read her books every night before she goes to bed. I'm the guy who's going to drive her to ballet classes and gymnastics and play dates. I'm the guy who will teach her how to walk and to drive and to say no to boys who want to kiss her. I'm that guy. I'm the dad."

I nod, tears coursing down my cheeks. Life is so crazy sometimes when it takes a person by the throat like this and just throws him to the mat. No one can fight like Destiny. Destiny wins every round, every match, every time.

"What I need to know is, what does it make you?" Tarin asks.

"What do you mean?" I swipe at my tears, but new ones are immediately there to replace them. Both of us are a mess.

"Before all this you were my forever girl. We were going to live in Chicago together happily ever after. But there was no Geneva in the mix when we made those plans. Now there is. And as much as I love you, I can't give her up. I'm all she's got, and even though she's really, really tiny, I already love her." His voice cracks on the last words and his chin drops to his chest. "I don't know how all this shit happened, Scarlett. I'm so sorry."

"You're sorry because you don't want to be with me?"

He looks up, anguish making his face twist. "No! Jesus, I want to be with you more than anything! But I just know … or I figured

… the last thing you'd want to do is be around Jelly's kid. She wasn't … she wasn't the best person in the world and I know you didn't approve of her."

"You make me sound like a monster."

He takes my hand in his and holds it tight. "I didn't mean it like that. I really didn't. You were right to be angry with her. She was a user and a loser in almost every way."

"No, she wasn't. Don't say that. Like you said, she had a hard life and she was a survivor. I can respect that, even if I didn't agree with her methods." I pull my hands back and put them in my lap. I can't look in his eyes anymore. "I'm hurt, though, that you think I'm the kind of person that could hold a person's parents against her. That I'd not like a tiny baby because I didn't like her mom much."

"No one would blame you if you did. It doesn't make you a bad person, it just makes you human."

"No." I shake my head emphatically. "That is bad person material, there. Babies are innocent. Anyone who dislikes a baby is an asshole."

Tarin laughs softly. "That's good to know … that you feel that way."

I look up and we stare at each other for a long time. He reaches over and wipes the tears from my eyes, and then I do the same for him.

"So where does this leave us?" I ask, finally breaking the silence.

"You have a choice."

My lips tremble. "I do?" I can barely get the words out.

"Yeah."

"Fine. What are my options?"

He takes my hands in his again. "Well, option one is you can stand up, walk out that door, and never see me or Geneva again. Free pass. No hard feelings, just me with a broken heart and a baby to take care of."

"That sounds like a pretty shitty option. I hope there's another one."

His mouth goes up in a half smile. "There is. Your second option is to stay here in L.A. with me and Geneva. We could live together and you could hang out with me while I take care of her. Or you could live close by and visit a lot."

My heart spasms with the pain that option brings. Maybe it should make me happy, but I want more. "Well, you've given me a lot to think about."

"Do either of those options sound like something you could do or want to do?"

"Maybe. But I want to know what *you* want me to do."

"Honestly?" he asks.

"Yeah. Truth. Truth … or dare."

He sits up straighter, letting my hands slip out of his. "Yeah, okay. Truth or dare." His sexy confidence is back and my body instantly responds. I have to wipe my mouth to keep from licking my lips in anticipation.

"You choose truth, then?" I ask. My heart is hammering in my chest. I can hear it in my ears.

"Of course."

"That's tricky you know. Asking for truth."

"So you've learned," he says, leaning in closer to me.

"I've played with the best," I say, moving in closer too.

"Go ahead then, do your worst. Ask your question and I'll give you the truth."

"Okay fine. What do you want me to do in this situation. With you and Geneva here. The whole truth."

"And nothing but?" he says.

"And nothing but."

He breathes out through his nose once, hard. "Okay. Time to man-up. I can do this. Scarlett?"

"Yes?" I'm so anxious now as I wait for his words I can hardly sit still.

"I want you…"

"Yes…?"

He clears his throat and then pulls at the neck of his shirt. "Is it hot in here or is it just me?"

I slap him on the arm. "Don't play. Answer the question."

"Question? Did you ask me a question?"

"Tarin, I'm warning you…"

"What was it again? I forgot." He's grinning now, begging to be tackled.

"I'm not going to touch you until you finish the game. Answer the question. What do you want me to do?"

"You're pushy."

"Answer it."

"I like pushy women."

"Answer it.

"I like to have sex with pushy women. In the family room. On the floor."

"Tarin!" I jump over and tackle him backwards into the cushions. Our faces are an inch apart. "Answer the freaking question or you're going to have to pay the forfeit."

"Oooo, I get to be your slave for a day and give you an ass massage? I choose forfeit. Uncle. I give. You win."

"No. The forfeit in *this* game is you get to be *Scott's* slave for a day and give *him* an ass massage. And fair warning … he has a hairy ass. Pimply too."

Tarin grimaces. "For reals?"

"For reals. Answer the question."

"Fine." He reaches up and kisses me quick. "I want you to move in with me and Geneva and play house with us."

I frown, scrunching up my eyebrows. "Define *play house* for me."

"Wake up, have breakfast, work out, walk the baby in the stroller, feed the baby, rock the baby, have sex with me while the baby sleeps, make some music together, walk the baby, feed the baby, rock the baby, eat another meal, have some more sex …"

"Sounds like a lot of work."

He smacks my butt. "You're a hard worker. You could handle it."

"Would it be me doing all that baby stuff?"

"We'd do it together. Team effort. Me and you. You and me. You and me and Geneva makes three." He grins.

I die a little inside at his adorably stupid expression. And then I think about the realities of that kind of life.

"I'm not sure I can do that, Tarin."

He freezes, his smile faltering. "What do you mean?"

I kiss him once, trying to ease the sting of my words. "What if you decide you're tired of me? Tired of being home instead of out on the road? What will you do then? Disappear and leave me to take care of her? Because as much as I like kids, I'm not sure I could handle that."

He shakes his head. "No fucking way. 'Scuze the French, but no. I'm not that kind of dad."

Just hearing that word makes my heart melt a little. *Dad.* I stroke the side of his face. "You're a dad now."

"Yeah. I'm a dad now. And I want you to be the mom."

I sit up all of a sudden, my heart going double-time. "What?"

Tarin sits up slowly, never taking his eyes off mine. "I want you to *really* do this with me. All the way. I'm the dad, you're the mom. Together. Us."

I frown, torn between crying, screaming, and smiling. I settle for the crying. "Will you please just tell me what the hell you're talking about? I'm so confused right now, I don't know whether you want a roommate, a mistress, a governess, or a wife. Seriously. Speak plainly or suffer my wrath. My sanity is questionable at this point."

Tarin stands up and pulls me to my feet. Once I'm there he drops down on one knee.

"Oh my god," I whisper. "What are you doing down there? Get up!"

He takes my hand in his and reaches around behind him. Out of his back pocket he pulls a band of gold with a diamond perched on top of it. His grin is a wonder to behold as he holds it up between us.

I can't breathe!

I can't breathe!

"Scarlett? Will you be my baby momma? The one who pulls me back from the brink and saves my soul when I'm about to toss it out with the trash? The lady who plays truth or dare with me and forfeits on purpose just so she can give me an ass massage? The girl who forgives me when I say and do stupid shit when I'm trying to be romantic? Will you be the one who goes to bed with me at night and wakes up next to me in the morning and kisses me regardless of my morning breath? Will you kick my ass in the boxing ring until we're old and gray? Will you…"

"Tarin…" I'm crying so hard, I can't speak.

"Okay, I'll cut it short. Scarlett, truth or dare?"

I stand stock still for a full ten seconds waiting to hear the voice of Austin's spirit telling me to run. But he remains silent. The only thing I can sense inside the headspace where Austin normally resides is peace and acceptance. I don't know if it's coming from him or my own heart, but it doesn't matter. I finally, for the first time in two years, feel healed and ready to move on with my life. How could I not with this beautiful man before me down on one knee?

"Dare," I say, the tears drying enough for me to speak.

He grins devilishly at me. "Wise choice. Okay, Scarlett …? I dare you to marry me."

I nod at Tarin, my smile hurts it's so big. "I'll take that dare."

"Good. Glad you said that, because I got this rock on sale and they said they wouldn't take it back. And besides, I'm really not all that into ass massages. I just said that before to con you into telling me your inner secrets."

He slides the ring on my finger, and only when I'm sure it's on good and tight do I grab a pillow and conk him over the head with it.

CHAPTER
FIFTY-FIVE

TARIN AND I ARE STROLLING down the sidewalk, taking turns pushing Geneva in her buggy. The rings on my left hand sparkle in the late morning sunlight.

"So Scott's moved on to his next project, huh?" Tarin says, his arm draped loosely over my shoulders.

I look off in the distance at the sound of a small engine coming our way. "Ask him yourself," I say, pointing to the blue Vespa zipping down the street.

It pulls up next to us, its rider flipping up the visor of his helmet.

"Yo, yo, yo, happy family, what's up?" Scott grins, making his eyes crinkle. I can't see his mouth, but he's pretty much smiling all the time now, so I know it's there. He's on top of the world, making serious cash money with finishing up Tarin's job and now heading into his next one. And this one's even more high profile.

"Nice ride," says Tarin, nodding as he takes in the gleaming powder blue metal and leather seat.

"Yeah, it gets about a hundred miles to the gallon. Very enviro-friendly. Plus all the ladies like it, so …yeah."

ELLE CASEY

"What up? Moving on to your next project?" Tarin asks.

"Yeah. Should be pretty decent. Can't share names. Confidentiality agreements and so on, you know the gig." He pushes his scooter forward more so he can look in the buggy. "How's my goddaughter doing?"

"She hasn't changed much since you saw her last night," I say, rolling my eyes. He sees the baby as much or more than I do. Baby fever is running rampant in the Kilgour household, and I still can't stand the idea of Scott moving out. Luckily Tarin's on board with a semi-permanent houseguest.

"They grow so fast," he says, sighing. Slapping his visor down he finishes off with a salute. "Later, peeps. Keep it real. I'll be in touch."

Tarin and I wave as he buzzes off. I laugh when he almost loses control and ends up in someone's driveway in the process of recovering. He waves back at us to let us know he's okay.

"Are we sure the Vespa's a good idea for him?" Tarin asks, looking back over his shoulder at Scott's departing form as we continue our walk.

"Who knows? As long as he stays in the neighborhood streets, I don't think he can do too much damage."

Geneva opens her pretty blue eyes and looks up at me. I have to stop and pick her up.

"You're going to spoil her picking her up like that all the time," says Tarin. There's no censure in his voice. He knows his words are wasted on me.

"You can't spoil a baby with love." I tickle her chin as I walk and she rewards me with a goofy baby smile. "She just smiled at me again."

"Doesn't count unless someone else sees it."

"Ricky confirmed it yesterday," I say, still tickling her chin. I cannot get enough of her beautiful face. People can say what they want about Jelly, and the tabloids sure have done a lot of gossiping about her life and tragic death, but she sure makes beautiful little girls. No one can argue that, and if they even try, they're going to have to deal with me. Scarlett Kilgour does not play when it comes to her daughter.

"You paid Ricky off with cupcakes, so that doesn't count."

Geneva blinks at me, her impossibly long, black eyelashes in stark contrast to her milk-white skin. "Are your camera batteries all charged up? I want to do another photo shoot later after her nap."

"The other eight we've done this week weren't enough?"

I look over at him. "Am I being annoying? I'm sorry. I just can't get over her, Tarin. She's just …"

He leans in and kisses me loudly on the side of the head. "Shush. I know what you mean. The batteries are charged and ready. I feel a really good portrait coming on."

"Really?" I grin up at him. He makes me so happy. I never in my life thought I'd feel like this with another musician who makes beautiful music.

"Yeah, really. Mother-daughter style. It's going to be iconic."

"Iconic," I say, feeling the warmth of love travel my veins. "I like that."

"I like *you*," Tarin says, dropping his arm to my waist. "My wife. Mother of my child."

"My husband," I say, leaning into him as we walk. "Father of my child."

A whisper comes on the breeze to my ear, filling me with happiness. I recognize the voice. It once made beautiful music too. *What a kickass family you make together, Scar. Good job. I'm proud of you.*

I respond silently in my head. *Thanks, Austin. I'm proud of us too.*

What to read next …

For more of the humor, romance, and writing style you enjoyed in *By Degrees,* try the Rebel Wheels series. There may be some guest appearances in this series by certain characters you've come to know. Enjoy!

Or, for a romance based in NYC, try Love In New York

Being an independent author, I depend entirely on *you*, the reader, to get the word out about my books. If you liked this book, won't you please leave a review online and recommend it to a friend? The more you spread the word, the more books I can write, and nothing would please me more than to put a new book in your hands every single month.

I read all my reviews!

Find more Elle Casey books at the following retailers:

Amazon
iBooks
Barnes & Noble
Google Play
Kobo
Walmart
Your Local Library via the OverDrive ebook platform

Want to get an email when my next book is released?
Sign up here: www.ElleCasey.com/news

ABOUT THE AUTHOR

Elle Casey, a former attorney and teacher, is a NEW YORK TIMES, USA TODAY, *and Amazon bestselling American author who lives in France with her husband, three kids, and a number of horses, dogs, and cats. She has written more than 40 novels in less than 5 years and likes to say she offers fiction in several flavors. These flavors include romance, science fiction, urban fantasy, action adventure, suspense, and paranormal.*

A personal note from Elle ...

If you enjoyed this book, please take a moment to leave a review on the site where you bought this book, Goodreads, or any book blogs you participate in, and tell your friends! I love interacting with my readers, so if you feel like shooting the breeze or talking about books or your family or pets, please visit me. You can find me at ...

www.ElleCasey.com
www.Facebook.com/ellecaseytheauthor
www.Twitter.com/ellecasey
www.Instagram.com/ellecaseyauthor

Other Books by Elle Casey

CONTEMPORARY URBAN FANTASY

War of the Fae (10-book series)
Ten Things You Should Know About Dragons
(short story, The Dragon Chronicles)
My Vampire Summer
Aces High

DYSTOPIAN

Apocalypsis (4-book series)

SCIENCE FICTION

Drifters' Alliance (ongoing series)
Winner Takes All (short story prequel to Drifters' Alliance,
Dark Beyond the Stars Anthology)
The Ivory Tower (short story standalone, Beyond the Stars: A
Planet Too Far Anthology)

ROMANCE

By Degrees
Rebel Wheels (3-book series)
Just One Night (romantic serial)
Just One Week
Love in New York (3-book series)
Shine Not Burn (2-book series)
Bourbon Street Boys (4-book series)
Desperate Measures
Mismatched

ROMANTIC SUSPENSE

*All the Glory: How Jason Bradley Went from
Hero to Zero in Ten Seconds Flat*
Don't Make Me Beautiful
Wrecked (2-book series)

PARANORMAL

Duality (2-book series)
Monkey Business (short story)
Dreampath (short story standalone, The
Telepath Chronicles)
Pocket Full of Sunshine (short story & screenplay)

www.ingramcontent.com/pod-product-compliance
Lightning Source LLC
Chambersburg PA
CBHW021522250626
47154CB00006BA/1936